"WHAT DO YOU OFFER ME?"

Sabrina did not make the mistake of thinking she had won. She was gambling with the devil and she knew it. But if she could hold her own with him long enough, she might induce Jack to help her to achieve her needs. She had sworn the night she left London that she would do whatever it took to gain Kit's freedom. No hazard would be too great. So then, why not wager her reputation against the viscount's expertise? It was a risk worthy of her goal. And, unlike the viscount, she had every intention of cheating him of the very prize she was about to offer.

"I need to win a small fortune. Five hundred pounds would suit me nicely."

"I see. And if you win?"

Sabrina found she could not look directly at him and hoped he would assume it was from modesty rather than dissembling. "If you require it, instead of a hundred and a quarter of my winnings, I shall give myself to you for exactly one night."

THE GAMBLE

Laura Parker

Zebra Books
Kensington Publishing Corp.
http://www.zebrabooks.com

ZEBRA BOOKS are published by

Kensington Publishing Corp.
850 Third Avenue
New York, NY 10022

First Printing: May, 1998
10 9 8 7 6 5 4 3 2 1

Printed in the United States of America

Prologue

London, October 1740

Like many a worldly Lady of Quality in London, Lady Deborah Morley professed a mild curiosity to lay eyes on the new Viscount Darlington despite—or more rightly because of—his reputation for wildness and brash conduct. Bold fellows were always of interest to bored ladies who lived by their wits and bodies among the pampered pups of the English aristocracy.

The novelty of Lord Jack Laughton lay in part in the fact that he had been reared on the Caribbean island of Barbados. Come to London some months earlier to inherit his title, his singular purpose in remaining in town seemed to be to flaunt his contempt for the conventions of the English Beau Monde. This explained why London was agog with gossip concerning the doings and dealings of the mysterious expatriate.

Of greater import this morning was the fact that Lord Chichester, Lady Deborah's lover, had challenged the viscount. This had followed Chichester's neglected wife's spiteful claim that Darlington had comforted her in her husband's absence from her bed.

Lady Deborah's small mouth firmed with smug satisfaction. The claim was outrageous! Lady Chichester did not possess the body or manner to satisfy her own husband, let alone attract a man of the viscount's notorious tastes. What concerned her was that despite Lord Darlington's public assertion that he did not know Lady Chichester, her husband had refused to rescind his challenge. The West Indian was said to be as fearless as he was proud. He had taken up the gauntlet though there was no cause.

That aside, Lady Deborah was prepared to be disappointed by the viscount. She was prepared to observe and yawn at his boorish behavior. She was even prepared by boudoir gossip to feel a slight lustful shiver for the primitive islander. After all, she was wanton at heart. She was prepared for every contingency of feeling except that which arose as she watched the new viscount handle a rapier.

The duel was being held in a clearing in the shadows of Whitehall, a favored spot of aristocrats who did not wish to journey from London into the country so early in the day. As the mistress of the challenger, she was there to urge Chichester on to victory over his opponent. Yet one good glance at the handsome face of Jack Laughton with its wicked scar that gave him a devilish aspect and her fickle heart switched sides.

It was no match at all. The viscount's mastery of the blade was dazzling. From the first clash of swords that rung with tinny scrapes and flashes of sparks in the milky blue mists of dawn, it was apparent that the challenger was sadly outmatched. The enraged husband of a silly, susceptible wife made poor sport for the Viscount Darlington.

Five . . . ten . . . twenty . . . in less than thirty heartbeats it was over. The quick graceful lunge under the challenger's arm, the soft cry of his surprise, the withdrawn point, a fatal collapse into the grass: all executed with chilling exactitude and very little fuss.

Lady Deborah knew she should have been shocked, enraged, despairing of her loss. Yet her gaze remained riveted on the slayer of her lover.

Pure female curiosity had made other women who knew better, as well as foolish ones who did not, stand and challenge a disreputable gentleman in order to draw his attention their way. But the rapacious hunger awakened in Lady Deborah's bosom had its roots in the admiration of one predator for another. As he turned from the man lying on his back in the dew-spattered grass, she stepped into his path and threw back the hood of her cape.

He paused, his rapier still unsheathed, the tip angled just above the damaging damp of the grass. The mists ripening with morning light revealed an attractive face of angular shadows. The nose was a trifle too long for true classicism, yet the mouth was mobile, sensual, patently mocking even in repose. Astonishingly, he wore his own golden hair unpowdered and tied back with a black ribbon. Beneath his jutting brow his beautiful hooded eyes blazed with the powerful vitality of life.

A strange thrill shot through Lady Deborah when he turned those light eyes on her. She inhaled sharply in the wake of the languid downward drift of his lashes as he surveyed her form. Oh, if only his touch were as stimulating! No Caribbean pirate or West Indian freebooter could have looked more imposing or less inclined to be cajoled by a woman's mere innocent flirtation. Luckily for them both she had no such insipid liaison in mind.

She felt the latent hum of violence in the viscount's stillness as she approached. His thin veneer of elegance was no more a part of him than his richly decorated clothing and, she suspected, just as easily shed. Like the blade unsheathed at his side he lacked only a cause to display the brutal, aggressive force that was his nature. Her lover had offered it and the cost was his life. She would make a better adversary.

When she paused within arm's reach he did not speak

to her, did not even offer her the civilized gesture of his hand or a smile, but turned his back and began a leisurely stroll toward the deeper penumbra offered by the spreading shelter of nearby ancient trees.

She hesitated only a moment, glancing back to where the physician and her lover's seconds were carefully bearing the fallen man toward his carriage. She should go with him, should be there to comfort, to whisper, to cry.

She turned smartly on her heel and hurried across the wet verdant turf after the vanquisher.

Exhausted, elated, and submissive, Lady Deborah lay in the forked roots of a chestnut tree. Her silk skirts were muddy and crushed about her waist, her bare thighs opalescent with dew and the essence of their coupling. She had been ridden longer, with more finesse, but never with such heat and power or repressed violence. Darlington had not made love to her but had taken her with the same devastating accuracy with which he had dispatched his opponent. She had not, as she intended, been his reward but his second revenge. In quivering new knowledge of herself and despite the intended degradation, she had enjoyed it. Exquisite sensation still ran like fairy flame beneath her skin.

The languor of what the French referred to as *la petite de mort* made her reluctant to even open her eyes. Speech was a supreme effort. "You have cuckolded a dying man."

The sound of his companion's voice rasped against the silence that Jack Laughton preferred after coupling. Deliberately, he finished buttoning his breeches before replying. "I imagine he would have preferred it that way."

"Have you no remorse, no regret?"

Interrupting his search for his coat, which he had discarded in his haste some distance away, Jack turned to gaze at the reclining woman. She rose to a sitting position, her generous bosom spilling from her unhooked bodice as she carelessly tossed her skirts down over her nakedness. She was lovely, had pleased him as well as many another. Despite that, he felt nothing for her, merely a vague momentary sense of respite from his surpassing indifference to the world. He did not know or care to know her name.

Involuntary emotion passed like a cloud shadow across his thoughts and was gone—yet he recognized it. "What use is regret? It is a meal eaten with a corpse."

Despite the rebuff she smiled at him, the edges of it licked by covetous desire. "Will I see you again?"

A wolfish gleam entered his silver gaze. "No, my dear. I never sup twice at a dead man's table, however tempting the meal."

He saw the sudden wounding of his rejection in her light eyes and then just as quickly a readjustment of her emotions into ones of anger and resentment. Ah yes, the woman scorned. He knew that face as well as his own. "Someday you will meet your match, Darlington, and she will roast your heart and eat it while you watch."

"What a charming demise you devise for me," he answered with a hint of amusement. "The exercise should prove stimulating for the pair of us. I eagerly anticipate the arrival of this she-devil."

Jack strolled rapidly away from the woman who began shouting invectives at his back, feeling once more a sullen moodiness closing in around him.

Since his return to London he had not grown accustomed to England's wan climate of incessant chills and gloomy mists. Yet nothing had sufficiently moved him to consider leaving the misty isle. Nor could he account for the sudden whim that had made him decide to sail for London after twenty-two years' absence. Perhaps it was only idle curiosity. What he had discovered upon arrival affected him less than most supposed.

His detested father had been dead three years and for an equal period of time the Darlington solicitors had been searching for him in order to bestow the news that he was the new Viscount Darlington.

Neither discovery held the drama it might have for another man. His solicitors were confounded by the laughter that greeted the news of his father's death. In the months since, his squandering of what should have been a sizable fortune had repeatedly scandalized them. They cautioned him not to spurn the legacy his title bestowed upon him. They thought to appeal to his noblesse oblige. Unfortunately for the viscountcy, he had none.

Jack absently rubbed the C-shaped scar that curved under his right cheekbone, a habit that betrayed his rare moments of agitation. A title and estates could not blunt his father's more enduring legacy: his mother's murder and his own disfigurement.

Damn them all! They need not know what aroused and directed him. He never explained himself, nor rejected a slight.

He had grown to manhood in the West Indies amid a passionate Creole society that held sway even in the British territories like Barbados, a world where a high-spirited lust for life and an easily offended pride were badges of honor. Born with a natural if aloof arrogance, he had quickly discovered reasons to become handy with a sword and pistol. From Port Royal to New Orleans, when liquor flowed and passions were aroused, a casual remark or the smallest slight could result in a duel between friends. Experience had taught him to never back down, ever show mercy, or ever let an enemy go unpunished.

In comparison, life in London bored him. Gaming offered the only source of relief for his apathy. When winning paled, he began to play ever more recklessly until now he lost more often than he won. Strangely enough, though he might soon again be poor, his title offered him the same protection it had once offered his murderous sire. His shortcomings were seen as rights of his birthright, his excesses his due, his guilt pleasures the way of the world. The duels he had fought since his arrival were of note only because dueling in England was rare. Men of reason, he was told, demurred from the exercise. They brought suit in courts of law!

Jack cursed under his breath. He had not meant to kill Chichester. He had executed the disarming maneuver dozens, nay, hundreds of times. If his foot had not slipped an inch in the dew-slick grass, the fool would be alive instead of a blot on his conscience.

As for the man's mistress . . . now there was a predator, ever ready to seek the advantage in a situation. Chichester had not bled his last drop before she had hiked her skirts in invitation to anoint the conqueror. Lust had had little to do with why he had succumbed to her embrace. Rage over a needless death had spurred his action. The interlude had blotted out, if only for its duration, the deed.

Perhaps his detractors were right and he would soon come to a much-deserved bad end. He was bored with his life, bored with the prospect of his future. Yet he was young, not quite thirty. And so he would remain in London, caught between ennui and the malicious delight he took in ruffling the feathers of his detractors by claiming their gold at the gaming tables and their women in the boudoir. Clasped to England's cold bosom, he was in perfect harmony with his own dissatisfaction with life, and with himself.

As Jack neared his waiting carriage, an imposing black silhouette detached itself from the shade of a nearby tree trunk. The full morning light fell upon him, yet the silhouette remained ebon. The man stood six foot six, his skin smooth and glossy black as japanned wood. Though his clothes were European, his features were an exotic mixture of slanted black eyes, broad nose, and generous mouth chiseled in high relief topped by a cropped cloud of frizzled black hair. When he spoke his words came forth in a deep baritone of perfect English. "You are well, my lord?"

Jack smiled at his personal servant, the only person in

the world whose good opinion he valued. "Yes, Zuberi. Without a scratch." If one discounted those left by the lady, he mused.

Zuberi answered Jack's smile in kind, and it brought into focus the pleasing shape of its owner's features. "The enemy is vanquished."

Jack sighed. "Alas."

As they moved in together toward the carriage, the opening notes of a lark's serenade floated down to them from a branch.

Jack paused and lifted his head. A rare genuine smile touched his lips as the fatigue of another sleepless night momentarily fell away from him. As the melody repeated itself in the cool crisp air, he found himself thinking the most unusual, nay incredible, thought. He did not know what joy was.

Most men claimed to have found whatever joy they possessed in the arms of a woman and named it love. If there were such a woman who could rouse and arouse him from the galling monotony of his life, then he would gladly stake everything he possessed for a taste of that joy though it ultimately cost him his life.

"The she-devil," he murmured under his breath. Yes she would need to be able to hold her own against him.

Chapter One

Sabrina Elizabeth Lyndsey stood in the cold dark gallery outside her cousin's door, waiting for a summons. Clasping cold hands so tightly her knuckles ached, she struggled against the panic slowly gathering within her.

Let it be over, she silently prayed with a strange sense of resignation. *Whatever is to come, let it be over quickly.*

She had thought herself well rid of her guardian, Robert McDonnell, when, in August, business for King George had taken him to Scotland, a land so remote in her mind as to seem a foreign country. He had returned unexpectedly tonight and, as luck would have it, in time to learn of an indiscretion that was certain to land her in disgrace . . . or worse.

The weight of her twenty years of life sat heavily upon her slender shoulders, but Sabrina possessed too much of the Lyndsey spirit to be completely cowered by circumstance. 'Twas not the first time she had disgraced herself. Nor was it the first time she had had to face the forbidding Calvinist cousin into whose care she and her ten-year-old half brother Kit had been placed after the plague took their father's life the previous year. For the past year she and Kit had been subjected to Cousin Robert's strict scrutiny, disapproval, and sermonizing. During that year, with a determination matched only by her arrogance, she had spent her energies upon foiling her guardian's efforts to break her will.

Yet—by mercy's grace!—she had never before been caught out in a matter so recklessly indiscreet.

Sabrina tossed her head, sending ripples through the mane of blue-black hair falling loose about her shoulders. Whenever possible, she avoided the "mackerels" with their sprays of wheat meal, preferring a wig when public appearances required her to appear with powdered hair. The age admired fragile pale countenances, shy melting glances, and rosebud mouths: small, pursed, and delicately shaded. Her wild dark hair framed a face with wide-set violet eyes beneath markedly winged black brows, long straight lashes that added a veil of mystery to her extravagantly pretty looks, and a mouth voluptuously full and red. Cousin Robert disapproved of what he termed her provocative features, which he warned could work against her reputation.

A sly smile curved up the corners of Sabrina's mouth but it held no warmth. Cousin Robert's concern for her reputation stemmed from his own pompous, self-serving ambition. He was not above exposing her to whispers and rumors when it came to his own desires. Though she was a commoner, daughter of a merchant, she was also an heiress. The man who wed her would gain the vast Lyndsey woolen fortune and a considerable portion of the West Country.

As with all young women, she was bound by custom to wed where her male parent or guardian saw fit. To help further his own political ambitions, Cousin Robert was determined that she wed a peer of the realm.

Sabrina pulled her cloak more tightly about her, hoping yet knowing she could not forever hide what lay beneath.

In one matter only was Cousin Robert right. There was

a wildness within her. It clawed and fluttered in desperation to escape the vexing lassitude and despair that ruled her present existence. She could not explain the restlessness, the indescribable need to be caught up in life, however trite and venal her method. That restlessness had led her to join in the night's mad scheme.

Sabrina smirked. Of course, the blame for her conduct could as easily be laid at Cousin Robert's door. It was in the role of countess's companion that she had dressed up in borrowed gentleman's finery and a moldy full-bottomed wig and set out to prove that she was as brave as her aristocratic friend.

Because the association was seen as an advancement of his own social stature, Cousin Robert had approved of her becoming the Countess Lovelace's companion. No doubt he would have rescinded his consent had he discovered how much alike the two young women were in temperament and their need for constant diversion. Or, how freely the canary and madeira flowed in the countess's home. Or, that gambling occupied most of the lady's evenings. The countess even occasionally staked Sabrina to modest bets.

All of a sudden Sabrina's stomach cramped. She clapped both hands to her mouth, but it was too late. A loud undignified belch worthy of a trencherman escaped and echoed down the long empty hall.

As chagrin vied with amusement, she smothered her laugher in her palm. Truth to tell, she was a trifled foxed! No doubt of it! The grip of "demon spirits," as her uncle called liquor, had made her think she and Countess Lovelace could get away with visiting a tavern along the Thames dressed as gentlemen.

If only she had run at the first sign of trouble. But she had been transfixed, appalled, and fascinated by the unexpected arrival at the tavern of London's most notorious rake.

* * *

The Stag Horn was one of many such taverns that stood within hailing distance of both the London Tower and the Thames. For two hundred years those ancient alehouses, leaning crookedly upon one another like tallow candles set too long by the fire, were the favorite gathering spots for sailors and unemployed soldiers of fortune. Crammed into their narrow common rooms, men drank their fill while trading tales of battles fought and women conquered.

Further down river, Parliament's lords and commoners met and squabbled among themselves over King George's rights and theirs. But here, within the shadow of the Tower Bridge, untutored men of humble birth kept suspicious company with adventurous Dandies of noble heritage who sought amusement among the lower classes. The only thing these men had in common was boredom, and a fondness for drinking and quarreling.

The drinking was hours old by the time Sabrina and Lady Charlotte arrived. Afraid their voices would give away their disguise, neither she nor Lady Charlotte traded more than speaking glances and the occasional whisper. For once they were overawed by their own audacity.

The Honorable James Branston had suggested a masquerade as penalty for Lady Charlotte Lovelace's gambling debt to him. Sabrina disliked him least of the countess's many male admirers because his boyish good looks seemed to hide nothing more sinister than a predilection for pranks and a weakness for gambling. He had even offered to accompany them in order to see the challenge carried out.

Ale had never tasted so crisp and refreshing to Sabrina as it did in that smoke-filled room that stank of humanity and perdition. She watched with wide eyes and listened intently to the crowd, seeking to commit to memory the lewdest of the jests and the bawdiest of the ditties she

"Ma foi! A colonialist joins us!"

The startled pitch of the voice crested over the crowd, subduing it in the backwash of cackling laughter. "No paint. No powder. He lacks the manners and the delicacy required of a gentleman. His kind are no better than dogs!"

"What folly!" Lady Charlotte gasped as Sabrina, equally alarmed, turned her head in the direction from which the insult had sprung.

Several noblemen occupied a nearby table, dressed in the exaggerated style of elaborate, banded silk coats, buckles, braiding, and frothing lace that marked them as "macaronies." Lady Charlotte had remarked upon the group when they first entered the tavern but the powdered and rouged Dandies were so far into their cups that she had decided there was no need for concern about being recognized by them or even approached.

Now one of them lifted his tankard. *"Salute!* A plague on all colonialists!"

The rejoining, "Here! Here!" of drunken approval from his cronies reverberated through the common room, attracting the tavern's other denizens, who turned curious gazes on the tableau.

Sabrina held her breath as the viscount turned to survey the five men, wondering why any sane human being would wish to antagonize this supremely self-possessed stranger.

After the briefest of considerations, the viscount looked away from the table, apparently prepared to ignore them. Yet as he walked past, one macaroni stuck out his leg, blocking the way with a gold-buckled, red-heeled shoe.

"But observe. The fellow's as brown as a seaman." The challenger half-turned to catch the eye of a companion and winked. "My dear fellow, do you know what they say about West Indians? The tropical sun makes them all quite mad. Without culture or good society, they are reduced to ignorance and superstition. I hear they even practice witchcraft. Picked it up from the Africans they import."

"How positively droll that the colonials of the Caribbean should be so influenced by savages one would assume are their inferiors in every way," remarked another.

"Unless it be true," added a third, "that they are the mongrel pups of depraved fornicators."

Chuckling, the self-designated leader looked up at his prey. "I've heard their women are all ugly, thin-tittied hags. I'd sooner mount a goat! What say you to that, colonialist?"

The viscount laughed, the sound short and contemptuous.

The last and silent member of the dandy's party suddenly leaned forward toward the challenger. "Chris!" he said with a worried expression. "Do you not know whom you address?"

The leader tossed a contemptuous glance over his shoulder. "A colonialist. What of it?"

" 'Tis Lord Darlington."

Once spoken, that name seemed to cast a spell of utter silence over the tavern's other patrons.

The news had no such impact on the challenger. He rocked back onto his rear chair legs as he looked up at the man before him. "So you're Darlington. Should I be impressed?"

Sabrina watched in rapt fascination as Lord Darlington picked up the man's tankard of ale, took a leisurely sip from it, and then flung the rest into the face of his detractor.

With a roar of rage the sodden gentleman arched forward to set the front chair legs back on the floor. The viscount was faster. He lifted a foot and set it against the wedge of seat showing between the macaroni's spread thighs and shoved, sending him tumbling backward onto the floor.

" 'Tis no wonder the English aristocracy has no luck controlling their colonies when you observe their way with ale," Darlington commented to the room at large, then turned away.

The comment set the patrons rocking with laughter.

Their mirth was cut short by the pungent profanity that erupted from the gentleman who sat on the floor mopping up his ale-soaked lace. All heads turned expectantly toward him.

A shiver of excitement passed through Sabrina, for even she knew that the gentleman must now respond to the viscount's insult or live with the pain of his public humiliation.

Tossing away his ale-soaked handkerchief, the dandy struggled to his feet with the help of his companions. Then, flanked by them, he rushed the retreating man and caught him by the sleeve, forcing him to turn around.

"God's body, but you're an ugly rascal!" he crowed when his eyes came to focus on the viscount's face.

Something less than a smile traced the viscount's lips. "And you, sir, are a drunk. 'Tis a failing that may save you from gray hairs." His silver gaze measured the distance to the man's dangling sword arm, the fingers of which twitched in uncertainty. "But, I pray you, find some other executioner. I've killed once this day. My bloodlust is surfeited."

The announcement electrified Sabrina, as it did the crowd who backed away from the two men. She rose to her feet and this time Lady Charlotte did not attempt to stop her.

"You will not stand to a challenge?" the dandy shouted in false bravado for as his hands twitched, his knees trembled.

The viscount made a short gesture of dismissal. "I refuse."

Sabrina expelled a breath of relief as Darlington turned his back on his enemy and strolled confidently toward the exit. She was about to smile in approval when their gazes met.

For no more than the length of a checked step his incisive pale gray stare bored into her. In that moment she wondered if his gaze had sliced through her disguise, through the silk and lace and full-bottomed wig to lay bare the furiously beating heart of the woman beneath her corsets. The sudden vulnerability of that exposure and its wonder provoked in her a hard shiver that was not all trepidation.

Until this moment, she had not met a man in all London that she might admire. Now she felt the stimulating presence of this man that led men to envy him and women to succumb.

A moment later he turned to the door and went through it.

She slumped back against the filthy wall, uncertain of whether she was glad or disappointed that he had not spoken. She had seen in his face an expression that contained no emotion, no anger, no fear, and no interest in whether its possessor lived or died.

A moment later the tavern's company erupted in chaos. As if failing to have the fight they have spoiled for, the company decided to create a release of their pent-up expectations by venting it upon their own.

"Come, quickly!" James Branston shouted and they ran away from the fracas.

It was pure bad luck that their retreat from the tavern had been intercepted by the night watch, whose attention had been drawn by the tavern brawl.

The opening of a door on the hall interrupted Sabrina's reverie and Mrs. Varney, her cousin's housekeeper, stepped into the gallery.

"Mr. McDonnell will see you now," she said with distaste in her voice.

Ignoring her, Sabrina stepped across the threshold into a well-lit room.

Like many wealthy practitioners of Calvinist austerity, Robert McDonnell denied himself all public show of riches yet did not stint upon his private pleasures. The fire was thickly piled with coal. Enough candle wax burned to illuminate a far larger room. Near the fire, he sat ramrod straight in a high-back chair, soberly attired in a buff brown suit with plain white linen. He was square and well fed. Only the severity of his temperament betrayed his extremist views.

Sabrina noted these things at the edge of her thoughts, for her cousin was staring at her with eyes as dark as ink as they took in the leather boot tips showing beneath her cloak. "Well, mistress. Let's have a good look at you."

Certain he would order his servants to strip her if she refused, Sabrina threw back her cloak defiantly, revealing what lay beneath. Mrs. Varney's indrawn breath hissed like a snake in the silence.

The sight of his female relation dressed in a gentleman's silk coat and breeches set her guardian's lips aquiver. He blinked rapidly as he took in the details of lace ruffles, leather boots, and even an ornamental sword.

When she could stand the suspense of his silence no longer Sabrina said carelessly, "You need not have worried that I'd raided your cupboard, cousin. Our tastes are *très* dissimilar."

He started at her bold words. "Is this an example of what London has taught you? That you are no better than—than . . ."

She saw a speck of spittle fly forth as he fumbled for words. It seemed he did not possess the vocabulary to describe his abhorrence of what she had done. " 'Tis the device of a slut!"

Sabrina held her head high though she flushed deeply at the deprecation. " 'Twas no more than a bit of foolery, cousin. 'Tis all the rage among London ladies."

"The rage of harlots, I've no doubt! No lady could ever conceive of so disgusting a display. Whose garments do you wear, mistress?"

Resentment throbbed inside Sabrina. If her cousin cared to look he would find Lady Lovelace's family crest embroidered inside of the clothing she wore. That she must not allow. "I did not inquire. I stole them from a laundry line."

McDonnell's lids flickered again. "I demand the name of the person who tempted you to this."

She shrugged elaborately and wrapped her cloak about herself, emboldened by the liquor singing in her veins. "Betray a friend? Would that not be unchristian?"

"Don't blaspheme!" He rose from his chair, his jowled face livid. "You are in dishonor and disgrace."

Sabrina hid a hiccup behind one small hand. If this was the best threat her cousin could manage, she had wasted a good quarter hour in needless worry.

He pointed a finger at her. "If you had not been recognized as a lady of Quality, do you know where you would be at this moment?"

Sabrina held back the tart observation that she would most probably be safely abed. He wanted contrition. She would give it to him because the ale that had earlier made her merry was now making her woozy.

She lowered her head, her thick lashes sweeping over smiling violet eyes that would certainly give her away. "I beg your pardon, Cousin, and swear to never again be found out in folly."

She turned abruptly to Mrs. Varney. "Send my maid to me with an ewer of hot water. I should like a bath before I retire."

"We are not done, mistress!"

Sabrina turned back to her cousin, one black brow arched in imperious inquiry. "Must there be more, cousin? The evening has left me most dreadfully dull. I assure you, I shall make a more worthy recipient of your wrath in the morning."

Her unrepentant tone enraged him. "God curse your impudence!"

The moment the words were out, she noted, he seemed to regret his excess of feeling and subsided into his seat. "I have heard it preached many times that the devil makes wickedness attractive in order to entice the virtuous. I am forced to conclude that you have been fashioned for the sole purpose of corrupting souls. I would not doubt you have made a bargain with the Great Deceiver himself."

Sabrina felt the sting of that accusation to the soles her feet. "You would not dare speak such insults to me were I a man."

McDonnell banged the arm of his chair. "You forget that britches do not make you a man!"

The anger drumming at Sabrina's temples redoubled. She had seen a man in action this night with whom she would gladly trade places, be it with her soul as the bargain. Lord Darlington would have made very short work of her cousin! Aye, he would have seen her guardian cowered and begging for mercy!

". . . shall be married at once, to a man with a heart harder and a resolution stronger than mine."

Sabrina shook her head slightly to clear it, so caught up was she in her own thoughts that she had heard only the tail of her cousin's pronouncement. "What is this?"

McDonnell's expression remained a study in distaste. "It will not longer be my duty to chastise and humble your proud spirit for the sake of your soul. On the morrow I shall accept Lord Merripace's offer for your hand."

Sabrina felt as though ice water were flung in her face. "That old reprobate? He's trice my age and his drool smells of snuff. I will not marry him."

"You have no choice."

Sabrina's smile turned sharp at the edges. "If you attempt to force me into marriage, I shall tell Merripace myself what occurred this night. And make no mistake, when I'm done telling the tale he will not wish to wed me. How then, cousin, will you dispose of me in a light favorable to your plans?"

McDonnell rose from his chair and this time approached her. "You dare threaten me?"

Sabrina hesitated. She had suspected for some time,

though she could not prove it, that her cousin was in league with those who plotted behind Sir Robert Walpole's back. Court politics had never been of interest to her yet she was willing to use any cudgel that came to hand to beat back the fate he planned for her.

"I know very well that you back Sir John Barnard's attacks on the king's man, Walpole, for his lack of vigor in pursuing a war against Spain. I have heard you and the men who come here to meet under the shroud of night deplore the king's signing of the Treaty of Seville as a craven policy of conciliation with Catholic France and Spain."

Assured by the rapid blinking of his thin-lashed eyes that she had hit upon the truth, and thereby a weakness, she advanced a step toward him. "If you force me to wed, cousin, I shall use my acquaintance with aristocratic friends to find an excuse to appear before the king's eye. There I will denounce you for the intriguer you are!"

His arm snaked out so quickly Sabrina did not have time to dodge the blow. His palm struck with stunning force across her face, knocking her back a step. Her bootheel caught in the hem of her cloak and she tripped and fell, as he did nothing to try to prevent it.

"Whore! Devil's consort! You will not defy me in this!"

Sabrina stared up at him from the floor, her battered cheek cradled in her hand as she blinked back the tears of pain she could not control. "Touch me again and Lord Lovelace will hear of it."

His expression altered, becoming once more a remote mask of ruthless but deliberate disdain. "I do not think so. In fact, I'm certain no one shall hear anything from you again for quite some time to come. In order to protect you against your own worst proclivities I have no choice but to remove you from all influence outside my own."

Sabrina held her breath. If he consigned her to a madhouse or house arrest with his Calvinist kindred, as he had Kit, she would run away.

"You will be sent at first light into the care of my ailing Aunt Thaddeus, who resides in Bath."

Sabrina dropped her lashes over eyes she knew were suddenly too bright. Her delight nearly betrayed her as a smile struggled on her month. She was being sent away from London! No torment that, no ignominious banishment, but freedom! Her guardian hated the country. He would never come to Bath. He had unknowingly granted her her two most fervent wishes in the same breath. She was leaving London—and escaping the possibility of marriage!

She knew better than to acquiesce too quickly. " 'Tis autumn. The roads will be muddy, travel difficult. Bath will be damp and full of gouty nobles seeking the cure."

"Things to be endured." He sounded inordinately pleased by the hardships she had mentioned. "A chastening of the body may improve your soul. Mrs. Varney will, of course, accompany you. I recommend her piety and humility as a pattern for your own life."

"Sir, you are too kind," Mrs. Varney gushed. "If I can be but a pale example of the exemplary conduct shown by you, sir, I should be grateful to the Almighty."

Sabrina disliked toads in any form and spies even less. She glanced pointedly at Mrs. Varney. "The highways are scarcely safe this time of year, cousin. The gazettes are full of tales of travelers who have been accosted by every sort of brigand and highwayman."

"Highwaymen?" Mrs. Varney repeated in a faint voice.

"You will needs provide us with an armed guard," Sabrina continued. "I hear they are for hire quite reasonably."

"God alone shall protect the righteous," Cousin Robert intoned.

"Then Mrs. Varney will feel herself well-protected against the likes of 'Black Jack' Law." Sabrina offered the shaken woman a malicious smile. "Black Jack is said to be most hospitable to his female victims. He rarely steals more than their virtue."

"That will be enough of that!" Cousin Robert bent a blighting glance upon his ward. "You will go to Bath and Mrs. Varney will accompany you."

Sabrina held her tongue this time because, in point of fact, she was too glad to be leaving London to care to destroy his design. Only one thing more would make her life complete. "May Kit visit me there?"

Sabrina stiffened as her cousin's dark eyes, which had blazed moments before, grew distant and chill. "You do expect that I will reward you for this night's work? I am sending you away that you may neither speak to nor see anyone until after you are wed."

He stared at the young woman at his feet, an unholy amusement kindling in his gaze. "Besides, they tell me your father's bastard is ill again and unfit for travel."

Sabrina rose to her knees, her pain forgotten. "Kit? What's wrong with him?"

He gave her a pitying look, his voice laced with scorn. "How kindly you speak of your father's by-blow."

Sabrina rose with surprising grace, if a little unsteadiness, to her feet. "Kit's mother and my father were wed."

His voice did not rise to her challenge this time. "Not according to God's law."

Sabrina met his stare with flat determination. "Handfast has been sanctioned for generations in the West Country."

"The king saw fit to rule otherwise," he said in a dismissive tone. "Your father's bastard has been disowned."

The king's verdict was less than three months old and galled Sabrina still. "You were behind that deed, as well. It could perhaps be rescinded were the truth known. The king would be interested to know that by denying Kit his birthright, he has allowed you to fund your causes against him with my father's fortune."

"Your reckless words simply prove my point. As for the bastard, I am considering sending him to the workhouse. My patience with him is at an end."

Sabrina blanched. "Consignment to a workhouse would kill him."

"Mayhap so," he rejoined with a small smile.

In that moment Sabrina understood she had made a mortal enemy.

All feelings of concern for herself dissolved. There was only one person she loved in this world and that was Kit. After the death of his mother, she had cared for him and been as much a parent to him as any. She had ached and fretted over the parting from him this last year. Now he was in mortal danger and she, feeble female that she was, was his only hope for rescue.

Swallowing the bitter bile of resignation she lowered her head and said in a tight voice, "Very well, I'll go to Bath."

Seemingly pleased to have wrung a rare concession from the proud girl, he nodded. "There you will remain until the marriage contract has been signed. 'Tis hoped you would learn a degree of humility from an isolated contemplation of your former life. Anything less and you may depend upon it that you will never see your father's bastard again."

Sabrina abruptly turned her back and walked away, no longer able to endure the sight of him. She paused when she reached the door and glanced back over her shoulder to where her guardian stood staring after her.

"I will find a way to best you, Cousin Robert," she said under her breath. "I swear upon my father's grave! Even if I must seek aid from the devil himself!"

Chapter Two

"Hold there!" cried the Lovelace butler as the masculine intruder made to push past him.

He put his arm out to block the entrance to the earl's Hanover Square residence, but the "gentleman" struck him on the back of the hand with the spines of a very feminine ostrich feather fan, and cried in a throaty contralto, "Stand aside, Geoffrey!"

The poor man's eyes widened in uncharacteristic surprise. "Oh! 'Tis you, m'lady!"

"Of course, 'tis I."

Lady Charlotte Lovelace sailed past her startled butler into the front hall to the accompanying swirl of a voluminous black cape and the powdery scent of a gentleman's full-bottomed wig.

As she continued in an elegant glide toward the dining salon, the butler scrambled ahead of her to snatch open the doors to allow her entrance.

Once inside the dark-paneled room she stopped short. One glance was enough to reveal her worst fears—here was indisputable proof of her earlier activities.

Surrounding several card-strewn tables, rush-bottomed chairs had been pushed back in haste, evidence of her guests' abrupt departure. Sputtering tapers still cast flickering reflections in the pewter surface of candlesticks and flatware. The ruins of her four P.M. supper, the fashionable hour for dining in town, had congealed on platters and plates and in spatters upon the linen cloth of the long center table.

"Geoffrey!" she called in her carrying voice. "Geoffrey!"

"Yes, countess?" the butler replied from a safe distance in the open doorway.

She made a short sharp gesture with her fan. "What is the meaning of this? Why has the table not been dealt with?"

Geoffrey said soothingly as he approached, " 'Twas on your ladyship's instruction that the table not be cleared each evening until after his lordship has returned for the night."

"Ran is not yet home?"

The brightening of her spirits revealed itself in her extraordinarily blue eyes. In hopes of inspiring jealousy in her often-absent husband, she had for weeks deliberately left evidence for her own abandoned pleasures. But tonight she wished him to think her as solitary as a pigeon in a parsonage.

"Then there is still time to reap victory from what I deemed certain defeat. Clear the table at once."

"Yes, my lady." Geoffrey tried not to stare at the slightly askew wig upon the countess's head. Because she was a tall woman, he had to lift his chin in order not to seem to be peering at her from beneath his lids. "His lordship has just sent word to you to expect his return shortly."

"Shortly?" The countess's cerulean gaze recalculated the possibility of removing the telltale signs of her former company. Yes, it could be accomplished. "Then why do you stand there? Have the table cleared. Immediately, do you hear me!"

All too well, thought the much put-upon butler. His mistress of eleven months was always clear in her needs and wants, though she changed them with even more frequency than her gowns. "It will be done, my lady."

"Another thing." She swung her head toward the old retainer, meeting his eye with a frankness most ladies would never have thought to spare an inferior. "Upon his lordship's return, inform him that I have retired for the night and bid him not to disturb me. 'Tis imperative! Disaster shall befall all of us if you fail me!" With a sweep of her great cape she turned and departed the room.

As he rang for the understaff, abed this last hour, the Lovelace butler wondered how it would all end. He had witnessed during the earl's rollicking bachelorhood rows between Lord Randolph and several jilted mistresses. One had involved an intoxicated duchess with a predilection for throwing breakable objects. Yet he had never met a lady to equal the new countess. Her titian hair, when a wig did not muffle it, was proof not only of her temper but also of a will to match. Only the earl, being the sort of man he was, could control her. Yet it was clear that things were at a sad state between the pair.

It was common knowledge that the earl had married for that rarest of all reasons, one that the nobility considered the frailest foundation for such an alliance. Lord Lovelace had married for love. Yet, after the first blissful weeks, things had deteriorated with a shocking rapidity. Their lovers' spats had become more frequent and sustained. Of late the respectable old residence had rung regularly with the sounds of their quarreling.

Geoffrey shook his head as he bent to pick up the ostrich fan the countess had dropped. It was like her to abuse so elegant a bit of frippery. The earl could be equally negligent, leaving behind him a trail of mallaca canes, jeweled snuffboxes, and the occasional glove. The trouble was they were both like children, headstrong and unable to admit to error and apologize. Her ladyship had too much money, too much time, and too few interests to occupy her, while the earl was far too preoccupied with the affairs of state and therefore sadly neglecting his pretty wife.

The butler frowned as he fished a snuffbox with the initial "M" set in diamonds on the lid from among a pile of cards and chips scattered on one table. Sir Millpost's, no doubt.

He did not approve of all the countess's guests, especially Sir Millpost, an acquaintance of Lord Lovelace's bachelor days. There was a gentleman more than willing to incite a slighted wife with the *on dits* of the less respectable members of the Beau Monde. Yet her ladyship had not, for all her youth and recklessness, seemed the sort to be taken in by rakes and rogues.

Perhaps he had overestimated the countess's good sense. For had he not just been shocked to glimpse Lady Lovelace's legs encased in a gentleman's blue silk breeches and white silk stockings? What his lordship would make of that he did not wish to imagine!

A quarter of an hour later, Lotte, as Lady Charlotte was referred to privately by her husband, reclined in an elegant sprawl of dishabille upon the pile of pillows propped on her bed. Minus the wig, her natural titian-hued curls fell in artful arrangement about her perfectly sloping shoulders. The sensual lines of her voluptuous body were merely suggested beneath the folds of her silk wrapper. The expression on her face, a trifle wide at brow and jaw for fashionable beauty, suggested boredom. Beneath half-moon brows, her clear pansy-blue eyes reflected an inward preoccupation while her mouth was set in a contemplative pout. No one who might chance upon her reverie would suspect her of the mischievous nature that had fueled the evening's escapade. Yet her air of careless indifference was a well-practiced pose. Behind her serene expression, Lotte was furious.

It was Jemmy's fault!

A pucker of annoyance momentarily marred her boredom. A fine cockscomb he made! James Branston had run away like a green maiden when the night watch unmasked their little ruse. If sweet Sabrina Lyndsey, her young companion, had not had the wit to suggest a bribe to the guard then they might have both been hauled before a magistrate. As it was, the guard had insisted upon accompanying them to their homes.

Lotte closed her eyes as the first stirring of emotion rouged her cheeks. As if Ran was not already completely out of charity with her over her extravagance, her gambling debts, her choice of friends and, not least, her failure to conceive again.

Lotte's eyes snapped open, her soft mouth crimped in one corner by anguish. She was sorry she had miscarried the child conceived in the fourth month of their marriage. Yet the nine weeks leading up to the loss had been terrible enough. The constant sickness, the plaguey poor feeling, the debilitating exhaustion, and then the sudden sharp pains knifing through her and the blood, so much blood! She knew then how much worse the pregnancy might have been. Her own mother had died giving birth to her.

No, she did not want to conceive again. Had consulted a midwife in Hackberry Lane for advice on how to make certain she would not. Of course, she had not told Ran what she was doing. He talked constantly of having a child.

A shiver passed over Lotte's skin as delicately as a ripple on a still pond. What her husband would have had to say about that she could not bear to entertain. He was cool enough toward her as it was.

A fresh sense of unease gripped her. Hugh Millpost had passed on the news to her as a bit of idle gossip, as if he supposed she must already be aware.

Ran had taken a mistress!

"I do tho admire your huthband's tathe in women," Millpost had whispered in her ear between sets of cards, his speech impediment serving to make his tattle all the more venomous. "Hith stamina wath alwayth rumored to be prodigiouth. Two redheads, yet! My dear, you muth find a match for the pair of grays he purchased for her. They tho perfectly compliment her new carriage. But hith choice of lodgings . . . even Queensbery ith more particular about the location of hith mithrethes."

Lotte snapped her mouth shut before a profanity could escape. It was bad enough Ran neglected her shockingly for his political friends. Now he had openly set up a mistress. She had no reason to doubt it. Rumor carried by Millpost was always wickedly precise. There had been mistresses before their marriage, for Ran was too virile a man to live otherwise. But that he had taken another, before a year of marriage was up!

Lotte made a moue as she rearranged the folds of her Chinese green silk wrapper to cover her bare legs. No, she would not think about that any longer.

All their troubles were the fault of his friends, she was certain of that. They saw to it that he was too occupied by political intrigue to provide her with protection and advice, and keep her out of trouble. He must dine with those who thought themselves superior to her because they spoke of treaties and war over their partridge, and of alliances and tendered bills for the House of Lords over port while she nodded off out of boredom. How she hated them all! A proper husband would have been here tonight to prevent his wife's folly. She was innocent, completely above reproach in the evening's events.

As she liberally applied this salve to her stinging conscience she dipped into her bonbon box, choosing a candied orange rind coated in marzipan. There was only one more tiny cloud on her horizon. How would she ever raise the money to pay her gambling debts?

She had taken up gambling in order to occupy her lonely

nights and, as usual, she had been losing badly tonight. When the evening's losses were tallied, hers were the heaviest, to Jemmy Branston. Lingering after the others he had repeated an idle bit of gossip that certain London ladies had been sighted on the town dressed up in their husbands' clothing! He then proposed to cancel her debt if she enacted a similar masquerade. The risk had seemed slight compared to what Ran's reaction was likely to be when he learned the extent of her gaming debts.

Lotte sighed as she bit into the almond paste confection. Of all her husband's faults, and as his wife she could attest to the fact that he possessed many, she found his righteous indignation the most galling. She could but agree with Viscount Darlington. The gentleman had only a few nights earlier pronounced her husband's manner, "a trifle high in the instep for an earl."

If only Jack had not appeared so unexpectedly at the tavern on the Thames, Jemmy might have kept his head to a better degree. But Branston was like most young men, in awe of the brashly confident viscount. Oh, but he had behaved magnificently at the tavern in turning the tables on those besotted fellows! If Darlington had been with her this evening things would have ended much differently.

Lotte's mouth softened as if in expectation of a kiss. Bitingly witty and sinfully attractive, though icily disdainful at times, Lord Darlington was the only man other than Ran who made her heart beat a little faster. Of course, she loved Ran. Yet no lady liked to be neglected and she was certain she had detected a glimmer of interest in the viscount's silvery gaze.

Once Ran had been her most ardent swain. During their courtship Ran had on one occasion slept in her father's garden below her window because he said he could not bear to be parted from her even for a night. Once wed, he had pleasured her in ways that she had never even known to dream of. But his ardor had cooled during the eleven months of their marriage, solidifying lately into a very millstone of husbandry. Now some carrot-topped doxy was receiving his ardent attentions.

"A pox on wedded bliss!" she muttered darkly.

"I greet you with equal felicitations, sweet wife."

The familiar baritone voiced from the doorway brought Lotte into a sitting position. There stood her husband, looking as splendid as ever in a masculine habit of deep green satin and dripping French lace at neck and cuffs, a fashion he preferred over the more austere English style. His wig was queued back with a black ribbon, the new English vanity.

Yet it was the man himself, not the trappings of an aristocrat, who had held her in thrall from the first. He was tall and lean, which made him appear even taller. Harshly handsome with bold nose and firm mouth, here was the only the man she had ever invited into her full embrace.

Struck by the heat that had always enveloped her whenever he entered a room, Lotte leaned back, allowing her wrapper to slide open on a provocative length of gartered thigh. "Oh, 'tis only you."

His gaze narrowed in speculation upon her immodest display. "Whom else were you expecting, Lotte love?"

Lotte sent him a wary look from beneath seductively lowered lids. Whenever he called her "Lotte love," they were certain to have a nasty row. Dear lord, had he heard?

"No one unless, perhaps, my maid," she managed to say without a tremor.

He took a step inside the room into which she had pointedly not invited him, his gaze lingering long enough in the room's deepest shadows to enrage her. Did he really think she had a secret admirer tucked away in a corner?

Gathering her courage, she decided to sling the first stone. After all, what had she to lose? "If you've come home to scold me, you may save your breath. Your disaffection with me is legend. You need not refine upon it tonight."

Lord Randolph Lovelace's plum brown gaze returned to his wife. Lounging in her bed with her red-gold hair undressed and tumbling about her lovely shoulders, her skin gleaming enticingly in the candlelight, she looked both innocent and sluttish all at once. Swept by a sudden familiar sense of longing and rage, he could not decide whether to rush over and embrace or throttle her. Instead, he retreated into the role of mocking husband.

"If I am disaffected with you, Lotte, then it is by your doing. You will insist upon surrounding yourself with companions who are beneath you. Without exception they are either idle, dissolute, incorrigible gamblers, or all three into the bargain."

Lotte pretended to be absorbed in the exact twist of the curl she fingered. "I can't think who you might mean. They were friends of yours first, Ran."

"Not Darlington."

"No, Darlington is a particular friend of mine," she answered smugly. "But certainly Millpost was counted among your acquaintances. I vow I am as afraid of the baronet's vicious tongue as anyone is. Half the Beau Monde goes in fear of that most accomplished gossip. The other half entertains him shamelessly in hopes of learning the fearful secrets of the first half." She cast a coquettish glance her spouse's way. "I prefer to be among the second half."

"Millpost is a malicious talebearer. Do you think any word you slip in his ear is not privy to all of London within the hour?"

Lotte reached for the lace handkerchief tucked into her décolletage, relief tugging the corners of her mouth into a smile. If Ran could make conversation about Millpost, he had not yet heard of her little escapade. "You are too harsh. Perhaps he does tattle, but what of it?" She glanced up at him with the first flirtatious curl in her smile. "Admit, he tells delightful stories. So droll, don't you know."

Her husband eyed her coldly. "I've informed Geoffrey that Millpost is no longer to be given entry into my house during my absence." Even as she went stiff in rage he continued in his most haughty voice. "Added to that list shall be any person who has been in regular attendance at your salon parties."

"You cannot do that!" Lotte rose up on her knees, her wrapper sliding open from the knot in the belt in an inverted V that revealed all but the apex of her thighs. "You've no right!"

"As your husband I have every right." He offered her the first smile of the evening and it made her shiver. He was angrier than she had first supposed. To judge by the set of his jaw and glint in his dark eyes he was furious, a judgement she had been able to render with ever more frequency these last months. "I may do anything I wish, dear wife. This is my house."

Lotte tossed her head and retreated into an ordinary wifely compliant. "I do believe you are foxed. Yes, that would explain your boorish attitude. You will drink until your manners are drowned." She sniffed deliberately. "I put to you, my lord, that your own acquaintances are a poor influence upon you."

His smile widened and she knew at once her error. She had handed him exactly what he most wished for, an opening to discuss her own habits. "It is equally obvious that your acquaintances are a dreadful influence upon you."

He came forward slowly, the suspense made all the more terrible until by the time he reached the bed Lotte was visibly trembling. She saw him slip a hand into his coat pocket and then withdraw several bits of paper. With a gesture that was an insult all its own, he sent the papers flying across the distance to land on the coverlet between her spread knees.

"Gambling debts!" he said between his teeth. "Did you think I would not learn of them so soon? Or were you foolish enough to hope I would not learn of them at all?"

Lotte did not reply as she picked up the slips, for they both knew that she would have preferred the latter choice.

"Compliments of Branston," he confirmed for her startled gaze. "Met him in the street an hour ago. Babbled something about a mere dustup and then he said to consider them paid. Would you care to explain?"

Lotte raised shock-widened eyes to her husband's and saw confirmed in his expression that he knew everything, had known everything before he entered her room.

"My wife," he continued in a deceptively soft tone. "My bride, abroad in London's dark dangerous streets, dressed in the breeches of a man and the silly notions of a peagoose.

"Lotte!" The exasperation of the word flared full in his scorching gaze. "Have you no better sense or understanding? Or is one year in London enough to totally corrupt your character?"

Lotte's eyes narrowed like a cat whose mouse had just escaped. "You dare call into question my character when 'tis yours the public makes free with these days?"

To her amazement, Ran blushed. "I have seen the latest gazettes. Caricatures are a politicians' bane."

"Do you think I give a fig for what the gazettes make of your politics? I do not. If that were all!"

"All?" he questioned carefully. "Is there some new scandal to which I am not yet privy? Pray speak plainly."

The chance to wound him was too much for her to resist. Lotte subsided onto her haunches with a melodramatic sigh, her head drooping as she applied her handkerchief to the corners of her eyes. "Very well, if you must have it baldly put to you, if you must see me shamed, if you must—"

"Lotte," he said with a familiar edge to his voice, "I've no patience for soliloquy this night."

"Very well." She looked up at him over the edge of her handkerchief. " 'Tis well known, 'tis nothing less than tittered about in the streets that—that, oh! That you have taken a mistress!"

The entire sentence, hiccuped sobs and all, played back through Ran's thoughts before his lips twitched. "Is that all?"

Her head jerked up, her dispirited maiden pose forgotten. "You mean 'tis true? How dare you stand here in your wife's bedchamber and admit that you have taken a mistress!"

Ran sighed, abashed at last. "You are right, of course. Indelicate of me to acknowledge her. But, Lotte, see reason—"

"Reason?" Her voice rising higher in the end of each word, she sprang forward, her generous bosom straining against the open neckline of her wrapper. "You dare! Dare stand before me, unrepentant? And expect me to be reasonable?"

Ran winced at the shriek of the last word. He had never much cared for his wife's shrill tone when angered. He liked it less and less with every minute. But what shook him more was the slowly mounting realization that he had, perhaps, made the biggest mistake of his life in marrying her. He had suppressed the feeling again and again these last weeks, but he could no longer deny it; his marriage was a disaster and he was at a loss to understand how it had come about.

A man fully conversant in the ways between men and women, he had not known he could feel such depths of tender passion for any living creature until he met Charlotte Samuelson on a spring afternoon riding through the parklands of Somerset. She was beautiful and tall with the vivid coloring that turned all heads. She moved with a sylph's grace and the voluptuous languor of a woman meant to be loved, and often. Yet it was her gaiety and goodness of spirit that had invoked within him the desire to possess her over every other consideration. And there were many.

His family had reminded him that the Samuelsons, once mere squires raised recently to the rank of baron, were not his equals in wealth or rank. His political allies had cautioned him against allying himself with a woman whose family peerage was not important enough for a man with his political aspirations. More candid friends suggested that perhaps a country girl would not be clever or sophisticated enough to hold her own among his London set. They, at least, had been proven correct.

Lotte's indifference to his political dealings, her dislike of his professional associates, and her disdain of his many social duties had seemed merely a matter of adjustment. His professional life could be every bit as tedious as she claimed, yet he had expected she would perform her obligations for the sake of his career. When she refused, after the miscarriage of their child, to any longer accompany him on his nightly outings, choosing instead the company of acquaintances he would rather she snub, he had consoled himself with the thought that she was clever enough to avoid entanglements which would reflect badly upon herself. Now it seemed he was wrong.

She entertained frivolous people. Worst of all, she had become a gambler—a very bad gambler. Her debts had raised the brows of his solicitor. To make matters worse, she had begun denying him access to her bed from time to time. Her actions at first surprised, then hurt, and finally angered him. The bride he had chosen in love to be the mother of his children now looked no more warmly upon his embrace than any loveless alliance he might have chosen.

Yet looking at her now, with her glorious hair undone and her bright eyes full of tears of self-pity, he felt ever more strongly the wild desire to rush to her side. He ached to press her down on the bed, to embrace her naked body and make her weep and moan with equal desire, and then when they were both satisfied he longed to cry, "For God's sake, Lotte, let us stop this madness! Let us forgive one another and promise not to quarrel ever again!" The paradox held him immobile.

Lotte saw reflected in his handsome face the struggle taking place within him but could not fathom the reason behind it. The more he stared harshly at her the more convinced she became that her rash actions this night had evaporated whatever love had remained between them. The thought truly frightened her and she struck out against it.

She wrapped her robe tightly about herself, her voice dripping with sarcasm as she said, "If you have said all you wish to say, certainly there must be some bill, some matter that would better occupy your thoughts than your wife."

"Lotte, I—" He broke off, looking distracted. "Yes, you are right. I was to meet Lord Darlington at Lincoln's Inn Field."

"Jack?" Lotte said with some malicious twinkle in her gaze. "I don't doubt you will find his company preferable. I certainly would find his preferable to yours."

Something in her tone brought him up short. He had heard there were rumors circulating about the address Darlington was paying his wife but had never given them credence. Anywhere Darlington went, dark rumor sprung up in his path like poison mushrooms. Yet now, he was forced to put a new interpretation to Darlington's attentions to Lotte. Perhaps she was encouraging them.

But no, surely his lovely, silly bride would not be so remiss in her duty to him to provide first an heir? Or would she? That would explain why she sometimes spurned his advances when once she had welcomed his embrace at all times.

A lover! The ugly suspicion took root instantly in his mind and grew with the rapidity of a morning glory vine.

Fury shook him, uncalculated, unreasoned, irrational. He took a step back from the bed and then another, afraid for her in his rage. "Until you have come to your senses, you are confined to this house. And hear me, Lotte. You will obey me! Or else!"

"Or else? Ran?" But she was too late.

He did not hesitate in his step as he strode across the room to the door that connected their bedchambers, unlocked it, and then slammed it behind him with such fury that the chandelier a floor below could be heard tinkling in the sudden silence.

Lotte collapsed in hysterics that lasted a full half hour. At the end of that time she felt much better, so good in fact that she rose and rang the bell for her maid.

The lassitude of an hour earlier evaporated with her rising fury. When she arrived, Lotte ordered the sleepy maid to pack her for a long journey and then began impatiently prowling her room.

She would not remain beneath the roof of a man who was so unfeeling and cruel! She would not allow Ran to treat her like an errant child or shut her up like a broken bit of crockery he no longer wished to look at. She would not simply subside into the role of neglected wife. She loved him too passionately for that. She would run away! Yes, that was what she would do!

Feeling the packing was progressing much too slowly, she began jerking items of clothing from her armoire and casting them about the room as she plotted her escape. She had heard the spa town of Bath was a pleasant place in the off-season and that gambling there was free and easy. If she remembered correctly, the Lovelace family even kept a house there. She would wile away her time until her husband came to his senses. That would require that he leave his precious House of Lords to come to collect her—if he still wished to have a wife.

"Now we shall see what is most important to you!" she said as she tossed a shoe at their connecting door.

Chapter Three

From the pit to the servants' upper galleries, the theater at Lincoln's Inn Field was filled with customers who had come to watch the pantomime of *Orpheus in the Lower Regions.* It was the most talked about production of the season, rumored to have cost Mr. Rich, the director of the theater, more than 4,000 pounds sterling.

Certainly the enormous serpent slithering from the wings, accompanied by startled male gasps and feminine shrieks from the audience, appeared to be worth a hefty sum. Covered in shiny gold and green scales with brilliant crimson spots, it boasted fire-bright eyes, lethal-looking fangs, and a hiss of unnerving realism. The clockwork machinery required to automate the beast was first-rate. It crossed the stage with a sinuous grace not unlike its natural counterpart, a fact that did not go unappreciated by the spellbound audience.

Yet in the velvet-hung boxes of the theater, where a profusion of high-backed gilded chairs offered luxurious seating for noblemen and women who were not their wives, the topic of interest was of a decidedly different nature.

All along those expensively adorned tiers the scintillating whispers circulating behind lifted hands and discreetly spread fans concerned one of their own. According to the latest *on dit,* the subject of that conversation had proved himself just that very morning to be every bit as deadly as the serpent occupying the stage.

The murmur of voices grew in volume as the ears of those distracted from the production pricked up at snatches of conversation here and there.

"—Darlington in Lord Revoit's box!"

"Give's a man a start, that scar."

" 'Tis the first letter of the word 'cursed'."

"That scar?"

"—his own sire done it."

" 'Pon oath!"

"The late viscount suffered delusions—"

"Still, a peer and all, not much to be done."

"—ran mad, convinced the boy was not his but Satan's spawn, he murdered his wife and—"

"—sought to put the mark of Cain on his own son with a knife."

"—sent to relatives in the West Indies for safekeeping."

"What could one explain his peculiarities. His own hair! Not at all *à la mode.*"

"—wild from the first, they say. Ran away from his guardians at thirteen."

"Lived among the pirates, privateers, and gamblers of the Caribbean."

"Wild, m'dear!"

"—and women!"

"A positive satyr!"

"A renowned duelist."

"Surfeit of madness there?"

"Believe it."

Accustomed to the sly glances and scandalous whispers that often accompanied his public appearances, Jack Laughton sat like stone. The only sign of unrest were his long hard fingers tapping an impatient tattoo on his bronze silk-clad thigh.

Unlike his companions, he was not even mildly entertained by the spectacle. He felt only faint annoyance eddying through his haze of intoxication. When the serpent sank its dagger-like fangs into Eurydice's enticingly bared neck, it dawned on him that he knew the actress, intimately, and that her neck tasted of greasepaint and sweat.

As the beast sluiced away, its deadly deed accomplished, Jack considered dispassionately the fact that every man present believed him to be as cold-natured as that mechanical reptile. Upon rising at five P.M. he had responded to the news that Chichester had, indeed, died from his wounds with the order that the widow be sent the standard funereal arrangement and his wishes for a speedy recovery. Even his admirers blanched as he recounted the tale at supper.

Bitterness curled Jack's upper lip, making the seam in his cheek more pronounced as the audience oohed and ahhed in lamentation over Orpheus's lost love. To his mind the aristocrats seated about him were nothing more than carrion birds dressed in exotic plumage. Rings adorned their sharp talons and practiced smiles blunted the wicked curves of their beaks. Yet their fixed-eyed stares betrayed them to be every bit as heartless as vultures who sought in every glance a sign of weakness among their own. They fed daily on the misery of their neighbors, spicing their mealtimes with gossip of others' frailties and shames and misfortune.

They might linger in sentimentality over this gaudy sham of mythology and yet they rallied around a duplicitous social order that had required for the sake of primogeniture that society protect a murderous nobleman at the expense of justice for his dead wife and abused son. Only in their fear of appearing equally vulnerable were they banded together. Let them talk. They feared him and, for now, that was enough.

"Darlington!"

Jack looked up with faint disinterest at the tall man who had entered the box. "Lord Lovelace, we had despaired of your company this evening," he murmured with just enough apathy to make a mockery of the greeting. He turned to the younger of his two companions. "Be a good fellow and provide Lord Lovelace your chair, Alan."

The younger man grinned amicably and rose. "Do join us, Lord Lovelace. The pantomime has just ended and the best part's about to begin. The gladiators' spectacle is next."

"Promises to be of the rarest sport," added Lord Revoit, who made up the third member of the party. "A healthy wager by you would be welcome, Lovelace."

"I do not bet," Randolph returned shortly.

Jack's interest quickened as he turned a deceptively languid gaze on the earl. Lovelace's patrician features were more drawn than usual, as if he were struggling to keep his temper at bay. It was an interesting possibility Jack could not resist putting to the test.

"We've seen damned little of you these last weeks. Your lady wife so opined over supper but recently."

Randolph accepted the seat, then said peremptorily, "You dined with my wife tonight?"

His clipped tone drew Jack's smile. What had lovely naughty Lotte been telling her prideful spouse that should have him looking like a cock with his tail feathers caught in a stile? Just for the devilment of it, Jack drew out his answer. "You have my compliments of her. Not three in London can equal your wife's charm or her complexion. Alas, Lady Charlotte and I did not dine together this evening. Believe me, I would not abandon so charming a companion for an evening elsewhere."

Randolph held himself in check though he longed to bodily attack the man whose sardonic wit seemed always to hold him up to faint ridicule. Yet how alike was his *bon mot* to Lotte's chastisement. When had Darlington become a rival for his wife's affection? And just how successful had he been? The questions roiled in his belly but he would not give them voice. "I have informed my lady wife that we shall no longer be at home to her greater circle of acquaintances. Your name adorns our list of visitors inconvenient."

Jack noted the sudden twitch at the back of the box and turned to find Hugh Millpost standing there, eyes wide with intrigue. His often silent approach had served the gossipmonger well on this occasion. There would be no need to inform anyone of Lovelace's action. Millpost would make certain the *on dit* accompanied every cup of cocoa served to the Beau Monde at breakfast. A pity, Jack thought. Lovelace should have had the presence of mind to spare his wife the embarrassment.

Randolph, too, had noted the presence of another but gave the tongue-wagger the cut direct by not speaking to him. He could not dismiss the man, but he did not have to encourage him.

He turned back to Darlington, his voice distinctly lower. "I expected to find Branston here. Or was he too fatigued by the night's earlier adventure to join you?"

Too shrewd to rise to the bait of the earl's tantalizing question, Jack yawned. "The fellow's a noncock and a fool."

Randolph could but agree with that assessment of Branston, yet he did not make the mistake of applying the label to Darlington. Though his drunken state was obvious from his flushed face and lazy posture, the viscount retained a shrewd calculating gaze and the superiority of self-possession. He might detest the man, disapprove of and resent him, but he did not underestimate him. If Darlington had set his sights on seducing Lotte then he would not easily be distracted.

"Oh, but look here. Didn't I predict there'd be rare sport tonight?" Sir Alan said as the curtains again parted. A surprised cheer went up as two women emerged from the wings of the stage, each carrying a three-and-a-half-foot, two-handed sword.

"What's this?" Randolph asked, jarred momentarily out of his own dark thoughts.

"Women gladiators?" Lord Revoit gave a harrumph of discomfort. "All but unheard of."

As soon as they reached the center of the stage, the two women bowed deeply to the audience in show of deference.

"This is preposterous!" Randolph voiced in irritation.

"They make a change from ballerinas," Jack drawled, his mood improved by the chance to further goad the earl. "Conveniently, they provide the usual stimulation." He leaned forward in feigned interest of the proceedings on the stage. "Observe how the short petticoats leave the limbs free while the bodices hide only the summit of their delights."

"And they wear different colored ribbons," Sir Alan offered in the spirit of amiability. " 'Twill make it easier to tell them apart."

Jack shot the younger man a disbelieving glance. Far more obvious demarcations than colored ribbons were the differences in size and hair color between the two women. One was amazingly stout with a shock of dirty blond hair scraped back from her face and tied with a bit of red ribbon and the ham-like arms of a coal miner. The other, russet-haired and clearly a dozen years younger, was tall and broad-shouldered, but much more slender.

The older woman stepped forward first and snarled at the younger woman, causing her to falter back a step. A ripple of self-conscious laughter skirted the crowd and was quickly silenced.

The impressive muscles in her arms were apparent as she raised over her head her sword. The three-inch wide blade was dull for most of it. But the last six inches caught and reflected the stage lights with the telltale gleam of a well-honed edge.

" 'Ere ioy stands, luvvies!" she cried in a gin-blurred voice. "Give us a coin afore ioy gives ye a show. Guaranteed spectacle." She jerked her head toward the younger woman and curled her lip. "Ioy'm a smithy by trade and will make quick work o' the Irish drab. Ask me 'usband. Beats 'im every mornin' just to keep me hand in!"

The boastful claim drew laughter and a few coins that sailed past the apron of the stage to ring merrily on the boards.

As the blond bent over to scoop out the coins, the younger woman strutted forward and gave the larger woman a wallop on the buttocks with the flat of her sword. "Shut up, ye ole sow!"

The bigger woman roared her chagrin as she straightened. "Sneakin' lil' whore! I'll chase ye clear back to the fey isle ye sprung from." She swung her sword violently at the younger woman, who sidestepped it with ease.

"Sure'n I'm spry enough to keep ahead of the likes of ye, ye anvil-handed English cow!"

The younger woman's sally elicited a light shower of coins on her side of the stage.

"Thousand pounds on the Irish girl!" Lord Revoit proclaimed with a shout of glee. " 'Twill be worth it to lose if she lands even one good blow. Who'll take my wager?"

When no one answered, Millpost moved from the curtain at the back of the box, his carrion bird beak of a nose twitching in excitement. "Lord Revoit's wager will not go taken?"

"I'll not wager tuppence on so tawdry a display," Randolph answered and rose abruptly.

He again drew Jack's sardonic gaze. "Are you leaving, Lovelace? The fun is only beginning."

A muscle ticked in Randolph's jaw. "On the other hand, I am unastonished that this spectacle of female depravity should arouse a man of your tastes."

The warm breathy roar of the crowd momentarily swept over them as Jack considered his options. Lovelace was no fool and only a fool phrased himself so carelessly that his words might be mistake for an insult. Yet he offered him that possibility. "On this occasion I shall bow to your judgement of the proper pursuits of womanhood."

Randolph's expression betrayed his inclination to repeat his insult, but he said, "As I do not share your predilection for bloodshed, I withdraw my hasty words."

Millpost craned his neck forward, all gleaming yellow teeth and reptilian smile accompanied by a faint malodorous whiff of digested cheese. "A wager! That ith how gentlemen thettle their acrimony. Will you not acthept a friendly wager from Lord Lovelace, Lord Darlington?"

Randolph suddenly remembered a bit of gossip Lotte had let drop a few days earlier. Darlington's finances had suffered a reversal of fortune which a steady stream of loses at the gambling tables were aggravating. A final staggering loss, one he could not easily repay, might turn the trick of driving Darlington in humiliation out of London.

"Very well, to indulge you, Darlington, I will make a wager with you alone. What say, ten thousand?"

Jack felt a faint flush of gambling blood creep up the back of his neck. Ten thousand! That amount would settle his debts—if he won. If not . . .

The whispering of warning returned, swift and urgent. Yet, he had never been a man to abide curtailment of his desires, even if the suggestion came from his own conscience.

"Ten thousand, you say." His voice was absolutely steady. There was no flicker of fear or greed in his expression. Gambling might be his passion, but it was a bloodless, cerebral activity at which he was exceedingly good. "Why not twenty?"

"Jack you can't—" Revoit's soft-spoken alarm was silenced by a quelling glance from Darlington.

Randolph's expression eased into warmth for the first time. "Why not, indeed." He indicated the stage with an economic sweep of his arm. "Choose your champion."

At last Jack found his full interest drawn to the stage.

The referee, who carried a long staff, was calling out the rules of the battle. It was his job, he said, to separate the two should blood flow. The winner would be determined by the first to draw blood three times, unless one combatant cried halt sooner. Despite her cockiness, the redhead appeared more than a little afraid of the older, stout-bellied woman. Her sword trembled in her grasp as they slowly circled one another. The crowd's merciless mirth urged her on to what most likely would be her doom.

"The Cockney slattern," Jack said suddenly.

"Done!" Lovelace pronounced the word in satisfaction and turned to leave.

"You awe not abandoning youh enterprize, milord?" Millpost exclaimed in disappointment

"I've no interest in the outcome. The sole purpose of my bet was to accommodate Darlington." Randolph's gaze flicked briefly over his adversary. "I expect you will wish to collect or settle the debt before noon?"

Jack met the full hostility in his opponent's gaze with his usual pose of indifference. "At your service, Lovelace."

Jack turned back to the spectacle with only half interest, for it quickly became clear the battle had been choreographed. As the first blows were delivered with the broad sides of their weapons, landing an equal number of times on both, it occurred to him to wonder if Lovelace were already privy to the outcome. He rejected the thought at once. That supercilious stickler for propriety would never be party to a rigged contest.

Something akin to amusement struggled in Jack's chest. Perhaps he could afford Lovelace's high morals if he also had his deep pockets! To redeem his blackened character, he should reconsider wedding the wall-eyed termagant with a hundred thousand a year who had pursued him shamelessly last year in Tortola. Nay, not even for two hundred thousand!

His guffaw of immoderate laughter drew the quick sidelong glances of his companions, but no questions.

On stage the Englishwoman suddenly roared, lifted her broad sword over her head, and brought it down with a vigorous slash that drove the Irish girl backward so quickly she trod on the toe of her own shoe. The girl shrieked as the blade passed within inches of her nose and then sliced into the arm she had raised in protective instinct.

"Halt!" cried the pikeman who moved to separate the bleeding girl from her attacker.

Half the audience crowed their delight, showering the Englishwoman with shillings and half-crowns that she wasted no time in collecting and stuffing into her bodice.

" 'Twould seem your bet's assured," Revoit remarked at Jack's elbow. "Lucky thing. As I recall, you haven't twenty sovereigns to your name at present."

"I had not expected there to be real blood drawn," Jack murmured with a frown.

"Why, these drabs are accustomed to hard knocks. They receive worse when falling down drunk," Sir Alan replied jocularly, as if to convince himself that the wounding was part of the mummery.

Jack did not answer.

Once the Irish girl was bandaged and the Englishwoman fortified by a bucket of ale graciously offered up from an admirer in the audience, the referee called for the battle to recommence.

Each now carried a dagger with which to fend off blows. The women circled one another warily, calling out curses and jeering the audience who alternately encouraged and derided them.

Jack noticed how the Irish girl kept her dagger close to her body with her wound-weakened arm. He knew he should be delighted by that show of weakness. His champion would easily pick her off and he would go home with his financial problems solved.

Instead, he drew his chin into his collar as his fingers

again tapped an impatient rhythm on his knee. This was no sport. This would be a massacre and he no longer wanted any part in it.

Cautiously and then ever more vigorously the women engaged one another with slashes and jabs until their bodices darkened with their exertions and droplets of sweat flew from the ends of their tresses as they swung and swayed, groaned and cried out.

The crowd's hurrahs and cheers became disappointed hoots and catcalls when the pike bearer moved between the two women and ordered them to opposite sides of the stage. There the daggers were exchanged for wicker shields. The Englishwoman again drank a large glass of spirits.

When the pikeman called them to combat for the third time, the Irish girl paused on her side of the stage to tuck in a loose end of her bloodied bandage.

Seeing an advantage in the moment, the Englishwoman charged with the wicked edge of her blade. A cry of warning from the crowd jerked the girl's head up just in time.

She raised her wicker shield to take the brunt of the attack and desperately twisted her body away from the deadly edge. The force of the blow sent her reeling away in a spin that ended when she crashed into the scenery at the rear of the stage. The canvas backdrop, freed by the impact, collapsed upon her.

Seizing the advantage, the Englishwoman took the flat of her blade and delivered a stunning blow across the top of the younger woman's head. Certain of her victory, she then cast aside her armaments and moved to the center front of the stage, lifting her arms in victory and signaling for more tribute.

Several assistants raced out from the wings to help untangle the fallen girl. Once freed, she scrambled to her feet and stood a moment, shaking her head like a colt trying to toss a bridle. Then, to the surprise of every soul present, she launched herself, unarmed, at her opponent.

The attack sent both women sprawling onto the boards. Immediately, the girl swung a leg over the panting woman's belly. Yelling invectives, she grabbed two fists of hair and began banging the woman's head against the wood floor to the bloodthirsty delight of their audience.

Winded by the fall, the larger woman thrashed about under the weight of her opponent like an overturned turtle before she gathered breath to cry out in an ale-slurred voice, "Ioy give!"

As hoarse cries of triumph and surprise rang in the rafters, Jack knew that he had made a grave error. Yet, for the moment, the loss did not seem important. He, too, had been caught up in the rare sight of a weaker soul besting impossible odds. He moved to the near end of his box and tossed the winner the full contents of his pocket, twenty gold sovereigns.

"Are you mad?" Revoit cried. "She's just made you a pauper."

"Demme, Jack, if that ain't a daring bit of generosity," Sir Alan pronounced in tones of frank appreciation.

"You flatter me," Jack answered silkily as he stared down at the stage onto which he had flung the last of his wealth. The Irish girl, bleeding from a dozen small cuts, was staring agape at him.

Sauntering out of the box, he had the sudden sensation of having stepped off a precipice into the open air.

He was broken. Cleaned out.

So, why then, was he smiling?

Chapter Four

"You witnessed the battle of the gladiators?" Jack called above the din of the crowd pouring from the theater.

Zuberi inclined his head then interposed his formidable bulk between the surge of the crowd and the viscount and spread his arms. Without so much as a word, a breech opened in the swift current of humanity around the six foot, five inches of silver and black livery, forming a channel that led directly to the curb and the coach that awaited them outside the theater.

"I partook of a seat in the servants' galley, my lord," Zuberi continued in the formal, slightly archaic speech that was his own as he fell in step beside his lordship. "I was most anxious to witness the mighty victory of the chosen one."

Jack paused before the coach and turned his head toward his servant, a quizzical look on his face. "What chosen one?"

Zuberi's smile was as moonlight in his midnight face. "The female with the splendor of the sun in her hair and the spirit of the lion in her chest. Who could gaze upon her and not see the blessings of the spirits shining within her?"

"A man whose gaze was blighted by French brandy," Jack replied drolly.

"You, my lord, bet against the flame-haired girl?" Zuberi's often-passive face was expressive in his amazement.

The reminder skipped like a stone on the surface of Jack's ennui, casting up ripples of faint annoyance. "The lesson is learned. The price was twenty thousand sovereigns."

Zuberi sucked in a great breath. " 'Tis a handsome sum."

" 'Tis a veritable Adonis gilded in my coin."

"My lord! Viscount Darlington!"

Jack turned slowly, recognizing the ring of challenge in that pronouncement of his name.

"Lord Priestley," he said icily as he spied the short, powerfully built baron of middle years. The man's badly squashed nose, the result of an encounter with an iron door at the age of twelve, made him instantly recognizable. He was known throughout London as an inveterate bully, yet Jack could not remember any encounter between them that might have set up the man's ire this night.

"You are Lord Darlington, are you not?" inquired Priestley's younger and more slight companion.

Jack turned on him a glacial stare. "You are not known to me, sir."

Though the younger man flushed, he rallied quickly. "I am Sir Alfred Ashewood, a cousin of Lord Lovelace's, and a friend in all matters."

"I see." Jack gave him a second disinterested glance though he had long since noticed the youth's brash stance with hand on his sword hilt. Lord, the youth would not live out the year if he so swaggered about Jamaica.

When Jack neither added to his comment nor moved so much as an eyelash, Priestley cleared his throat. "Lord

Lovelace expects that you will wish to accompany us at once to his home in order to discharge your debt."

"I think not." Jack's voice was singularly devoid of encouragement. "Good night, gentlemen. I am late for another more entertaining appointment."

Priestly moved as though he would block Jack from entering his coach. Just as speedily, Zuberi stepped between the two noblemen, silent and impassive, yet as effective a checkmate to provocation as a knight on the chessboard.

Jack offered his servant a wry glance, then entered the coach without even glancing back at his would-be escorts.

When Zuberi had done likewise, Jack rapped briskly on the coach's roof to indicate he was ready to proceed. Once the coach lurched away from the curb, Jack reached to open the lantern to dispel the gloom. " 'Tis a witch's tit of a night from which even the moon hides."

"The moon always follows the sun," Zuberi pronounced solemnly, as though he had followed his master's thoughts.

Jack smiled slightly. "Had I but your calm acceptance of life, Zuberi. You are exempt from all contingencies of pain and longing and remorse and suffering."

"One man may suffer much and understand nothing from it, my lord," Zuberi responded as he draped a bristling robe of black bear fur over the viscount's legs. "Another man may sit upon his reed mat and watch the day struggle with its own loss. Verily, the moon will follow the sun."

Jack absently rubbed his throbbing brow with long lean fingers, his thoughts returning to Priestley's appearance. It seemed that Lord Lovelace worked with a surprising rapidity when he found cause. The pair had, no doubt, been sent by the earl to provoke him to admit to the debt he could not pay. But why?

Lotte. He had no doubt Lovelace's actions were the results of some contretemps with Lotte. Though he discouraged it, she had recently begun confiding in him her unhappiness with her husband's neglect. Did Lovelace now suspect that he was seeking the role of his wife's lover?

An unholy expression moved across Jack's face.

If only Lovelace knew the truth! His interest in Lotte was not in the least carnal. The source of his chagrined affection was not love, not even lust, but a far more unnerving sensation. Lady Charlotte Lovelace reminded him, inexplicably, of his long dead mother.

The first time he had entered a salon in which she was present, her rich laughter had risen up and snared his attention. Even as he glanced in her direction he expected to sight another of London's pretty, self-indulged ladies. But then he had spied her. Her back was to him, but the graceful arch of her bare neck and shoulders had stirred to life within him some inexpressibly dear, if faint, memory. His breath had caught and his stomach had constricted in shock while tears pushed hard at the back of his eyes. It had taken all his will to keep from rushing up to her and . . . and what?

The sudden sentiment had appalled him, he who prided himself on being void of emotions. Yet he could not look away from her. Even as he neared her and knew her to be a stranger . . . something that bespoke of another attachment too dim to be completely recalled, yet too indelible to be completely forgotten, remained.

In the months following, with the hope of mastering the resonation of tenderness her presence inevitably caused him, he had pressed his acquaintance to become part of her dull cadre of friends. She had proved to be as kind as her smile though not at all his type. Even so, he could not now shake the disquieting feeling that she aroused by her mere appearance.

The London residence he had inherited contained only one badly damaged and deteriorating portrait of his mother. It showed a quiet, self-possessed woman, looking frail in a brocade gown styled in the manner of a score of years earlier, her reddish hair piled up and unpowdered.

The woman in the portrait did not possess Lotte's surpassing beauty nor vivacious temperament, yet the link remained. His only consolation in his self-embarrassment was that no one else knew of his feelings.

Now her husband wanted his money, or his blood. For himself he would meet and best Lovelace without qualm or regret. But he would not risk making Lotte a widow. He was a gambler and no gambler went against his instincts without courting disaster. He knew, instinctively, that he must not cause Lotte pain.

He leaned suddenly toward his servant. "Zuberi, I've no choice but to leave London, tonight."

As their gaze met across the short distance, Zuberi nodded slightly but his black eyes were more serious than before. "A man must sometimes unmake his life that he may begin again the journey to himself."

A wicked grin hoisted one corner of Jack's mouth and he struck the larger man a blow on the front of his shoulder with the flat of his hand. "Perhaps you should have remained with the bishop to become a priest, Zuberi. Your unorthodox sermonizing might have lured even me to church upon occasion."

Zuberi straightened as much as the low curvature of the coach ceiling would allow. " 'Twas the expectation of my first master who offered me, at the tender age of six, to the bishop of Barbados as atonement for his sins. For seven years I studied the Bible, prayed, and learned to make sums that I might keep records for the rum distillery which the bishop operated. Alas, my wretched sinfulness caused me to be sold away."

Jack offered him a fellow sinner's smile. "As I recall the tale, 'twas your distinct fondness for women that ruined you."

Zuberi's handsome face split in a sensual, full-lipped smile. "Nature flourished early in me. The bishop's cook ruined me for the church but not for life, my lord. At twelve years of age I was sold into the household of a sugarcane widow whose husband had recently perished from the yellow fever. She called me her little blackamoor after the Parisian fashion, and dressed me in silk turbans and brocade vests that I might fetch and carry in style for her wherever she went."

The twinkle in Zuberi's sloe-black eyes was apparent even in the darkness. "But I grew so quickly, my lord, that she soon found other uses more reasonable to one of my new stature."

Jack chuckled, "I can well imagine, my grandly-proportioned friend."

Zuberi again inclined his head, an action that often sufficed for speech when he wished to be tactful.

Zuberi was no longer a slave, though he had been one when Jack won him on a bet with a Louisiana planter three and a half years earlier. An abolitionist by inclination rather than politics, Jack had freed the man on the spot. In gratitude, Zuberi had offered to serve as Jack's personal servant. Now, as viscount, he had a dozen servants to do his bidding. A new thought struck Jack. "Have you ever thought of returning to your homeland, Zuberi?"

Zuberi shook his head. "I should not know it nor it I. My mother once told me it was a sign that I would journey much in my life but never set foot on the soil of my ancestors. I long to sail again on the great sea to the islands of my youth." The smile returned to his voice. "In Barbados the air is perfumed with the warmth of the sea and the earthly delights of fruit and flower. There the wind carries the breath of the sun even into the shadows. And the soil, it is as brown and fertile as its women."

"I envy your concept of paradise," Jack murmured. "I'm told I have inherited several holdings in the West Indies, interests my Royalist grandfather established with Lord Willoughby and then saw restored after the defeat of the Commonwealth. Perhaps I will one day join you on your voyage westward." A glimmer of the rogue brightened his gaze.

The larger man smiled. "My people believe in the Old Ways, which say that, of all God's creatures, woman is the most perfect. 'She maketh glad the heart of Man', so even your Bible says. We say it is for man to seek the most fertile field upon which to sow his seed."

"In that instance, I should be glad to do my part of the plowing," Jack responded and then yawned, feeling the tug of sleep at the corners of his thoughts. Perhaps he would not leave tonight— No, if he tarried Lovelace would no doubt send his henchmen to beat upon his door. "Son of a whore!" he muttered darkly and reached again for his brandy.

He was not a man given much to thoughts of his own morality. But the day's events had left him feeling as if he had taken a fork in a road before he had noticed there was a choice before him.

He allowed himself a final sip of brandy from his silver flask before saying to his man, "You shall remain in London until you hear from me."

"You are embarking on a journey?" Zuberi's handsome, broad-featured face split in a grin so irresistible that it soured Jack's mood even further.

"Nothing so romantic. I hear the spa town of Bath has the best gambling to be found outside London. I am in need of a chance of air. It will do as well as any place."

Zuberi's expression resembled a mask carved from the monkey-pod wood of the islands. "The moon always follows the sun."

Jack grunted as the coach lumbered down the lane. Zuberi's statement did not seem a heartening one but rather a warning of the wages of sin.

It was an hour when nocturnal creatures feel the pull of their lairs and cockerals twitch in unconscious anticipation of the morn. It was an hour when men may think themselves exempt from the strictures of the mortal world, when reason slumbers and fantastic desires awaken and stretch in anticipation of mischief. It was an hour in which Jack Laughton did his best and most diabolical thinking.

"What would you have a man do who has lost his last shilling?" Jack spoke to the vast empty highway of the Great Western Road as he rode purposely through the deep blue night silvered at the edges by a dawn not yet born. "What indeed?"

The exercise and chill had brought him to a state of semi-sobriety, the worse part of any debauch. He was sober enough to feel every jolt of the road in his knees and spine. He was sober enough to comprehend what his defiant gesture hours' earlier had cost him. He was sober enough to be galled by the fact that he had turned his back, for the first time in his life, on a challenge. And for the most prosaic of reasons, gallantry toward a woman.

He was also sober enough to know that he must find a way out of his predicament before Lovelace finished him in society by publicly branding him a coward and a defaulter on his debts.

Since he felt he did his best thinking when he was not quite sober, Jack decided to remedy his regrettable state. He reined in his horse, pulled from the pocket of his coat a flask, and drank deeply from it. The contents slipped familiarly down his throat, warming as it went straight to the pit of his empty stomach. After a moment, and two swallows more, his serviceable if threadbare pride cloaked his chagrined thoughts in the need for action.

The remedy to his troubles lay in discharging his debt as quickly as possible. A sudden withdrawal from town for a few days could be explained away by a vague reference to an ailing country relative. But only if he returned with a full purse. Once he had paid Lovelace, he would be able to bow out gracefully from their quarrel.

Jack closed his eyes in sullen reflection. He was being a fool! Why should he protect Lovelace? Why should he protect Lotte at the expense of his own pleasure? She was, after all, nothing to him but a dull reflection of an even duller memory.

He sank his chin into the folds of his collar and jerked his tricorner hat lower to stave off the chill eddying about his neck and ears. There was another fly firmly ensconced in the balm needed to soothe his troubles. That fly was destitution. He needed a stake in order to gamble in Bath. But where, oh where, was he to find such a stake?

After a moment he lifted his head and sniffed the air like a hound on the scent. The fresh chill of October and the sharp grassy odor of harvested hay stung his nostrils. Nothing, yet surely something more than his own dissatisfaction with himself carried on the wind, his keen senses told him. What?

Then he heard it. An unexpected sound came faintly but distinctly on the breeze, pricking up his horse's ears as well as his own. This time he did not doubt his senses. He reined in his mount to glance back over his shoulder.

The black hulk of the traveling coach was all but indistinguishable from the tenebrous forest from which it had emerged. Backlit by the silvery hem of predawn, the occasional golden flashes of shuttered lantern light marked its progress across the heath.

"Some other desperate soul aflight," he murmured as he leaned forward with a reassuring pat for his horse's neck.

None but the desperate or those on secret missions dared travel this lonely stretch of road at night. Every sort of thief from footpads to well-mounted highwaymen traversed the deserted stretches of Hounslow Heath betwixt dusk and dawn. The sensible spent their nights at inns where the most dangerous thing likely to accost them would be bedbugs. Who, then, was so desperate or secretive as to risk being abroad at this hour?

Curiosity was an emotion that seldom visited Jack, yet he backed off the highway and into the shadow of a lone larch tree to await the vehicle's approach. The merry sound of the harness bells, so at odds with the eerie silence of the surrounding night, quickened his whiskey-soured spirits as the coach approached. Who, indeed, traveled this night?

The richly appointed traveling coach rolled past him without recognition of his proximity. As it passed, light from the lanterns pegged on either side of the driver's seat twinkled in the polished brass and silver trimmings, advertising the wealth of the occupants.

Cinderella's coach could not have appeared finer in his envious gaze, or riper for the taking. The vehicle was without a guard, who usually rode with musket at the ready.

A guileful smile lifted the corners of Jack's mouth as he stared after the vulnerable equipage rolling down the empty highway. Then he glanced up at the sky quilted with stars but showing at its eastern hem the beginnings of the dawn.

When in his cups his late grandfather had loved to boast of his years as a "knight of the road." Like many Royalist Cavaliers dispossessed of their estates and property by Cromwell's Commonwealth, Jack's grandsire had turned to highway robbery in order to survive until the monarchy was restored. Those Royalist Cavaliers had, according to legend, stole only from their enemies, the supporters of the Commonwealth.

Even now, generations later, the highways of England remained dangerous places where less honorable men than his grandsire sought profit in robbery. The most notorious brigand of the day went by the sobriquet Black Jack Law. Handbills circulated throughout the countryside, offering a hefty bounty for his capture. Too bad he had not encountered the highwayman. He could use the reward.

Perhaps it was the dregs of the liquor or perhaps it was the fatalistic sense that he could sink no lower in his own estimation. Whatever its source, a demonic urge struck Jack, the wild desire to prove to himself how reckless and profoundly daring he could be. He was scion of an ignominious family lineage renowned for its debauchery and madness. What if *he* turned thief for a night?

What if he took a few bob from these smug, well-padded travelers who thought their fortunes kept them immune from the vagaries of the world? He would then have a stake for gambling in Bath, and relief from the tedium of his travels. After all, Black Jack Law was not the only fellow who gave no quarter to title and privilege.

"All the devils in hell could not fashion a sweeter bargain," Jack murmured in a voice gusted by laughter.

He tucked the switch of his golden hair up under the brim of his tricorn and then unbound his lace-edged jabot and tied it over his lower face, obscuring all but his eyes. Then he reached into his coat and withdrew his pistol, primed and ready against night predators, one of which he was about to become.

With a furiously beating heart, he set his spurs into his mount and shot off down the road in pursuit of the retreating coach.

Chapter Five

The bounce and buck of wooden coach wheels over the cobblestone road, pocked with wheel ruts after a recent rain, would seemed to have made sleep impossible for all but the inebriated or the unconscious. Yet Mrs. Varney had long ago succumbed to slumber, snoring like a bellows with her arms wrapped about her thick frame as her head bobbed in slack-jawed time to the rocking coach.

Much too angry to sleep, Sabrina cast a withering gaze upon the sputtering wick of the coach lantern that threatened to leave her at any moment in complete darkness.

She had gone to bed after the terrible interview with her guardian too angry to consider that he would carry out his threat this very night. Yet hardly had her head touched the pillow before she had been rudely awakened by Mrs. Varney and told to dress for traveling, per Cousin Robert's order.

To guard against the chill night wind whistling noisily through the crevices of the coach, Sabrina wrapped herself more tightly in her voluminous cloak lined with fur. The silk dressing gown and spool-heeled satin slippers she wore beneath it were fit only for the trip she had taken downstairs to inform her cousin that she was refusing to leave before morning.

Her cheeks flamed as she recalled how he had coldly ordered two footmen to deposit her bodily into the traveling coach. It galled her to remember how she had twisted and fought the two young men, seething yet helpless as they bore her down the front steps and placed her in the coach like a sack of meal.

While she had waited in the damp night air, the sleepy coachman had lashed her belongings, hastily thrust into trunks, on top. Only at the moment of departure were her cloak and bonnet handed through the doorway by her guardian.

His expression had been a composite of fury and triumph as he shouted, "You will learn humility, my girl, or you shall suffer even greater miseries than this!"

Sabrina twisted the soft velvet cloak fabric between her hands as unshed tears burned her eyes. How dare he bundle her out of London in the middle of the night! If he thought banishment from London would make her more amenable to marriage then—

"The devil take him!" she whispered angrily under her breath as she canted her head so that the wide brim of her velvet hat eclipsed the shadow of the woman opposite her. Cousin Robert thought her willful, self-indulgent, and spoiled. She might be all that yet there was more to her character than a computation of vices. She had used her sleepless hours since leaving London to scheme her escape from his control.

She would seek asylum with her mother's brother, Mister Everett Butler, who resided in the Massachusetts colony in the New World. Until Cousin Robert forbid it, she had corresponded regularly with him. Surely, when their uncle understood the peril in which she and Kit stood, he would allow them to take refuge with him. Yet she could not wait for her uncle to act. It would take weeks for a letter to reach Massachusetts and then weeks more for him to come to her aid if, indeed, he chose to do so. No, she needed a quicker means to save Kit.

With calm deliberation she listed again the tasks required to save her brother. She would need a means to get to Scotland, a way to free Kit, a coach to bear them to a coastal town, and then enough money for passage to America.

Money! The need for "the ready" was the sticking point of every aspect of her plot. She had none of her own.

Sabrina shifted her position against the hard, horsehair-stuffed cushions in search of the impossible, a comfortable spot, and felt a sudden jab in her right buttock. Reaching round she made a discovery. Stuck into the pocket of her velvet cloak was a large French playing card decorated with a hand-painted face of the Jack of Spades.

"Black Jack," Sabrina murmured as she ran a tapered nail buffed smooth as a pearl across the painted face. She had plucked the card from the deck as a souvenir of her first gambling success. She had thought then that she could never gamble again, the risk having made her heart palpitate to the point of pain. But Lotte Lovelace had lured her back to the tables several times since. Though she did not like to lose, she found she enjoyed the occasional win.

After a sharp searching glance of the sleeping Mrs. Varney's face, Sabrina surreptitiously drew forth the cause of the remaining lump in her cloak though she already knew what it was. Tucked into the lining was her pearl necklace!

The necklace consisted of a string of inch-long perfectly matched pearls from which hung a large baroque pearl drop the shade of iridescent smoke. Those smoky depths were lost now in the folds of her cloak, where she had hidden it from the possibility of drawing Mrs. Varney's gaze. Yet as she ran her fingers lovingly over their surfaces, she could visualize the faint sheen of shell pink and sea green that sunlight would reveal on its surface.

Her fondness for them had nothing to do with their

value. They had been an extravagant gift from her father on her sixteenth birthday. They were the only things of value that she had successfully hidden from Cousin Robert when he had come to Cornwall after her father's death to claim such things as pleased his eye and his greed. The rest of the Lyndsey jewels he kept under lock and key in his home. By custom only married ladies were permitted to adorn themselves in gems. Perhaps, when she wed—

"Never!" she muttered.

She picked up and reexamined the playing card. As it provoked new thought, her smile gathered strength and beauty, transforming her from a pretty young woman into a singularly lovely one. She would gamble for the money she needed!

Keeping company with Lady Lovelace had provided her with many opportunities to advance her worldliness. For instance, she had heard more than one guest remark upon the fact that for years the spa town of Bath, under the leadership of Beau Nash, was a veritable gaming paradise. Gentlemen and ladies, the nobility and gentry all gambled together in the spa town with an egalitarian abandon unheard of in London.

As Mrs. Varney snorted in her sleep Sabrina tucked the necklace into her bodice. She refused to worry about how she would gain entrance to the gambling tables while under the watchful eye of Cousin Robert's relative—or whether she would win. Since luck had provided her with the jewels she would otherwise have been forced to leave behind, luck would certainly prevail in her worthy cause. Of course, she would win. She must!

No sooner had she sat back in much improved humor than the dilatory sounds of plodding hooves and creaking wood were suddenly disturbed by the percussive report of a pistol.

"What the dev—" Sabrina began, only to be cut off as the coach lurched and the horses abruptly picked up their pace under the crack of the whip and frantically bawled orders of the coachman. The action sent her flying from her seat into the lap of the startled Mrs. Varney, who let out a whoop of surprise at being so unceremoniously awakened.

"The horses have bolted!" Mrs. Varney cried and flung both arms about Sabrina.

"Nonsense!" Sabrina shouted back and tried to disentangle herself from the older woman. "I'm certain I heard a pistol shot!" The realization brought a gleam of mischief to her gaze. "Oh, Mrs. Varney. I do believe we are being attacked!"

"Dear lord! We shall all be murdered! Or worse!"

Sabrina did not respond to this strange bit of logic. She was more interested in the driver's ability to handle his team. Surely it would be possible to outrun the marauder. After all, the horses were still fresh and a highwayman was not likely to give chase for long for fear of being exposed to other journeyers on the road. The chance to torment her companion would be worth the rough ride.

"Let us hope that your piety is enough to save us!" she shouted at the dumbstruck woman.

She then subsided to listen intently as the driver urged his steeds forward, for the marauder clearly continued to give chase. After a few seconds more of bouncing and lurching, she cursed under her breath her guardian's frugality. He had told the coachman not to stop the nights at coaching inns but to drive them straight through to Bath, saving them both money and time. Though her only thought had been to terrorize Mrs. Varney, every seasoned traveler knew that a coach on the road at night was likely to attract the eye of nefarious souls. Had she been given time to pack, she would have brought along her father's brace of pistols, for she was a superb shot.

Just when it seemed they might indeed outrun their pursuer, the coach lurched again, careening off the built-up cobblestone road onto the treacherously soft dirt shoulder where it teetered on two wheels.

Whispering a rare prayer, Sabrina grabbed a strap to keep from being tossed against the canted side door while Mrs. Varney clung to her by the waist. After a quivering moment of uncertainty, the coach slammed back down on all four wheels with a sickening crash that splintered wood and sheared off pegs. Moments later she heard an approaching rider, then a man shouting for the coachman to stand down. More threatening shouts were exchanged as she scrambled to the window to peer out. The prospect of dawn made the world outside faintly lighter than within the interior of the coach, but she could not see the man whose weight caused the carriage to suddenly sway nor the ensuing skirmish that took place. She heard the whistling of the coachman's whip, a cry of rage, and then finally the thud of a body fallen to the ground.

"They've killed the coachman!" Mrs. Varney whispered in horror. "We're next!"

"Do shut up!" Sabrina snapped. Yet the hair at her nape stiffened when, after several seconds of silence, the latch on the coach door creaked under the pressure of an unseen hand. Until this moment she had not truly thought they were in danger. An instance later the door was flung open.

"Deliver over your valuables, and quickly!" declared their assailant in a remarkably fine masculine voice.

The first thing Sabrina noticed was the business end of a pistol thrust through the opening. The second was the dimensions of the pistol's owner. Silhouetted against the faintly glowing sky was a tall, broad-shouldered man in a tricorner hat.

Steadied by the reality of his commonplace appearance, she rose from her knees and flung herself back into the shadows of her seat, more annoyed than frightened. "You, sir, are mistaken in your quarry. You'll find no booty here worth your efforts."

She saw the pistol jerk as if its owner had been startled by her pronouncement, then it disappeared from the breach. In its place was thrust one of the coach's exterior lanterns. The bright splash of yellow light from its vented opening lit up Mrs. Varney's features and she screeched as if the light scalded her.

The pistol again appeared, the barrel wagging at the older woman. "Step down, madam. At once!"

"Oh, please, sir," the woman whimpered. "I beg you in the name of heaven, do not shoot!"

"I have no such violence in mind," the highwayman replied in dry humor.

"You sound the gentleman," Sabrina observed from her shadowed corner. Though, of course, the linen he had draped over the lower half of his face made it a trifle difficult to tell precisely how cultured his voice was. "No gentleman, nor one who pretends to the title, would accost defenseless women."

The outline of his tricorn angled in her direction. "You are precisely the sort of easy prey a man such as I would wish to accost. Do not disappoint me."

Sabrina set her jaw against his presumptive tone. "I care nothing for your desires, fellow. You are thief. No doubt you shall soon end your days as you deserve, as gallows meat."

He swung the lantern around so that the light fell across her, momentarily blinding her. "Damnation!" she heard him mutter from the other side of the light.

Apprehension raked her resolve but Sabrina refused to retract her remark. "I am chilled to the bone and should like to be on my way. Be good enough to carry yourself off."

The haughtiness in her voice elicited only silence as once more his pistol barrel beckoned the passengers. Sniffling and murmuring a prayer about the mercy due widows and orphans, Mrs. Varney scrambled down the steps he unhooked for her and descended.

A moment later the lantern and the shadow of the man

behind it again appeared in the doorway, this time with a free hand extended in assistance. "Now you, my lady."

Sabrina did not flinch as the light again included her in its scope. She saw the sense in doing as he asked, even heard the civility in his request, but she had been bullied once too often this night. She folded her arms and turned her head away, offering the concealment of her hat brim as insult. "No."

She did not anticipate the powerful arm he slid about her before she could stop him or draw back. Even as she gathered her breath to scream he lifted her clear of the doorframe and pulled her out into the night. In three short seconds he had undone what it had taken two winded footmen considerably longer to accomplish.

For the instant she was held aloft by that strong arm clasped about her waist, she experienced the unprecedented sensation of being pressed against a firm, amazingly strong man who smelled of good brandy, fine tobacco, and some indefinable but pleasant scent. Could it be that highwaymen used lavender water?

"Stand up, my lady."

Too surprised to do anything but obey him, Sabrina discovered to her chagrin that the ground was within easy reach of her satin-slippered feet. Worse yet, the only reason she had not realized this before was because her arms had at some point inexplicably wound themselves about the brigand's neck. Annoyed, she released him with a suddenness that set her hard on her heels on the stony road.

He turned at once to hang the lantern back on its peg near the coach door. As its light finally included him in its glow, her eyes widened in astonishment at the richness of his clothing. His brown velvet "justaucorps": a collarless, full-skirted outer coat sporting a double row of ornate, hammered-gold buttons down the front and fastening its deep cuffs. His under jacket was embroidered creme brocade. Even his silver-spurred boots were so polished they gleamed faintly in the gloom. She had expected a brigand would be as filthy and disheveled as his character.

Frowning at her discovery of this sartorial splendor, she glanced upward at the linen mask that obscured most of his face. No powdered curls peaked from beneath his tricorn. Yet why should so well-dressed a man forego a wig when all but the most indigent wore wigs, even if they were made of goat's hair, horsehair, or even vegetable fiber? Or had he stolen this finery from an earlier victim and neglected to take the poor soul's wig?

Fresh misgiving welled up but she squashed the feeling with ruthless determination. No robber masquerading as a fop would cower her. Just let him try!

When he noticed her stare, he turned toward her. "Look your fill, my lady. You will find little to remember me by."

As he spoke he moved closer until she gazed directly into the finest pair of eyes she had ever beheld. They were light in color, large and lazy-lidded with surprisingly thick lashes that swept downward at the corners. She could not say why those eyes fascinated her. Maybe it was because they seemed to mock her. It was as though he dared share a private jest with her that she could not yet understand.

"Will you know me again?" He stood so close she saw his breath stir the cloth draped loosely over his nose and mouth. As vividly felt as the persuasive force of his touch, his presence seemed to rule the very silence of the night. Never before, not even when her guardian had raised his hand to her, had she felt the full vulnerability of being female. That sense of vulnerability angered her and in a reckless attempt to subdue it, she struck out boldly. "I shall remember enough to see you hanged."

Genuine fear sped through her as he swiftly reached out to her a second time. He did not, as she half-expected, grasp her by the throat to throttle her. He merely snatched her hat from her head by its floppy brim. He did not speak but his gaze lingered on the heavy fall of ebony tresses that he had revealed. She nearly reached up a hand to push the wanton waves from her shoulders but did not want to betray her discomfort at his perusal. Let him look his fill, as she had, and be done with it. She was up to the challenge. To prove it, she tilted her chin up defiantly.

His hand moved again to catch in his palm the end of one of her elaborate curls, as complicatedly furled as an ornamental curlicue. As he did so his knuckles brushed ever so lightly against the fullness of her breast. The touch was shocking for it reminded her that she wore no corsets, not even a chemise. Now he knew it, too.

His gaze rose abruptly from her hair to her face.

Though as vain as any pretty woman, Sabrina did not see any sign of admiration of her beauty reflected in the mercurial depths of this stranger's light eyes. She felt as if she were being weighed and accessed with dispassion. A muscle at the corner of her mouth quivered. Why did he continue to stare as if he had never seen a woman before? Or was he contemplating something sinister?

That thought roused her from her momentary silence and she reached up to flick his hand from her hair with a scornful gesture. "Never touch me again."

"But you are so very delicious, my lady." His careless phrasing made mockery of the compliment. Though he did not move even an inch away, he did not attempt to touch her again. "Since you will not permit an exchange of pleasantries then I must press you for your gold."

Something in his words, in his appearance, struck her as oddly familiar. And then she knew why. "But I know who you are!"

A menacing glint flashed in his gray gaze and was gone. "Indeed? Just who do you think I am?"

The belated realization that sharing her discovery might not have been wise made Sabrina blush hotly. If she had not, hours before, tormented Mrs. Varney with the idea she might never have thought of it at all. "You are Jack Law."

The declaration came forth so softly the breeze all but stole the words away.

"How came you by this conclusion?"

His mild response bolstered Sabrina's composure. After all, there was only so much fear she was willing to endure for the sake of a highwayman. "Your reputation is well-touted by your victims."

"What reputation would that be, my lady?"

She shrugged extravagantly, annoyed that he was once more the inquisitor. "Rumors are that Jack Law is not really a common highwayman at all but a wealthy aristocrat who robs travelers for the thrill of it. While other noblemen are content to keep to the meadows in pursuit of a fox, he chooses for his stalking fields the byways and highways of England."

" 'Tis a pretty tale." The sound of derision had many chords in his voice, Sabrina decided. "And you equate us upon such slim observation? I am charmed."

She folded her arms under her bosom, determined to meet him word for word. "I do wonder at your lack of caution, Mr. Law. After all, 'tis you who give yourself away. Your coat is more costly than my cloak. The lace of your jabot is the finest quality. Most telling of all, your speech surpasses the king's own son. A clever man would better disguise himself."

As she spoke, the gleam of admiration at last entered those remarkable eyes. "Surely there is more?"

Switching tactics, she reached out and casually rested her left hand oh so lightly on his velvet cuff, seeking to take advantage of his admiration. A year in London had taught her that besotted gentlemen always did her bidding. " 'Tis said you once allowed a new bride to keep her wedding ring when she told you it was the only thing of value she had ever owned."

Once again Sabrina found herself looking into his quicksilver eyes warmed by admiration, and felt triumph slip into her hand. But when he reached out and clasped her hand in his before she could avoid his grasp, she knew she had miscalculated.

She attempted to snatch her hand back. Instead, his lean hard fingers forced her unwilling hand to his face as he bent his head over her hand in salute. The courtly gesture startled her, as did the brush of linen covering his mouth, and the unexpected damp rush of his expelled breath through the cloth.

Remarkably, she found herself thinking, *I should like to know this Jack Law better.*

A moan from the coachman who lay in a heap near the right rear wheel broke that strange, inexplicable, wholly inappropriate spell. Sabrina blinked as though freed from blinders.

He straightened to his superior height and said abruptly, "I regret the need to cut short this charming interlude." He turned from her and held out his gloved hand to the older woman. "You, first. Hand over your jewels and money."

Mrs. Varney dug into her pocket at once and produced a jingling purse that she held out like a supplicant offering. "I have but forty pounds, sir."

Sabrina smirked as Cousin Robert's money disappeared into the robber's pocket. That smirk dissolved as he turned to her.

"I've not so much as a ha'penny," she answered in clipped tones, annoyed to realize he still intended to rob her, as well.

"You must have some small bauble about your person," he countered. "A brooch from a suitor perhaps, a strand of pearls upon your majority? Some little something?"

His all-too-accurate supposition that she possessed pearls spurred her indignant reply. "If I possessed such things, be certain I would not hand them over." She turned to climb back into the coach.

He caught her by the shoulder, his fingers griping tight

the folds of her cloak as he forced her back to face him. "Then be good enough to shrug free of your cloak."

"I—I will do no such thing!" She swallowed back the burst of rage that fed her stammer. He seemed to be reasonable as long as she remained so. "I shall catch a chill."

Something akin to amusement again struck sparks in those gold-lashed eyes. "You will. Or I will strip it from you."

With a begrudging admiration for a superior force, she unhooked the heavy clasp that held the cloak closed at her neck and swung the garment from her shoulders. "I expect you to return it, and quickly."

He caught it in one hand as she tossed it to him and then felt along all the seams. When he was done he looked her over again.

Sabrina was surprised by the tremor of emotion that passed through her as his gaze skimmed her slim figure. The night had quickly prickled her skin with goosebumps and there was a fair amount exposed upon which it might do its work. The Chinese silk wrapper she wore was held closed by a mere series of pink satin bows that began at her waist and rose to the lowest point of her cleavage. Dressed in negligée with her unbound hair tumbling free over her shoulders, she knew she looked more like a wanton who had just stepped from her bed than the weary traveler she was.

Contrary to her impulse, she controlled the urge to turn away from him as he regarded her with his singular attention. He was not the first man to ogle her bosom, she told herself. She could almost guess his salacious thoughts. Ordinarily, a gentleman's prurient leer inspired only her contempt. But something in this man's gaze forestalled her attempts to despise him. Her heart beat in a strangely unfamiliar pattern that caught its rhythm not from fright but the elation of the risk.

"Now then, I will have your wrapper."

"Absolutely not!"

"Then I will help myself."

Indignation flamed in Sabrina's cheeks. She was no maid or underling to be ordered about, even less the cowering maiden. Yet, more than any insult to her modesty, she feared he would discover the necklace tucked into her bodice. She had kept them safe for more than three years. She would not simply give them over to a common thief!

As he took a purposeful step toward her she balanced a fist on each hip, uncaring that the action lifted her bosom precariously to the brink of her neckline. "Enough of your threats, you yellow-spined, dim-witted jackanapes! We have given you what we have! Find other prey. We are done being afraid!"

She turned away and then swung back to add in afterthought, "You cannot be Jack Law. You are a miserable failure of a highwayman!"

"Miserable failure?" He spoke softly, as if the dawn itself might shrink away before the release of his rage. But there was no temporizing of the look in his eyes as he closed the distance between them.

Sabrina held his hard, unencouraging gaze. "Do your worst."

"My worst?" He cocked his head slightly, as if she had posed a challenge requiring thoughtful consideration on his part. "What, I wonder, would you consider my worst?"

She did not flinch this time as his free hand slipped down about her waist. She felt his fingers spread over her lower back, impelling her forward until the front of her wrapper brushed his waistcoat. Emotion passed through those bright eyes, hard and disturbing where minutes before they had been kindled by personal warmth. Know him better, indeed! Mercy's grace! What could she have been thinking? At the last moment her courage failed and she tried to wrench away as he bent his head to hers.

"No need to be coy at this juncture," he whispered through his mask into the hollow of her right ear. "You would know the stuff of which Jack Law is composed? I offer you a taste."

He jerked down his mask a scant instant before he turned his head and his lips found and locked on hers.

She knew she should have protested, cried out and kicked, clawed and bit him. Yet her treacherous body did not respond to a single urging of its own defense.

From deep inside her, a place where a year of unhappiness and frustration had simmered and smoldered, an insidious rebellious voice whispered, *Let him! Let him defile you! Learn what it is to lie with the devil. And then we'll see if Cousin Robert can keep to his plans to marry you off!*

That thought forestalled her protest just long enough to make it unnecessary.

The pressure and texture of his lips upon hers was unlike any touch she had ever entertained of Satan. His lips were warm, despite the night air, and firm and smooth as the finest silk. She had been kissed before but the pressing of slightly damp flesh had always left her repelled and unmoved.

The touch of Jack Law's mouth was altogether different. The embrace of his lips seemed the warmest, most inviting place in all the dark, chill dawn.

Her world careened crazily on waves of pleasure as his arms went about her. She gasped as he licked her lips with slow, confident strokes. Her knees weakened, threatening to tumble her until her hands reached and found mooring in the sleeves of his coat. Her nails curled possessively into the plush. She had not known she could feel such things. So this was a kiss. In the hands of Jack Law, a kiss was the most potent temptation she had ever known.

His hand found her bodice and then the heat of his kneading fingers spread through her clothing, making her breast ache with bliss and shame.

Her conscience struggled vainly once more. *This was madness, surely. You risk everything by acquiescence.*

Yet the strict urgings of reason could not hold sway. She

wanted only more of the glorious, disconcerting thrall in which this stranger held her. For that she was willing to risk even ravishment.

As if he read her thoughts and found them exactly to his desire, the highwayman suddenly lifted his head. "So, there beats within the heart of m'lady a rake!" he murmured against her ear.

As he swung away from her with triumphant laughter, Sabrina felt as if he had slapped her. No worse, he was laughing at her. Ridicule was the one thing she could not, would not tolerate.

She saw her moment and seized it. With both hands she dove for the curved pistol butt he had hooked over the edge of his coat pocket when he had embraced her. Her fingers wrapped quickly about it and then she jerked, tearing fabric as it came free.

He moved quickly but she was the quicker, backing up even as she lifted the barrel and leveled it at the middle of his chest. "Be gone! Before I do you mortal harm!"

For the space of two heartbeats he stood before her, backlit by the halo of lantern light, and then he swung away. Only then did she realize he had shown his face to her. But she had been too intent on aiming the barrel steadily to notice any distinct feature in the gloom.

"Coward! Blackguard! Villain!" Her heart beating in exultation to see him, the would-be vanquisher, at last on the run. Kiss her, would he? Make her quiver with never before felt desire? Humble her? She would see about that!

He made the saddle in one graceful leap and dug his spurs mercilessly into the flanks of his steed. It was a beautifully executed maneuver that she would have admired had some ancient, predatory instinct not informed her that he was getting away. The pistol came to life in her hands as if by its own volition.

She saw the rider jerk but his horse did not falter as it ate up the ground swiftly putting distance between them.

"Miss Sabrina!" Mrs. Varney rushed up to her. "You could have been killed!"

"Posh!" Sabrina answered smartly. "My father taught me to shoot when I was but six years of age. I believe I winged the villain." She smiled in satisfaction. "Impress me, would he? Rather I have given him something to long remember me by!"

Chapter Six

Sabrina stood in the doorway of a cottage whose lintel barely allowed her to stand upright. She had been set the task of watching for the sedan chair that would bear her hostess—and gaoler—Mrs. Thaddeus Noyes to her daily ritual of bathing at Queen's Bath.

Her first two weeks in The Bath, as the locals referred to it, were nothing short of disaster. Not only was Mrs. Noyes all that Cousin Robert had led her to expect in the way of piety and disapproval of worldliness, but the woman was a recluse. Sabrina had not set one toe into society since her arrival. Not only that, her hopes of meeting an acquaintance of the Beau Monde in the lane had been scotched by her location, as far from the heart of fashionable society as possible.

Mrs. Noyes' drafty stone cottage was set in the oldest part of town, located near the town's medieval East Gate and not far from the Abbey. Adjacent to an alley on one side, it was hemmed on the other by a row of ancient, half-timbered cottages whose residents kept piggeries in the rear. The windows were tiny and few, giving the cottage the feeling of being perpetually in the shade. The only concession to modernization had been to have the once beaten-earth floors paved with slate stones. Mrs. Noyes proudly boasted of the efforts of the Master of Ceremonies of Bath, Beau Nash, who had seen to it that the spa's streets were no longer filth-laden gutters brimming with the refuse of chamber pots and entrails from butchers' shops.

An appreciation for these better times was lost on Sabrina, who pressed a scented handkerchief to her nose whenever she looked out. Early drizzle had left the neighborhood overhung with trapped coal and wood smoke, and the faint stench from the fisheries located on the nearby river. Despite the inclement weather, the neighborhood's denizens thronged the muddy lane before the cottage, along with carts and barrows and barking dogs. The neighborhood was no better than the notorious rookeries of London.

A plaintive yowl of hunger directed Sabrina's gaze downward.

"Oh, and what do you suppose you are doing?" she asked the tabby cat who was weaving a friendly greeting about her ankles.

The feline had wandered in over the threshold the day after Sabrina had arrived. Despite the order to destroy it from Mrs. Noyes, who was terrified of the "slinking beasts!" Sabrina had not done so. Instead, it pleased her to secretly outwit the old woman by keeping the kitten hidden in her room.

Sabrina picked up the purring puff of brown, orange, and white and scratched behind the delicate ears of the kitten, feeling the bony skull in some alarm. There was little to steal to feed the tiny one.

It had taken no more than a few days to discover that Cousin Robert's parsimonious bent was far exceeded by that of Mrs. Noyes' miserliness. Not a scrap went to feed the animals she kept at the rear of her little cottage if it might be tucked into a pie. Not a crumble was left to the foraging of mice when it might be softened with a drop of milk or sherry and fashioned into the vile concoctions Mrs. Noyes called bread puddings.

"She eats much and nastily," Sabrina confided to her only friend as she climbed the narrow, crooked stairway that led to her bedroom. Being country-bred she had never developed the overly refined sensibilities of some city-bred ladies. Yet she had quickly met her fill of coarseness and meanness in this household.

"No need to mind my figure here," she murmured. She could scarce abide to swallow a spoonful of any course at the table. As nothing was allowed to go to waste, for fear of offending God's benevolence, Mrs. Noyes consumed every bite. No hog in her yard grew as round and corpulent as the owner herself.

"Now shoo!" She bent at the waist to drop the kitten lightly inside her door and then made certain this time that the latch was set. Secret acts of rebellion were no good unless they were kept secret.

"Sabrina? Do I hear the sedan chair?" inquired a querulous voice from below.

"Miss Sa-brin-a!"

The sound of her name was like the meshing of unoiled gears. With jaw set Sabrina tiptoed back down the stairs. Despite Cousin Robert's design, she was determined not to resist the role of menial to this woman of no taste and less refinement.

"Miss Sa-brin-a!"

As the third cry went up from the room at the rear of the cottage, Sabrina spied with relief the thin girl with lackluster brown hair trailing beneath her cap who was Mrs. Noyes' servant.

"Sophie, see to your mistress. I shall await the chair."

"Yes 'um," answered the much put-upon maid.

As the girl moved to do her bidding, Sabrina noted her ill-fitting black gown, rusty with dirt and soot and mended in so many places it resembled a patchwork quilt. Surely there was a castoff among her things that the girl might have. Or would Mrs. Noyes usurp the gift? Sabrina smirked. It would require three of her gowns sewn together to cover the obese woman.

"Miss *Sa-breee-na!*"

Sabrina poked her head once more out of the doorway to escape the screeched summons. No doubt Mrs. Noyes would take and sell any gown offered to the maid. Her stinginess seemed exceeded only by her greed.

Not a moment had been lost in posting a letter to London detailing the "infamous doings" of the highwayman who had relieved Mrs. Varney of her purse. Set to the task, Sabrina had dutifully written out Mrs. Noyes' demand for a replacement of the funds which were to have been used to ease the introduction of two more into her household.

Sabrina's lips twitched. At least there had been one bit of satisfaction resulting from the robbery. Mrs. Varney had been sent forthwith back to London by the incensed Mrs. Noyes. "Can't abide a body without the wits to guard her own pursestrings. Imagine, offering good gold after bad deeds!"

Unfortunately, Sabrina mused, she had not been allowed to pen her own opinion of the incident. She would have liked to entertain Lady Charlotte with the droll tale of her brush with Jack Law.

"Such things as ink and foolscap be costly," Mrs. Noyes had answered in denial of the request.

Sabrina suspected the hand of her guardian in the plot to deny her paper and quill, which effectively cut her off from the outside world.

At least the incident had left her armed. The highwayman's pistol lay together with her pearls under a loose floorboard in her room. If need be, she could rescue Kit by force.

Her winsome smile turned guileful. She rather liked the idea of dressing up as a thief and brandishing a pistol about. She had certainly learned how to swagger by having observed the cocky, self-confident marauder. Insolent and contemptuous of the very ancestry rumor gave him, Jack Law rebelled against the prevailing order. In that, she found a sympathetic heart.

Jack Law had been much in her thoughts these last days. She told herself it was because her life was dull and idle. She was confined in cramped quarters with nothing more to occupy her than cross-stitching, which she hated, and bible study, during which she invariably nodded over the psalm she was daily set to read and memorize. Little wonder she preferred to ruminate over a pair of wicked silver eyes!

The memory of those dawn-reflected eyes haunted her as surely as the touch of his hard arms and the effortless power of his kiss.

Sabrina turned her face from the doorway, overcome by a sudden shyness she could not account for. Jack Law was not the first handsome man she had ever encountered. Why, for all she had seen of his face he might not even be handsome. He might have teeth as bad as Sean's, her father's groomsman, or a nose like a cauliflower.

Yet she could not quite believe that. His voice had been too persuasive, too confident of its charm. By his manner, he was not accustomed to being denied by women, even aristocratic ones. He had handled her familiarly and lifted her out of the coach without a thought for her supposed august personage.

"Even if he were as handsome as Adonis, I should not have been moved," she whispered to herself.

Yet she had been. With his extraordinary manner and his civility sleeved in the threat of violence, Jack Law had touched her, made her tremble, and desire more. The moment he released her she had instantly missed the warmth and strength of his touch.

What if he had not released her, what if he had gone on kissing her, holding her, turning her bones to aspic?

What if he had then pulled her down onto the ground with him, and lifted her skirts and . . . she had not resisted?

Instead, he had laughed at her. She burned even yet with the memory. He had found her ridiculous in her passion. How lowering! How mortifying!

"There you be, Miss Sabrina!"

With a guilty start, Sabrina turned to the doorway and found Mrs. Noyes had entered the room.

"What folly be this, miss? You've the morning's full light and yet are neglecting your study."

Though broad of face the woman's features were squeezed into its middle by nature's sly hand. When her expression registered disapproval, as it did now, her eyes and nose and mouth seemed to disappear into fleshy puckers. "The reading of a psalm would benefit to pass the time while you serve at your observation post."

The muscles in Sabrina's throat locked. It was hard to assume humility when gall was all she felt. To disguise her struggle, she lifted her handkerchief to her lips and coughed delicately into it.

"A cough!" Mrs. Noyes' cry was clear in its accusation of displeasure. "You have a cough!"

" 'Tis nothing," Sabrina answered. " 'Tis the wretched air. The street reeks."

"Do not deny it. You've brought a London disease beneath my roof," the woman continued as she waved Sabrina away with a hand while she took a step back, the folds of the loose gray flannel gown she wore billowing about her like a thunder cloud.

Among Mrs. Noyes' dislikes, and there were many Sabrina had quickly learned, there was nothing she abhorred more than illness. The constant fear in her life was that she could run afoul of some noxious affliction that would carry away her life.

"I'm perfectly fine," Sabrina maintained with a spurt of temper. "I am never ill."

Mrs. Noyes shook a plump finger at the younger woman. "Sir Holly's theory is that those in robust health are the first to succumb to illness. He would treat your affliction with severe measures."

The man who came once a week to physic her hostess with nostrums and pastilles said to ward off everything from the pox to the gout was, in Sabrina's opinion, a quack. Yet Mrs. Noyes lived by his every whim. "I do not wish to see Sir Holly."

"And so you shan't!" the woman retorted. "I've not the means to afford the care." The woman peered suspiciously at the healthy swelling of Sabrina's bodice as though she might spy out some symptom through the corsets and gown. " 'Tis naught to be done but to the Pump Room for you, my girl."

"The Pump Room?"

"Aye, a dose of the waters is said to cure consumptive chests, a touch of the flux, even the rheumatic fever. To the Pump Room with you, today!"

Sabrina nearly laughed aloud, amazed at her own lack of shrewdness. Being a healthy young woman it had not occurred to her to fake an illness, until now. Half of the visitors to Bath came for the healing properties of its hot springs while the other half came for conversation and entertainment and play. Both could be found mingling together at the famous Pump Room. If she were allowed to visit there regularly she was certain to meet a London acquaintance whom she could persuade to introduce her into the card salons about town.

"You are absolutely right, Mrs. Noyes. We must go to the Pump Room this very day." She coughed deliberately this time, hiding her smile behind her handkerchief.

The woman's face registered alarm as she backed up yet another step. "*I* cannot go with you. My health requires strict adherence to a regimen, a bath in thermal waters then an hour in bed to sweat out the noxious properties which Sir Holly is persuaded are the cause of my bilious stomach."

Even better, thought Sabrina. "I suppose it is not unheard of for a young lady to take the waters alone, if it were a matter of her health," she surmised aloud. From the corner of her eye she saw the older woman blanch at the suggestion.

She coughed again, a little more heartily this time. "Of course, I will do as you think best." She stopped to catch her breath, as if the effort of speech had winded her. "I will try my best not to sicken further for I would not want Cousin Robert to learn I've become ill while in your care."

"The cost of taking the waters is excessive," Mrs. Noyes, responded doubtfully, staring at Sabrina as if she thought she might detect a deterioration of the young woman's constitution as they conversed. Then her expression cleared. "You are Robert's responsibility and 'tis therefore only right that he should incur the expense." Her face became a quilt of smiles as she added, "I see no need for hiring a sedan chair. A brisk walk is good for the lungs. Sophie will accompany you."

She swung away from Sabrina, the gray flannel she wore billowing out about her like sails caught by a freshening breeze. "So-phie! So-phie!" she called in the very timbre used by the local pig men when summoning their hogs to trough. "So-phie!"

Sabrina briefly closed her eyes against the shrill note in the summons, more than mollified by the promise of the immediate escape about to be hers. A morning, an hour even, on the town and she would find some way to make good on it. She must.

"Yer chair be waitin', mistress," the maid said as she appeared, unexpectedly, in the front doorway.

"Dawdling in the lane!" Mrs. Noyes cried, her features recomposing into the more comfortable expression of disapproving tyrant than that of benefactress. "We'll just see about that. But first you must accompany Miss Sabrina to the Pump Room. She is sickening with some retched disease."

She turned a doubtful eye on Sabrina, whose struggle

with her laughter had turned her complexion quite pink. "Aha! You are flushed." She hurried to the doorway, which she had to turn sideways to exit through. "It must be a fever coming on! I knew it! You must go the Pump Room at once! If the waters do not have the desired effect, you will be bundled back to London in the morning!"

That threat stiffened Sabrina's determination. The only place she would be going when she left Bath was to Scotland, for Kit.

Chapter Seven

Jack Laughton suppressed a sigh and drained the third of the three glasses prescribed as a dose of the waters. As he did so the faint aroma of hard-boiled eggs assailed his nostrils, the notorious odor of the spa waters.

"Must be good for one," remarked Lord Healy, a viscount of the Irish peerage, before sipping more tentatively at his third glass. "Shouldn't think a fellow would drink it elsewise."

Companions since supper the night before, they were visiting the Pump Room on their way to bed rather than upon awakening, as were most of the room's visitors this morning.

The Irishman twisted his lips after another taste. "Whiskey's my preferred medicinal. Sets up a stomach after a fine meal. How's the arm then?" He glanced with sympathy at the arm that the English viscount had been favoring since they met. "Damned unlucky, I say, to be tossed by one's own mount."

" 'Twas more unlucky for the beast, I assure you," Jack drawled as he gazed at the ruddy-faced young man whose lips were pinker than most girls' were. "Sold him the very next day to a tanner," he lied. "Promised me a fine purse in return for the use of the hide."

The nonchalance of Darlington's tone made Healy wonder whether the Englishman were joking or serious. To cover his disconcert, he chuckled. "In the market for a new prime bit of blood, are you?"

"Perhaps." Jack's lazy-lidded gaze continually roamed the room in search of stimulating company, company of the petticoat variety. What he had seen of the spa's feminine population since his arrival two days earlier had only mildly affected his curiosity. None had aroused his libido.

"If that be the case, I've a filly—"

"Please." Jack held up a languid hand. "I've heard tell of your Irish stables, Healy. May you have better fortune in the choice of a wife."

Lord Healy choked on his water and eyed his companion with resentment, not seeing the jest in this offhanded slight of his prize horseflesh. Darlington's genial yet unsmiling countenance offered him little assistance to move past the possible insult.

Being a peer in the lesser Irish ascendancy, Healy had not known of the English viscount before striking up a casual acquaintance fueled by mutual interests. Those interests were a desire to gamble; at faro, ombre, basset, whist, cribbage, or any other nightly variation of gambling that involved the shuffling of cards.

As a long time visitor to The Bath who had only once ventured as far at London, Healy felt much honored by the viscount's marked attentions. So much the better that those attentions were due to the fact that as an inveterate gambler he knew where the richest hands were played and had introduced the viscount to a few of them. Yet now he wondered if he had not caught an adder by the tail. There seemed something decidedly sinister about the gentleman and the scar he bore upon his otherwise exceptionally attractive countenance.

Startled by the direction his thoughts had taken, Healy glanced quickly about the Pump Room that was continually filling and emptying through all of its five arched doorways.

At that moment an unusually attractive lady sailed in. All heads turned curiously for like the unconventional Viscount Darlington, she wore her glorious pure gold hair unpowdered. Otherwise she dressed in the height of fashion in a silk gown of pale green, the bodice and sleeves of which were lined with scarlet and trimmed with gold. Ribbons streamed from her sleeves and cascaded from her tightly laced bodice. The effect was a summation of the woman herself: stunning, surprising, and wholly theatrical.

"I'd wager the society of Bath provides as good a show as any in London," Healy remarked. "To wit, the females."

The lines of faint boredom did not leave Darlington's face though he, too, watched the progress of the beautiful woman toward the well. "Alas, no lady moves me to abandon my position at the bar."

Healy did not dare question the viscount's sincerity only, silently, his taste in women. Then he spied another beauty and nodded ever so discreetly in her direction.

Jack turned toward the subject and smiled slightly. He knew her, quite well in fact. When last he saw her she was a French marquise's mistress. Perhaps times had changed or her circumstances were less secure, for the bodice of her pale pink gown was cut so low that it displayed the upper crescents of her rouged nipples—an open invitation for new admirers.

"What a magnificent pair!" Healy breathed in awe.

"Agreed." Jack inclined his head in acknowledgement of her. Immediately, she winked at him behind her fan. "Ah," he voiced regretfully and shook his head.

"Was that not an invitation to delectation?" Healy questioned in puzzlement.

"If you care to have your exploits gazetted to the world next morning. For her, gossip exceeds every other passion. A night in her arms will be repaid with amusing anecdotes told to your friends and enemies of the activities in which you indulged, how vigorously, and at what length." To augment the implication, he measured a length between his hands.

An embarrassed giggle burst from Healy. "But what of that lady, the one in the lavender sack gown?"

"Ah, Lady Dahlia." Darlington bent a jaundiced gaze on his companion. "She breeds upon mere flirtation. She has borne five children by five different lovers."

Healy promptly dismissed the lady in question. "I don't suppose the exquisite Venetian soprano?" he questioned hopefully.

The viscount again inclined his head with the briefest of smiles, this time at the lady of golden curls and impudent glances who had been eyeing him with equal frankness. But under his breath he said distinctly, "Poxed."

"Poxed?" Healy's voice faltered off key. "But there's no sign, no—"

"There will be. She wears too much powder. The skin has begun to rot."

The casual cruelty with which Viscount Darlington dismissed those women gave Healy a second sharp jab of trepidation. The Englishman was without sentiment or pity.

All at once Darlington's bored expression vanished, replaced by the singular regard certain species reserve for their objects of prey. Intrigued, Healy turned his head to follow the direction of that penetrating gaze.

A young woman had entered the Pump Room. She stood inside one of the arches, her hands clasped before her, a picture of modesty in a yellow sack gown of sprigged India cotton. She was half turned away as, he supposed, she searched for a parent or an ailing relative. Though she was a charming sight he would never have supposed Darlington's taste ran to the virginal line. Then she turned full face toward him and Healy drew in a sharp breath of astonishment. Surely it was her gaze that had arrested Darlington's attention for it now did his own.

Raven brows winged up over wide-set eyes so vivid a shade of violet as to be noticeable from across the Pump Room.

"You will excuse me," he heard Darlington say.

Startled back into self-awareness Healy took a step after the viscount. "I say, do you know her?"

Jack did not answer but continued purposefully across the floor toward the young woman in question.

Yes, he thought, as the heat of indignation swelled within his chest. He did know who she was. This was the obstinate young woman whom he had robbed and who had in turn shot him for his trouble!

More than that, they were not strangers. He had recognized her the moment he had opened her coach door.

Jack expelled a curse in a quick breath of annoyance. What unfortunate luck that he had chosen to rob a coach containing someone known to him. More foolish yet was the risk he had taken in stealing a kiss. In that moment his face had been exposed. The only question remaining was had she recognized him?

Although he had been introduced to Charlotte Lovelace's young companion months before in London, he had never taken pains to give the girl his attention. It was not until three days after the robbery that he had finally placed her face and recalled the chit's name. It was because of her hair. She had always been powdered or bewigged in the countess's presence. But the night of the robbery her hair was worn loose and unpowdered, a midnight curtain of cascading ebony ringlets that had struck him as somehow more suggestive than nudity.

His lip lifted in the suggestion of a sneer. Her name was Lyndsey, Sabrina Lyndsey, heiress to a merchant's fortune. A commoner had shot him!

His gaze raked insolently over her. How could this mere girl have relieved him of his weapon and then, with only dawn's light to guide her, had made of him a perfect target for her maidenly fury?

The wounding had so mortified his pride that he had delayed his entry into The Bath. Instead he had paused at a coaching inn to nurse his pride more than his arm. The flesh wound was healing, yet it throbbed in sympathy to his indignation over the incident.

Had the folly been any other man's he would have laughed. However, at stake was his own very thorny pride and he saw little humor to be had in the situation. He had risked more than injury in robbing that coach, he had anted up his pride, and lost. This time she would find him a more formidable adversary than at their last encounter.

"Miss Lyndsey," he began formally as he reached for her hand. "Well met, our happy reacquaintance."

"Sir?" As her violet gaze turned full wide upon him and he felt a rare jolt of surprise. The arrested expression in those eyes fringed in thick black lashes seemed to touch him in a quite vulnerable spot. Did she recognize him?

He took her hand and briefly brought it to his lips. As he did so he noted that her expression remained one of wonder with no trace of fright or concern. No, this was not the reaction of a girl reencountering her assailant.

"I am desolate," he murmured as he stole a lingering glance at her bosom. The memory of a soft kiss stirred in his memory. He did not, as a rule, enjoy kissing. Odd that he should recall hers, both in taste and texture. "Alas, you do not remember me."

The smile Lord Darlington offered Sabrina might have caused a lesser maiden to flee for her life. But she had been too afraid that she might not recognize or, in turn, be recognized by anyone on her first venture into Bath society to take exception to his approach. "Oh, but I do know you, my lord."

"Do you?" His tone was one of polite inquiry though steel framed it. Perhaps he had not yet won through.

"You are Lady Lovelace's friend, the Viscount Darlington." Sabrina finished her declaration a shade more subdued than she had begun it for a slight frost now laced the nobleman's gray gaze.

"Rather say I am the countess's supplicant puppy and you've a better description of my plight," he answered. His practiced voice gave lie to every outrageous syllable. "I am honored that you remember me."

His effort to charm her momentarily disconcerted Sabrina. She had not forgotten for one instance his constant snubbing of her in Lady Charlotte's salon. Yet she was grateful for this pretense to an acquaintance now. What fortuitous luck that he had deigned to recognize her in public. It would give her an instant profile in town that no amount of mere wealth could. Yet she suspected that he would quickly rescind his patronage if she did not make an impression upon him.

She lifted a gaze bright with mischief and met his calm expression. "Who could forget you, my lord? Once made your impression is indelible. 'Tis, of course, on account of your countenance."

The simple gallantry Jack was about to speak in reply died on his lips. He had lived too bold and intemperate a life to be easily swayed by unexpected events. Yet, for the space of two heartbeats her frankness took him aback. A merchant's chit had mentioned a disfigurement that not even his noble acquaintances dared allude to in his presence.

He reached up as though he would touch the scar, yet he merely sketched the sickle shape in the air before his cheek. "You find it—disturbing?"

"To the contrary." Sabrina's smile found its full glory. "I should not imagine, once a person has a moment to become accustomed to it, that your scar would disturb her any more than it does you."

"I see." Jack wondered at her purpose. She spoke neither artlessly nor from gaucherie. She was deliberately provoking him. It was a tribute to her success thus far that he remained in her company, for his purpose was accomplished. He no longer doubted that she had glimpsed his unmasked face. That fact, like his scar, would not have gone unremarked upon by this bold miss.

His gaze flicked discerningly over her, remarking with the eye of a libertine the flush beneath her flawless skin and the rapid pulse at the base of her throat. She was attracted to him, a fact that neither impressed nor emboldened him. However tempting a morsel Miss Lyndsey might be, innocents were not his style. Now that he thought of it, he suspected that she had shot him, not for the forty guineas he had taken, but for the simple liberty of the kiss he had stolen.

The scar on his right cheek twinged as it sometimes did when he was roused by unpleasant memories. Had a gentleman fired on him he would have sought retribution with the lethal tip of his rapier. At that, a wicked idea formed wholly and complete in his thoughts.

Would it not then be perfect revenge to repay an insult from a female with thrusts of a more personal nature?

He dismissed instantly any inkling of misgiving on the subject. He did not believe in pity, did not subscribe to it nor expect it in any part of his life.

Jack glanced down with new interest untainted by sympathy at his possible quarry. Her eyes were wide upon him, too wide for modesty's sake. Though she looked the picture of innocence in her cotton gown and demurely covered and powdered hair, he knew her as the ebony-tressed temptress of the highway. Seduction of her would be a simple matter. Even now she was trembling ever so slightly with the delicious temptation of desires she might not even yet recognize as carnal interest.

Virginal excitement. He had never experienced it. Perhaps it would be more entertaining to make her fall in love with him. His triumph would be complete when he abandoned her to her disgrace, smug in the knowledge that she would never know why.

"Allow me to escort you to the Pump Room, Miss Lyndsey, that you may partake of the waters."

"I—oh, must I?" Sabrina wrinkled her nose. "I should prefer to be away as quickly as possible. The place smells of rotten eggs."

"That is the spring water," he answered and calmly reached out for her hand. As he tucked it into the crook of his arm, he added with a mocking lilt, "I assure you, you shall find the taste equally disagreeable."

"Then I must hope to find the company in The Bath much the opposite," Sabrina answered pertly though she did not have the nerve to glance up at him this time.

He was much too close and she was vaguely aware of an antagonism in him she had not felt moments before. Where her fingers lay trapped in the crook of his brown velvet sleeve his warmth penetrated with disquieting affect. It marked a reminder that the day was cool and, more disturbing, that the man was not. It recalled vividly to her mind the powerful arms of the highwayman who had swept her first from her coach seat and later into his embrace.

She glanced sideways at the viscount, noting that his profile was quite attractive. Was he as skilled a lover as Jack Law? His reputation certainly made it seem a possibility. Lady Charlotte's friends recounted Jack Laughton to be a thorough profligate as well as the most accomplished gambler in London.

The feel of a man's hard heavy body pressing into hers had quite astonished Sabrina, as had the wet silk and sinewy force of his licentious tongue. She had been mortified and enraged by the highwayman's liberties, yet also, if she were to be perfectly honest, thrilled by it all.

Faint surprise sped through her. She had never before thought of any man in such an intimate fashion! Now she was making comparisons between two of them! Perhaps Cousin Robert was right. She had no shame.

That thought drew a smile from her.

"You must be the possessor of charming thoughts. Would you care to share them?"

The sound of Lord Darlington's voice startled her. How could she have forgotten her purpose in coming here so quickly? She would be called back to Mrs. Noyes' soon enough where she could brood at leisure over her highwayman. Now she must say something that would plant the seed of her interest in gaming with Lord Darlington. Of course! She would recount how she lost her money at the hands of a highwayman.

"I was remembering my journey to Bath, my lord." Sabrina put a small sigh in her voice. " 'Twas an onerous one plagued by bad roads and the specter of a highwayman."

"A highwayman, Miss Sabrina?" He drew her to a halt by the simple act of pausing himself. "Do tell me. Were you robbed?"

"Why, yes. I was."

"How very trying for you." Something less than sympathy colored his voice. "Of course, you have reported your loss to the authorities?"

"No." The arch of surprise in his brows annoyed her. "There was no need. He took little of value to me."

"Indeed? And yet you tremble to speak of it." He placed his hand over hers as he leaned slightly toward her. It seemed by the gesture that he grew in height and size, blocking from her view all but the fringes of the Pump Room. There was no place to look but up into his light eyes—strangely misty like the day. "You must have been truly frightened by the scoundrel."

Sabrina stared at him, for a moment confused by the difference between his solicitous words and the expression on his face. There was no genuine concern or kindness in his polished voice or warmth of true interest in his gaze. His gray eyes were as serene as a still pond, and just as unfathomable.

"I was not, at first. Though he demanded that I hand

over the sum I had intended to use to amuse myself at the card tables of Bath." She weighed her words against any alteration of his countenance and found only disappointment. He might have been a marble bust for all the feeling he exhibited. As a gambler she had hoped that he would commiserate over the loss of another, even by a thief. "But then the villain announced himself to be the infamous brigand Black Jack Law."

" 'Twas rash of the fellow," Jack remarked with a touch of a smile. Clearly she was a novice at intrigue. Her attempt to solicit his sympathy was too broadly played. But then she was about to learn about manipulation of feelings from a master—himself. "Do tell me more."

Satisfied to have retained his interest, Sabrina continued. "He was a braggart, to be sure. I've heard he fancies himself highborn. 'Tis preposterous. 'Twas manifest he is not of noble blood."

"Truly? And how did you come by this judgement, Miss Lyndsey?"

Sabrina did not miss his subtle reference to her own untitled state and knew she had made a blunder. She sounded supercilious when she had meant to sound worldly. "Do you not hold the opinion, my lord, that only an untutored rogue and coward would threaten helpless females?"

His lips arched in a thin smile. "Helpless? Certainly, as you are here to tell the tale, you were more than equal to the matter?"

"I will allow to a most providential bit of good fortune though I've told no one else but my hostess of it." She lowered her voice in the hope that by confiding in him he would feel bound to offer her aid. "I was able to steal the rascal's pistol. And though you will not own it, I quite believe I shot him!"

"A most unfortunate circumstance for the poor brute," he murmured.

"He more than deserved it," she declared hotly, annoyed that he did not praise her intrepid nature.

Jack's smile curled at the edges, caught fire by unholy amusement. "Such a violent young lady. You quite astonish me. Or perhaps there was just cause for your ire."

He bent close to her ear, almost brushing her lace cap with his lips as he squeezed her fingertips. Whispering low in a tone that had encouraged more experienced women to abandon good sense and divulge to him their most damaging secrets, he asked, "What nefarious deed did this outlaw accomplish that you should in recompense seek his life?"

As intimate as a lover's caress, the warmth of his breath played across Sabrina's left cheek. What "nefarious deed," she wondered, would best suit her desire to gain his sympathy? "Well, he . . ."

"Yes?"

"He insulted me," she finished weakly.

"I see." He moved back from her, as though to show that he knew he had pressed her too hard. "You may not wish to refine too much upon it, Miss Lyndsey. 'Tis well-known that highwaymen take gross advantage of the young females who are at their mercy."

"The highwayman took no more liberties with us, my lord, than to relieve me and my companion of our purses."

"Most curious. And just the two females at his mercy?" Jack allowed his suspicion a moment to fester in her thoughts. "I've heard of this Jack Law. He is notorious for his romantic conquests of his victims."

He lowered his gaze deliberately to her neckline and was rewarded by the deep flush of emotion he spied there. Really, this was no challenge at all. The chit was too easily moved. "Women are seldom eager to admit that he has stolen from them something infinitely more valuable than gold."

In mounting frustration Sabrina realized that he had formed the opinion that she had been ravished and worse, to judge by the censure in his words, he found that to her discredit. She could not leave him with that impression. Perhaps, for all his repute as a rake, he was also a prude.

"Jack Law was a gentleman," she replied calmly. "I think it cannot be but that he is a true gallant forced by extreme circumstances of which we may never know to earn his keep on the byways."

It was also the first guileless statement she had made, Jack thought. How very satisfying that it was said in his defense, though she did not know it. So she believed in the romantic fantasy of knights-errant. Poor child. She would be his by the end of the week.

He patted her hand, which lay just inches below the wound that she had inflicted upon him. "Then may he draw so lovely and persuasive an advocate as you, Miss Lyndsey, should he come to trial. Else you may be certain, Jack Law shall swing by his gallant neck."

"Did someone mention Jack Law?"

Sabrina looked round at this new voice to find that a young, ruddy-complexioned gentleman had approached them.

"You did," Jack responded. "Miss Lyndsey's coach was met by a brigand on the road from London." He glanced down at Sabrina. "Allow me to present to you Miss Lyndsey. Miss Lyndsey, this is Lord Healy, Viscount of Greybriar, in Ireland."

Even before the introduction was done Jack looked off with a quick flickering of a smile that caught the attentions of both his companions. "By your leave. I see the day is not yet a loss to me."

Without even a salute of her hand, he lifted Sabrina's hand free of his arm and walked quickly away.

"Wretched manners," Sabrina remarked before she could stop herself.

"You must forgive Lord Darlington's abrupt nature, Miss Lyndsey." Healy smiled at her, his interest in her fueled by Darlington's own. "I believe it to be my most fortunate gain that we've been abandoned by our mutual friend."

"Lord Darlington is no friend," Sabrina countered in pique. "We but share a slight acquaintance made in London through a mutual friend."

"A lady, I'll wager."

"Yes," she answered more sharply than was wise.

Darlington had dropped his interest in her as quickly as he had sought it. Though she knew it to be the very worst action a lady of pride could choose after sustaining a gentleman's snub, she turned her head to search out the direction of the viscount's defection and encountered the second surprise of the morning.

"Why, that is the Countess Lovelace!"

Chapter Eight

"Countess Lovelace."

Lotte Lovelace turned from her contemplation of the ornamental shrubbery growing in pots just inside the archway of the Pump Room, her brows arched in censorious inquiry against the person who had dared make free with her name in public. Her expression warmed the instant she beheld the gentleman crossing the room toward her.

"Darlington," she murmured in delight and shooed away the maid who had accompanied her.

Turning her full attention on the viscount, she recognized in him at once the signs of a night's dissipation. The heavy fall of lace from his jabot and at his cuffs had wilted in the dampish air of the autumn morning. His scar was a little more pronounced, etching a pale crescent through the golden stubble of his night-grown beard. His mouth, usually held in check by a habitual sneer, was softened by weariness. Or could it be genuine pleasure that showed to full advantage its sensual contours?

Lotte's heart stumbled at the thought.

Lud! She had forgotten that quickly the impact Jack

Laughton had on her feminine pulse. Yet, she was no fool, for all Ran thought of her. She knew it was no mark of distinction for a lady to have had the privilege of allowing the West Indian viscount to comport himself with lewd intent between her thighs. If rumor were at all reliable, he was equitably disposed to all offers.

No, she would never mistake his interest in her for genuine affection. He would know her infatuation for what it was, take her if she so recklessly allowed it, and then treat her as he did his other conquests, with faint contempt for their own weakness. For there was one thing she had perceived of him from the first. Darlington loved nothing and no one, least of all himself.

Still, it was such delicious fun to flirt outrageously with him and see that fire of desire burn into those strangely light eyes, even if it were insincere. It had been weeks, nay, more, since Ran had looked at her as a woman; adorable, desirable, eager to yield only to him. The throb of her pulse might be only nature but it was a comfort in her life, a life that had recently gone inexplicably, horribly wrong.

As he reached her, Lotte held out both hands to him along with a smile flushed by her most recent thoughts. "Lord Darlington! Whatever can this mean, to find you in The Bath?"

"Whatever you choose to have it signify, Countess." He took her hands in his possessive grasp. "So long as the words you use to describe the event are delighted, charmed, and pleasured to be again in your presence."

Lotte laughed. It was an arch remark that did not overstate its purpose with flowery embellishments. Contrary to the smug opinion of most gentlemen of the Beau Monde, truly accomplished rakes such as Darlington were rare commodities even in London.

Jack lingered a fraction longer than was proper on the backs of each of her slim hands so that Lotte's cheeks blossomed with roses by the time he was done. He lowered his lids as he straightened up to shield the intensity of the sentiment he suspected his gaze revealed. "Ah, Countess, the day improves by the minute."

"La, my lord, you are as free with your compliments as the spring with its rain. They fall indiscriminately upon all, do they not?"

"Countess Lovelace? Please forgive my temerity."

The viscount and countess turned displeased faces to the interrupter of their *tête-à-tête* but Lotte's expression did a rapid reversal into a smile. "Dear little Sabrina Lyndsey! It is you!"

Lotte reached out to pull her close so they could exchange kisses in the French fashion, on both cheeks. "Sweet child, whatever are you doing in Bath?" A sudden hectic flush entered her cheeks as she lifted her head and gazed eagerly about the room. "Don't tell me! Lord Randolph has brought you with him as a special favor to me."

"Alas no, my lady," Sabrina answered, surprised that the countess would make such a conjecture. "Yet it is most fortunate that we have met today. Most fortunate." She cast a doubtful glance that fell just short of the viscount's face. "I must speak with you, privately, please."

Sabrina's plea brought a renewed frown to Lotte's face but it cleared almost at once. "The very thing, my dear. But first allow me to present you to Lord Darlington. Darlington, do say you remember my little companion, Miss Lyndsey."

"I've had the pleasure," he answered lazily, not bothering to even glance at Sabrina. "It seems providence has been kind to us both this morning, countess."

"Yes, it is providence," Lotte concurred. She noted Sabrina's rising color at the viscount's slight. Yet she was never one to imagine discomfort when it might be ignored. She squeezed Sabrina's arm to reassure her and continued in a lighthearted manner. "Fortune smiles most particularly on me these days. The most enviable run of luck at cards has been mine since arriving in The Bath."

She laughed gaily, the kind of feminine laughter that though not loud enticed masculine heads to turn in her direction. "I positively believe I shall leave the town and my friends beggared."

"An enviable position, indeed," Jack answered.

"You need put forth little effort, Darlington," she assured him. "Of an evening, Bath seems rife with plump pockets. However, there's been too little to occupy my days. Now that you and Sabrina are here, I am saved from this interminable dullness!"

She hugged Sabrina a second time. "I am so very happy you've come! We shall make a party of it." She cast an encouraging glance at Darlington. "The viscount may join us, to keep us from lamenting the lack of an escort."

"I am yours to command," he returned with unusual warmth.

"I've a house in Kingsmeade Square." She lowered her lashes and then lifted them. "You may find me dining in this evening."

"Then I shall bid you *adieu.*" He gave her a respectful bow. "Miss Sabrina," he added with a lessening of warmth to match the sketchier bow he offered her.

"What a very odd gentleman," Sabrina declared when he had turned away.

Lotte gave Sabrina a sharp glance. "I do not find Lord Darlington's company taxing. Quite to the contrary. He is most stimulating company. No doubt when you have been wed a year," she added wistfully, "you will appreciate for the better the viscount's unique qualities."

She linked her arm familiarly through Sabrina's, as if she were herself a young maiden just debuted instead of a well-married matron of the aristocracy. "But I will own, I can't imagine why Darlington would cut you." She chuckled at Sabrina's look of surprise. "Yes, of course, I noticed. A blind man would have."

Sabrina blushed. The viscount had publicly snubbed her after minutes' earlier making her the object of his attention. She had felt summarily dismissed, like a precocious child whose antics had served to amuse until adult company had come along to supplant her. "I am, after all, a commoner," she reasoned aloud. "Quite beneath his regard."

"Rubbish! The viscount never allows station to dictate his tastes in feminine beauty." She hugged the younger woman's arm with her own. "But Sabrina, dear, you must be on guard with gentlemen like the viscount. He is notorious for his . . . well, perhaps I shouldn't . . ." She pinkened. "Just think of him as a hawk. One observes such a creature with an admiration for its magnificence and beauty. But one approaches it with the knowledge that its talons are deadly and its beak can rip tender flesh from the bone."

An apt analogy, Sabrina agreed but she knew better than to express any interest in the disreputable nobleman. Lotte was keen-eyed and sharp-nosed when it came to affairs of the heart. "I doubt I shall have the opportunity to use your sage advice, Countess, yet I thank you for it."

"Oh, you shall see Darlington again, and soon." She smiled with mischief. " 'Black Jack' has promised to call on us!"

"Black Jack?" Sabrina repeated in surprise.

Lotte laughed. "It is naughty of me, I admit, but I am responsible for the nickname. I remarked upon it the very first time that I laid eyes upon him. It must be quite some six months ago, now. I was playing a hand in Lord and Lady Greenwich's card room when he entered, dressed all in black and his skin as golden as one of those colonial Indians one hears about. 'There's the Black Jack I've been looking for,' I whispered to my partner. I'd been in want of the Jack of Spades to complete my hand, you see."

"How droll," Sabrina answered though she had no charitable thoughts to spare the man.

"One must own," Lotte continued in a rapturous voice, "that he is the most dashing gentleman of one's acquaintance."

Sabrina glanced sideways at the countess. Really, she could not understand Lotte's besotted expression, certainly not when she had a perfectly good, wealthy, and handsome husband in her pocket.

Annoyance flared to impatience when from the corner of her eye she spied Sophie entering the Pump Room. The maid motioned for her, the agitation in her furtive summons apparent. No doubt the time allotted her to visit the spa room was up. "Confound it all," she muttered.

"What is it, dear?"

To cover her slip, Sabrina turned a bright smile on the countess. "My hostess considers promptness to be among the chief virtues. I must leave now but I promise to come and see you very soon. Perhaps tomorrow, if it pleases you."

"Don't be silly. You are welcome any time. In fact, you must come with me in my carriage. I insist upon seeing you home."

Sabrina hesitated only a moment. She did not look forward to the trek home through winding streets wet with rain. "Oh, do you suppose I might?"

Lotte offered her a dazzling smile. "I shan't accept anything else. You have yet to tell me what you are doing here in The Bath and why you did not mention the proposed journey before you left London. Come along, I did not wish to take the waters in any case. My stomach has been delicate of late. I can't account for it but I'm certain those noxious waters will not improve it."

"But that is dreadful news," Lotte declared when Sabrina had informed her of the reason for her sojourn in Bath. "Lord Merripace is the last sort of person for you."

"Then you do not think my aversion to this marriage to be wrong-headed?" Sabrina asked in an encouraging manner.

"Indeed not," Lotte answered. "The marquis has buried two wives already, which would seem enough for any man. There are daughters, three of them. All older than you, I believe, though in truth I do not know them. I suppose he is considering a third marriage because he has no heir as yet."

"I have set eyes upon him only once," Sabrina said. "He smells of snuff."

"I wish I could claim your slight acquaintance," Lotte allowed with the frankness that was her nature. "Merripace is one of Lord Randolph's political allies. Ran tolerates the marquis because of his influence in the House of Lords. But marriage to him would be quite another thing."

"He is very ugly."

Lotte glanced at her companion with renewed sympathy. "If it were only that, my dear. I sat beside Merripace at dinner once and it quite spoiled the meal. His linen was dirty, his lace a disgrace. He does not subscribe to the modern toilette of the weekly bath. He told Ran he believes that bathing disturbs the bodily humors and allows in disease." Lotte wrinkled her nose. "No doubt he is not in error to a degree. The third remove at dinner had barely been placed before me when I saw with my own eyes a louse dangling from his wig in hopes of finding more wholesome prey."

Sabrina shared Lotte's reaction of a shudder.

Lotte reached out and gave Sabrina's hand a squeeze. "Oh, but you cannot be forced to marry him, dearest. Your guardian will surely come to see reason in your refusal."

Sabrina reclined against the satin squabs of the countess's carriage seat. "You do not know Cousin Robert."

"Perhaps if Ran . . ." Lotte began only to shake her head. "Or perhaps not. My husband is a positive stickler for the rules. He might advise that if your guardian has no objection to the match, no objection should be made."

"I shall not be forced to wed, even if I am beaten and starved."

Lotte's gaze settled on her younger friend with the appraising acumen of a lady sizing up the value of a diamond diadem. Though her sympathies were with Sabrina, she could well imagine Ran's argument in favor of Lord Merripace's suit. After a moment's thought she, too, could see the good to be had for her friend in making such a match.

"You do see the honor such a proposal does you? After all, the marriage would set the ascendancy of your family. Only think, Sabrina! You'll become a member of the aristocracy."

That thought considerably brightened Lotte's point of view. "Why then, we would be equals. We could go everywhere together, the opera, the king's balls, everywhere! Your children will assume titles, your grandchildren may aspire to a greatness unexpected until now." She flushed. "I mean you no offense, my dear, but without a match such as this, you are doomed to remain a cit."

The suggestion that she should consider trading her freedom for a coronet fanned the flames of Sabrina's mutinous fervor. "A title means nothing to me. Nothing, do you hear me!"

Lotte's red-gold brows lifted in offense. "Why such heat, Sabrina?"

"I mean no offense to you, my lady. Yet when I think of Kit and how he may be suffering—" Sabrina paused to control the sentiments that urged her toward another outburst.

Despite the fact that Ran thought public displays of tender-heartedness were undignified, Lotte could never bear to see a friend in distress and not offer comfort. She leaned forward and caught Sabrina's hands in hers. "What is it, dear?"

Sabrina shook her head, not wishing to reveal all her troubles at once.

Lotte shook her impatiently by the arm. "Come, I cannot help you if you will not be frank."

Sabrina looked up at the frank blue gaze regarding her and smiled despite her distress. "Very well, Countess. I've not told you everything."

"There's more?" Lotte's china blue eyes lit up in anticipation. Although she was a loyal and trustworthy friend, there was little in ordinary life that she enjoyed more than gossip and contretemps, especially if she were one of the lucky few in possession of the true facts. "By all means, enlighten me. I cannot provide you good counsel unless I am privy to the whole tale."

Sabrina was surprised by her own reluctance to reveal the truth. "I believe our guardian means my brother harm."

Lotte's mouth formed an O of astonishment. "Surely that cannot be."

"Kit is the rightful heir to the Lyndsey inheritance. Once he reaches his majority, he will be able to challenge our cousin's claim of his illegitimacy."

Lotte's expression reflected her doubts. "Now Sabrina, that matter was settled by the king himself months ago. Kit was the result of your father's liaison with his mistress and is therefore not entitled to tuppence."

" 'Tis a lie. I saw my father and Kit's mother married with my own eyes. Yet as a woman I could not appear in a court of law without my guardian's consent. I believe Cousin Robert destroyed documents and threatened my father's servants into silence. That is how he succeeded in having Kit disinherited."

"You make grave accusations, dear."

"I've more to make. Kit is a frail child. The Scottish clime to which our guardian has banished him is little more than a death sentence." Sabrina took a deep breath in anticipation of voicing thoughts she had never before given the breath of speech. "Cousin Robert would like nothing better than for a chill or the ague to carry Kit away." She met her friend's bewildered gaze. "I believe he would have Kit drowned or smothered if he thought he might get away with it."

"Sabrina!" Lotte's tone expressed the full extent of her shock.

Sabrina answered with perfect calm. "If I do not marry Merripace as my guardian wishes, he will allow Kit to die. He said as much before exiling me here. Do you not see my dilemma?"

"I see 'tis a devil of coil," Lotte allowed. She sank back against the satin bolsters to give her present thoughts deep consideration.

Finally, when two tiny indentations had marked her brow for some seconds, she shook her head and released the nether lip she had sucked in during her deliberation. "Alas, what can you do, Sabrina?"

"I am determined to steal Kit away from my cousin's care."

Lotte felt astonish register anew. "To what purpose, Sabrina? Do but think. You shall be found out and dragged home in disgrace that may forever shadow your life. Would it not be better to marry and then petition your new husband to take Kit into his care?"

"Do you think Lord Merripace will welcome in to his home the one person who might later challenge him for the rightful guardianship of my inheritance?"

"I had not thought so far as that," Lotte admitted, for keen analysis of difficult matters usually gave her the megrims. But Sabrina was her friend so she did not, as was usual, abandon her efforts at critical thinking. "If Kit were to receive the benefits of his wealth through your largess, could you not persuade him against the need to claim it outright?"

Sabrina shook her head. "I do not hold so good an opinion of my future husband as you do. Why should Lord Merripace take in a commoner's bastard? It would be an intolerable reminder to him that his new wife's antecedents are not all they might be."

Lotte waved this objection away with a flutter of a perfectly manicured hand. "Mayhap Merripace can be won over. Maman says a man may be won over by any woman of good sense and right determination." She frowned, wondering why she had failed so miserably to follow that advice. Thoughts of Ran so depressed her that she immediately dismissed them.

"Think of it. Once you are wed you shall have a fortune at your disposal. I shall help you, of course, to set up your home, plan your first ball, oh, so many things!"

"I'd rather be poor than wed," Sabrina answered.

"That is because you have no experience of destitution," Lotte snapped, thinking of her own upbringing in genteel poverty.

"I am determined on this point," Sabrina rejoined. "I will do anything, suffer anything, to save Kit's life, even if it means leaving England forever."

"Bosh! No one wishes to leave England. Wherever else is there?" Lotte asked with the certainty of one who knows her place in the world. "I will not further your aspiration in that direction. The sensible thing would be to set yourself to the task at hand. A son, Sabrina! Give Merripace a son who will inherit the title and the fortune you bring him."

Even as the final words of wisdom tumbled out of her mouth Lotte recalled again the episode of Merripace and the louse, and shivered. "Oh, very well, you are correct. It is an untenable position for you but I do not see how you may win against your guardian. Perhaps if you were to win the affections of another noble suitor . . ."

Sabrina shook her head. "Gentlemen seem to me of a breed. All are hypocrites, liars, and deceivers. None may be trusted." She gave a quick disarming smile. "Your own dear lord is the exception, of course."

"Perhaps not," Lotte murmured, forced to think again of her betrayed feelings. "But I promise I will speak to

Lord Randolph about your dilemma." She added darkly, "Directly we are speaking again."

"Is Lord Lovelace not in Bath with you?"

Lotte lifted suspiciously shining eyes to her companion. "No, for you see, my dear, I have run away from London."

Sabrina's own extremity of circumstance was momentarily forgotten. "But, Countess, why?"

"Because Ran—Lord Randolph has taken a mistress!" Lotte was determined not to burst into tears but she did, great heaving sobs that quite surprised her in their violence and duration.

"My poor dear lady," Sabrina crooned in comfort as she held her weeping friend in her arms. "Men are rotters! The lot of them! How can your husband so mistreat you when it is so very plain that you love him more than life itself? Hush, Lady Charlotte, hush. You will make yourself unwell."

"Lotte," the countess answered on a hiccup. "If we are t-to be confidantes, you may ca-call me Lotte."

"Very well, Lotte," Sabrina replied soothingly. "But I am perfectly certain his lordship will rethink the matter and come to his senses. A mistress is but a passing fancy, as soon forgotten as last week's gossip."

Lotte dabbed at her flowing eyes with a handkerchief. "If that were all." She shrugged helplessly. "But it is not. There was a terrible fight. He mentioned divorce."

"Divorce?" Sabrina echoed with the faint awe of one repeating a curse.

Lotte nodded vigorously. " 'Tis all on account of my wretched streak of bad luck at cards. Lord Randolph would not forgive me for losing what to my mind is a very small, well, nearly small sum."

"You say you are winning a fortune here in The Bath," Sabrina reminded her in hopes of consolation. "Surely Lord Lovelace will be mollified by that news. You can repay your debts from your present winnings."

Lotte lifted her tear-streaked face. " 'Tis a lie. I've lost more here in Bath than my previous debts in London. I only said I was winning to—to—" She blushed like a maid caught with a footman. "To impress Lord Darlington.

"Ran shall be furious when he hears," Lotte continued, unable to halt her confession now that she had begun it. "If he should refuse to pay, I shall be forced to sell my jewels. How can he be so hard-hearted? A mistress! Upon whom he spends his money. Just so! Yet, he will not pay his own wife's small debts. 'Tis atrocious! I shan't be treated this way!"

The weeping continued some moments longer until the coachman pulled before the address given.

"Oh, are we arrived?" Lotte questioned, pulling suddenly out of her friend's solicitous embrace. "I can't think why I—I so lost control." She produced a slight abashed smile. "Everything ha-has been so-oo topsy-turvy. I cannot eat. I do not sleep. Of late, I am ill upon every awakening."

She pressed a hand to her feverish cheeks and took a deep controlling breath. "One hour I think I shan't go back. Even if he should come to Bath on bended knee with abject misery in his tone. The very next I think my heart shall crack if he does not come for me today. I am like a weather vane in a storm, buffeted this way and that, and never certain of any direction for long!"

"You must not despair, Lotte." Sabrina cast about in her thoughts for a suitable antidote for the countess's tears. "Lord Randolph would not like to see you in such a state."

"You are right, of course you are." Ever aware of her appearance, Lotte quickly smoothed tears from each cheek with her handkerchief and smiling with false brightness said, "There now, I'm ready. You must think me the veriliest ninny to be drowned in sorrow when 'tis the happiest of coincidences that we have found one another."

The liveried footman had stepped down and unlatched the carriage door. When he had let the steps down, he offered his hand to Lotte.

She slid forward on her seat to exit but paused in the

doorway with only her head poking out. After a significant pause, she drew in her head and turned to Sabrina. "Surely you do not stop here?"

Sabrina nodded, resolute in her embarrassment. "Alas."

The countess's expression was priceless in its dismay. "But the lane is small and dirty and . . . common!"

Chapter Nine

Positioned on a settee in the countess's bedchamber, Sabrina languidly stroked the kitten she had brought with her from Mrs. Noyes' residence. Upon cue, she coughed dutifully into her handkerchief.

"No better. I do declare it, you are worse!"

Lotte turned from her vanity toward Sophie, whom Mrs. Noyes sent daily to inquire after Sabrina's health. "You may tell your mistress that you have seen her and that Miss Lyndsey is no better."

"Yes, m'lady." Sophie bobbed in deep curtsey, as overwhelmed to be in the presence of a countess as she had been three days ago. "But Mrs. Noyes suggests that Miss Sabrina return today."

Lotte held up a hand for silence. "Do not babble, girl."

She turned back to a contemplation of herself in the gilded frame mirror above her dressing table as her maid put the finishing touches on her coiffure. "My felicitations to your mistress. May she not be further plagued by illness visited upon her household."

With a languid movement, Lotte reached to extract a

coin from the silver dish that also held her tortoiseshell hairpins. Without even glancing at it, she allowed it to casually slip from her fingers.

Sophie leaped to retrieve it, a ritual begun three days earlier. When she attempted to hand it to the countess's maid, Lotte flicked her fingers in dismissal. "I am far too busy to collect trifles. Keep it, girl."

"Yes, m'lady!" Sophie squeezed the coin with the desperation of one who thought it might jump from her fist. "Only what do I tell my mistress?"

Annoyed by the girl's persistence, Lotte sought to catch Sabrina's eye through the medium of her mirror. The sight made her lips twitch. The younger woman's complexion had crimsoned from her efforts to control her laughter.

She pretended to regard her guest's mirthful expression in mock alarm. "Why I believe, Sabrina, you are flushed. Feverish, I am tempted to call it. Declining, I'm all but certain of it."

She glanced again at Mrs. Noyes' maid. "I had not thought of it 'til now. But as you come daily into Miss Sabrina's company *you* might well carry disease back to your mistress's door. Therefore you are banned from my home until I am certain the danger of infection is past. Tell your mistress the ban shall last a fortnight, at least."

"Yes, m'lady." Sophie bobbed another curtsy and backed out of the door as though royalty had dismissed her.

Lotte turned her attention to her "declining patient" who yawned and stretched like a cat that had finished a delicious dish of cream. With a twinkle of amusement in her eyes she said, "You seem lethargic. Shall I send for a physician?"

Sabrina shook her head as she rearranged the folds of her borrowed blue silk wrapper embroidered in gold and red butterflies. "Quite the contrary. I am feeling quite fit."

"Really?" Lotte's signature red brows expressed guarded hope. "One does wonder what to think. One moment declining, the next positively spry. Might it be delirium taking hold?"

"Oh, I hope so," Sabrina answered.

A quick exchange of glances was all that was needed and the two young women broke into gales of bright feminine laughter. Their delight in bamboozling Mrs. Noyes was with them still.

Sabrina had suspected that Mrs. Noyes would not be pleased to find her in the company of another when she returned from her first visit to the Pump Room. That displeasure, however, had turned to obsequious delight when she had discovered her charge's companion was an aristocrat.

"A countess! In my home!" the older woman had exclaimed to those passing her door before setting about to make a complete toady of herself. Sophie was ordered to bring the best chair in the house from the woman's bedroom into the parlor so that Lady Lovelace might sit upon it. Ale and cakes the likes of which Sabrina had never before known to exist in the household had appeared as refreshment. Cringing in embarrassment, she had stood silently by while Lotte allowed herself to be fawned over in a manner she suspected the countess despised.

The interlude might have served no other purpose than as an instance of absurdity if she had not taken it upon herself to cough loudly in hopes of bringing to a close the quarter hour's exchange.

"You are still ailing!" Mrs. Noyes had cried in accusation. "Go to your room, at once! And there you must remain!"

Lotte, quick to spot a weakness, had observed in her most authoritative voice that Mrs. Noyes was very brave to house contagion beneath her tiny cramped roof. With equal alacrity, she pointed out that her home in Bath was both spacious and compartmentalized. A person might be quite ill in one room yet never infect any other member of the household. Before Mrs. Noyes could insert a word, the countess had risen to her feet with the firm declaration that she would take Sabrina to stay with her. It was the least she could do.

Mrs. Noyes' halfhearted protests were quickly overridden when Sabrina provided a few sneezes and coughs as counterpoint.

The countess's adroit handling of the woman impressed Sabrina. Yet after three days of freedom, she was no closer to finding her way into a gaming salon than before. That must change.

"I am so very weary of lying about indoors," she said with a sly glance at her hostess. "I feel as caged as a menagerie beast. 'Tis a very pretty cage, to be certain," she added to remove the sting from her complaint.

Lotte beamed. "Do you like the new drapes? I thought as long as we were to be ensconced in Bath for some days we should enjoy it. I may make a few other changes as well."

Sabrina glanced at the accoutrements of the countess's boudoir, which included rose silk bed hangings, oriental carpets and hand-painted French furnishings, and wondered what else could possibly be added. The house itself was newly built on the large square called Kingsmeade, part of a set of houses fashioned from the local golden-white Bath stone by the famous architect John Strahan. She knew this because, much to her surprise during their journey across town to the countess's residence three days before, she had been subjected to an unexpected lecture of the city's architecture by—of all people—Lady Charlotte.

Lotte had animatedly pointed out the differences between Wood's style, which was decidedly more Palladian than Strahan's more traditional baroque facades. Strahan, according to Lotte, was John Wood's greatest rival in his efforts to build the city. St. John's Hospital was Wood's work, as was the home of the Avon Navigation Company and Combe Down quarry owner, Ralph Allen. Kingsmeade was Strahan's.

It seemed that, for all her seeming disinterest in weighty

matters, Lotte had acquired in a very short time an astonishing breadth of knowledge on the subject of architecture. She had a keen grasp of the mechanics of it as well as an understanding of the merits of each design. In recent days, she had even begun to sketch ideas for remodeling the Lovelace mansion in London. Perhaps the lady's life of indulgent idleness was at an end.

Sabrina frowned with a sudden dire thought. If Lotte suddenly took it into her head to go home to her husband before she had introduced Sabrina to the gaming society of Bath, her own plans would collapse. Time to nudge her friend.

"If only I had your wherewithal, Countess." Sabrina sighed dramatically. "I, too, should set up housekeeping in town where, of a certainty, Kit would receive proper care. Yet I cannot be content for even a moment while Kit is counting upon my rescue."

Lotte turned back to her table so that her maid could pin atop her powdered curls the addition of a lace cap. "I do not, as you well know, share your reasoning in the matter of your brother's safety. However, were I possessed of the ready, you may be certain I would have loaned it to you. I am still prepared to help in any manner I may."

Sabrina sat up. "Then help me in the manner I need. Introduce me to a place where I might gamble and win the money I need."

The countess frowned. "That would not seem a sound plan, if my luck at the tables is any measure."

"I have no choice," Sabrina answered. "Good or bad, my luck is all I possess."

Lotte smiled. "Very well, I was about to tell you in any case. I've accepted an invitation to a small party to be held this evening."

"A card party?"

Lotte inclined her head in dismissal and her maid, chosen for her discretion as well as her skill with a lady's toilette, melted away into the shadows. Only then did she swivel about on her tufted seat.

"An evening of gambling hosted by one of Lord Randolph's distant cousins. Unknown to me personally, of course. There are dozens of cousins. The Lovelace family breeds excessively, if you ask my opinion. I'm afraid the stakes will not be high. With the passage of the odious Gaming Act last year, high stakes gambling has been curtailed in public places. Alas, it has had a dampening affect on even private parties." She wrinkled her nose. "I'm afraid that is Lord Randolph's fault. He backed the bill. Still, the party marks a beginning."

A frown again puckered her brow when she picked up a hand mirror and was momentarily distracted by her reflection, which was as pale as a tallow candle. She sighed. "I had expectations that Darlington would have favored us with a visit by now."

"I do not see what difference the viscount's attendance could make," Sabrina retorted.

Lotte reached to dip two fingers into her rouge pot, intending to improve upon her maid's efforts, but then thought better of it and abandoned the effort. "In order to enter one of the private salons where the stakes remain unlimited we must have an escort."

"I would prefer it not be Lord Darlington," Sabrina said crossly though she, too, had briefly entertained hopes of his patronage.

"You've never said why you disapprove of Lord Darlington, above the ordinary gossip, I mean."

"The ordinary gossip is enough to influence my opinion."

Lotte canted her head toward the younger woman. "Sabrina, what is this new pout? Though you do not wish to marry Lord Merripace, it cannot follow that you must not wish to fall in love."

Sabrina smoothed the shiny surface of her borrowed

finery. "I dare say I cannot comprehend the meaning of the word love."

"Gammon!" Lotte lifted a hand heavenward as her eyes followed. "Surely you have felt a thrill when a certain gentleman's gaze meets yours? How, if he but chances to touch your hand, your heart leaps?" Her lids fluttered down as a secret smile softened her mouth and filled her cheeks with the glow that had been missing. "One day there will come a moment when you know with absolute certainty that your life will never be complete if he does not kiss you!"

Sabrina made a sound that was far from concurrence.

Lotte opened her eyes, her wistful expression altering to one of wonder. "These feelings *are* known to you?"

Sabrina shook her head. "Not a one."

Lotte's azure gaze drifted down upon her friend in a kind of benediction as she said softly, "You will."

Sabrina shrugged, unconvinced. "There's only one who occupies my thoughts and affections and that is Kit." Her mouth softened. " 'Twas kind of you to allow me to write to him and stamp it with your crest. Perhaps it will be delivered to him for the very reason that there is no outward sign of my hand in its composition."

" 'Tis nothing to frank a letter for a friend. However, I can't say that I changed my opinion of your plan. Running away never solved anything."

Sabrina forbore to remind her benefactress that she had done exactly that in deserting London without telling her husband. The subject of Lord Randolph was not one that the countess cared to discuss unless she brought it up. And when she did, inevitably, the scene ended in tears. In fact, these past days, the countess seemed more fragile of constitution than Sabrina in her most persuasive pretense at illness.

"How is your digestion today? You were quite ill at breakfast."

Lotte blushed. " 'Twas nothing. A spoiled kidney, perhaps. I cannot think why I ever liked them. The smell is enough to quite revolt one's system.

"I shall send my maid to attend you when I am done dressing," Lotte continued quickly. "I can't imagine what your guardian was thinking to send you off without one. Clearly the man has no experience of ladies. I suppose one must be grateful that he had packed a few of your gowns. Yet you will quickly run short once we are out in society. You may borrow whatever you need from my closet."

"You are too kind," Sabrina answered though the offer had its limitations. When she stood the hem of the wrapper puddled about her slippered feet, testament to the fact that the countess was tall with a spectacularly voluptuous figure, while Sabrina was petite and less generously contoured.

"Do not forget your clogs," Lotte called after her. "A gentle rain has begun."

"Anything else?" Sabrina inquired politely.

"Yes, wear your green and pink stripe silk gown. As I recall, Darlington is partial to stripes."

"Darlington again," Sabrina muttered as she strolled through the dressing room that separated her room from her hostess's. Nothing concerning the viscount was of the least interest to her. His conduct toward her had been nothing short of galling. No amorous advance from him would ever move *her* to pine for his kiss.

Sabrina brought her fingers to her lips. She had not slept a night since arriving in Bath without the specter of Black Jack Law to keep her company. Always the dream was the same: the meeting, her anger, his threat, the kiss, the pistol shot. The *crack* of that pistol shot always awakened her.

The outlaw who had ridden into her life out of the moonless night still fascinated her. She had only to close her eyes to recall the impression of his mouth on hers, the firmness of his lips, smooth yet exciting. She had only to hold that memory to her to feel a strange yet deep stirring. Was this unaccountable sensation the pang of desire the countess had hinted at?

She snapped her eyes open and snatched her hand from her mouth, faintly ashamed to realize that she was atremble.

"Out! Out!" she commanded the highwayman's memory and twisted her toe into the plush as if she could grind all thoughts of him into the carpet.

That forbidden moment, the pressure of those lawless lips, had lingered in her memory far beyond its importance to her!

"Most honored to make your acquaintance, my lord." Squire Threadlesham beamed up at the tall nobleman to whom he had just been introduced by their host, Sir Avery Lloyd. "Most honored."

He bowed a second time. The action launched an assault by his ample belly upon the buttons of his clothing, which provided a valiant effort to keep closed the front of his vest. His ruddy cheeks bloomed as he realized he was being rewarded with silence by the viscount. "Only wish my Bess weren't abed with the very rheumatism which brings us to town. When she learns she missed out on the honor of meeting a genuine member of the peerage, she won't be fit to live with."

"Hectoring hens, every one," barked their companion and host Sir Avery, an elderly knight of three score years.

He pronounced this opinion with faint contempt for the swarm of ladies streaming past him into the salon of his Bath residence. He glanced at Lord Darlington. "Not my usual style, mixing gentry with the titled. But my wife insisted. Things are done less formally in Bath. Been listening to that damned Nash fellow again."

"Don't expect a nobleman of your estimation often lends his consequence to affairs of this sort," Threadlesham remarked in the outrageous hope that the viscount would contradict him and asked to be allowed to call on the ailing Mrs. Threadlesham. To his disconcertion the viscount had yet to address a word to him of any sort. The introduction elicited only a lift of golden brows and the firming of a handsome masculine mouth into what might only in extreme generosity be termed a smile.

"Never made the acquaintance of a member of the peerage before," Threadlesham continued nervously. "No indeed, unless one considers a baronet, no, of course you wouldn't. But Sir Avery is a right stouthearted gentleman. Fought off Jack Law with nothing but a cane."

For the first time the glance of indifference lifted from Jack's tarnished-silver gaze. "He was attacked by the highwayman?"

"The very soul," Threadlesham answered, pleased to have found a subject worthy of the nobleman's response. "The Knight, for all his bravery, lost his silver buttons and buckles, a brand new watch, and a considerable purse. Said he recognized the brigand from a reward bill posted in the tavern of a coaching inn. Brave to make a fight of it."

Jack's lips twisted in amusement. He could better imagine that the old fool had given up his goods while watering his breeches.

"Have a care when you leave the spa, my lord. The byways hereabout are dangerous. Jack Law wouldn't think twice of attacking a person as august as yourself."

Yet as Threadlesham eyed the aristocrat's ruthless expression, he revised his opinion. The viscount's icy disdain and wickedly curving scar would give even the most unregenerate miscreant pause.

"Damned rascal should be hung!" Sir Avery declared in distracted annoyance.

"The very thing, Sir Avery, the moment we catch him."

"Catch him?" The older man cocked his head in question, much as a dog might. "Demme! What's to do but he ain't been nabbed before now?"

Threadlesham looked sheepish. "The thing of it is, Sir Avery, Jack Law's reputation has gained such polish every venial villain 'twixt London and Cornwall has taken to claiming the sobriquet as his own. 'Twas reported just last August that Jack Law had robbed five different coaches on five different lanes in two different counties on the very same night!"

"Busy fellow," Jack murmured.

"Hang 'em all!" Sir Avery declared gruffly. "Bound to be among the coffin meat sooner or later."

"A young woman in the Pump Room declared but recently that she had been robbed by the fellow," Jack offered in a bored tone. "Perhaps you should engage her services. She claims to have shot the brigand with his own pistol."

The two men standing with him guffawed their disbelief.

Threadlesham shook his bag-wigged head. "Mind, I do not say she was not robbed but had it been by Jack Law, she would not be boasting of it. Take's advance, they say." He made an obscene gesture with his hand.

Sir Avery extended his gold snuffbox toward Jack and flicked open the lid with a thumbnail. "Have a touch of snuff, Lord Darlington. Bucks up a man's courage for these damned tepid affairs. Can't imagine why a man of your ilk chose to attend."

Having involved himself in the business of taking a bit of snuff, Jack was spared the need to reply. As a rule, he detested snuff but it gave him something to do while his patience learned a new degree of self-possession.

On one point Squire Threadlesham was correct. Ordinarily he would not have considered an appearance at a party sponsored by a rusticating lady with too little to occupy her too small mind. Yet, on this occasion, he had actually finessed an invitation.

He looked across the main salon until his gaze narrowed

in on a figure, seated among the feminine flock, dressed in striped pink and green silk. Sabrina Lyndsey. He was here because she was here.

He had deliberately stayed away from her for three days to enhance the suspense of their next meeting. He had set himself a task, to humble Miss Lyndsey. Tonight, he would begin that campaign.

He had watched her for the past half-hour, secure in the knowledge that she was totally unaware of his presence. He had recorded her smiles, absorbed the way words formed on her soft round lips. He had committed to memory the exact arch of her neck and gentle inward slope of her back from shoulders to waist, registered her every elegant gesture against the future. Never again would she be within his view and he not recognize her immediately, though she be no more than a silhouette thrown upon a window shade.

Why? Because it pleased him to know more about her than she would ever know about him. For instance, he had learned that when she was nervous she often turned away from the object of her fear. Was it a deliberate provocation, a demand that the offender work to recapture her attention? Twice she had turned her back on Jack Law. Yet, she had not turned away after he had kissed her. She had struck out at him. That was the reaction he intended to provoke in her again. He had not interest in the innocent-seeming miss he observed this night. He wanted to again match wits with the vixen of the highway.

It rankled to admit it but a quite extraordinary thing had happened to him as he lay in wait for Miss Lyndsey these last three days. He had thought constantly about her.

Few women occupied his mind past the hour of their usefulness, and fewer still lingered in his thoughts when they were no longer present. He was not accustomed to lingering preoccupation, or even lingering lust. Yet, at the end of each evening he had found himself pondering the mystery of a pair of violet-blue eyes and wondering about the woman behind that gaze.

It must be that he desired revenge more than he had suspected. Yes, that was all.

His smile warmed as his gaze wandered from Sabrina to an inspection of Charlotte Lovelace. Resplendent in a gown of palest pink silk that made luminescent her flawless bosom and shoulders, she was infinitely more beautiful and naturally more elegant than any other lady present. That fastidious prig of a husband did not appreciate his good fortune. She would be a pleasure to seduce. Yet he was determined to spare her from the folly of entering into an affair with him. He had few scruples, none of them connected to the usual rules of polite society, but he held fast to them in his fashion. Because she reminded him of the only person he had ever loved, Lotte was inviolate.

His eye caught the swaying movement of pink and green silk as Sabrina rose to follow several other women into the card salon. He had been aware of her jealous reaction to his warm greeting of Lady Charlotte in the Pump Room. He had even tested that suspicion by snubbing her in Lotte's presence and been rewarded by the snap of anger in those violet eyes that gave away too much of her feelings.

Had she been experienced in the art of flirtation she would not have given herself away so readily. She was a novice at the game of seduction. He was not, as she was about to learn.

His left arm just above his elbow throbbed a little, a palpable reminder of the reason for his pursuit. Patience was the first line of assault on a proud heart. He would use Sabrina Lyndsey's pride to bring her down and before he was done she would even thank him for it.

When he had sniffed and sneezed and dusted away a sprinkling of snuff from his jabot with his handkerchief he said abruptly, "Excuse me," and walked away from the startled knight and squire.

Chapter Ten

Sabrina sat at a table for four, her cheeks flushed from concentration and annoyance. The countess had staked her with what she had regretfully termed a "pauper's sum" of fifteen guineas. Yet after no more than an hour's play the pile of bank notes and coins by her left elbow easily amounted to five times the original. She should have been delighted but the triumph was an experience she wished fervently would end.

Two of her fellow players, both gentlemen, had picked up on her excitement at winning and it had sped through them as a frissom of sexual invigoration. Or perhaps it was the canary that they had been liberally imbibing which fueled their libidinous attention.

"My dear Miss Lyndsey, you're a deal too coming for me," said Lord Quince without rancor.

Sabrina offered him a frosty smile. "You are too kind, Lord Quince. I confess I am not a very skilled player for I've had so little opportunity."

"Who needs skill when lucks sits at on your shoulder?" remarked Mr. Shelby.

"Envy that rascal the view." Lord Quince winked at Shelby. "Fine pair of tits on the filly, what?"

The glance Lady Quince leveled at her husband should have singed his wig.

"Miss Sabrina is indeed favored by the stars," Mr. Shelby concurred as his face pinkened at the bottom rather like a turnip.

"By all the graces," conceded Lady Quince in ill humor and then gave forth a distinctive belch that perfumed the table with sour spirits. "Shall we play another hand?"

"Indeed, m'lady. The very thing." Mr. Shelby offered her a slightly stupid smile. "After all, I've still a few coins which Miss Sabrina may wish to make hers."

"If her luck holds," remarked Lady Quince sourly and reached for the tumbler that a servant kept full of wine.

Sabrina clasped her hands together to keep from obeying the impulse to pluck the bank notes from her pile and tuck them in her bodice. It would be poor manners to remove the possibility that they might be won back though she had no intention of wagering a single shilling of the evening's profit.

As Shelby dealt the next hand, a heavy foot nudged Sabrina's under the table. Her smile stiffening, she inched her foot away. The foot pressed harder, causing her to look up into the leering drunken countenance of Lord Quince.

He grinned at her, revealing ill-fitted brown-stained teeth. "Nary a man—er, hand has been more eager to fall to your grasp. You'd prefer livelier sport, I'll wager."

"You mistake me entirely, sir," she said shortly and glanced away.

Damn his impudence! His evening coat was spoiled by several moth holes and his wig, over-curled and under-powdered, was a dozen years out of date. With a large-veined nose sporting a strange dark growth on one side, how could he possibly think himself a source of fascination for any woman?

Yet vanity was not always harnessed to good sense, Sabrina supposed. He was of that variety of English lord who preferred horses and hounds to the fashionable doings of the Beau Monde. No doubt he believed a loud voice, vulgarity, and despotic constitution were equitable replacements for manners, culture, and a pleasant appearance.

"Whiskey, hounds, and the hunt, that's enough for any man," Lord Quince had declared at the onset of the game, "That, and a bit of muslin sport."

Well fortified by spirits, he had taken every opportunity during their card play to lean in her direction, supposedly to peek at her cards yet his gaze never rose from an insulting appraisal of her bosom. Once, when a coin slipped off the table into her lap he had grabbed and squeezed her thigh under the pretext of trying to catch it.

Perhaps it was ungracious to wish to blazes the very people who had made possible her evening's good fortune, yet she wanted nothing more than to leave the room and forget their existence.

She sent a pleading glance Lady Charlotte's way but the countess, seated at another table at the far end of the room, did not chance to meet it. She seemed inordinately absorbed in her own hand. By the look of the quilting between her auburn brows, her game was not going at all well.

"Are you wagering, Miss Lyndsey?"

Sabrina blinked and returned her attention to the cards she had been dealt. "Why, I suppose so, yes."

"Not I." Lady Quince rose though it was difficult to judge that at first, for she was so short that standing made no great difference in her height. "I've had quite enough. Lord Quince!" Without parting, she turned and left the table.

Relieved, Sabrina dropped her hand and rose. "In such case, gentlemen, I think we should adjourn."

"Are you done fleecing your betters, Miss Lyndsey?"

That voice! Sabrina swung around, her heart pounding in unexpected fear and delight. The delight died a precipitous death at the sight of the man who stood behind her chair. "Lord Darlington."

"You need not be so demonstrably happy to see me," Jack remarked of her sudden crestfallen expression.

"Rather I am unmoved by the thought, my lord," Sabrina remarked coolly, totally out of charity with the entire evening and equally exasperated with herself. How could she have mistaken the viscount's voice for another? Jack Law, even if he were a nobleman, he would have better sense than to tempt fate by confronting one of his victims in public. Yet, for one all too brief moment that is exactly what she had thought was occurring.

Sizing up the stranger, as a rival to his nonexistent claim on her, Lord Quince's tone was distinctly belligerent as he stepped between the pair. "Miss Lyndsey doesn't appear to be cheered by your company, sir."

Darlington gave him no more attention that he might have a moth flitting past. His silvery gaze remained on her. "I have come expressly to play a hand with you, Miss Lyndsey."

"You would find little joy in it, my lord," she said carefully. He was, after all, her superior and if her snub were observed she might soon find herself *de trop* in Bath society. "I am not equal to your skill."

Amusement tugged at the left side of his mouth. "Is that how you choose your partners, only those you believe you can best?"

Sabrina shot him a murderous glance as her two gaming companions stiffened at the implication. "Nay, my lord, for then I should never play cards at all."

He inclined his head. "A pretty save. One might even say a clever one."

"Who the devil are you?" demanded Quince.

Sabrina turned to the slighted man in faint annoyance with all concerned. "Permit me, Lord Darlington, to introduce to you Lord Quince and Mr. Shelby."

"Darlington?" Lord Quince barked, determined, it seemed, to make fresh headway toward disaster. "Don't know a Darlington. Ain't even wearing a wig. Should that name be known to me?"

His rapier-sharp gaze trapped the countrified peer in its gleam. "I could make it so, with pleasure."

Darlington's tone stirred the hair on the nape of Sabrina's neck. "I'm certain the baron would prove amicable to another hand of cards," she suggested into the short silence.

"He may prove himself amiable by favoring us with his absence."

Lord Quince harrumphed but did not offer a challenge for the danger that ran like a deep current through the viscount's bored speech had cut through his alcohol fog. Defeated, he looked like the puffed-up drunken lecher he was. "Damnation, me wife's waiting. Another time then, Lord Darlington."

As he turned away he caught Sabrina by the arm just above the elbow and pinched it hard. "Look to your own, Miss Sabrina. That London rake is after more than your shillings. Red-gold, that's the coin of his realm."

Sabrina did not respond to his vulgar warning as he sauntered away.

Jack turned to the remaining man. "You will now equally oblige me by removing yourself."

The contempt in the compelling glance that Jack turned upon the commoner so weakened his knees that Shelby stumbled a little as he backed away.

"That was very rude of you, my lord," Sabrina said softly as she extracted a silk scarf embroidered in gold thread from her chair and draped it about her shoulders.

"Then I am mistaken and you enjoyed being pawed by that manure-reared bully."

Sabrina smiled in spite of herself. "I did not think anyone noticed."

"Then you must revise your opinion, Miss Lyndsey. We were all aware." He sat down before lifting his gaze significantly to hers. "The company found it most entertaining to witness the torment of a pretty helpless creature."

Surprise lifted Sabrina's expression. "You make me sound a victim."

"I thought you a silly young woman to put up with it."

The set-down stung even though it did not surprise her. Lord Darlington seemed incapable of civility. No other man in the room would have continued to sit while a lady stood in his presence. Yet she was discovering that she enjoyed measuring her wit against his. "I can't then imagine why you should bother to speak to me."

"Can you not?" He shuffled the gilt-edged playing cards with remarkable ease, his long fingers moving swiftly in patterns of long familiarity. "I like to test the odds in every situation. For instance, my mere presence at your side offers the room more reason for speculation. Ladies who are long in my company are usually suspected to have forfeited their good sense or their good reputation. Which will you be accused of forfeiting, I wonder?"

Unperturbed, Sabrina turned a smile of complete confidence upon him. "All this may be accomplished by so small a thing as sharing a table with you? I am impressed by the potency of your reputation, my lord."

His gaze flashed something—amusement?—and was gone. "You are not afraid of me? I rather thought you would be too proud to realize your full danger. I am grateful to learn that it is so."

If he hoped to trip her up, to make her agree to something that she misunderstood, he was doomed to disappointment, Sabrina decided. "You expect me to now play cards with you?" Sabrina said as he began dealing hands.

He looked up at her. "Do you always require reassurance, Miss Lyndsey? 'Tis a tiresome habit more in keeping with a young woman who believes her charms insufficient to retain a man's attention. As any quizzing glass can assure you of your beauty, your petulance gives one the impression that you are querulous by nature."

"For a gentleman known to be both dangerous and ruthless you sound remarkably like a nanny and a scold, my lord," Sabrina returned with some heat and sat down.

He glanced across at her and the merciless expression in his gaze was for once absent.

Sabrina drew a breath of astonishment. She had forgotten that he did not smile. The emotions that most often shaped his mouth were contempt, disdain, aloofness, or mocking sneer. Yet in this moment, the amusement that animated his face could be labeled friendly.

He was sinfully handsome. Why had she not noticed so before? Perhaps because she had been too preoccupied with her own concerns on the only other occasion they had stood face to face, in the Pump Room. Lords were, to give their due, routinely described as handsome. But with Lord Darlington, the designation was appropriate. She had not noticed before that he was soberly dressed in black with few touches of lace. By denying the fripperies of the day, the force of the man alone came fully into play.

A strange thrill moved through her as she regarded him with a consideration she had never before shown any man. The wide forehead and jutting brow balanced his bold nose and gave his lean cheeks and hard chin a counterpoint. His deeply hooded eyes held a fascination that was equal parts engaging and sinister. It was not a tender face or a perfect one, but so wholly masculine in its sun-bronzed leanness that by contrast the features of every other man present seemed to be made of unbaked dough.

A woman's scream fractured the moment like a brick striking a panel of glass. Even as the shards sliced through the spell of sensual awareness, Sabrina rose to her feet, half-aware of an alarm she could not name. She found the cause when she turned and saw that the group of players at the far table was focused on one of their own, who lay sprawled on the carpet beside her chair.

"Lady Charlotte!"

There were advantages to being a man, Sabrina mused not for the first time as she balanced Lotte's sleeping head upon her shoulder to cushion her from the worst jolts of the carriage ride. The dear lady had fallen asleep the instant the carriage pulled away from the entrance to Sir Avery's home. Their fortunate escape from prying eyes and rumor-mongering whispers had been made possible by an unexpected savior. Lord Darlington would not have been her candidate for role of Good Samaritan, yet he had been impressive in the role.

She had rushed to Lotte's side without a thought for anything but to reach her. The poor countess looked like a rag doll sprawled on the carpet in her finery, her head cocked at an awkward angle and her gown wrenched out of line so that one of her generous breasts had spilled free of her neckline, revealing its ruby nipple.

Sabrina had torn her scarf from her shoulders and laid it discreetly over her when it seemed the rest of the company was too aghast or titillated to come to Lotte's aid.

Only Lord Darlington had acted with a cool-headed swift efficiency that left no doubt among the gawkers that he had taken the matter in hand. In quick succession, he had ordered spirits of camphor to revive her, lifted

Sabrina out of his way, and then bent a knee beside Lady Charlotte, lifted her still senseless, and braced her against his chest.

When the spirits were waved under her nose and she came round, he asked in a quiet authoritarian voice if she were in pain, feeling ill, or any other kind of distress.

Lotte fluttered her lashes then opened eyes that seemed to have grown too large for her delicately featured face. She stared uncomprehending at the viscount for a moment, and then blushed deeply when she realized who bent so closely over her. "My lord, what is this?"

"Not what you imagine or I should desire, Countess."

He smiled at Lotte, exhibiting a protective tenderness Sabrina suspected few women had ever received from him. Her gaze went from him to Lotte and a deep shock of awareness and alarm swept her. How fondly the countess gazed up at the viscount. How solicitous he was as he lifted her carefully and easily from the floor. He held her high in his arms, balanced against his chest for what seemed a frisson-charged eternity before turning to deposit her back into her chair.

It took no imagination to decipher the whispers among the witnesses who had crowded around this tender scene. The murmur on every tongue matched her own suspicions. They must be lovers or would-be lovers betrayed by this simple incident.

The suspicion nibbled at Sabrina's peace again now as she regarded the viscount who sat opposite her in the countess's carriage, silent, still, and as much at ease as a buccaneer who had captured his prize.

In the feeble light cast by the coach lamp she could see that he was deep in thought. His mouth was a tight, straight line, his golden brows bunched tensely atop his nose. The deep-set eyes were hooded more than usual and the dull gleam of his natural hair gave him the aura of being an altogether different being than the ordinary people who inhabited the town. The conviction grew within her that he was a very dangerous and a very bad man.

Unlike other unfeeling noblemen who used their elevated status to exploit and discard the weak and inferior, Lord Darlington acknowledged no hierarchy in his world save himself. He was the plunderer, every other creature potential quarry.

The Beau Monde recognized it as well. That fact had been borne out when he had tersely called for Lady Charlotte's carriage. Despite the sputtering protest of their hosts, who belatedly offered the countess a room for the night, he had not even bothered to repeat himself. He had assumed, as was the case, that Sir Avery's servants would do his bidding over their master's. When he was satisfied that Lady Charlotte could stand, he had helped her to her feet and escorted her to the door with an arm wrapped with intimate familiarity about her waist. The most brazen of the curious had followed them to the threshold and so knew what everyone who cared to soon would, that the viscount had accompanied the countess home in her carriage.

A chill that had nothing to do with the brisk autumn night sped through Sabrina. He wanted Lotte. Poor foolish, lovely Lotte. She needed protecting against herself.

Feeling far less cool and composed than she appeared, Sabrina hugged the exhausted woman in her arms a little tighter. He would find no welcome in Lotte's home this night. Let him try to take advantage of her, she thought with a natural antagonism against all tyrants. Just let him try!

"You should take better care of your lady."

The accusation voiced suddenly in the silence disconcerted Sabrina. Though she had been thinking along amazingly similar lines it rankled that he should accuse her of disinterest in the countess's welfare.

"Lady Charlotte is not in my care. We are friends."

She saw him glance out of the window as though something had caught his eye. "She brings you into her household and treats you, a commoner, as an equal." His gaze returned to her but it was insultingly unfriendly. "These things are unprecedented in most aristocratic households. Do you not think that obliges you to her in some manner?"

His words were like the flicks of a whip's tip against her conscience. "I assure you—"

"Don't assure me." His leg stirred and his knee came into accidental contact with her skirts. In that instant a charge like static jumped between them. She recoiled instinctively from the touch but he seemed not to notice.

His voice was sharp with reprimand. "Lady Charlotte is a tenderhearted creature, often showing kindness to those whom she should offer reticence. Do not abuse her kindness. Care for her as you would one you held genuine affection for."

Shocked out of consideration for her inferior position Sabrina erupted. " 'Tis you who abuse Lady Charlotte's goodness! Do you think I did not see, do not know? You would prey upon her weaknesses when she is most vulnerable."

He did not react as she expected. The tension in him inexplicably eased. "What weakness would that be?"

"You must know that she and her husband have separated in rancor."

"Alas, no." His gaze shifted again to the all but nonexistent view beyond the carriage window. "I do not give a damn for rumors of domestic acrimony."

"I suppose not, as you are to blame."

His head whipped around. "What did you say?"

If looks could do violence she would have been in great jeopardy, Sabrina supposed. Only a drunkard like the bully at the Thames alehouse would have failed to realize the power behind his intimidating stare of storm gray.

She swallowed, trying to keep her voice to an angry whisper that would not awaken the countess. "Do not mistake me for a brainless chit, my lord! I know you have seduced Lady Charlotte away from her husband."

His gaze did not flicker. "You are wrong."

"Am I? Did I not see with my own eyes tonight how adoringly she looked up at you when in a weak moment she forgot you were not alone?"

His lips twisted in scorn. "What you saw is no one's business."

"I rather think Lord Lovelace would disagree," she rejoined.

He moved so quickly that she had no time to gauge his intent before he gripped her knee, the fingers curling about it until they exerted a painful pressure despite the layers of gown and petticoats. "I warn you this once, Miss Lyndsey. Do not meddle where it does not concern you. I will have no mercy if you attempt to oppose me."

She was not certain if he then leaned forward or if his stature in her eyes seemed to grow in proportion to his threat. All at once she was aware of every line and angle of his ruthless expression, of silver eyes glowing catlike in the dim light. Her shudder of fear caused the countess to stir slightly.

She did not like to be afraid. It made her angry. And that made her brave. "Well then," she rallied at her most haughty, "I think I have my answer."

"You have!" He bit off the last of his retort as he released her and leaned back.

For the duration of the ride, Sabrina gazed unseeingly out of the window. She felt raw, quivering, and wholly unsettled by the presence of the viscount. Were there other men who so convincingly conveyed the potency of intended violence without raising their voices? She had never met one. Compared to the viscount's icy rage, Cousin Robert's bombastic threats seemed little more harmful than the blustering gusts of the spring rain.

She did not mean to laugh. It simply escaped.

Though she kept her face averted she felt his gaze upon

her, hard and smooth and cold as the touch of frosted glass. But that is not what suddenly sobered her. While she did not fear Cousin Robert, there was one who had cause to fear greatly.

"Kit," she whispered so softly that it could not quite be heard.

The viscount was through the door the instant the carriage stopped rolling. He handed Sabrina down by grasping her about the waist and setting her on the walk. It was an impartial touch he might have used to convey a child to safety, but Sabrina felt the heat of his hands wrapped strongly about her and then the abrupt return of a chill when he released her.

Not waiting to be told what to do, she hurried up the steps and rapped sharply on the door. It seemed an eternity before she heard footsteps in the hall on the other side. By then the viscount, who once again held the nodding countess in his arms, was cursing softly but so virulently that Sabrina found herself both impressed and in wonderment at what several of the words meant.

The servant who came in answer to her knock was dressed in bedclothes and nightcap. Uncertain of the identity of the late-night guests, he opened the door only a few inches. "Yes?" he inquired in a sleepy voice.

"Make way for your mistress!" Darlington ordered loudly and kicked the door wider with his foot as he entered.

Sabrina swept in behind him, equally opinionated about what should happen next.

"The countess is feeling unwell," she informed the servant. "Wake her maid at once. Be certain she brings with her a small glass of milk laced with brandy and a hot water bottle. What are you doing?" she demanded of the gentleman who had continued on ahead of her.

Darlington turned and looked down at her from the

second step of the sweep of stairs that led to the first floor. "Taking the countess to her room."

"You cannot do that."

"No?" In another older age, his imperviously lifted brow would have been enough to send some poor wretch to his demise, she did not doubt. "Then who will? *You?* This elderly stick of a servant?" Not waiting for whatever feeble protest he suspected she would feel obliged to make, he turned and continued to climb.

"Does he know where to take her ladyship?" the servant asked in concern.

"Certainly not!" Yet curious to learn the truth for herself, Sabrina followed quickly after him.

Moments after the small entourage had disappeared at the top of the stairs a rap at the door caused the servant to open it again.

"Evenin' to ye." The man on the doorstep, dressed in a heavy shapeless coat, doffed his knit cap. "Bein' as I saw the gentleman carrying the lady inside, I was wonderin' if ye be in need of a physician? Five bob will fetch him."

"That won't be required," the servant answered coldly.

"That so? My mistake. Only that gentleman, that wasn't his lordship now was it? Done a spot 'o work for Lord Lovelace a time or two. He don't wear his hair natural, being a lord. Will the gentleman with the golden mane be needin' a sedan chair then? Can whistle one 'round the corner for five bob."

The servant shut the door in the stranger's face without comment.

Instead of anger, this action elicited a cackle of glee from the stranger.

"Got ye, I have!" Archibald Foibles rubbed his hands together. His London contact would be impressed. London agents were thought superior to those in rural areas because their exploits of tracking and informing were more readily circulated in a town like London, where gossip among those who used their services spread their reputations.

Well, the Beau Monde would soon learn a new tune with a new name, Archibald Foibles. And he would earn a pretty penny for his trouble!

"Foibles on the job! And 'ee knows what's o'clock, guv'nor!"

Chapter Eleven

Exhausted by the evening's misadventure and half-asleep on her feet, Sabrina did not expect to find anyone waiting in the hallway when she exited the countess's room nearly an hour after their arrival. Yet, cloaked in the shaft of moonlight streaming in through the oriel window at the end of the narrow hallway was a masculine figure.

She stopped short, the candle in her hand flickering uncertainly as dreamlike fabrication vied for reality. For an unnerving moment she was stricken with a sense of memory come to life. A profile of features too quickly glimpsed to be identified, the tilt of the head, the very stance of the silhouette etched in darkness were so compelling that a thrill of anticipation sped through her. "Jack?"

The man turned abruptly toward her from his contemplation of whatever lay beyond the bay window and the slanted white lit up his saturnine features. "She is settled?"

The cold formality in that voice was unmistakable. This was not "Black Jack" Law but the aristocratic Lord Jack Laughton. Of course it was Lord Darlington! Who else would be in the countess's home?

"Yes, and sleeping."

Cross-purpose feelings assaulted Sabrina, stinging her with rebuke of her fanciful thoughts. Jack Law! Absurd! The two men shared a vague similarity of physique and a disturbing gray gaze. As for the rest, she must have been dreamwalking. "She says she was merely exhausted by the long evening."

"Good. Then we may speak frankly." He came forward and took her by the elbow and steered her toward the stairs. "The salon below will do for our purposes."

She did not protest his high-handed assumption that she would do as he directed. He was a man accustomed to ordering menials about. She wondered again just how familiar he was with the countess's spa residence. She had not been able to confirm his knowledge of the location of Lady Charlotte's bedroom. Unlike the sleepy servant who had come to the door in answer to her knock, Lady Charlotte's personal maid had been awake and awaiting her mistress's return and was therefore stationed at the head of the hallway when the viscount appeared with her ladyship in his arms.

Annoyed, Sabrina wondered why Lord Darlington continued to hold her arm. At first she had assumed he was steadying her as she descended the stairs into the penumbra of the unlit entry. Yet even after they reached the bottom and her candle threw out a sufficient if unremarkable light across the floor, his hand continued to closely cup her bare elbow. It was more than an impersonal touch, it seemed a possessive one. She tested the tension in his grip and discovered he did not mean to release her.

How odd of him, or did he assume his charms were equally irresistible to both commoners and countesses? His fingers danced on the skin of her inner elbow, a most sensitive place, she realized as anger spurted through her. If he thought to toy with her, he had a surprise in store! Poor Lotte, to think she was besotted over so unrepentant a rogue!

When they reached the salon she forcefully pulled free of his hand under the pretext of reaching for the door latch.

There was no fire in the hearth, nor had one been laid that evening since the countess had planned to be out. As she stepped inside the chilly room cast in black shadows it seemed somehow isolated from the rest of the house. The feeble light from the candle she carried could not chase away the blanketing gloom. Yet when she moved quickly across the room to a candelabra and leaned her lit candle toward the wick of the first taper, the viscount said crisply, "Leave it unlit. 'Tis a waste of good wax."

Given the direct order, she set her single lit candle on the table and turned to her unwelcome companion. "What short subject have we to discuss, my lord?"

For a moment she thought he would not answer her impertinence. He had moved beyond her candle's aura and stood like some judgemental shadow near the cold empty hearth. Only his hair gleamed warmly like old gold in the shadows. "Is the countess prone to collapses?"

"Quite the contrary." Sabrina softened a little. So, he was genuinely concerned about the countess's well-being. "As long as I have known her she has enjoyed remarkable good health. She is wont to brag of her stamina on the dance floor and laments the fact that Lord Lovelace does not much care for the exercise."

"A pity for her." She thought she detected disapproval of the earl in his voice. "Yet she has been less well of late, am I correct?"

"Nothing to cause concern, before tonight," she answered thoughtfully. "She has complained of a sensitive stomach this last week."

"These gastric upsets." His voice sounded weighted with considerations to which he was not giving breath. "Do they occur continually or most often in the morning hours?"

Sabrina nearly smiled. He sounded quite like Mrs. Noyes' quack, though in actual fact she suspected the viscount would make a better physician. He, at least, was listening to the answers while Mrs. Noyes' man often seemed to be listening to the music of the orbs as she droned on and on in complaint.

"Most often upon awakening. Just this morning her breakfast proved too onerous a burden. Why do you ask? Do you believe that it might be serious?"

"Is she prone to tears? Excessive emotion? Does she perhaps speak of someone in particular at these times?"

"She is never hysterical, my lord," she maintained in stout defense of her friend. What was his purpose? All at once it occurred to her to wonder if he hoped to judge the effect of his absence upon the lady. "Why should such things interest you?"

He stepped toward her and into the candle's glow that made of him a bronzed being, from his golden hair to his tawny skin. "Perhaps distraught is too strong a word. Would you say she is mercurial of mood, sensitive to innuendo?" He spoke as if she had not voiced a single question of her own. "Does she rise later and retire earlier than in London?"

"Bath is a less formal place than London. Would you not agree?"

"But there is a new pattern in her behavior, is there not?"

Annoyed with his refusal to even acknowledge her questions, Sabrina decided not to answer any more of his. "Is there some malady which fits your description, my lord?"

"Not a malady, precisely . . ." There was definitely a note of reluctance on his part.

"Then what? Do you suggest I send for a physician?"

"I suggest you inquire of the countess her wishes, on the morrow."

He turned away and moved briskly toward the door, as though he had learned what he desired. There was just one problem, Sabrina thought in exasperation—she had not learned anything!

"Really, my lord, 'tis a most vexing business. Will you not explain yourself a little?"

He stopped short at the door and turned so that the golden globe of the candle's glow once more lit up his face. Earlier in the evening she had for the first time thought him handsome. Now she found herself thinking that his scar was so far from a detriment to his attraction as to be part of it.

"I never explain myself, Sabrina."

She stiffened at his familiar use of her name, a familiarity that in this case defined her status as inferior.

"I bid you a goodnight. I am late for an assignation. I have not lost my taste for the gaming tables."

"Oh. Oh!" Sabrina felt her heart drop into her shoes as she patted futilely the pockets within her gown. "I left behind my winnings!"

"How very remiss of you."

She glanced at him in reproach. "Quite so, my lord. But no matter. I shall go round to the hostess in the morning. Surely someone will have put it aside for me."

"You suppose wrongly." He turned from the door, his purpose of leaving seemingly forgotten for the moment. "Someone will have helped himself to the good fortune caused by your error."

"I don't believe you." He was amused once again at her expense. "No one would steal my winnings."

"Of course they would. Shall I prove it to you?"

He came purposefully to where she stood and reached into his pocket, then extracted and laid on the table before her a handful of bank notes and coins.

Sabrina glanced from the money up to him, with a sense of bewilderment. "You? You took my money?"

His smile was gone. "I reaped the benefits of a neglectful winner."

"I cannot believe—" All at once she smiled, feeling quite silly. "But, of course. You are teasing me."

Something flickered in his expression. "Shall I make

myself clear?'' He scooped up the coins and repocketed them.

Sabrina blushed deeply, ashamed to have been caught in this predicament by the shrewd and judgmental man. ''I concede your point, my lord. I was exceedingly foolish to leave the money unattended and I promise you I will take better care of my winnings in future.''

''I should hope so. 'Tis a costly lesson for you.''

''What do you mean?''

''Only that I have no intention of returning your coin to you, Miss Lyndsey. Losers weepers, finders keepers, I believe the old rhyme goes.''

Sabrina stared at him, clearly astonished. ''You mean you will not return my money when you've just boldly declared that you stole it from me?''

''I mean precisely that.'' His expression revealed no emotion whatsoever.

''But, why there must be nearly a hundred pounds!''

''A fifty-pound note, two tenners, and six guineas, to be precise,'' he finished politely.

Sabrina flushed. ''How dare you!''

''I dare a great deal.''

Something in that phrasing in that cool, polished, unperturbed voice silenced Sabrina's next sally. She believed him. He would keep her money and if she dared accuse him in public of the act, he would laugh in her face and defy anyone to question him. He knew, as well as she did, that no one would. ''You are a scoundrel, my lord!''

He gave her a short, mocking bow. ''See that you remember the lesson, sweet. I stomach no scruples in taking what I want.'' His gaze found and took hers prisoner. ''And I never ever suffer regrets.''

There was nothing she hated more than humbling herself, yet she could not allow her hard-won funds to leave in his pocket without at least trying to redeem them. ''My lord, that money is all I have in the world.''

He was silent for a moment, dangerously so. ''Do not

underestimate my intelligence, sweet. I know you are heiress to a vast fortune."

"Then you know that my guardian controls the purse strings."

"I see. So then, he disapproves of your gambling?"

"He does not know," she said simply.

"Indeed, I thought not." He came toward her, his expression emotionless but his voice all persuasion. "What motivates this urgency for money? Is it for the thrill of the gamble? Does your heart beat a little faster each time you wager?"

He took her hand in a formal gesture and pressed it between his lean fingers. "Tell me you are driven by the reckless desire to risk everything on the possibility of the loss and I will believe you. You've had that thrill of victory tonight. What matter a few coins more or less?"

Sabrina considered many responses and realized at once that begging would not win his admiration. He admired strength. "I need the money."

"For new baubles?" His gaze lowered meaningfully to her expensive gown. "Does your guardian's disapproval extend to your extravagance at the modiste's?"

Her chin lifted in instinctive response. "Can the reason matter?"

"Not in the least."

"Then, as a gentleman, you will return my funds."

He released her hand and ran his palm up her arm to her elbow, which he cupped in a sensuous caress. "I'm no gentleman, pet. Haven't your friends told you that?"

Sabrina experienced a quiver of unease laced with an unexpected thrill. She had not expected he would touch her so personally yet she did not draw away for fear he would think he had frightened her, which he had. "I don't always listen to gossip."

His gaze liquefied with a heat unconnected to compassion. "You should, you should."

Sabrina cast her thoughts wide, seeking a witty reply. "If

I did then I must surmise that you, whatever else you fancy yourself, are a man who does not like to be in debt to anyone."

"You think not?" The brief but reflexive tightening of his fingers on her elbow betrayed his surprise. Yes, she had chosen the right course!

"I believe you might be willing do me some small service in return for the funds with which I have gifted you."

"You gifted?" His eyes narrowed. "I stole, you mean."

She took a step back from him and his hand slipped free of her arm. "I prefer to think of it as a gift, in return for the favor you are about to do me."

"You're a strange sort of girl. I am intrigued."

She looked up into his molten gaze though she felt as if she were leaning over a precipice. "Then you agree?"

"I'm least inclined to grant a boon when I already have what I want." He patted his pocket in case she might mistake his meaning. "What would you require of me, if I were so inclined to offer aid?"

"I need your help."

He chuckled, amusement laced with disbelief. "Mine is the very last sort of help you need."

"You are wrong. You know a great deal about a matter which is very important to me."

"I'm flattered. What, Miss Lyndsey, do I know a great deal about that so fascinates you? No." He placed one long finger against her lips as she opened her mouth to speak. "Permit me to speculate. Life offers me so little in the way of diversion and I do appreciate a good riddle. You must be aware of my reputation?"

It was a question for which he did not wait upon a reply.

"I am reputed to be little more than a serpent wrapped around the coronet of a viscount. The West Indies are full of poisonous vipers, you see. Rumor claims I have shed the skin of my fellow Englishmen and become a reptile of the tropics. Those I account my acquaintances will tell you my clothes and smiles do not sufficiently cloak my cold-blooded nature. You have heard this?''

Sabrina gave a slight nod in answer.

''Yes, I'm certain your tender ears have been filled with dire warnings against my lascivious inclinations. Do you know I am deadly with a blade? That I've killed twice in a fair contest of skill?''

Again Sabrina nodded. Though she had not been told of the duels, she completely believed him.

''Still you seek my aid. I am baffled, unless . . .''

He was close, too close. He lifted his free hand to her cheek, grazing it with the back of his forefinger. The deceptively gentle caress sent a strong tremor through her that he must have felt through his fingers because his smiled. ''Ah, now we come to the point. You have heard something more than the common gossip.''

She backed up a step and he followed, step for tentative step, until they were caught up in a strange dance of advance and retreat as he spoke. ''Perchance you have spoken with ladies of my intimate acquaintance. They would tell you different tales.''

''What would they say?'' she asked quickly, reluctant to reveal her awe of him. Yet she was daunted by his low melodious voice that struck her courage like a pelting of smooth hard stones. She was accustomed to dealing with inexperienced or easily discouraged swains. This man was an altogether different article. Though he had not yet done anything strictly wrong, she felt as if her honor were at stake.

''My conquests will tell you that they have never known such pleasant company. Never known such proficient skill.'' His voice lowered, the words finding a deeper timbre as his eyes held hers captive. ''Never served such demand. Never realized there existed within them such reciprocal sentiment of carnal feeling for a man.''

''I fear I fail to understand you, my lord,'' Sabrina murmured as the back of her hips came up against the sideboard standing against the wall. She could move no farther and they both knew it.

"Do you? I wonder." He found the curl lying in the curve of her left collarbone and began to toy with it. "Can you be that naïve at eighteen?"

"Twenty!" The spoken number had a hectic quality to it because he was swishing her curl slowly back and forth along the sensitive skin of her neck. A ticklish brush up the side to just under her earlobe made her set her teeth in her lower lip to keep her from giggling or fleeing. Equally detestable displays of vulnerability, she warned herself.

"Ah, then twenty." He leaned closer to her, if he were going to kiss her.

She did not move, could not look anywhere but into his compelling silver gaze. Strangely enough she could hear her blood rushing in her ears, could feel the weight of each heartbeat inside her chest, could feel her own breath pass softly over her lips as she expelled it.

So this was how truly accomplished rakes behaved. It seemed he possessed some art that made a woman so intimately aware of herself that he needed not do anything to send her seeking and searching for more.

She lifted her chin in invitation though he had placed no compelling finger beneath it to urge the action. She felt her lids drift down over her eyes so that she need not face the moment of surrender, and then the heavier stir of his breath sent a quiver across her lips.

At the last moment he turned his head aside and she felt his mouth slid along her cheek before he whispered directly into her ear, "What do you require of me, pet?"

She did not like the diminutive but she let it pass because she found she could barely stand. He was leaning over her, forcing her into a backward arch so that the furniture at her back was her only support her.

Sweet reason! She did not dare touch him! Yet this insanity of feeling he stirred up in her urged her to do exactly that, to reach out and place her hands on his shoulders, to curl her head forward and lay her lips on his and learn what it meant to be seduced by this master rake. No, no! That is not what she wanted from him. What had he asked? "I want you to teach me how to gamble—no, how to win."

She had never thought to see him surprised, yet the incredulous look that came into his face quite amazed her. For an instant his eyes widened and his mouth loosened as if to draw breath between his lips and then he leaned back from her and erupted in laughter, harsh mocking laughter that made her face burn.

She sidestepped away from him, then turned her back. "I am pleased to provide such diversion for you, my lord. If you allow it, I will withdraw, for I am quite weary."

But he blocked her path, his movement so swift that she did not have a chance to evade the arm he thrust out. When she turned away he thrust out his other arm, effectively trapping her along the wall between his spread arms.

"Teach you to win!" he scoffed. "Have you no understanding of what it is to gamble? By its nature there remains always the element of chance."

Sabrina set her jaw. "I am not entirely unfamiliar with the concept. Yet, I have heard it said that a true gambler knows ways to curry the favor of chance."

Jack wondered if she had ever realized how lovely she was. Did she know how compelling her voice was, how tender her mouth, how appealing her violet eyes? Everything about her was encouraging him in his duplicitous endeavor. "The only true way to curry luck is to cheat, sweeting."

"Then teach me to cheat."

She answered so readily that he suspected she had expected his answer. He supposed she had been spoonfed enough ill-character observations of him that she would suppose him capable of all and any crimes.

"As it happens, I do not cheat."

"So much the better," Sabrina murmured in relief. "Then teach me to play cards as well as you."

He dipped his head, entrapping her in his gaze. "What is to be my reward for this office?"

"I will share a—a third of my winnings with you."

"That is a foolish offer." His tone was sharp. "Do you not require every penny? You should offer me something less valuable than your hard-won coin. What is of less value to you? Your reputation, perhaps? Your honor? Your virtue?"

The conventional suggestion did not shock her. It seemed all men came to that proposition sooner or later. "I should imagine, my lord, if half the tales told of you are true, you have a sufficiency of women willing to bed you."

"Ah, but that is beside the point." The mocking cadence was back in his voice. "I am a man of wide and generous but often fickle appetites. I am likely to crave that which is not presented." Once more he leaned toward her until his mouth hovered an inch above hers. "If you were to offer yourself to me, I should not stint upon savoring so lovely a morsel as yourself."

Sabrina's mouth thinned in anger. What a fool she was! To think he might have been in the least serious. Seduce her? That was the very last thing she would ever allow.

She placed a hand flat against his chest and though she did not push, she applied a resisting pressure. "I have no interest in bedding you, my lord. And I am disappointed that you cannot think of a more creative and remarkable inducement."

"I am a simple man of simple pleasures." His smile gave lie to every syllable.

"It seems a simpleminded pleasure, my lord. You are reputed to be a gentleman who thrives on risk, the recklessness of chance."

He pulled back a fraction, the better to look into her eyes. "You have a purpose in your challenge?"

"I value myself more highly than you might believe. Your help is a beginning, but I require results."

"This beggar would ride a rather fine horse?"

"Precisely."

"What do you offer me?"

Sabrina did not make the mistake of thinking she had won. She was gambling with the devil and she knew it. But if she could hold her own with him long enough, she might induce him to help her to achieve her needs. She had sworn the night she left London that she would do whatever it took to gain Kit's freedom. No hazard would be too great. So then, why not wager her reputation against the viscount's expertise? It was a risk worthy of her goal. And, unlike the viscount, she had every intention of cheating him of the very prize she was about to offer.

"I need to win a small fortune. Five hundred pounds would suit me nicely."

"I see. And if you win?"

Sabrina found she could not look directly at him and hoped she would assume it was from modesty rather than dissembling. "If you require it, instead of a hundred and a quarter of my winnings, I shall give myself to you for exactly one night."

Jack knew he should have been amused, triumphant, scornful of her foolishness in that she had offered him the very thing he wanted most from her. But he felt strangely disappointed by the offer. It reduced her to the level of the dozens of duchesses, countesses, and baronesses who nightly paid their gaming debts with boudoir trysts with those to whom they were obliged in debt. He had expected more of her.

Why? Why expect more of anyone than you expect of yourself? he mused cynically. Would it have made his revenge any sweeter to debauch innocence? Though her face might be worthy of adorning an altar, she possessed the ripe curves and lush bosom of a wanton. He should rejoice that she had willingly offered herself to him. And when he was done, she would have no reputation, no honor, and no understanding of the true cause behind her downfall.

He touched her again, this time impartially, brushing a lock of hair from her forehead. "Wash this powdered filth out of your hair. I much prefer your natural ebony shade."

"How would you know my—?" Something in his expression stopped her protest. "Very well, though people will remark upon it."

"That is the point. If you are to fleece this spa town of its gold, you must devise as many distractions as possible. Where I will take you, the formality-conscious Beau Nash will not be there to bar the door." He smiled and it was as cold as his heart. His fingers slipped from her face to the top of her properly cut neckline, which he rimmed with a finger. "Buy a more daring gown. Modesty will not serve you."

His fingers spread across the full swells straining against her bodice and traveled leisurely downward. " I don't suppose you have any jewels? A pity. Still, you will not need them if your gown is cut with sufficient cunning." When his fingertips reached the edge of her neckline he curled them inside and felt for an instant the moist warmth welled between her tender breasts.

Even as Sabrina drew a breath in umbrage, he lifted his hand and moved away. He had strolled all the way to the door before he turned back to her. "Tomorrow afternoon I shall call upon you. Be ready. I will not cool my heels upon your tardiness."

Sabrina wondered dazedly if this was what she wanted, after all. "What shall I tell the countess?"

"Nothing. I shall see to that matter myself. I do not like tale-bearers or prattling women."

"I am neither."

A moment earlier she had thought he might force himself upon her. Now he surveyed her with all the warmth he might have shown a lapdog. "See that you do not yield to the temptation. It is an all too ubiquitous failing of your sex."

"You are hateful, my lord."

"It will serve you best if you remember that."

When he was gone, Sabrina stood along time in the silent gloom feeling sorely abused and neatly caught by circumstance. The wager she had made with the Viscount Darlington might well be the biggest and most dangerous gamble of her life.

Chapter Twelve

The sudden cry on the street was cut off abruptly but its shrill of terror was enough to penetrate even Jack's brandy-laced thought.

He shook his head like a dog upon awakening, aware more of the rough trot of the bearers of his hired sedan chair than of the cause that had aroused him. Upon leaving the countess's residence, he had repaired for an hour to a tavern where in a private parlor and with a bottle of brandy as solace, he had sulked.

The second cry was more subdued than the first, but he recognized it as female.

Even as he did it, Jack wondered why he bothered to jerk aside the curtain meant to veil him from the worst of the town's smells and sounds. But once he did, his quick gaze immediately spied the altercation ahead in the lane dimly lit by a smoking torch.

A gentleman in satin coat and lace made a threatening gesture at the young woman who was being held with her arms pinned back by a second man. The pantomime played out quickly as the gentleman struck the girl two vicious blows, one to the face and the second to her middle. It was just the sort of tableau that should have gone unremarked by a jaded soul like himself, who was accustomed to encountering examples of life's brutality on any corner. He did not feel particularly like playing Sir Gallahad. But he did not like the odds nor the nor the fact that it was a woman against two men.

"Halt!" he cried to his startled bearers and stepped out of the chair the instant they set him down. Belatedly, he realized that the altercation was taking place on his block, not far from the door of his Bath quarters. Even as her pitiful cries echoed in the lane, Jack saw an imposingly large shadow emerge from a doorway in the middle of the block.

"The devil!" he exclaimed in ill humor. He recognized the girl's would-be rescuer as none other than his man Zuberi.

"Fool! They might slay . . ." Jack let the thought trail off. He doubted any ten men could do Zuberi substantial harm as long as it remained a hand-to-hand fair fight.

Then he saw the narrow gleam of a deadly blade being unsheathed by the well-dressed brute who turned to face the unwelcome Zuberi and his disinterest in the fight evaporated. Zuberi was not a man who feared much, but even he was at a disadvantage with a yard of steel.

Ignoring the protest of the chair bearers that they had not yet been paid, he strolled purposefully toward the fray.

Personal fear did not enter his thoughts as his drew his pistol from his pocket and advanced on the melee. Neither courage nor conceit fueled his lack of trepidation, only a hard-earned confidence in his own mastery of the situation.

The man in the velvet evening coat and Zuberi were slowly circling one another. Zuberi's long arms were stretched out before him to fend off the expected thrust of a blade. The other man stood apart, heaping invectives against the girl who was kicking him with a viciousness that Jack surmised would leave the fellow black and blue shins.

The girl broke free then stopped short and screamed when she noticed his approach.

That was a damned silly thing for her to do, Jack thought indifferently, considering that the weapon he held was drawn for her benefit.

"Which of you gentlemen prefer to be shot first?"

The two men started at the pleasant sound of a gentleman's cultured voice addressing them. The one with the sword quickly lowered it while the other grabbed and thrust the girl before him as a shield. Why had she not run, Jack wondered in exasperation. Stupid goose!

"Evenin' guv'nor," cried the velvet-coated gentleman with the drawn sword. "We was after savin' the poor girl from bein' attacked by this black savage. Just gon' to show 'im a thing two about manners." Jack was now near enough to see the man's smile pleat the pox marks on his face.

" 'Tis a lie!" cried the girl whose arms were painfully pinned back by the other man. "They're after murderin' me 'cause I won't go with 'em!"

" 'Ere now. None of that," the man answered almost casually as he delivered to her a stinging slap with the back of his hand. Zuberi made a sound very much like that of a bellows put to sudden great pressure.

Jack stifled a yawn. "I'm equally uninterested in the points of the quarrel between you. Simply choose which of you must die in order that the chit may be released."

He pointed his pistol at the velvet-coated man, who immediately dropped his sword. As the barrel moved toward the chest of the other man, he backed away from the girl so quickly it ratcheted up a smile at the corners of Jack's mouth. "That's as I thought. Zuberi?"

"Well met and a great good evening to you, my lord," the servant intoned with a warm wide smile of greeting.

"I suppose you are now sufficient to the matter?"

Zuberi's face altered to one that made Jack glad he had never gained the larger man's rage.

"Well enough." Jack grasped the girl by the arm and

pulled her ruthlessly from the lane toward his door. "Don't look back," he snapped when she twisted in his grasp. "You won't like the results. Zuberi will, in his own inimitable words, smite them hip and thigh, and a rare hash he shall make of them."

With the sounds of a beating at their backs, Jack and his freed hostage entered his abode.

Five minutes later, during which time Jack had consumed a bumper of brandy, Zuberi entered the tiny salon of Jack's rooms, his face as unmarred as before. Only his torn shirt and bleeding knuckles gave any indication that he done any other than return from a stroll through the park.

"I should like to propose, Zuberi," Jack began in a frosty tone, "that we refrain from further altercations in the lane. The neighbors may begin to suspect that we are barbarians rather than simply Barbadoans." As he spoke he moved forward and extended to his servant a glass of brandy.

"I am pleased to see you looking well, my lord. I have this fortnight longed for our reuniting." Zuberi took the glass and after a brief pause to received Jack's assent, turned it up and drained it in one thirsty swallow.

"Wirra! And where were ye afore now?"

The sound of the heavily Irish-accented feminine voice caused both men to turn around. Standing in the doorway with a hand on each hip was the cause of the street brawl. The left side of her mouth bore a bleeding bruise. A raw patch in her scalp showed where a fistful of vivid red hair had once been. Her bodice was torn in three places and little more was left of her shredded skirt than a scrap of linen. Altogether she presented a perfect caricature of a street slattern.

Something familiar about her, thought Jack as she marched up to Zuberi.

"Leaving me to fend off every sort of durty haythurn from the gutter, that's what!" She poked the huge man in the chest. "A pox on ye!"

"Mistress, please allow," Zuberi began with the most tender of looks at her. "My lord Laughton, viscount of Darlington, I beg the humble opportunity to present—"

"So this is himself, is it?" She made a gesture toward Jack, but she was plainly addressing Zuberi. "Did ye ken me for a fool? I'm no so green as that. I'll not be tradin' me vartue for the likes o 'im!" She turned to leave.

Before she could take more than a step Zuberi scooped her up from behind.

"Put me down, ye great black beast from hell!" the girl screeched

Wincing, Jack watched his servant struggle rather vigorously with the girl and wished himself anywhere but here.

Without asking his master's permission, Zuberi finally managed to deposit the mad-as-a-wet-hen girl on a chair. She was up in an instant and halfway across the room by the time Jack blocked her path.

For the first time Jack studied her face and it drew him toward her with a frown. "Have we not met before?"

She hesitated only a moment and shoved him hard. The brandy had made him less steady then he knew and she passed him in a flash.

When Zuberi moved to give chase, Jack put a restraining hand on the larger man's arm. "Leave her. 'Tis clear the wench knows nothing of the kindness done her or believes herself to have been better served by a thrashing than a rescue."

His disdainful remark brought her to a halt three steps from the door. "Honest hard work never put fear into the likes of me," she said proudly. "But I'll not go slaypin' with this dodgey gentleman."

"My master would not have you," Zuberi replied with quiet dignity. "You look no more toothsome than a rat come into the house through a crack. Though I vow you're not so ugly that my master may not require a second look when you've been properly cleaned and dressed."

A smile, which he refused to give life, tugged at Jack's

mouth over Zuberi's over-generous compliment. He proclaimed in withering tones, "I never embrace the Irish. They're even more unpredictable than savages."

"Aye, and what of it?" the girl responded roughly. "For all that, I'm a respectable lass, I am."

"The fair green isle, home to my first master," Zuberi intoned so rapturously one might have thought he was on intimate terms with that verdant isle. He moved closer to the girl, his dark eyes all but devouring her. Strangely enough, she did not seem to diminish when measured beside him. The thought struck Jack that she was quite a bit taller than she had appeared when he had approached her on the street. Something, certainly, familiar in that height and hair. Perhaps if he had consumed less brandy it would come to him more quickly.

"I did not like much about my first master but I did admire his tales of his homeland." Zuberi lifted one large hand, as if he could not bear not to touch her. Yet his gesture stopped short of the tangle of vivid hair that tumbled about her shoulders. "I most especially liked those of St. Patrick's way with snakes. You have met him, perhaps?" he questioned with the guilelessness of a child.

The girl blinked. "Know Saint Patrick? Is it that mad you are, Mr. Blackamoor?"

"If this touching little scene is done," Jack said in a drawl that precluded any other choice, "I will continue my journey to bed."

The girl looked at Zuberi and he returned her look. The pair were clearly infatuated, Jack thought scornfully and wondered at the attraction. For the girl, certainly, but Zuberi's women were usually more voluptuous and patently feminine.

"Verily, I am ashamed that I did not come to escort you home." For such a large man Zuberi sounded remarkably contrite. "But I could not leave when my lord was expected. Yet I vow I never brought you here for his delectation, oh champion of the Gladiators."

Jack's head whipped around so quickly his mind reeled from his liberal application of liquor. "Gladiator?"

Zuberi dragged his gaze from the girl and Jack would have sworn, if it were possible, that the large man blushed. "I am guilty, my lord, of a most indulgent vice. I went back to Lincoln's Field Theater every day for a week after your departure from London. Three times, my lord, I witnessed this wondrous lady hold sway over her opponents, vanquishing both large and ferocious harlots."

"Don't tell me, you were so stricken by love for this female Hercules that you absconded with her." Jack's voice dripped with sarcasm.

"Oh no, my lord. It was my great and bountiful joy to offer her employment when she was defeated."

"Lost a battle did she?" Jack thought fleetingly of the twenty thousand pounds that she had once cost him by not doing so.

"Never. I was thrown out for winning," she answered with all the indignant wrath of a disaffected duchess. "Me manager wanted me to toss the fight, only I wouldna'."

"I see," Jack murmured though he did not understand, nor did he care to.

"She is a champion. Champions do not choose defeat," Zuberi agreed. "I told her my master can find other work for her." A great smile of satisfaction spread across his face. "And so I brought her here to you."

Jack allowed himself a second deep swallow of brandy before saying to Zuberi, "As you have brought her here without my permission, she is now your problem. I expect you to deal with it without resource or reference from me."

The girl eyed him equally hard. Irish contempt, he thought. And then she turned to Zuberi. "I'm that sorry I called ye a beast. But you will own you are black."

"No?" Zuberi's face was as expressive as a mime's. "Are you certain?" He lifted back his free arm to inspect it. "Oh, you are right."

"Daft man!" The girl giggled self-consciously. "You are a fey spalpeen."

His brow furrowed. "Is this good?"

"Well, it's no so bad as it might be."

Zuberi's handsome, broad-featured face split in a grin so irresistible that it soured Jack's mood even further. Yet they seemed no longer aware of his existence. His gaze cut briefly to the girl who was now tucked under the branching shadow of the enormous man's long arm. The devil! She had, he was certain, already seduced his man!

Chapter Thirteen

London, November 1, 1740

"You win again, my lord!"

Gwendolyn Carrington's sultry voice was laced with petulance. "That makes fifty sovereigns I owe you." She leaned back suggestively against the satin squabs of the bed that served as their card table.

It was clear from an observation of the unbroken, smooth curves of her body that she was without stays. Being free, the easy play of her fine figure was revealed beneath the clinging lines of her silk maroon dressing gown. Her gaze, at once sensual and practiced, gave away her position as a mistress. To whit, she was mistress of the Earl of Lovelace.

"Can you think of no more just repayment, Lord Randolph?"

Her fine attributes so temptingly offered would have seemed enough of an invitation for any man worth the designation to a dalliance far more enjoyable than cards.

Randolph smiled at her indulgently. "Shall we try

another hand? Your luck may yet turn." He reached for the deck of hand-painted French cards.

His lack of response poured gall into Gwendolyn's already wounded pride. This self-imposed celibacy of his had lasted more than a fortnight. It was all very well that he was generous in his keeping of her, for he had rented this small but well-appointed house, and provided her with a carriage and pair. Yet she had once thought the better part of her luck to be in snaring a young, handsome, and thoroughly virile protector. For once she had expected to thoroughly enjoy her service on her back. Yet, the earl had not bedded her above three times before having lost interest in the activity she loved best. He had remained so capable of resisting her charms that she had begun to worry. Did another besot him? Was he thinking of turning her out for another, or was he being tempted away? No matter. Tonight she was determined to win him back into her bed and into her avidly accommodating embrace.

She fluttered a hand at her neckline, inviting attention to its daring depth. "Do you not find the room much too warm? I fear the fire is too well-banked."

When he did not look up from shuffling the deck, she reached out and snatched the deck from him, then tossed the cards clear of the bed onto the floor.

"See here, Gwen!" he began in faint annoyance but then he smiled and threw up his hands in defeat. "Very well. No more cards. I really should go."

"Must you?" Smiling at him, she slowly tugged loose the first two ribbons of celestial blue, which held close her bodice. Twin breasts pale as alabaster and crowned by rosy nipples pushed into view.

Alas, the view could not persuade Randolph away from his morose reflection. Lotte had run away from him. Everything and everyone reminded him of that vexing fact.

Gwen saw his expression darken and hoped it was an indication of the struggle taking place within him to remain with her. To add to the enticement, she twitched open her dressing gown, unveiling small round knees and slender calves sleeved in blush silk stockings that were an erotic study worthy of Hogarth or Rowlandson.

Though she could not know it, her dimpled knees only reminded Randolph of Lotte's, whose were as smooth and blushed as ripe peaches.

Undiscouraged, she slid one leg over the other before allowing her knees to part her gown and expose two deliciously plump thighs gartered in garlands of pink roses and trailing pastel ribbons.

The display recalled to Randolph's mind the first time Lotte had allowed him to undress her, a thing she had been quite averse to in the beginning, though they had been wed a week. She had informed him that her mother warned her against such practices, even between husband and wife, because it encouraged the formation of lascivious appetites.

Thank providence she had been right, Randolph mused with a rueful smile.

Encouraged by that smile, Gwendolyn toyed with the ends of her golden hair that hung in ringlets down her bosom to her waist.

Ran, who had chosen Gwen precisely because her hair was not that unusual, suddenly pictured brilliant red curls framing a face at once pretty but also clever. He could recall in vivid detail the feel of their springy silkiness when spread across the pillows or entangled about him in the delirious moment of climax.

The lustful look that came into his eyes emboldened Gwendolyn's hopes. She reached up and ran a forefinger down the cleft between her breasts.

"I am desolate to think you should not be paid in a timely fashion for your luck this night."

Her finger drew little circles on her skin and then plunged beneath the only ribbon of her bodice left tied. "Are you quite certain there is *nothing* I might offer in recompense?"

The smile she bestowed upon him might have given life to a man of four score years. It certainly stirred Randolph's already burgeoning organ, which thoughts of Lotte had begun. He watched in growing interest the play of her fingers on her skin as she offered him a demonstration of the kinds of things in which he might himself indulge. Yet his reflections remained steadfastly upon the libidinous games he had taught his own wife.

During those first weeks of wedded rapture he had learned that Lotte was all that was natural, uninhibited, uncalculated, and free from artifice. Not long after persuading her to allow him to act as her maid on those occasions best suited to the desire, he had entreated her to pose for him. Though she had been easily dissuaded from her notions of modesty in the matter of her husband's enjoyment of her body, she maintained that such naked games be done at night and by the light of a single taper. She did it, giggling and reluctant as first and then with more spirit and coquettish joy.

She would strike a posture with her petticoats lifted above her knees, or in her corset with the strings of her chemise loosened by his hands and for his benefit. When she had grown more courageous, she would stand before him in just her chemise that she shimmied down from her shoulders to her bosom and then to her fingertips before she stepped out of it.

What delight to find her inventive, as when one night she had gone up ahead of him and she surprised him by being at her bath when he came in. The naughty suggestion that he join her, all her own, had changed forever his perception of the uses of their tub.

Her fundamental aptitude for pleasure had never been equaled, certainly not surpassed in his experience. She was all he wanted, or ever . . . would . . . want.

And that was the trouble!

Lord, but he missed Lotte!

Ran stood up. He would go and bring her back!

"What are you doing?" Gwendolyn cried out in exasperation.

"I'm leaving." Distracted by his thoughts of the details of his departure, he did not even stop to kiss her before he reached for his coat. "Another evening, Gwen. I promise you may recoup your losses."

She quickly sat up, not bothering to pull her wrapper closed. "Is there something I've done that displeases you?" She looked hurt, her lower lip protruding seductively. "I would do anything." She lifted eyes swimming in tears. "*Anything* at all to please you, my lord."

Ran stared at her sybaritic nakedness and wondered if politics and loneliness had addled his brain. Why should he not indulge himself with his mistress? It was the thing. Every gentleman who could afford it, and many more who could not, kept a woman on the side. Mistresses were *de rigeur,* nay, expected of a man of his station and wealth and looks. She was young, lovely, deliciously naked, and eager to please.

It did not work. No amount of rational, reasonable thought could stir his lust to the level required to entertain the provocatively revealed creature before him. He wanted Lotte and no other.

"Do forgive me, Gwen. I shall find a method to make it up to you." He turned and was through her bedroom door before a hastily thrown slipper struck it with a force that made him wince.

An hour later, Ran sat with his bumper of port in the darkness of his library. He had not bothered to stir the fire to life when he returned home. The cool darkness suited his mood and helped to cool his libido which had shown remarkably poor timing by belatedly asserting itself once he had left Gwen to her own devises.

He was going to Bath tomorrow. His personal servant had been set the task of readying him for first dawn. The only question that he could not yet answer was how he should treat Lotte once he found her.

He had known her whereabouts from the very beginning. Only his quixotic Lotte would have announced to his butler, the most loyal member of his staff, that she was running away and that he was on no account to tell his lordship.

Randolph's lips twitched as she recalled his butler's exact recitation of the encounter. "Her ladyship's express wishes were that you not be apprised of her forthwith departure from this residence nor that you should learn that her trunks are to be sent to the Bath. Therefore, I beg you lordship, question me no further on the subject."

So Lotte had run away. Well, he might have expected it. He had spoken very harshly to her that night. Once past his husbandry fury over her daring, he had thought perhaps it would do them both good to have a separation. Once alone in a town where she knew no one and forced by her own self-imposed exile to remain in hiding lest a sighting of her be reported to him, he believed she would soon see reason and return. Certainly he was not about to hie off after her like a lovesick calf. He had his reputation to think of, and his position as head of his household. If he could not manage a wife, how would he ever retain the respect of his servants or gain that of his children?

Ran smiled as he took a satisfying sip of his port. He wanted children, as many as Lotte could successfully manage to produce. He had hoped they would be parents by now. It had grieved him greatly when she had miscarried their first. Yet he had been so certain she would be breeding again by now.

The sound of the bell by the front door rang hollowly through the still house. Ran did not bestir himself. If it were Gwen come to scold him, he would simply refuse to see her. He was not by nature a rude or callous person but he did not like scenes. If only Lotte were as sweet as she had been in the beginning they might not now both be miserable and alone.

He had finished his port when a light knock sounded at his door. "Enter."

His butler appeared in stocking cap and nightshirt. "Beg pardon, my lord, there's a person below who insists that you will want to see him, no matter the hour."

Ran sat forward abruptly. "Willows!"

"Aye, my lord, that's the name he gave."

"Show him up at once."

Two minutes later Mr. Willows appeared in the wake of Ran's butler. A short man of compact body, he wore a neat but inexpensive wig that capped a face with a ruddy complexion, bulbous nose, and small pinched mouth. At first glance he might have been mistaken for a tradesman, tailor, haberdasher, or any of a hundred other burgers of the merchant class. But the telling sign was in his eyes, which were dark, bright, and constantly moving. Mr. Willows' job was to observe, to watch and notice, to ferret out and search for things and people. In short, he was a detection man. In theory Ran detested spies, but he was also a realist and knew they had their uses.

Ran did not move from his chair. "I presume by the hour of your call you have important news, Willows."

"Good evenin', yer lordship." Willows spoke with the easy informality of one long accustomed to dealing with the private and often sordid lives of the aristocracy, his exclusive clientele. He pressed his tricorner to his chest as he executed a bow. "I do indeed have news. It came by messenger within this very hour."

Ran steepled his fingers before him as his elbows rested on the armrests of his chair. Now that he was determined to go and retrieve Lotte himself, he felt a little ashamed of hiring men to trail her. Though, at the time, he had told himself it was for her protection rather than to keep tabs on her actions. A lady traveling along would be easy prey for all manner of villains.

"Tell me."

Willows nodded. "I knew you'd be the sort to have his news fresh. Willows, I says—"

"Yes, yes." Impatience flicked through Ran's voice. "Get to the point, man."

"The very thing, your lordship." Willows began to dig around in his waistcoat pocket, producing from it a pair of spectacles and then a missive. As he unfolded the paper he said, "Your lady wife remains in Bath, my lord."

"Just so. You must do better if you expect my thanks."

Willows glanced at the earl over the rims of his spectacles. "Indeed, my lord. Not to worry. There's far better fare, if you take my meaning. My man Foibles is a fellow as can be counted upon to be as discreet as he is thorough."

"Such as?"

"I've details of the countess's recent activities. Willows' gaze slipped sideways away from the earl's. "This last week there's been a change in the countess's situation. She weren't, after a fashion, alone."

Ran sat forward, his steeple exploded by an impatient gesture. "What, exactly, do you mean?"

Willows adjusted his glasses. "Here it is in Foible's report."

"Report?" The idea of a document containing a list of his wife's movements disturbed Ran. "You've written it down?"

"Not to worry, my lord." Willow's small mouth pursed. "Writin's safer than you might think in my occupation. Ain't many fellows as can read and write. Foibles knows his letters and figures. Can on occasion pass for minor quality, a useful talent for a man in our line of work. Ah, here it is."

He cleared his throat and began to read. "The countess had taken into her home a young woman of mysterious origin, who is frequently seen in accompaniment with the countess."

"My wife going abroad? Where to?"

Willows made a small shrug with his shoulders. "The

usual, my lord. The Pump Room, public breakfasts, the occasional service at the Abbey."

Ran relaxed. "It that all?"

"There has been a recent change." Willows seemed to need to consult his paper a second time. "On the evening of Thursday the twenty-seventh day of October in the year of our Lord—"

"Get on with it!"

"O' course, my lord. The countess, hm, ah . . . yes, here it be. "The countess was seen to gamble in the home of Sir Avery. At the hour of midnight she was accompanied home in the person of a gentleman of Quality who bore the countess from her carriage to her door in his arms.' "

Ran shot up from his chair in spite of himself. "He what?"

Willows tapped the paper with his finger. "It says right here he bore—"

"Give that to me!" Ran snatched the parchment from the man's grasp and stared at the scratch marks. "A gentleman of Quality by his bearing and in spite of the lack of a wig upon his flaxen— Flaxen." Ran squashed the paper between his fists. "Darlington!"

"Didn't get his name, my lord, but Foibles will remain on the job until he ferrets it out."

"That won't be necessary. You are dismissed!"

"But, my lord, there's services as a man like meself—"

The terrible expression on the earl's face squelched his final remarks. He hastily stepped back and removed his spectacles to his pocket, which seemed at the moment a safer place than his face.

"Takes some that way," Willows would later remark to his wife. "The younger gentlemen never quite believe it's possible that their wives might forsake them for another though they feel free to roger anything in petticoats. Makes a man wonder, don't it?"

Randolph followed Willows to his door and when he was through it shut the door in the man's face.

"Darlington!" he whispered darkly as he stared grimly off into the distance. He should have known!

Darlington had disappeared from London the same night as Lotte, yet the connection had never been made in his mind. After all, he was responsible for the challenge that he thought had sent Laughton into hiding. That the coward might have taken his wife with him had never crossed his mind!

Ran let out a primitive groan that bared his teeth.

It was the one thing he had not, would never have, considered possible. Lotte had run away with another man? No, not another man—Darlington!

Had they planned it? Had the idea of an elopement been in the works even before their row of a few weeks' earlier? Had they been lovers plotting their escape while he was cooling his heels in the hopes that she would get over her infatuation with the West Indian?

Every conjecture cut into his soul like the lash of a saber. Blood began to flow and his heart to beat so heavily that a faint red veil seemed to lower before his unseeing gaze. How could she? With Darlington, that elegant, debauched butcher! He could kill them, kill them both!

Chapter Fourteen

Bath, November 5, 1740

The private salon was awash in the myriad colors of gowns and formal coats, of laces and jewels, elaborately coiffed male wigs and tiny ruffled feminine caps on close-stacked feminine curls. Rouged cheeks and scarlet lips complimented rice-powdered countenances. Artfully cut patches of black velvet or silk lay provocatively near an attractive eye or lip, or poised upon the summit of a darlingly revealed bosom; all accoutrements meant to distract and entice and lure the opposite sex.

There was much laughter and gaiety. The room resounded with raised voices. The occasional thrilled cry of a winner or groans of disappointment were underscored by the exertions of a small chamber orchestra set in a galley above. Yet, for all its beauty and glitter and semblance of culture and refinement, this was a gaming hell.

The faces of the room's occupants were hard with concentration, their smiles oiled by guile, their eyes glittering with covetousness. One and all, they radiated the fever of self-interest. But it was not the preening heat of sexual awareness. Of genuine interest only to both men and women was the dice or cards spread upon the green-baize card tables, which were scattered through the opulent room like small verdant oases amidst a sea of Beau Monde regalia.

"So, what say you, my lady?"

Sabrina glanced up into the cynically amused expression of Lord Darlington, her escort, and wondered again at her temerity. It was one thing to gamble among Lady Charlotte's friends. It was another to enter a gaming salon from which society would bar her if it knew she was neither a mistress nor wed. Not that she would give Darlington the satisfaction of knowing her agitation. She turned coolly away from him. "I say, my lord, that we should find ourselves a seat and begin the evening's enterprise."

"So anxious, my pet? I'd have thought you would wish to observe the play before you entered it."

His hand on her elbow tightened just a fraction. "There are no innocents in this room. The boundaries of class are abandoned at the door. The squire's wife, the earl's married daughter, and the duke's mistress are equals within these walls. A love of gambling is their creed and their common bond. Do not be mistaken. The most virtuous countenance among them hides the heart of a predator who is a better competitor and more skilled at dissembling than you."

She glanced sideways. "If you hope to frighten me away, you will be disappointed."

"Good." The wolfish gleam in his eye reminded her that for him this was nothing but a game, a distraction he could tire of at any moment. Whether he won or lost, he gambled only for gold. She had a brother's life to stake—and, if she won, her virtue as a debt to be collected by the man by her side.

She felt his hand at the middle of her back impelling

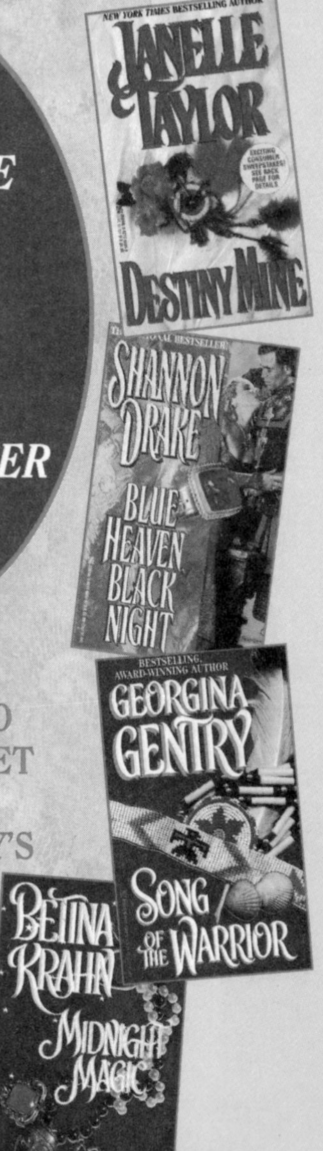
NEW YORK TIMES BESTSELLING AUTHOR
JANELLE TAYLOR
DESTINY MINE
SHANNON DRAKE
BLUE HEAVEN BLACK NIGHT
BESTSELLING, AWARD-WINNING AUTHOR
GEORGINA GENTRY
SONG OF THE WARRIOR
BETINA KRAHN
MIDNIGHT MAGIC

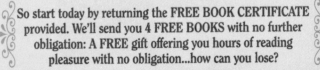

her forward. "You have only to choose your part this night and we may begin."

She again glanced his way. "What do you mean?"

"Egalitarianism among the classes requires the safeguard of illusion. Many here have adopted a sobriquet for the night."

"What is yours?"

He gazed down at her, a cool assessing expression on his face. "I do not bother. My reputation speaks for itself. You, however, may wish to distance yourself from it."

"Why should I want to do that?"

He looked at her like a puppy that had learned a new trick. "I was hoping that would be your reply. So then, we shall allow people to draw their own conclusions."

Something in his tone made her ask, "What will that be?"

She decided that she preferred disdain to the unholy smile he now bestowed upon her. "Why, that you are my current mistress."

Sabrina tossed her head and looked away, feeling the unaccustomed weight of her own long dark tresses freed to cascade over her shoulders and down her back. Though she was not the only female present wearing her natural hair, it was the addition of rice powder to her cheeks and rouge to her lips that made her feel conspicuous.

That feeling was encouraged by the many frank stares in equal numbers of envy and lust that were following her progress with Lord Darlington into the room. Her gown of midnight blue was cinched in the waist tighter than usual, the lowered neckline a scandal that she would not have dared in London. The heavy collar of pearls about her neck did not so much fill in the expanse of her bosom as attract the eye to it. Certainly they must think her Darlington's mistress. She alone knew that she intended to deprive him of that prize.

If only he had offered her some assurance of her beauty, she might have felt more certain of herself among this glittering crowd. To her consternation, his only comment upon viewing her when he came to pick her up had been a brief widening of his eyes followed by the careless comment, "You will distract the easily smitten."

Unfortunately, she was not equally unmoved by his nearness. She could no longer look into his dark face with its cool, privately amused mien and not be reminded of the bargain between them. Ever since she had offered herself to him for one night in exchange for his help she could think of little else but what she would do if he forced her to pay up. But it was not enamored enchantment. She sensed, despite his seeming disinterest, the disturbing notion that he would demand his due whether she won or lost.

They touched only where his fingers spanned her elbow. Yards of silk and lace and boning and ruffles and padding separated her from him. Yet, she seemed alternately scorched and chilled by his presence, a quixotic combination of physical heat and haughty aloofness. How very odd it was, to feel suffocated by his mere presence.

Where was her spine, her contempt for him? Even as she had struck the bargain with him, she intended to cheat him. If only he would step away, she thought with a sudden flushing through her body, she could concentrate on the genuine problem at hand.

She glanced doubtfully up at him and the moment's panic eroded as she realized that he had not noticed her agitation. Resplendent in a gold silk coat and black breeches, he was studying the room through those silver-bright eyes, which did not include her in their perusal.

There was no emotion in his lean, sun-bronzed face and she wondered momentarily if he ever sought relief from this gaudy yet empty existence. No, of course he would not. He was a viscount. However idle and indulgent his life might be, he would know nothing of loneliness or sorrow or regret, or impotence before life's greater forces. From his auspicious birth his every whim would have been catered to. Even now, he thought he had taken control of her scheme to raise money for herself. Let him. He would be the very last soul to whom she ever told the truth. It was the last and only hold she had over her own destiny.

Perhaps she worried needlessly.

For exactly two hours each afternoon for nearly a week she had sat with him at the tea table in Countess Lovelace's salon while he showed her how to cheat at cards. He had taught her how to palm a card, especially handy when one needed an extra trump or to come ace-high in a tie. He had taught her how to deal from the bottom of the deck when one had glimpsed the nether card and saw an advantage in possessing it. Each day when he left her he had ordered her to practice until his return the lesson of that day. Even without his prompting she would have. Yet never once during their lessons had he touched her, spoken charmingly to her, or even indicated that he thought of her as other than an apt pupil for this brand of licentiousness.

Or, perhaps, his interests were otherwise engaged.

A physician had come to examine the countess the morning after her collapse. After he left Lady Charlotte had locked herself in her room and not reappeared for the rest of the day, though Sabrina had heard her weeping on and off until after midnight. When she finally did appear next morning, she was as wan as a wax figurine. She had refused to answer any questions about her health yet claimed she was too unwell to venture beyond her door. Even so, she had welcomed the viscount into her private chamber on several occasions.

Sabrina considered yet again the troubling possibility that they were lovers. At the very least the countess seemed to possess a surfeit of affection when it came to Jack Laughton.

Unable to still her curiosity, she said casually, "I trust we did the right thing in leaving Lady Charlotte alone."

Jack glanced at his protégée, his face betraying none of

the feelings her beauty aroused in him. "You cannot help with what ails her."

She turned to him. "Has she confided to you what is wrong?"

"No."

It was a syllable meant to end the discussion.

Jack steered her toward the table he had selected with more care than he would have for himself. He did not know what motivated her desire to win a fortune. He suspected it was simply the thrill of the game. He wanted her to experience that thrill and not be called a cheat because of it. Therefore he had chosen a likely bevy of quail as her first targets.

To his surprise and satisfaction, she had a natural talent for cards. But the urge that motivated him was far from altruism.

From the night they had sealed their bargain, he could think of nothing but her. For days as he sat so quietly and passionless across from her, pretending that cards brought him to her side, he had endured the sight and smell of her until it had teased his lust to breaking point. Minute after minute as she sat chastely unaware of his scheme, erotic images cascaded through his thoughts. He mentally peeled her gown from her shoulders and buried his face in the warm, fragrant skin between her breasts. He imagined how it would feel to touch and kiss and suck from her all resistance, until he had roused her equally to his need. Would she simply follow him into that sweet agony of desire? Or would she be afraid, reluctant? Would he need to tease and gently caress from her the passion she did not yet know existed within her? Or would she capitulate freely, offering drowning wet kiss for kiss, touching him boldly and stroking him hungrily until he entered her and gave them both what they most desired?

She was naturally sensual; her every graceful movement, her wit, and the way she looked at him when she thought he did not notice told him he was winning her without even a touch. He would let her have her victory before he took his.

He maneuvered her quickly and efficiently across the crowded room to a table near the back where three gentlemen and two ladies sat playing ochre.

"Good evening, Healy. May another join you?"

"Lord Darlington!" The Irishman was on his feet in an instant but his gaze traveled to Sabrina's face and then swept downward in an appraisal that left the young man's mouth softly agape. "Won't you be introducing me to your lady, my lord?"

"I was contemplating it, but it seems you might drool upon her."

The fair-skinned man blushed painfully. "Hardly fair, Darlington!" He winked at Sabrina. "We Irish reserve our best manners for the ladies."

"In that case, I'd be obliged if you would see to my sister-in-law." Jack ignored Sabrina's amazed glance as he released her arm. "Newly arrived from an Atlantic crossing. Expected to squire her about. Naturally, I loathe these family duties." Without a backward glance, he turned and sauntered off.

Sabrina stared after him in silent fury. How dare he leave her in the company of the only other person in Bath whom she had met before. A head of hair devoid of powder and a little rouge would not be enough to fool a flea. Had Darlington forgotten the Pump Room meeting with Lord Healy, or was this a deliberate trap, the beginning of another of his humiliations?

"Lady Laughton?"

The name was repeated before Sabrina turned toward the Irish peer, a bewildered look on her face.

Healy smiled his most charming smile. "I beg pardon, my lady, but I assumed being a relation to the viscount you were a Laughton. Lord Darlington didn't, after all, finish the introduction."

"No, he did not." Sabrina extended her hand, prepared

to brazen out the encounter until Healy called cheat. Perhaps she could then persuade him that it was merely a jest on the viscount's part. "How very nice to make the acquaintance of a friend of Jack's."

He did not blink at her intimate use of the viscount's first name, seemingly too engrossed in the exact location of the ornate pearl drop resting in the cleft of her bosom. He took her hand and bowed formally over it. When he had straightened he stammered. "I—I didn't quite catch the name."

Sabrina smiled wryly. Perhaps she had no reason to fear recognition. She had not worn anything so daring as this gown to the Pump Room and—really!—the man had yet to look above her collarbone.

She choked on the very idea of Darlington posing as her brother-in-law. "The viscount is often abrupt. I find it a tiresome affection when it's done purely for the effect it has on others, don't you? We are not blood relation. Only by marriage, distantly."

"But—?"

"I never take him seriously. Do you?"

"Well, I—"

"Sister-in-law, indeed." Her chuckle again drew his gaze to the now quivering pearl. "Jack's foolish attempt at claiming ownership, I should think." She gave a little sigh of tolerant exasperation. "I am a widow."

"I see, I do, indeed." Healy's eyes filled with a new understanding. If she was not Darlington's blood kin then she was fair game, providing Darlington was not his competition.

Unlike the lady, Healy did not share an appreciation for the viscount's wicked sense of humor. He glanced back over his shoulder just to make certain the viscount had left the vicinity before he turned to pull out his chair for her. "Do join us, Lady—"

"Luck," Sabrina supplied with a merry laugh as she promptly occupied his seat.

"Well!" Mischief kindling in his green eyes. This was one member of the Darlington clan whose sense of the absurd he shared. "I've always wanted to court Lady Luck." This time he did not attempt to disguise his ogling of her bosom. "Say you gamble, my lady."

She offered him a suggestive glance. "In more ways than one, Lord Healy."

"The answer to a man's prayers, my lady," he returned warmly. "Allow me to introduce the other members of the party."

As Sabrina nodded through the round of introductions, it was all she could do to keep from glancing in the direction by which Darlington had left. *I don't need him,* she mused silently. *I can do this. I must. For Kit!*

There had been no word, no answering letter, from her brother. Despite the pretense of illness, she was certain Cousin Robert would not long allow her the freedom of Lady Charlotte's household. Worse, any day he might send for her to come to London to be wed. Tonight was the only chance she would have to win a hefty sum.

She picked up the first card dealt her and saw that it was the Jack of Spades.

"Black Jack!" she murmured under her breath. This was a sign of luck, surely. Yes, she would be as bold as the highwayman himself.

Chapter Fifteen

"Queen high!" Sabrina declared as she spread her winning hand upon the verdant napped-wool tabletop.

Her pronouncement was followed by a nice round of applause from the small gallery of players who had abandoned their own tables in order to follow the extraordinary luck of the newcomer amongst them.

For the last hour of the three-hour play, Lady Luck, as the precocious cardplayer continued to call herself, had amassed from the modest start of fifty pounds nearly five hundred.

"Lady Luck, you are well dubbed," Healy answered with an admiring shake of his head. "The Little People themselves could not curry the favor of gold any the better."

"I'm flat, as well," declared Lord Cray, the gentleman on his right.

"I am in need of a change of partners," responded the only other woman remaining at the table. She eyed Sabrina with clear envy. "You are as fortunate as you are lovely, my dear. Only reflect that neither endures."

As she rose, one of the gentlemen from the throng

surrounding them pulled back her chair for her and then quickly deposited himself in it.

At the very moment the gentleman's posterior touched the chair, a rough masculine voice exclaimed, "Demme, sir! Move you aside. I want a seat!"

Sabrina glanced up into the face of the owner of that bombastic voice and saw beneath an elegant wig the beefy features of overindulgence. The man's eyes were small and black, their gaze frank with insolent curiosity as it met hers.

"Gad, but you're a winsome filly."

Sabrina looked away at once.

"Damme, spirited too!" he voiced with relish. "I will have a hand at this table." Without waiting, he grabbed the back of the newly seated gentleman's chair and jerked it back meaningfully. "Take the air, sir! I will play the lady."

As Sabrina watched, the man hastily abandoned his place and then she glanced again at his usurper. He wore a blue coat with silver scrollwork down the front, but the elegant coat could not disguise his essential boorishness. The ruby stickpin in his jabot and the huge diamond in the ring on his right forefinger were at odds with his thick neck and brutish countenance.

He smirked and jerked his head toward her. "Evening to you, m'dear. May I join the table?"

He seated himself in expectation that there would be no objection.

Sabrina rose from her chair and announced to the table. "I'm afraid I do not play with strangers."

When the boastful man had stood up again, he grabbed the padded shoulder of the gentleman nearest him. "Introduce me to the lady, Cray."

Lord Cray did so. "Sir Alan Buckley, allow me to introduce our guest for the evening, just arrived from the Indies, I'm told. Lady—er . . ."

"Lady Luck," Sabrina supplied succinctly. She sat down and reached for her goblet of wine, intentionally preventing Buckley from reaching for her hand. "A name which means as little to Sir Buckley as his means to me."

Undismayed by her manner, Buckley chuckled. "Allow me to change that impression. Demme me, ma'am. You're about to play cards with the gentleman who has this very day apprehended the notorious highwayman Black Jack Law."

"Lady Luck, you've spilled your wine," Healy exclaimed.

Sabrina glanced down at the scarlet creeping across the green baize from her overturned goblet. "So I have," she said without emotion.

As a servant appeared at once with a linen napkin to sop up the spill, Sabrina lifted her gaze to the smirking man. This man had apprehended Jack Law? That seemed impossible.

"I surmise you've heard of the culprit, my dear?"

"Indeed, we all have," Healy answered, to be convivial. "A most notorious fellow. Rumored to be a gentleman of Quality."

Buckley rolled his eyes in the Irishman's direction. " 'Fraid that's nonsense," he said coolly. "He'll swing as the baseborn miscreant he is." He rubbed his hands together. "Dash it all! The demnition of a convict has set up me appetite for sport."

Sabrina jerked her head up from a contemplation of her scattered thoughts. "How can he be condemned if you've just arrested him? Surely there must be a trial?"

A puzzled look came in Buckley's black gaze. "What need for a trial when the truth's been thrashed out of him?"

"What?" Sabrina's voice wavered on the single syllable. Her hands clenched in her lap. "You beat a confession out of him?"

Buckley grinned, hugely enjoying her attention. "A heavily muscled arm and a coachman's whip can mete out justice quicker than a moldy judge."

Sabrina shivered. "You killed him?"

"Never a bit!" Buckley's thin mobile mouth widened like a chasm. "Needs to learn not to be impudent, ain't he? Won't be protesting his innocence and threatening the general public again. But I left enough for the hangman's gibbet."

"That is disgusting!" she exclaimed before she could stop herself.

He eyed her up and down without rancor. " 'Pologies, o' course. Got to respect a lady's sentiment, demme, or where does any gentleman stand?" He did not seem the least bit regretful to Sabrina, but smugly superior. "Now, let's have no more nonsense. Deal the cards, m'dear."

"I will not play you, sir." The disdain she felt was undisguised as she rose a second time. "Excuse me."

"Gently, m'dear." Buckley bounded to his feet "Naturally, delicate sensibilities overwrought. Jack Law himself would tell you, 'twas no more than his due. Had to keep a criminal in his place, that's all."

Sabrina tried to keep her voice level but it was frosted with dislike. "All Englishmen are owed the right of a fair trial, Sir Alan. All men, even the guilty ones."

She sensed the mood of the crowd was growing restless with their dissension. Not because they believed her to be in the right or even because she thought the sentiment of the crowd was with her; she knew too clearly that it was not. They were here to play cards not deal in politics.

He smiled in conciliation. "If more Englishmen believed in the law, m'dear, we would have less Jack Laws. But a rabid dog must be put down before he infects others."

She heard the assenting murmurs of those surrounding their table. Of course, they would be relieved that one more threat to their way of life had been removed from their midst. None of them had met him or had shared his kiss. To think of the dashing highwayman utterly defeated, bloody and battered . . .

Sabrina reined in her wayward thoughts. She must be mad. Had she not herself taken aim and fired at him?

Oh, but it felt as though her heart were being ground under a bootheel! Must not think of him. Must not!

"Lady Luck?" Healy prompted.

Sabrina turned to find the Irishman studying her in concern. "Are you unwell, lady, or do you refuse the challenge?"

Sabrina blinked. "What challenge is that, Lord Healy?"

"Mine," Buckley said promptly. "One hand, 'tis all I beg. Double your winnings and take home a bit of Sir Alan's blunt."

"Double?"

"The very thing, Lady Luck." Buckley reared back on his heels, a shrewd smile on his face. "Name the game, m'dear. Name the stakes. Buckley will accept it, double or nothing."

For one fantastic moment, Sabrina nearly offered to wager her five hundred against Jack Law's life. Absurd! She would be thought worst than a sentimentalist, she would be considered a fool. No matter the outcome, she knew the felon would not be freed.

Anger swamped her. Had she not been sent to Bath because of matters she could not control? Jack Law had lived his life as he chose, knowing full well the price he would have to pay if caught. Then there was Kit, her poor innocent Kit, whom she could free, but only if she amassed sufficient funds.

"Double or nothing?" she asked sweetly as she resumed her chair. Buckley nodded. How could she refuse? A doubling of her winnings would allow her to leave Bath on the morning coach.

"Very well, one game."

Buckley reached for the cards before Sabrina intervened. "I believe, sir, it was my turn to deal."

He frowned, his hand hesitating over the stack as confirmation whispered through the crowd, then pushed the deck in her direction. "Well, m'dear, I can't contradict you."

She played her first hand conservatively, watching and counting just as Darlington—who seemed to have disappeared—had instructed her. A few tense minutes passed before she realized that she not only held the card Buckley most likely needed but that she was going to win.

When she spread her cards to reveal the winning hand, she saw his small eyes all but disappear beneath the brooding jut of his prominent brow. He gnawed the corner of his lower lip as she raked in his bank note, bringing her winnings just shy of one thousand pounds.

Unexpectedly, he burst out in laughter. "Double or nothing again!"

She hesitated.

"You're not the kind to take a man's money without giving him the chance to win it back, are you, m'dear?" His mouth formed a smug line.

Don't be a fool, she told herself. Yet the gazes of those surrounding the table seemed to pin her in reproach. From one thousand she might reap two! It was a more than generous wager. Besides, Buckley played badly, negligently, due no doubt in part to the amount of drink he continued to swill through their play. Luck was with her.

And, in the deepest secret heart of herself to which she would not quite admit, she wanted to exact revenge for his treatment of Jack Law. She would best him the only way possible.

"Very well," she heard herself reply and knew she could not take it back.

The swell of voices at her back attested to the fact that gambling fever was contagious. Within minutes the onlookers were firmly ensconced in two camps, those who backed her to win and those who chose Buckley as their champ.

This time he dealt the hand and the moment she saw how he handled the cards, she knew she had made a serious error. When the cards were arrayed before her, he looked up and smirked. His look must have been as merciless, she thought with startling clarity, when he ordered Jack Law flogged.

He had cheated! She saw it happen. Did not anyone else?

She turned blindly toward her backers and spied Darlington's somber face among them. Though the movement was quick and minimal she was certain she saw him give a tight negative shake of his head. Say nothing? He meant her to say nothing? Then he must have seen the sleight-of-hand that might defeat her.

She sat through the hand, going through the mechanics of the game, unable to believe she could have made so stupid a blunder. She was helpless to prevent him from besting her, not by skill but by guile.

The moment of defeat, when it came, seemed unreal. She was not now two thousand pounds to the good but a thousand pounds in debt, to a cheat and a scoundrel!

"Alas, not even Lady Luck is immune from bad fortune," Healy whispered sympathetically when the hand was done.

Sabrina sat like stone as Buckley accepted the congratulations of his fellow gamesters. The amounts of some of the side bets wagered made her loss almost insignificant by comparison. Yet, for her, she had lost everything. Gone!

"Bad luck, m'dear," Buckley offered with a conciliatory wink. "Care to attempt to clear your debt?"

"Luck is neither good or bad. It is either present or absent." Darlington's voice sounded much closer to Sabrina than before. Then she felt his warm palms cup her bare shoulders. "Come, cousin, you must be fatigued."

He drew her to her feet by the pressure of his hands and then she saw flutter past her shoulder a paper he tossed on the table. "I expect all debts are now settled."

"Don't carry her off." Buckley chuckled lewdly as he eyed Sabrina's bosom. "I'm certain the lady has her own charming ways of paying her debts."

She felt Darlington's fingers tighten on her shoulders

once more and wondered why he was cautioning her against a reckless retort.

"If rumor be right," he said in his familiar bored voice, "you are not a favorite of the ladies. They whisper it about that you are better at pulling a cork than sheathing your smallsword."

A hush fell over the room, an awful silence into which a gentleman's pride could forever perish.

But Buckley seemed to hesitate over the matter of a perceived insult. "If I knew you, sir, I might believe you were attempting to insult me."

Sabrina held her breath as Darlington said, "Then you must strive to know me better. I would not want you in doubt."

His hands slid down her arms to the elbows in a clear display of ownership that made her face burn. "Come, cousin. The company begins to bore me."

Chapter Sixteen

A thin gruel-gray broth of a dawn was breaking over the spa town. It had rained during the night. The streets and buildings were dark with slick snail tracks of moisture. Individual sounds echoed eerily through the empty silence. Leafless trees raked charcoal branches against the pearly sky.

Sabrina stood at the window of Countess Charlotte's salon looking out, trying to hold her mind back from the moment when Buckley had turned over his cards. The brandy in the goblet clutched in her hands had not been touched. Beyond the parted drapes a new day was breaking, yet she remained hostage to her dark musings on her mistake. She kept going over the moment again and again.

Suddenly she swung back from the window.

"You knew he cheated!"

Jack sat half a room away, legs stretched out before the fire he had laid himself. His brandy glass had been drained twice. He was considering a third refill when she finally spoke. He glanced up, no expression on his face. "What of it?"

Sabrina took two hurried steps toward him, her face reflecting in exquisite detail her distress. "Then you knew he unfairly took my money?"

She was backlit by the watery yellow cast of dawn, her curtain of dark hair blacker than night about her shoulders. She wanted comfort. He had comfort to give her, but not the kind she thought she wanted. So, instead, he gave her the truth. "What I know is that Buckley used the opportunity you gave him to relieve you of your winnings."

"You say it does not matter that he cheated?"

Lord, but her sweet voice was tragic. How he longed to reach up and pull her into his lap, to stroke the heavy curtain of her hair back from her cheeks so that he could find and kiss her mouth.

"Why did you do nothing? No, worse—you abandoned me!"

Throughout the entire evening he had only for a moment taken his eyes from her, and that was the cause of this present distress. Things had been going extremely well until nature forced him to go in search of a chamber pot, and he had returned to disaster.

True, he might have warned her that Buckley was a notorious if unproven cheat, particularly when playing women. Yet, he wondered if his warning would have prevented her from taking Buckley's bet. A gambler in the throws of the fever seldom listened to reason. Therefore, he would stick now to the rational points of his argument. "You say Buckley cheated. Did you not go there to do the same?"

He saw her stiffen in defense of the accusation. "I did not cheat."

"Did not need to resort to it, you mean." How narrow her waist was! He would, perhaps before the hour was out, span it with his hands. "If you could have, you would have cheated to win. As Buckley did. There is no difference between you, only he was the more clever charlatan."

She staggered back, as if his words were blows, and he

wondered at the source of the extremity of emotion that drove such a reaction. No, that was wrong, he only cared that she was agitated. The more distraught, the better for his plan. He was a master at turning the wellspring of emotion in a woman from one font to another. She needed comfort and he would give it to her, but only after she had vented the anger enough to accept the only kind of solace he was prepared to offer her.

When she had mastered herself she set her untouched brandy aside and faced him as poised as before. "Your accusation is detestable and unjust!"

Jack reached for her brandy. "Detestable, perhaps. Unjust? No. You, my sweet, became greedy." He took a quick sip, feeling in need of its bracing qualities. "Restraint is a valuable quality, I'm told. As I've never heeded it, I could not say."

She flexed her fingers into fists, too proud to rebuke his accusation a second time. It was not greed but enmity that had made her seek to best Buckley.

The man's self-congratulatory account of the brutal treatment the highwayman had received at his hands had appalled and repulsed her. Those feelings had made her lose sight of her nearly-won goal. As much as it galled her to admit it, when she had accepted his challenge to a second game of cards, she had no longer been thinking of Kit. She had been thinking of Jack Law.

Her thoughts now derailed upon the very logic that had driven her game. Mercy's grace! She had risked and lost everything . . . because of a stolen kiss on a moon-dark night.

Guilt swarmed over her in stinging nettles of shame. Everything lost! For the sake of a thoroughly unrepentant blackguard who no doubt deserved every punishment the law would exact from him. How could she have been so selfish, so foolish? Kit's future depended upon her!

Jack watched her expressions ripple and change like sunlight upon the surface of a lake, from righteous anger to stubbornness to doubt and finally to some private shame that made her drop her gaze before his. "I warned you, gambling is a game for the dispassionate dissembler."

Her gaze came shyly back to his as she spread her hands in a little pleading gesture. "I was doing so well. I had won enough!"

The simple gesture of surrender was right in line with Jack's expectation. He had never met a soul less able to disguise her feelings. She was ready to respond to any display of kindness on his part. Why then, he pondered absently, was he not feeling triumphant? "Pray tell me, when is enough ever enough?"

She turned away from him, not wanting to see his gloating expression. If only she had quit while she was ahead. If only she had not been blinded by feelings unworthy of her goal. Perhaps she should have stayed and played on. All she had needed to win was one more hand!

"There will always be one more hand."

She glanced back sharply, stung by his astute comment.

"The lament of the loser is always the same," he commented dryly. " 'If only I had not bet one more hand', or 'If only I'd had the wherewithal to wager one more hand.' 'Tis the siren song of chance, my sweet."

She crossed her arms under her breasts, lifting them forward, and it was all Jack could do to keep from reaching for her. " 'Tis a dirge you are much familiar with, my lord?"

"I've sung a chorus or two in my time."

He looked away toward the fire. But the image remained in his mind's eye of her superbly molded figure and the thrust of her beautifully rounded bosom. Did she know how effortlessly she taunted him? No, she would run for her life, and her virtue. He heard the tantalizing whisper of her silk stockings as she drew closer.

He looked up to find that she had moved to his side, exactly where he planned her to be, ripe for his ruthless brand of consolation. "The difference between us, sweeting, is that I can afford the loss, whereas you cannot."

Her face, lit by the firelight, crumpled in pain. "Do not remind me!"

"Struck a nerve, pet?" He almost felt sorry for her. She had fewer defenses against his manipulations than he had supposed. He had expected she would be more of a challenge. The seldom-roused emotion of pity insinuated itself into his feelings, but he squelched it. Where would the predator be if he backed off from weak or unprotected prey?

He gazed covetously at her, exchanging pity for purpose. "Why not confess to me the real reason behind your need for money? If it be an entertaining enough tale, it might just persuade me to loan you the purse."

"What is this?" She angled her head in defiance. "Will you now offer to loan me money? A week ago you would not return what was rightfully mine."

Touché. She had not lost her spirit, thank the gods. He had no taste for sacrificial lamb. "I never explain myself."

She hugged her arms to her breasts, and he watched, willing the fabric to lose its battle to contain its luscious burden. "Then neither will I."

"Pride is an expensive commodity. Are you certain you can afford it?"

He saw disdain reenter her gaze along with the wit he admired. "I am curious, since you know nothing of my plight and find my actions ridiculous, why did you pay my debt to Buckley?"

He swallowed the brandy warming on his tongue. "The simple truth? I prefer that you be in debt to me."

"Why?"

He stared at her, a burning seductive look that could not be misunderstood. "I don't think I'd enjoy you as much if Buckley had been at you first."

He saw her blanch and wondered how she could look

so erotically appealing and remain so naive. "That's disgusting!"

He shrugged. "My motives are no less honorable than Buckley's, only more honest. 'Tis common practice for ladies to redeem their gaming debts on their backs."

He saw her tight head-shake of denial as he drained the glass. "I have a suspicion you would have been insulted and called Buckley a cheat. And that, my dear, would have been to your detriment."

"What do you mean?"

"Buckley is the kind of brute who would have demanded retribution for your slander." He glanced up and down at her, deliberately making her aware of herself as a woman. "You are a commoner while he is titled. I've no doubt he would have resorted to rape and felt justified." Her look of outrage did not deter his speech. "I, on the other hand, want you in my bed for our mutual pleasure. The debt will end there, with one night."

"You are hateful."

"You've said as much before." He looked at her empty glass and wished it refilled. "Face the truth. You are a very bad loser."

"And you are—"

"Hateful." He looked up, tenderly amused, into her outraged expression. "I know."

Sabrina did not know why but the tender expression on his handsome face seemed more of an insult than any look before it. Her rage, already simmering, burst forth as she lifted her hand and stepped forward to strike him.

He was faster. He leaned in, grasping her swinging arm by the wrist so tightly she gasped in pain. "I don't like being struck. You wouldn't like what would occur if you did."

"Let go of me!"

"No, I don't think I will."

She stared at him, mute and furious, and he knew no man had ever physically assaulted her. Touching her now, feeling the surge of emotion that had set her atremble, he marveled at the power of self-control exerted by the men in her life before now. Alas, he lacked that control, and a conscience, and a heart.

He drew her down against him by her wrist and then snaked an arm about her waist to hold her there. "This, at least, is one debt you can pay yourself."

He saw alarm widen her eyes but she looked more abashed than afraid. "You've been wondering what it would be like to touch me." There was steel in his velvet voice. "Admit it."

"Don't flatter yourself!" She struggled briefly but did not say anything more.

After a moment he released her wrist and ran a hand up under the black fall of her hair to cup the back of her head. As his fingers spread through the silky strands, he pulled her fully into his lap until she sat on his spread legs. "I've been equally curious, Sabrina. Let us see what, together, we find mutually attractive in one another."

Sabrina braced a hand against his chest, telling herself that she would look ridiculous if she screamed and fought him. After all, they were beneath the Lady Charlotte's roof. He would not dare seduce her on the carpet. What harm then if he kissed her? Insufferable bore!

She looked across the scant inches that separated them into his triumphant smile. He thought himself irresistible, did he? She supposed she should be impressed to find herself in the arms of a viscount, yet it was very much the man she resisted, with his scented clothing and privileged airs.

Jack felt her animosity. It burned in her dark eyes and flushed her delectably trembling lips. The sight was quite arousing. Yet he knew better than to force her. He would show her what she thought she could resist and how absolutely futile resistance was.

His fingers moved to her chin, which he tilted up. "You do know how to kiss a man, do you not, sweeting?"

His thumb stroked her lower lip, a tantalizing feathery caress. Sabrina knew she should speak, say something biting and clever. But she could not think. Could not look beyond those silver eyes softening and heating with desire. And she knew then that her life was about to change forever.

She closed her eyes a moment before his mouth touched hers, hoping to blot out the actuality of the event. Instead, it exaggerated it.

His long, slow, drugging kiss went on and on. He clasped her head tightly, massaging it with his fingers, sending chills down her back and linen chasers of heat.

Sabrina felt oddly disconnected from her body until his fingers slid from her hair and rested ever so lightly on her breasts above the deep neckline of her gown. His touch was that of a man burning with fever. She held her breath as his lips continued to caress hers, softly, persuasively, nudging and rubbing, begging and provoking a response from her until she no longer wanted to hold back. Her mouth softened under his, lips molding onto lips until there was no separate space. She felt as if she were melting under his tutelage. The sensation was something new, so why this sense of vague remembrance? Was it dreamed of or only hoped for?

Behind eyes squeezed tight against the moment, she saw the rapturous darkness of a moonless dawn, remembered the whinny of impatient coaching horses, and the jingle of harness bells. The kiss, the kiss of the highwayman had stirred her like this!

"Come home with me." His lips formed the words against hers in a rough urgent voice. "Let us be alone."

Resisting the tug of desire-shocked senses Sabrina murmured groggily, "I can't."

His fingers spread possessively across her left breast and cupped its fullness through the cloth. "Then spend an hour here with me now. No one need ever know."

"No!" The very idea broke the spell of his kiss and, eyes snapped open, Sabrina sat upright in his lap.

His mouth was softly blurred by her kisses. "Afraid?"

Guilt and shame arrowed through Sabrina. She had never meant to keep her bargain with this clever handsome nobleman. Was she mad? "I don't want—"

"Liar." A fluid smile, more genuine than not, flowed across his mouth. "You want everything, things you do not even know to ask for. I can give them to you." His hand scandalously caressed her breast. "I can make you sing and weep, make you happy. Come home with me. Now."

The muscles of her face spasmed with emotion. "I can't!"

Sabrina did not cry. Neither Cousin Robert nor Aunt Thaddeus had wrung a drop from one eye. Not since the begrudged tears she had shed over her father's bare grave in Cornwall had anything or anyone driven her to a display of weakness for any reason. The expected yet uncontrollable fit of weeping that suddenly swept over her appalled her even as he gathered her in his arms.

"There, there, sweeting." Jack caressed her shoulders, amused and confounded by this ill-timed flood of tears. Virgins! Lord, how he detested them! "Do not fear the trembling of desire. 'Tis nothing that time and experience cannot master."

If he had hoped to console her to dryness, he found himself sorely disappointed. Her sobs were hard, tight, resentfully given up, if unstoppable. He wondered with his usual cool detachment if his lace would be ruined by her saltwater bath.

In his experience tears were the universal weapon resorted to by women whose position was otherwise weak. Therefore, he was never moved by such displays. Yet, when he reached up to smooth a hand over her bent head, he found that hand was shaking. It did not sound as if she cried often for she did it without much grace or beauty. As he stroked her dark hair, he found his thoughts stolen by images of himself wrapped in nothing but that shiny black fall and the knot in his lower belly redoubled.

With a stifled curse he lifted his hand away.

Ridiculous! His cronies would laugh themselves mad if they knew he was comforting his intended prey. What the deuce had he hoped to accomplish by pressing her here, in Lotte's salon? Swiving on the carpet was not his style.

No doubt of it! His lust for revenge upon her combined with his unexpected eagerness for her had addled his brain!

After a minute passed, reluctantly he admitted to himself that perhaps she was overwhelmed by something more urgent than the ecstasy he had produced within her.

He did not know why he decided to say the words. Yet he was certain he could accomplish, without bestirring himself too much, anything she might need taken care of.

"What will make you happy, pet? I swear I will help you."

She looked up at him, wariness and uncertainty and shyness all vying with the need to ask again for his help as she tried to master the sobs that escaped from her like hiccups. She looked like a half-drowned kitten as he retrieved and offered an already damp handkerchief. "Do you mean it, my lord?"

"Ask any favor of me, Sabrina."

She swallowed her tears and said with as much dignity as she could muster, "I want you to help me save the outlaw Jack Law from the gallows."

"That, I admit, is not the sort of favor I had in mind," Jack said quietly.

Chapter Seventeen

Jack considered half a dozen things that he might say in response, beginning with the fact that she did not know the real Jack Law. She had met, instead, himself in disguise. But curiosity is a powerful emotion, he was discovering. At the moment it was as powerful as his lust for her. She had come into his embrace with very little urging. No doubt, he could easily persuade her back into it. For the moment, curiosity to understand her reasoning proved the greater temptation.

He slid his hands from her hair. "You want this miscreant's life spared. Why, sweeting?"

He had not refused! Sabrina tried to disguise her elation with an indifferent shrug. "Because the fellow was kind to me."

"Kind? Did he not rob you?"

His sardonic tone was not lost on Sabrina. As she tried to rise from his lap he held her there by placing his hands firmly on either side of her waist. Strangely, she felt no desire to struggle. She turned her head to stare straight ahead into the hearth flames, choosing her words with care. "Yes, he did rob me. But he was not a wastrel. He was gentlemanly and civil and even—"

"Romantic?" Jack supplied.

She glanced at him from the corner of her eye. "I did not say that."

"There was no need. What but romance would cause a young woman of your station to remember kindly a scoundrel of the byways?"

"Certainly I am not so foolish!" The annoyance lacing through her was not, she knew, free from embarrassment. If only he would release her she might be able to think. The unfamiliar sensation of hard muscle and harder bone shifting beneath her petticoats was most distracting. His hands were persuasively warm about her waist and his kiss still lingered on her lips. She had only to lean closer to once again taste . . . No, she had indulged herself enough.

"My reasons are far from impractical. Yet they are my own and, as such, privy to none other."

"Is it his kiss you crave?"

The immediate blush, no more than a shadow creeping across her lovely profile in the firelight, astounded Jack. Mercy! She was half in love with a sham, a shadow, a make-believe! Truly, what man could say he knew the workings of a woman's mind?

To think he might have won the minx that night on the highway and saved himself the business of the last few days! So, she liked them deadly, disreputable, and villainous! And here he had been at odds to conceal his true character from her!

He laughed, clear, unfettered masculine amusement at his own lack of perception.

Sabrina winced, bitten to the quick by his mirth. "I think your sense of the absurd is misplaced."

This time as she tried to stand he did not stop her. In fact, he seemed in helpless thrall to his amusement. He leaned his head back to better allow the gusty sound to erupt.

She had thought him handsome before. With his face flushed by mirth and his features recomposed from sarcastic disillusion into genuine good spirits, he seemed both younger and less dangerous than at any other moment in their acquaintance. How was it that no woman had claimed his heart before this? Certainly, he must have captured many a lady's.

Those thoughts quickly evaporated under the new barrage of impproprietous chuckling that erupted when he had finally sobered enough to gaze up at her. After one sharp glance he inexplicably succumbed to another paroxysm of laughter.

"My lord," she admonished in resentment. "Your laughter will rouse the staff."

Reminded that they were in the home of another, he nodded and wiped a tear of laughter from his right cheek with a knuckle. "Do forgive me, sweeting. Life offers me so few opportunities to indulge my humor."

The gaze he turned on her was now as bright and mercurial as quicksilver. He held out a hand to her. "The very last thing I desire at this moment is to be disturbed. You are a novelty I do not intend to share with anyone."

Sabrina's heart doubled its beat in renewed hope but she quickly squelched the feeling that accompanied his words. The idle flattery of gentlemen had never before affected her. It must be the reaction of her nerves to the horrendous outcome of the evening that made her feel as though she must smile back at him or burst. Or perhaps it was simply her unexpected reaction to his kiss, that sham exercise of genuine feeling that he had so cleverly mastered. Perhaps when she had had more experience at kissing her odiously uncooperative feelings would not be so easily duped by a rogue's tricks. For even now those unruly feelings urged her to take his hand and lay her own upon his laughter-firmed cheek, to bask more fully in the scintillating gaze of his silver eyes. Then her pride reasserted itself and she was consumed by the urge to pound him with her fists. How dare he laugh at her!

She turned away toward the fire and extended her hands instead to the gentle flame. "It is late, my lord, and I am fatigued. As it seems we've nothing else to discuss, I will bid you goodnight."

" 'Tis dawn, sweeting. Too late for *bon nuits.* But what of Black Jack? Will you abandon him to his doom after all?"

"What do you mean?" She snapped at the hope he dangled before her despite her resolution to be rid of him. "Are you willing to help me?"

He dropped his hand of invitation. "I think, my sweet, that I just might. *If*—" He drew out the word in his taunting masculine drawl.

Refusing to acknowledge the quivering sense of vulnerability his teasing elicited, she clasped her hands together before her and swiveled toward him on the balls of her feet, a gesture as graceful as it was feminine. "I would have thought that a gentleman like yourself, who lives for diversion, as you put it, would find the notion of liberating a prisoner from his cell rare sport."

"Rare sport, indeed. Yet I should not like to find myself replacing him in gaol." He lounged back against one wing of the Queen Anne chair and slung a silk-stockinged leg over the arm. "The fellow means little to me. Yet I know he's of value to you. Just how valuable, that is my question?"

Without hesitation, she reached up and unhooked her pearl necklace. "I will wager Black Jack's freedom against these."

Jack regarded the luminous handful of pearls she held out to him as if they were poisonous. "What makes you believe that I would be interested in winning your baubles?"

"Rumor has it that you are with pockets to let."

He shrugged and slung an arm over the thigh of his

dangling leg. At once bored and at ease, he was the picture of an indolent aristocrat. "Life is full of idle rumor."

"Doubtless," she answered with acerbity. "Yet it would explain your knavish behavior in regard to the theft of my meager winnings."

The laughter-creased lines remained on his face. "If you believe I did that out of want you don't know me very well, sweeting."

"Perhaps not. But—"

"Enough of buts." He moved sharply, sitting straight up as a deep V formed between his golden brows. "Why have you not pawned your pretties yourself if, as you claim, you are in dire need of coin?"

Confound him. He saw all too clearly the illogical workings of her mind. There was no need to answer him, she reminded herself. Despite the warning in his burning gaze, she would not ignite from his wrath if she refused his request. Oh, but she felt the lick of flames as she stared into his eyes, and it was not altogether unpleasant.

"The necklace was a gift from my father. I had hoped to spare it. Now, I have no choice but to offer it up, as well."

He cupped the lavaliere dangling between two of her fingers. "My father gave me gifts as well." He looked up at her with a gaze that made her skin shrink. "Can you guess what it is? I keep it with me always."

Though she could not explain it, Sabrina's eyes darted to his cheek.

"I see you've been told."

"Your father scarred you?"

The shock in her voice instantly persuaded him that her horror was genuine. But he did not want her pity.

He released the large pearl, the muscles working beneath the skin of his jaw as if he were consuming a small but particularly tough piece of gristle. " 'Tis a singular gift from a parent, do you not agree? Less open to thievery or loss than, say, jewelry or a house. Though I must admit I've never been offered as little as a fat fart for it."

His gaze flicked sharp as a rapier point over her, backing off any impulse for sympathy. "Your pearls should bring you a good deal more."

After a moment's hesitation she released her grip on the strands so that they slipped free of her fingers and fell into his lap. "They are yours, if you will help me."

Jack held up the pearls toward the fire to better enjoy their beauty. They were extravagantly lovely, almost as lovely as their owner was. They belonged about her neck, shimmering against the satin-smooth contours of her breasts. Without the exquisite cushion of her skin they seemed cold, lifeless, bereft.

He turned back to her. "You are a terrible bargainer. Never pay your debts until the hand bas been played out."

"Hateful!" she exclaimed between her teeth. "I should not have expected anything else from you." She held out her hand. "Give them to me."

He offered her a reproachful glance. "Miss Lyndsey, do not insult either of us. You know my feelings in such matters."

He laughed as she snatched at her necklace, then easily reached to pull her again into his lap with an arm snagged about her waist. "Now, now," he taunted between chuckles. "Have you learned nothing, sweeting, of how to charm a gentleman into doing your bidding?"

She twisted around within his grasp until she met his mocking smile. Only with the greatest of effort did she subdue her desire to continue wrestling him, however futile it was. "You win, my Lord. I have nothing else with which to charm you."

"Such modesty does not become you. I like better your waspish side."

Her eyes narrowed. "Were I wasp I should be tempted at this moment to sting you mightily."

His smile widened. "Honey is more pleasing than stings.

Persuade me to give your pearls back to you." He held them at arm's length from her, the prize and the bait. Then he dipped his head quickly and kissed the summit of her breast presented above her neckline. "I dare you."

His warm kiss burned upon her cool skin as she experienced once again the thrall of being too close to him. She smelled the heavy spice of his perfumed clothing, even the faint scent of brandy on his breath. He thought himself invincible and irresistible. She would like nothing better than to show him that he was neither.

She reached up and braced both palms against his jawline, tilting his head back until it leaned against the chair back and he gazed at her along the line of his nose. He did not speak, yet those silver eyes flashed like lightning between the twin thickets of his dark gold lashes. Ignoring that too-bold gaze, she gently turned his face with her hands from side to side, studying the exact contours of his mouth as if they would give her clues to his art with a kiss. Then, because it was beneath her fingers, she glanced at his scar.

A gift from his father, he had said. The thought made her shiver a second time. It was not then carelessly or unintentionally given. What could a child possibly have done to deserve so permanent a reminder of his sire's wrath? She knew in an instant that the answer was nothing. He had done nothing, and yet it was his to bear all his life, that reminder of paternal displeasure.

She traced a finger ever so lightly along it. He flinched and raised a hand as though to deny her. But then his hand fell back as his lips crimped in the corners at some secret pain. The long-forgotten wounded child peeked out of those hooded eyes an instant before his lids fell shut, sealing out the world.

Was it this talisman of cruelty that had made him bitter? Had the cut gone deeper than the skin and injured his soul? Had he suffered rejection and scorn because of it? These fanciful thoughts intrigued her. Despite the smooth, pale scar sliding under her sensitive fingertips, she doubted a woman born would find him ugly. Nay, he was notorious for the number who found him exactly otherwise. So what, if not disfigurement, made his soul so bleak and his heart so empty? Each question that swirled through her mind brought another in its wake. What could heal so wounded a man? Could anything?

She had meant to kiss him, merely that. She had meant to put all her effort and slim knowledge into the art, into a contest of wills, hers to his. Now that was forgotten. The muscles ticking beneath her fingertips betrayed his agitation as nothing in their past encounters ever had. He was vulnerable. She sensed it as tactile sensation, but he was fighting the response, even to her simple human touch.

She leaned close, consumed with an overwhelming sympathy for the child who once lived within his frame. She nuzzled his mistreated cheek with her nose, feeling with instinctive tenderness an affinity for the child she would never know. She did know what it was to be alone and afraid, to doubt where there was need, to suffer at the hands of those from which one was to expect protection.

She shut her eyes and rubbed her cool cheek against his warmer one and thought of Kit, alone, afraid, who must be wondering if anyone in the world still cared about him. And she knew she would do anything to win this man to her cause, not because she had use for him but because she needed to know that not all were abandoned to their hopeless fates and that, perhaps, life had not been as cruel to her as she supposed.

She discovered his mouth almost by accident. The blind search for comfort ended in something else when he suddenly turned his head and brought his mouth under hers. For a moment, their lips merely made contact, the smooth surface of his firmed by emotions she could not fathom. And then hers softened and settled over his, gentling upon that hardened surface like a blanket of benediction to his defiance.

His lips parted in a whisper she could not hear but whose context was surrender, the willing giving in for the moment to something unexpected.

Her hands moved from his face to his shoulders, then one moved behind his neck so that she could cradle his face to hers. His mouth opened, engulfing hers in a powerful jolting pleasure that made her belly quiver. This time she did not pull away, she followed him, daring trick for trick until she at last captured his tongue in her mouth and sucked from it the sweet taste of desire.

The muscles in his shoulders became rock hard as he held himself still against something she did not understand. He did not touch her anymore. He had taken his arms from her waist and gripped instead the chair arms. This is what he had wanted, demanded, only minutes earlier. Now he was reluctant. He shuddered like a man in the throes of some enormous pain. Yet she went on kissing him. For now, after weeks of enmity and strife, all she wanted in the world was to continue kissing him, to kiss him until there was nothing left but this moment, this terrible wondrous feeling of dread, and the power.

She had never felt such influence over another creature, never before knew that she had at her disposal the means to move another being. What bliss, to make a man sigh!

Jack wondered at her power to wound him. He had not suspected that skill to be hers, the ability to reach so neatly beneath his guard and strike with deadly accuracy at his heart. No one since . . . since . . . no one.

He lifted his hands slowly toward her, aware with every ounce of rational sense left him that once he embraced her he would not ever be able to completely let go again. Better not to touch, not to want, not to surrender for even an instant than to live with the enormity of the want rising like lava from the depths of his soul.

So small a thing, so tiny, her display of compassion. Yet he had never before known the emotion in any guise. Women admired, adored, desired, or despised him. None of them had ever looked upon him and acknowledged in simple sympathy his humanity. Now Miss Sabrina Lyndsey had. And he would never forgive her for it!

Sabrina drew back first, the spur the smallest sound in the world. The cause was, perhaps, the scritch-scratch of mice claws in the wall or the spit and hiss of resin touched by flame. Some sound alerted her to their precarious situation. And she found she was not lost, not quite, to the world.

Jack opened his eyes and the full heat of his hunger flooded her. She had expected to be sliced to ribbons by his acerbic speech but now she was awash in a heat so finely wrought that even her toes curled in defense of the flame in those silver eyes.

"Stand up, Sabrina."

His voice was so husky she scarcely recognized it as his, yet she acted upon his instruction without hesitation, sweeping her skirts free of his legs even as footsteps came down the hall. Moments later the door to the salon opened and an amazed maid stuck her head in.

"Oh, beg pardon!" she exclaimed and shut the door so quickly Sabrina had no time to stop her.

"There," he mimicked in a girlish tone, "see what you've done to my reputation?"

She spun about to find the old amusement the only emotion in his perfectly composed face. "Well, weren't you about to say something of kind to me?"

She stared at him a moment longer. He looked as at ease as if she had just served him a dish of chocolate instead of a feast of stormy, passion-laced kisses. She, on the other hand, felt flush and damp in a dozen places. She knew from his expression that her face perfectly reflected her tumult. So what? She, too, had felt with her own hands and lips and body his response. His appearance might defy it yet she knew now that he was not unmoved.

She turned from his challenge. "I think I have nothing more to say to you."

"Then at last we are agreed." He rose gracefully in a single fluid movement that brought him to his superior height before her. Reaching up, he draped her necklace of pearls about her throat and then worked the clasp.

When he was done he touched the lavaliere and then trailed that finger down into the warm valley of her cleavage. "I will come to collect my prize when I have earned it."

She did not ask him what he meant. "I must speak with him."

He looked up from her lush bosom. "Oh, you will see your Black Jack Law again. That I do solemnly promise you."

"You understand your part?"

Zuberi smiled. "She understands perfectly, my lord."

"I can speak for meself." Alvy McKee, the Irish girl herself, had not softened a jot during her sojourn beneath the viscount's roof. "And I'm after sayin' I don't like it."

"Your opinion is of negligible importance, my girl."

Jack inspected her for flaws. Her face had healed during the past week to reveal the features of a pleasant-faced creature. With her wild red hair washed and pinned back beneath her servant's cap, she looked almost respectable. Almost. The stubborn set of her wide mouth, her remarkable height, and Amazonian proportions set her apart from the average timid, thin drab of an English maid. Moreover, even properly corseted and gowned in the dull garments of a maid, her figure and youth were undeniable.

She was right to suspect dishonorable intentions from men. It was upon just that appeal which his plan to free Jack Law depended. Yet it might easily misfire. If he lost the gamble they might be gaoled together by dawn.

He turned to his servant. "You have the message I entrusted to you?"

"May a thousand flies sting my flesh if I fail you," Zuberi replied.

"I doubt the measure will be necessary," Jack observed dryly. "But, if the lady agrees to follow my instruction, see her safely to the Coeur de Lion Inn before you attempt the more daring enterprise I've set out for you."

"You may depend upon your most faithful one."

Jack nodded and began pulling on his gloves, eager to be off. He was dressed for traveling in boots and leather breeches and a great winter coat to ward off the November chill. He had slept away the day, having given his night to the company of Sabrina.

Jack smiled cryptically. Was he the first gentleman to stage a gaol break in order to seduce a woman? Possibly not. If bards wrote true, men had over the centuries attempted any number of fantastical feats in order to win an hour between the thighs of their fair one, things which even the most inebriated fellow would not attempt. All in the name of love.

Jack smirked. Love! Hellfire and damnation! He was not in love. He was in rut for the most delicious young woman he had ever met. By morning he would be sated, avenged, and his own complaisant self again.

Sabrina had come to occupy his thoughts and actions more thoroughly than was wise. The lust he felt for her must be burned out. A night would be enough. Two nights too much.

That bit of self-awareness momentarily disconcerted him. Two nights too much? Why did he think that?

Shrugging off unaccustomed disquiet, he glanced again at his accomplice in the plot.

Zuberi had changed from his usual immaculate livery into loose-legged culottes, untucked shirt, and brogues. The poor man's garb only served to emphasize his exotic appearance. Certainly his proportions were more obviously revealed.

An ebony Hercules, Jack mused absently and then after

a second thought, glanced sharply at Alvy. The girl was eyeing Zuberi with all the tender admiration of a lady in the presence of her first beau.

Jack scowled at the pair. It seldom occurred to him to consider the private lives of his servants. Zuberi had an uncanny habit of drawing the amorous eye of the more adventuresome women wherever he went. No doubt the ex-gladiator was an agreeable armful in bed and Zuberi could swive her all he liked, with his blessing. But the exchange of calf-eyed glances did not bode well for his own purposes. He would not allow a street waif to steal his valet.

"You know what to do with the miscreant, should you succeed in liberating him?" he said crisply.

Zuberi tore his gaze reluctantly from Alvy. "Aye, my lord. I am to see him to freedom. You will be going now ahead of us to London?"

"No. I've business yet in town." He glanced again at Alvy. "When you leave for London, do not bring Alvy with you. Her accent is likely to draw unnecessary attention to our plot."

Stone-faced, Zuberi returned his attention to the viscount. "Is there any other way in which I might serve you, my lord?"

"See the matter through, that is all I ask." He glanced deliberately at Alvy and away. "I am depending upon you alone."

"I don't like him," Alvy declared once the viscount had departed. "What's wrong with me accent? 'Tis as proud a tongue as yours, I'm thinking."

"Ah, but his lordship is not to be doubted, loveliness."

"His eyes were as cold as the wail of a banshee. Me Da says there's spirits as walk the earth in the guise of mortals."

Zuberi's complexion grayed. "Do not speak of them! You will call them to you."

"Call who?" Alvy demanded.

"The dead who walk," the great man whispered.

"Wirra! Is what you're after callin' his lordship behind his back?" Her laughter was unexpectedly musical. "I'd like to see himself answer that."

Alvy's amusement could not sway Zuberi. He came up to her and put a long thick finger to her smiling lips. "Do not mock the spirit world, mistress. Another time I will tell you a tale of great horror, a tale told me by my own mother."

Alvy stared into the familiar dark face that had shared her pillow for the first time the night before and wondered how someone who looked himself like a phantasm come to life could believe as she did in so many ways.

She reached up and cupped his cheek. It still amazed her to find it smooth, though he said he seldom shaved. The beard of a man was a sign of his virility, her ma had once told her. Wirra! A mistaken measure, certainly.

She had never thought to lay with a man who was not hers, though it be only through handfast. Now she had given herself to a heathen. Her Da would have beaten her. Yet this man, with his dark skin and the strangely slanting black eyes and a smile wider than heaven itself, had been kind to her from the very first day. He had bathed her bruises, not once but twice, had fed her his share of the servant's rations and then gone back for more for himself, knowing that no one in the viscount's household would deny him.

How could she say no to him when he had come to her cot under the eaves of the house the night before and put his hand on her, startling her to wakefulness with its heat? How could she refuse the kiss he had so gently and sweetly placed on her mouth? How could she refuse his gentling touch as he stroked her from shoulder to hip and back, again and again until her blood sang some new tune?

If he had asked, if he had spoken a single word, she would have found a way to refuse him. But he did not ask. He never said anything, not when his kisses deepened and his arms tightened about her, or when he pulled her from her narrow pallet onto the floor beside him. He never asked or begged or demanded, just looked at her with such joy in his eyes and such happiness on his face that she could not find any words of reproach.

She had gone with him into the sweet bliss of desire, not knowing from one moment to the next if he would crush her to death or tear her apart in his need. He had done neither. He had cracked the world and shown her the beauty of its center.

And now she could no longer think how to breathe without being in his presence. "Ye won't be leavin' me behind, will ye, Zuberi?" Her face felt tight, her eyes hot with unshed tears. "Ye won't allow himself to part us?"

"Mistress Alvy darling," Zuberi intoned in his oddly formal way, "I may not disobey his lordship. He has spoken. It must be."

Despair sliced through Alvy. "What am I to do?"

He smiled. "I will persuade his lordship to send for you."

"What if ye cannot?"

He did not lie to her. His face lost its ardor and the solemnity of it pierced her heart.

Alvy snatched her hand from his face and then, thinking better of it, raised it to strike him smartly across his cheek. "That's what I think of yer promises, Mr. Blackamoor!"

"Wait!" he called after her as she started out of the room. "You have a duty to the viscount. He is depending upon us."

"Ye're his man, not I!" she tossed over her shoulder without pausing. "Bad cess to the pair o' ye!"

Chapter Eighteen

At first it seemed the room was empty. A mephitic gloom permeated everything with the damp sourness of rotting hay while an unseen bucket, called a *chaise d'aisance* by the French, offered the commingled stench of human feces and retching.

Shadows folded back upon shadows chased barely to arm's length as Jack held the lantern he carried aloft. Finally something moved in the far corner of the brick-walled cell, something humped and huddled. Larger than a rat, Jack readily surmised. Therefore it must be a man.

He had paid the guard a few coins into order to view the infamous Black Jack Law, much as one would at a menagerie of zoo animals in London. He was not the first to bribe his way into a gaol. The aristocracy and gentry considered the viewing of condemned criminals a great diversion, especially if the prisoner was in any way notorious. He, however, was getting very little so far for his fee.

''You, fellow.''

The shape convulsed as if in terror and Jack heard the faint clink of fetters. Damnation! Chains would make his task that much more difficult. Yet, he was not without resources. He fingered the heavy iron key in the pocket of his greatcoat.

He approached the still huddled figure. "If you be the highwayman who calls himself Jack Law, show yourself. Otherwise be damned to you!"

The harshly spoken words, though barely above a whisper, did the trick. The figure sat up, revealing much less of a man and much more of a boy than Jack had supposed he would find.

As he swung his lantern forward for a better view, the scarecrow figure threw up a bony hand to shade his eyes. The person before him was a gangly, very wiry youth of perhaps fifteen—no, fourteen. No beard smoked his lean cheeks. There was mud and blood smeared across his face, which distorted his features, and long ropes of tangled greasy hair lay limply on his thin shoulders.

Jack's brows lifted. What folly was this?

"Attend me. I will ask but once. Are you Black Jack the highwayman?"

The scarecrow's mouth began to work as if it were on rusty hinges in need of oil. Finally the voice that issued from it was as pathetic as it was hoarse. "I sweared I was. Only, God's truth, I ain't!"

"Then why did you say you were?" Jack prompted, accustomed by his own notorious life to dealing with knaves and chicanery of every stripe.

The figure struggled to his feet to the accompaniment of clinking chains, revealing an all but shredded shirt that hung in ribbons from his thin shoulders and wrists. Stains caused by, Jack surmised bleakly, any number of disgusting causes matted his breeches. Yet he waited with a patience neither of them could truly afford for an answer to his question. Finally the figure staggered about, revealing his back.

His thin back was a mass of crisscrossed welts blacked by dried blood from which matted wisps of straw protruded like grotesque whiskers. Jack winced at the sight, as eloquent an answer as any bard might have made him.

"The confession was beaten out of you." It was not a question.

He approached the boy cautiously but there was no need to expect assault, for the weakened boy collapsed, his legs folding under him, long before Jack reached his side.

"Can you walk?" He bent down to briefly to prod the prisoner's shoulder, feeling knobby bone beneath thin skin. "Your life depends upon it."

The boy's head jerked up and Jack found himself staring into bloodshot eyes of fearful blue tinged with a spark of hope. "I ain't guilty. That's not a word of a lie!"

Jack knew better than to offer the wretched boy sympathy. Only anger would give him the strength he needed to escape.

"Perhaps you are not guilty of the crime of which you've been accused. But do not abuse my wits with the notion you are innocent. You may answer me this. Why were you chosen to be hanged as Jack Law?"

The young man hung his head so low it seemed as if the weight of it would snap his wretchedly thin neck. "I cannot say."

"Who did you rob? Come now." Jack prodded him with his boot tip. "I'm not your confessor nor do I give a jot if you robbed the Queen herself. Only do not try my patience or I will wring your worthless neck myself and save the hangman's fee."

This got the boy's attention and he lifted his head again, anger burning now in those pain-rimmed eyes. "I stole a chicken. To feed me family. Da's gone and Ma's ailin'."

"A pretty tale."

The boy struggled again to his feet and in the meager lantern light his former sallow skin was ruddy with indignation. "I'm tellin' ye true, though ye see me hanged for it!"

Jack smiled. So the boy had spunk. He reached into his

pocket and withdrew the key, which he tossed at the boy's feet. "See if that affects the small miracle we're in need of. Do be lively, fellow. I've no desire to share your accommodations. The guard could return at any moment."

The boy scrambled in the fetid hay to pick up the key and awkwardly inserted it in the manacle that chained him to the wall.

Jack watched in weary resignation, faintly curious to know why so ill-suited a victim had been chosen to represent the swaggering figure of the country's most infamous highwayman. Nothing about the boy fit the image of the flamboyant, elegant, hale and hearty, and reputedly aristocratic Mr. Law. Even the age was incongruent. He could not imagine that this puling lad had yet managed to mount his first woman.

The distinct metallic click of the lock opening brought a smile to both their faces. "Give me that," Jack directed, holding out a gloved hand for the key, which he promptly returned to his pocket. "You are to remain here until the occasion arises when you see your moment for escape. Not a moment before, do you understand me?"

"I don't," the boy freely confessed.

Jack's smile was as brief as it was beautiful. "If you fail me, I'll dance a jig on your grave. Do you understand that?"

The boy nodded. "What do ye want o' me?"

Jack ignored his question. "Once you leave here, set out on foot along the byway to the south. A man as tall as an oak and dark as the night will meet you. You are to go with him and do exactly as he says." Seeing the guile of deception enter the boy's gaze, he added, "If you do not, he will murder you with my blessing." He shifted his greatcoat so that the younger man could see the pistol sticking out from his belt. "Now do we understand one another?"

The boy swallowed and nodded.

"Good." He turned and walked as far as the door before he thought to ask, "What is your name?"

"John."

Jack threw back his head in silent laughter.

Sabrina faced her hostess with a white face of barely contained rage. "So then, it has come to this. I will not do it! I will not!"

Lotte watched in mute sympathy as Sabrina crushed the letter between her hands. The girl had read to her the pertinent portions of the letter that had arrived the night before from her guardian. No innocent prisoner condemned to the gallows had ever looked more righteously indignant in her doom. Every rigid line of the girl bespoke her horror and disdain for the events about to overtake her.

"Perhaps he can be persuaded to reconsider," she said finally.

Sabrina turned abruptly from the window out of which she had been staring at the setting sun, the hem of her gown rustling as she began to pace. "He has signed the marriage contract. There will be no turning back. Cousin Robert and Lord Merripace will presently be in Bath and I am to prepare myself for the marriage ceremony forthwith."

"Surely he cannot mean to marry you out-of-hand, like some common— ah, some poor unbred chit." Lotte pinkened at her *faux pas* but continued in her line of thinking. "I shall insist on throwing the wedding myself. He cannot deny me, a countess, the pleasure of the exercise. But there are so many things to be done in order to host a proper wedding."

Nothing pleased Lotte more than the prospect of a party, even better if she were in charge of it. "If Lord Randolph had more amusing friends, I should find excuses to entertain frequently. But there, I stray. 'Tis late in the season. Everyone will have already abandoned London for the shooting in Scotland and will remain away until after the first of the year. I don't see how a respectable wedding can be arranged in less than six months." She smiled brightly at her device. "Engagements among the aristocracy have been known to endure some years before the ceremony."

"Cousin Robert will not be denied the ceremony," Sabrina answered shortly. "He's bringing a parson with him for the express purpose of holding the ceremony within the hour of his arrival."

"You don't say? He is remarkably formidable."

"For a commoner?" Sabrina suggested saucily.

Lotte dismissed the jibe with a feathery motion of her hand. "I am certain there are a number of capable people among the common stock." She smiled most persuasively. "Have I not found much good company in you?"

Sabrina redirected her thoughts from the trap that lay before her to her hostess, who looked remarkably fit in a gown of green and gold. "I'm glad to see your smile, Countess. You are feeling better?"

A dreamy absent look came into Lotte's face, making her seem a dozen years younger. "I suppose I am," she said after a moment. "I don't know precisely what I am." She added briskly, "But I do not wish to discuss it."

Nor did Sabrina. A few hours earlier in this very room she had believed that with Jack Laughton's help she would succeed in her plan to free Kit despite all barriers. Now, like the hot breath of the coach horses that were no doubt being whipped along the highway on the orders of her impatient guardian, she could feel disaster overtaking her.

She glanced down at the foolscap she had wadded up in her hands and wondered how much time she had left. A day, only a few hours? What was remarkable was that Cousin Robert had bothered to write at all. But then, he was ever seeking methods by which to chastise and humble her. Perhaps it pleased him to shrive her with the thought that doom rode hard upon the heels of its delivery.

"I have been ordered to return to Mrs. Noyes' cottage at once."

"I do not see why that's necessary," Lotte answered peevishly. "After all, I've not been well and need the comfort of your pretty face about me."

Sabrina smiled at this outrageous statement. "You are not an ailing housebound patient, Countess. Now that you are feeling well enough, you may attend the theater, or a musical evening, even play a hand of cards with any of the number of hostesses who've invited you out for the evening."

"A hand of cards would be nice," Lotte said wistfully.

Yet, in truth, she had found the idea of gambling less compelling with every day. There were other matters on her mind, matters that concerned most readily her absent and very silent husband.

It had come to her as she lay exhausted and miserable in her lonely single bed these past days that perhaps she had done wrong in running away. Perhaps she should not have abandoned Ran to the clutches of the scheming, conniving, unscrupulous wanton he had so thoughtlessly and foolishly allowed to ensnare him in her carnal web.

Poor darling, wonderful, dunce-headed Ran. She did love him, so much it was a pain in her middle, a sweet, deliciously sharp pain she would willingly die from if he would but hold her in his strong arms until she expired.

A brief knock at the door and the countess's bid to enter produced a servant girl with saucer-wide eyes.

"There's a very large and dark person at the servants' door, ma'am, who wishes to speak with Miss Lyndsey."

"A 'dark' person, did you say?"

"Yes, ma'am. Black as your shadow. Gives a person quite a turn, he does, ma'am."

Lotte's expression cleared. "But of course. That will be Lord Darlington's extraordinary personal servant. I believe his name is Zoo—? Que—? Hmm. It escapes me. Nevertheless, show him in."

"He won't come in. He said as much. Wants only to speak to Miss Lyndsey."

"I will go," Sabrina answered and hurried out of the room before Lotte could halt her.

Sabrina waited until she reached the gloom of the hallway to release her smile. Lord Darlington had news for her! As proud as the viscount was, it could only be good news. And that meant there might yet be a way to thwart Cousin Robert.

As she followed the maid into the depths of the servants' quarters, a place in this house she had never before visited, she wondered how Darlington had accomplished his task so easily and then chuckled. He was nothing if not masterful, a man who knew what he wanted and one equally adept at winning by charm or by force.

She had not been able to sleep at all after he left her. She had paced her bedroom seeking any distraction from the wild unruly fantasies that had seized her mind in the aftermath of their tempestuous embraces. Could it be that she was truly and deeply stirred by Lord Darlington? Had she, too proud to believe in love, fallen for the very last man she would ever have expected to elicit her most tender feelings? How foolish. How like herself!

Impulsive, rash, daring with more courage than sense, she had lived the last years of her life by whim and defiance. Yet her escapades of the past were nothing compared to risking her heart with a man like Jack Laughton.

She laughed suddenly, the pealing sounds ringing on the cold stones of the basement walls. It served her right. No, it was perfect justice. She who had disdained the very notion had fallen in—love? lust?—with a man who could love nothing and no one.

"He's just there, miss, in the garden," the maid said at last and stopped to point to a darkened hallway with the kitchen door at the end of it, ajar.

"Very well, you may go." Sabrina took the candlestick from the girl.

She waited until the maid's footsteps had retreated down the hall before she stepped forward and opened the door wide. At first she saw nothing. Disappointment arrowed through her, sharp as a needle's prick. "Yes? Hello? Are you there?"

The colossal form that appeared from the garden shadow snatched her breath. For the space of two heart-beats she did not recognize the form as merely human. And then he smiled, a wide generous span that steadied her nerves.

"I bring you greetings, mistress, from my lord," he said in tones so deep they seemed to resonanate in his chest. "You will do him the honor of reading his note?"

Sabrina stared at the man revealed by the limpid halo of her candle a few seconds longer, fascinated by the enormous, ebony-skinned man who spoke with great courtesy and good humor. This obliging man served the uncivil Darlington? It seemed impossible.

"Mistess, the note?"

"Of course." She took from his hand the small, folded scrap of paper.

The cryptic note read:

Come with the messenger. He is free. Proof awaits.

Scratched below it with the slash of a pen was a single bold "J."

She refolded the note and lifted her head with a smile. "Your lord is an intrepid and resourceful soul."

The large man merely nodded once with great solemnity.

"I am to come with you. But what shall I tell the countess? No, never mind," she added as her mind began to work.

She would tell the countess that she must inform Mrs. Noyes of her guardian's imminent arrival. That way she would be allowed to go out alone. "Wait here. I will be a few minutes." She smiled briefly at the huge man. "You *will* wait?"

"Like the night upon the dawn," he answered in his softly modulated basso.

Sabrina smiled in spite of herself. "You could give your master lessons in flattery."

Once up in her room she debated some minutes how to dress. In the end she chose the riding habit of a deep blue, which fortuitously her guardian had had packed for her. It was woolen and durable and would withstand a long journey through the bitter days of autumn. For she had decided what she was going to do. She would ride for Scotland with Black Jack this very night, if he would take her.

"He must," she whispered to the kitten that sat on her bed watching attentively as her flustered mistress hurriedly worked the last of the brass buttons through their holes in her tight-fitting jacket.

Rather than wait in Bath, as she had originally planned, while the highwayman found and brought Kit back here to her, she would go with the outlaw to Scotland and escape with Kit from there!

"It is a much sounder plan than you think," she admonished the kitten who had lost interest the process and turned to grooming one small paw.

Cousin Robert was on his way, might even arrive this every night. When he did, she would be gone without a trace or an explanation. Let him then try to wed Merripace to her shadow!

When she had pushed her feet into her stiff new riding boots and then packed a few essentials into her portmanteau, she knelt on the floor beside her bed and thrust her hands under the feather tick. She smiled as her fingers found and curled over the items she sought and then she pulled them out. Her booty contained her precious pearls and Black Jack's pistol.

"He will be pleased to know we are armed," she said to

the kitten who had come forward to rub her head against her mistress's cheek. "Oh, little one, I wish that I could take you with me, but where I am going there will be no room for kittens. The countess is a generous lady. She will see to your care." She bent and kissed the fluffy head. "Now, you must promise not to cry and rouse suspicions before morning. Promise?"

Jack waited in the shadow of the house across the square until Sabrina had stepped into the sedan chair Zuberi had purchased for her. He knew she was perfectly safe in his servant's care, yet he wished he did not need to make her wait for him even as long as it would take him to finish his self-imposed errands. Seeing the countess was the last of them.

As the bearers set off with Zuberi as escort, he noticed his servant carried a portmanteau. Doubtless, it belonged to Miss Lyndsey. He had noticed that she was dressed for traveling in a riding habit and the great cloak she had worn the night he attacked her coach. Yet there was no need for luggage on this occasion unless . . .

"What now does the minx have in mind?"

He crossed the square in long purposeful strides, uncaring that it might be noticed that the Viscount Darlington was paying a visit upon the Countess Lovelace. Whatever rumor sprung up in the wake of his footsteps on this night could only distract from his real intent this night.

"I do not ask for nor want your approval in the matter."

"She is so young, so innocent." Lotte emphasized that last word with a significant lift of her copper-bright brows.

"It is my intent that she shall be a great deal less so by dawn," Jack replied coolly.

His frankness drew a harsh glance from Lotte. The last thing she had expected when the arrival of Lord Darlington had been announced was that he had come to tell her that he was absconding with her companion for a night of debauchery.

"I cannot condone this. To admit to me that you intend to corrupt my companion!"

"Yet you do suppose that seduction at my hands will not be a fate worse than death?" The suggestion ignited and smoldered behind his light eyes. "At one time, you were the object of my dishonorable attention," he lied, in hopes of distracting her.

"Really?"

Lotte's guileless question drew his laughter. "You proved rather too great a temptation."

"I don't understand." She sounded injured by the idea that anything she might be should shoo him away.

He had come to be kind. "Let us just say that you are too good for me. I felt the danger of sentiment lurking behind the seduction." He smiled his most beautiful, heart-startling smile. "I am, as you know, heartless. You might have ruined my credit as a rake."

It was a pretty speech, unlike his usual acid-tongued remarks. Lotte could find no fault in it, nor any way to answer it in kind. He was, as she had always suspected, a shade too clever and irreverent for her. "You have a facile tongue, Darlington."

He took her hand in both of his. "Jack, for tonight. This one last time, let me hear you call me Jack."

She blushed the high strawberry color of which only true redheads are capable. "Very well, Jack."

"Ah, you see, a liaison between us would have ruined us both."

"You are a great flatterer and deceiver, my lord," Lotte answered with the proper amount of reproach due a gentleman who had propositioned a lady, however indirectly.

"I thank you for seeing me for what I am. And still liking me a little despite it."

"I suppose you had better go now," she said in a tone so regretful she blushed again.

Jack brought her unresisting hand to his lips and placed a lingering kiss on first the back of it and then the inside of her wrist. From the corner of his eye he saw her lips part as his own touched that sensitive inner skin and he chuckled inwardly. Perhaps he was being a greater fool than he realized. How ripe she would be for the plucking, if her heart did not belong to someone else.

He straightened quickly. "When do you intend to tell your husband?"

Lotte blinked rapidly, her red-gold lashes fanning her overheated cheeks. "What can you mean?"

"If the signs be right, you will in spring deliver to the earl his first child."

Her eyes widened alarmingly and then her mouth crumpled. "Oh! Oh!" She gripped his hand with surprising strength. "How did you know? It is common rumor even now?"

The sudden change alarmed Jack. " 'Twas a lucky guess on my part." As her stricken gaze swept up to his in trepidation he nodded reassuringly. "I played a long shot, Countess. But I am right, am I not?"

"Yes! Yes," she repeated more softly. "And I don't know what to do."

"Go home and delight your husband with the news."

She shook her head so vigorously her powdered curls raised a mist about her head. "You do not understand. He will not welcome it. That is, he might have, before now."

Jack said in his most jaded voice, "Then you have taken a lover."

"Not quite." She glanced up guilty at him. "We had a most horrible misunderstanding. And my gaming debts and . . . and other things."

She took a deep bracing breath. "Lord Randolph has taken a mistress. Yet he forbids me to console myself with friends!" A bit of the old provoking spirit flashed in her blue eyes. "I might have said something about someone else to lead him to believe that I would not sit docilely by while he dallies his fill."

Jack had played this scene too many times to appear innocent in the matter. It explained at once Randolph Lovelace's enmity and hunger to run him through. "Your husband believes we are lovers."

Lotte's legs trembled so hard she staggered. Even so, she angrily batted away Jack's hand as he tried to steady her.

"Oh, but this is a pretty coil!" She took several quick steps away from him toward the window at the front of the salon and then spun about. "I have done nothing—well, very little. And now I am ruined."

Jack hid his inclination to exercise his amusement at her expense. He could guess that Lotte had said and done enough to inflame her husband's ardor and jealousy. At the moment he would have liked to give her a good shaking for her foolishness. She was, after all, indirectly the reason he had left of London.

He approached and touched her gently, taking her by the upper arms. He was amazed when she came willingly in against him and lay her cheek upon his coat front.

"I thought Ran would have come for me long before this," she whispered unhappily. "He should have. A husband should pursue his wife." She hiccuped, but it sounded suspiciously like a sob. "Unless he no longer cares."

Jack cradled her head in one hand and patted her back with the other, feeling a thousand years older than the blithe spirit he held. "Go home, Lotte."

She shook her head, her expression that of a willful child. "I cannot go home to him. Not like this."

"He will forgive you."

"That is just the point. I do not want be to taken back because I am with his child."

Jack just refrained from pointing out the possibility that her actions had set the stage for her husband to doubt the veracity of her statement. Then again, Lovelace might not be as much a fool as most men. For Lotte's sake, he hoped that was so. "So then what will you do?"

She lifted her head but her eyes did not meet his this time. "I do not want to be with child. I am terrified of childbirth." Her voice dropped to a childish whisper. "I fear I shall die."

He had no ready answer for that. "I can only tell you how I would feel if you were my wife. I should want you back, whatever the misunderstanding."

He reached down and lifted her face by the chin. "Even your stickler of a husband must have enough manly lust left within him to know what he has found in you."

She smiled back, at first a bit wobbly but then more resolutely. "Do you really believe it?"

"Would I lie to you?" And then because he did not want to talk any more, he bent his head and captured her trembling mouth for a brief moment with his firm kiss.

When he lifted his head she was staring at him with a new and dangerous awareness.

He set her promptly to arm's length before he forgot he was playing the gentleman and advocate for her foolishly absent husband. "Now you go straight to bed and in the morning write that dullard you love to come and fetch you back to London. There will be time enough to persuade him of your value before you deliver your news to him."

"What of Sabrina?" The look in her gaze was frankly sensual. "You will treat her well?"

He lifted a single golden brow. "Do you still doubt me?"

She pinkened, her hand rising unconsciously to her lips. "No."

The tender scene played out in silhouette against the backlit lace curtains of the house on Kingsmeade Square had sliced to ribbons the heart of the one person in all the world who should never have witnessed it.

Lord Randolph Lovelace had followed Darlington from his apartments, having arrived in the lane of the viscount's address just as the gentleman was going out.

He had ridden night and day to reach Bath, only to discover what he was still prepared to disbelieve as truth.

Lotte and Darlington were lovers. Proof positive, seen with his own eyes, now stared him in the face. The embrace. The kiss. The tender parting. These could have no ambiguous meanings.

Ran watched the viscount descend the steps, his visit no more than a quarter of an hour long and played out in plain sight. The assignation had been minus the sweaty coupling, which in his feverish, tortured imagination must have taken place on every other night.

"How could she!" The anguished whisper tore from his throat. His good, sweet, wonderful Lotte. What could have tempted her into another man's arms? What had happened to their own consuming love? Darlington, he had come between them.

"I will kill him!"

Randolph reached for the pistol he had kept primed beneath his heavy coat, ready to fend off any assault upon the highway. Now he could imagine no sweeter revenge than setting its barrel against Darlington's temple and pulling the trigger. Vanquished, his rival would no longer be able to touch Lotte ever again.

He gripped the pistol butt, his hand trembling on the brink of the act. The sound of Darlington's booted footsteps ringing on cobblestone was the only sound in the square as the man neared his hiding place.

So near now, so easily accomplished, the surprise leap from the shadows, the lifting of steel and wood, the sudden pressure of metal against bone, the simple squeeze of the trigger.

The mad-blood haze lifted slowly from Randolph as Darlington turned the corner and strolled unknowingly past his own mortality and out of sight into the night.

He slumped against the stone edifice in whose shadow he stood, a broken, soul-weary man. He was no butcher. He could not kill in cold blood. Nor in raging temper. He could not kill what Lotte loved.

He found his sweating and shivering mount where he had tied it to a hitching post on the opposite side of the square. The horse whinnied its distress as Randolph mounted it but he was past caring. He ruthlessly turned the animal about and applied his spurs for speed.

If he rode the beast and himself into the ground, so be it. He knew he had to leave Bath on the very hour of his arrival or, despite his resolve, he might yet in some other less controllable moment kill them both.

Chapter Nineteen

Sabrina had not meant to fall asleep. How could she think of slumber when she waited for the arrival of Jack Law? Yet after the first hour of pacing the private parlor of The Coeur de Lion Inn, where every new voice or footfall beyond the closed door drew her attention, she found she could no longer remain alert. The wide width and welcome shelter of the Queen Anne chair set before the fire in the small drafty chamber beckoned.

Once settled in its deep seat with its tall back and wide wings gathering and holding the fire's toasting warmth, she felt her head droop. Just for a moment, she told herself as she tucked her feet up under her skirts. She would not sleep. And then her lids fell shut on memories she had forgotten and things that would never again be . . .

She stepped out of a window onto the rolling grassy lawn, slick and freshly cut and smelling of spring. As she did so, she heard her name being called through the upper story window of her father's Devonshire home. She threw back her head in laughter and then picked up her skirts and fled the petulant sound. Ah, but it was good to be home again!

When out-of-doors, she always ran. Her father said she would never make a proper lady until she was hobbled like a horse. But she did not care to be a lady, not ever. Now that she had seen London she was certain she would forever remain a hoyden.

She quickly gained the gap in the tall hedges that ringed the rear garden of the house and slipped through, not bothering to pause to unhook her sleeve that caught on a branch. She felt the fabric pull tight and then heard a faint ripping sound as it came loose. There would be the devil to pay. There was always the devil to pay from Prue, the nurse who had looked after her since the early death of her mother. But her father would laugh when she told him the story of her day's adventure. For she was certain it would be an adventure.

She ran past the rougher ground, heavy brogues slipping on round wet stones, until she caught sight of, gleaming though the trees, the river. The sun lay upon it, split into shining ribbons of gold by the breeze rippling the surface. She had come to dip her hands in the river, to splash it upon her sweaty cheeks and watch the fish jump and the gulls cry shrilly with excitement. Then she would sit on the bank and wait in the hopes she would see it.

This was the day, of course. It never kept a schedule, but that did not seem to matter. She always knew by the expectation that gripped her upon awakening when the red-sailed sloop of the privateer would appear in the distance.

Yes, there it was!

Moments after she had gathered her skirts and sat in the green-dappled shade to wait, the sloop appeared from a bend in the river. It was just as she remembered it.

Butterflies floated past her and the underwood to her back hummed with bees broken by the chatter of birdsong. She had eyes only for the graceful ship slipping silently upriver, away from the sea into which, just beyond her sight, the river spilled.

Most often it anchored off the far shore in the curve of the natural harbor where the river widened before its final plunge to the sea. Today it sailed on, coming in closer than ever before. She saw first a man in the eagle's nest. Then, as if it were a gliding swan, the ship turned broadside as it neared the shore, presenting her a full view of its deck, and the men standing there.

A premonition of wonder and fear struck through her, a strange elation and dread. There, standing mid-deck, were her father and Kit. They were smiling, the man's arm lying protectively about the shoulders of the thin frail boy whose fair hair tossed in the breeze.

Even as she opened her mouth to cry a delighted greeting, the ship canted and turned away, presenting its stern to her as the sails snapped and buckled and then caught again the freshening breeze.

She jumped to her feet, waving a frantic arm back and forth above her head.

"Wait! Wait for me!"

A draft of cool air whispering past her cheek roused Sabrina. Yet when she opened her eyes she could not be certain she had felt it.

The chamber was nearly dark, the fire no more than smoldering embers that threw faint light only upon nearby objects. She lifted her head, which felt woolly and thick as if she were sickening. When she tried to swallow she found her throat clogged and her chest oddly heavy, as if she had been running for a long time.

She sat up suddenly. How much time had passed? An hour? More?

She glanced toward the door to find it remained closed, as before. The shuttered window opposite her was equally shut against the night.

She felt his presence an instant before he spoke and yet the sound of Black Jack Law's voice was the most unnerving sensation of her life.

"You've been crying in your sleep, mistress."

"Have I?"

Sabrina raised a hand to her cheek and was startled to find it damp. She had been dreaming of Kit and her father and all that was now lost forever.

Embarrassed, she dropped her hand. The last thing she wanted was to seem weak and chastened before this wildly self-sufficient man. Though it rattled her confidence not to be able to see him, she did not turn toward the place from where his voice emanated. He liked mystery. She could be mysterious as well.

She deliberately leaned back into the contours of her wing chair. "I thought you might not come," she said with quiet dignity. "I had grown weary with waiting."

"I regret that. The delay was unavoidable." He sounded as though he meant it. Extraordinary!

He had been imprisoned and was now free. She did not know how to ask him what he had suffered so she simply said, "I was told you were beaten and tortured."

"An exaggeration."

"I see." The sound of his voice! Though muffled, she surmised, by the mask that he wore, it seemed hearty. Indeed, as if he had just partaken of a good meal and sufficient wine to thoroughly warm and satisfy his appetite.

Unable to resist, she leaned forward and turned her head in his direction. He appeared as a dark upright figure in a greatcoat with arms folded. He leaned a shoulder against the far wall in the deepest shadows created by the placement of her chair between him and the fire. She peered through the gloom, searching for the details of his face, yet they were blurred and indistinct. For all she saw of form and feature he might have been fashioned of coal. "Will you not join me by the fire, sir?"

"Not yet." There was amusement in his tone. A sign

that he was of a mood to be indulgent? "Considering our last meeting you can appreciate my predilection for anonymity."

"Very well." His reluctance was good, Sabrina decided, at least until they had struck the bargain which she hoped would make them accomplices.

"I am told you are responsible for my sudden liberation. May I ask why?"

She laughed self-consciously and slid her feet out from under herself, propping them on the brass fender before the hearth. " 'Tis a rather complex tale."

"I have time."

She had not had much practice at bargaining, but it seemed appropriate that she maintain a certain formality until she had extracted a promise from him. "I have need of a man of your talents."

"I am flattered." He spoke lazily, as if being saved from the hangman's knot was a customary service done him by young women of Quality. "Might I suggest which of my many good talents might best serve you?"

She ignored his innuendo. "I know which suits me. I have need of your talent for stealing things."

"What do you wish stolen? A new gown? A jewel? A kiss, perhaps?"

Sabrina surprised herself by chuckling. She had remembered him aright, a vain, strutting rooster who thought himself adored by women. The faint odors of leather, tobacco, and whiskey flowed from him to tease her nostrils. Strange, she would have thought he would smell of the malodors of his prison. "What I wish you to steal is in Scotland."

"That is a long, difficult journey."

"So I've been told," she murmured, thinking of the letters Kit had written her when first they had been separated. He had complained at length of the bad roads and multiple delays caused by broken wheels and impassable stretches that required them to backtrack sometimes for several days together. The cold of the too-short days of winter made his bones ache and the interminable nights with nothing to do but recite psalms and prayers seemed a cruel monotony to visit upon any lonely sad child.

"All the same, it is what I should like for you to do."

"You expect a great deal from a man you wounded with his own weapon."

She caught her breath. "Did I really wound you?"

He grunted. "Enough to leave a mark, not enough to incapacitate me."

"I am sorry. Truly."

As I view it, my liberation by you is no more than my due. By it we are made even."

His unexpected view of events surprised her but she was not without a persuasive logic of her own. "I was not responsible for your capture. Yet I came to your aid."

"With the help of a gentleman of great daring."

"I suppose so," she murmured, not wanting to think of Lord Darlington at this moment. "Since I have done you this good turn, you might repay me in the performance of an errand."

"To Scotland?"

"Yes. I wish you to go to Scotland and steal the most precious thing in the world to me."

"Precious?" A new note of coolness had entered his tone. "My lady is greedy for gain. A sentiment I can appreciate."

"Perhaps I should be more specific. 'Tis not treasure. In fact, it is not something I wish you to steal but rather *someone.*"

For the space of a few heartbeats, silence offered the prefect vessel for his surprise. "Go on."

"I want you to spirit my half brother Kit away from those who hold him under duress."

"You want me to kidnap your brother?" The surprise had not left his tone but the humor was fully back.

"It will not be kidnapping. Kit wants to come to me."

She sat forward again, making her appeal directly to the long, dark masculine form that hovered at the edge of her focus. "But he is weak and ill and cannot accomplish it alone."

"Why? What profit to you?"

"No profit to me. Rather I would see him profit."

Annoyed that he had yet to reveal himself, she sat back out of his view. Addressing his motionless silhouette was rather like speaking to an apparition.

"Kit is the rightful heir to the Lyndsey fortune, not I. It was only through the insidious lies spread by our guardian that the king was induced to declare our father's marriage to Kit's mother illegal and therefore Kit a bastard."

"Your guardian's purpose?"

"As I am a mere woman, he gained permanent control of my inheritance."

"An inconvenience to you, I see."

"More than an inconvenience." Her patience was beginning to unravel. "To further his nefarious political aspirations, our guardian has demanded that I marry where the dispensing of my dowry will gain him the most political influence."

"Does this influential fellow have a name?"

"Lord Merripace."

"Merripace." She thought he spoke the name as one familiar with it. Could it be true that he, too, was a nobleman?

"So then you will gain a coronet and a title, your guardian gains a powerful political ally, and Merripace gains the husbandry right to plant his seed in your ripe young body. Why should you wish to spoil this pleasant design?"

She clenched her fists to control her rising irritation with his raillery. How could she have forgotten how maddening this fellow could be? She supposed a man who lived by whim must find her concerns ridiculous. Yet they involved her very life. "I did not set you free to ply me with odious questions."

" 'Tis a fair question. Come, no one willing concedes a fortune for poverty."

"I would, for Kit. My brother has been sickly all his life. I suspect my guardian will allow Kit to die once I am wed. To spare his life, I would give up three fortunes."

"In that case, I want no part of your scheme."

Sabrina lurched forward in her chair. "What?"

"The night I detained your coach you stood up to me. You were strong and daring and reckless enough to wrest from life what it was unwilling to concede you. Now I find you a mewling, weak woman full-up with false sentiment."

"I am sorry to disillusion you," she said indignantly. "Not all of us can take to the road when our lives defeat us."

"Why not?" He sounded closer. Had he taken silent steps toward her while she spoke?

Sabrina considered his question. "What do you require of me?"

"A revelation of your true nature." Oh yes, he was much nearer now. His voice came from directly above her. "It will not repel me. Is it wealth you seek? Revenge against your guardian? Rebellion over his authority?" She sensed him leaning over the chair back, so close now she felt his breath chase shivers across her cheek. Had he removed his mask? "Or, are you in it for the sheer devilment you may cause?"

She closed her eyes, trembling despite the weeks of longing for this moment. If she reached out she could touch him. Shyness held her back, kept her from even gazing into his stranger's face. "Why do you seek to make my motives ugly and wicked?"

"Because," he murmured into her ear, "the truth is that life is ugly and the motivation of men and woman most often wicked."

Sabrina slowly shook her head. "Not in this, not where my brother is concerned."

He stepped back, withdrawing from her not only his

physical presence but also the spell of intimacy he had been weaving about them.

"From whence this sudden deep partiality for distant kin?" How scornful he sounded. "You have been content until now to entertain yourself in London with the likes of Countess Lovelace and her idle pack of gossiping gamesters."

Sabrina's eyes snapped open. "How could you know that?"

"Ask a magician how he accomplishes his arts."

"You've been inquiring about me," she said, unable to keep the smugness from her tone.

"I've done more than inquire. I've been watching you." His voice dropped into a lower register. "I have been your shadow these last weeks, scarcely more than an arm's length away."

His words were like a caress that made her shiver. "Then why did you not show yourself before now?"

"How do you know I have not?" The tone of his voice had altered again to something more familiar. "Perhaps you were too willfully blind to see me?"

Was that possible? She bolted upright from her chair. That voice was so familiar, so like—

"Darlington!"

"Stir up the fire, mistress, and then look your fill."

She reached for the poker then angrily jostled the logs until flames licked at the newly exposed surface of the wood. When she was done she swirled about, poker still in hand.

He stepped forward out of the shadow and everything she thought she knew about the last moments, and the last weeks, changed, utterly and forever.

He was dressed for riding in leather coat, suede weskit, and polished thigh-high boots with spurs. His golden hair gleamed—unmistakable—in the fire.

The sharp prick of disappointment brought new tears

to her eyes but Sabrina fought them. "Scoundrel! I suppose it pleases you to make a jest of me."

"No." He said the word softly but so persuasively that she wished she could read the truth behind his expression. All she saw in it was the aloof indifference with which he most often faced the world.

"I thought it time that you knew the true nature of the man you dubbed Black Jack on the highway some weeks ago."

"You cannot wish to make me believe that you—?"

"Precisely." He came forward, looking now far too handsome and far too pleased with himself. "I stole your housekeeper's pounds and pence."

"I do not believe you."

He paused within arm's length of her, amusement curving his mobile mouth. "Shall I kiss you again? Perhaps it will remind you, though I will admit to the dent in my vanity that it has not jogged your memory ere this."

Sabrina opened her mouth and then closed it, finally at a loss for the words. Could he be telling her the truth? Could Lord Darlington, a peer of the realm, have chosen to rob a coach, her coach, on the Western Road? "Why?"

"For the simple and expedient reason every man turns to robbery, Sabrina. I was in need of funds."

"You are a viscount." Her gaze was doubtful. "You are heir to vast lands."

"Not so vast, nor so wealthy. 'Struth, 'tis a sad and winsome tale. Your tender heart will approve of it," he said pleasantly and she knew he was about to make mockery of what came next.

"Until a year ago I was the cast-off son of a madman. Abandoned and poor, I lived on an island whose sole source of diversion for a young man without funds was drunkenness and gambling. Then—you will approve of the fairy tale quality of this next chapter—I inherited my lunatic sire's title. But old habits die hard and the madman's money weighed rather heavily in my pockets. I made it my sole purpose to live as far beyond my new means as possible. Alas, I succeeded rather too well. Until the annual annuity fills my coffers again, I am as clipped for farthings as any pauper."

Sabrina suspected a few painful truths lay beneath his disaffected words. "That was very foolish of you."

"A lesson that bears no repetition," he allowed with a small smile. "So, sweeting, now you know my secret."

"You are Black Jack Law, the highwayman."

He stared at her as if she had just grown a second head. "In all my life I've robbed exactly one coach. Yours."

"But, if you are not he, then who resides in the Bath gaol?"

"No one, any longer. I set the poor wretch free, as you asked."

"I did—" Sabrina found herself shocked by the news. "You set the real villain free?"

His brows rose imperiously. " 'Twas by your direct charge."

"Yes, but that was when I thought . . ." She paused to untangle her own thoughts. "The man who robbed me was no true villain?"

Jack laughed. She had managed to surprise him. "I will admit to a certain flattery in your defense."

It occurred to Sabrina that he might be lying. "Prove you are not the highwayman."

" 'Twas you who dubbed me Black Jack. I did not volunteer the name."

"You did not deny it."

"I was robbing you, sweeting. It did not benefit me to correct any misimpression."

"Where is the real Black Jack?"

He leaned an arm against her chair back. "I haven't the slightest idea. But the half-wit stripling they intended to hang in the real brigand's place should now be safely beyond the bloodlust demands of his betters."

Dismay informed her expression. "You mean the captive was not the real Black Jack either?"

"Alas, no. For a man whose reputation permeates the countryside, Black Jack has been oddly absent from the field."

Sabrina sank back down into her chair. "If what you say be true, then all is lost."

Jack came around and stood before her. How absurdly lovely she looked in her misery. From the moment he had spied her curled up asleep like a kitten in this chair he had been able to think of nothing else but how and when he would take her in his arms and make love to her. He reached out a finger to touch one dark curl. "What is lost, sweeting?"

Her expression was one of defeat. "I must find a new method by which to free my brother."

He lifted his gaze from a contemplation of the row of brass buttons on her bodice that he longed to unfasten. "You were serious then?"

"I beg your indulgence owing to the late hour, Countess, but is imperative that I speak with my niece and ward, Miss Sabrina Lyndsey."

Lotte adjusted her sleepy gaze to include the two gentlemen who had risen to their feet with her entrance into her salon. Roused from her bed just as she had drifted to sleep, she allowed her dream-filled gaze to wander from the tall stranger in severe Calvinist style who had addressed her without waiting for permission from his companion. A more conventionally dressed member of the Beau Monde, the gentleman wore a heavily brocaded coat with deep sleeves, silver-buckled shoes, and enough lace to keep his laundress busy for a day and a half.

She continued to gaze vaguely in his direction for he, at least, was clearly her equal. One of Ran's cronies, perhaps? His wig was the old-fashioned kind, long and thickly curling over his shoulders, all but hiding his features. Which was just as well, she decided as her eyes focused with more precision. His most distinguished feature was his nose. It was a large, red-veined, irregularly shaped protuberance that looked like a beet had been attached to the middle of his face. Clustered closely about it, his squinty eyes and sunken-prune mouth made small impression.

With the hauteur of which she was capable, Lotte lifted her chin and said disdainfully, "I do not recognize either of you fellows."

The portly gentleman stepped forward and made her an awkward leg. "Do you not remember me, countess? I am Lord Merripace."

"The louse bearer!" Lotte murmured under her breath. Like a splash of cold water, the news instantly awakened her wits, and her protective instincts. These men had come for Sabrina. Happily, she was not here. Yet she had no intention of volunteering even that much.

"I've a vague recollection of you, sir," she said aloud. "If you here to inquire about my husband, you will not find him in town."

"We've come—" the other man began impatiently only to be silenced by a glance from his noble companion.

"I am most anxious to see Miss Lyndsey," Merripace said, his mouth working in a manner that revealed to Lotte that he had lost the better part of his teeth.

"I do not permit my companion to receive gentlemen callers after we have retired."

"She has gentlemen callers?" the Calvinist inquired.

Lotte at last allowed her gaze to wander in his direction. "And you are . . . ?"

The man flushed more from anger than embarrassment, she suspected. "Robert McDonnell, my lady." He made her the slightest bow, so stiff she wondered if there was an iron bar stuck up the back of his horribly designed coat. He would have made a fine officer in Cromwell's

Commonwealth army, she thought with a shiver of distaste. "I have come to fetch my ward from under your roof."

"Have you, indeed? Why, may I inquire, should you wish to do that? We are of an accord which I do not wish disturbed."

Though the chill of dislike never left McDonnell's face, his voice softened with cordiality. "We are arrived on the pleasantest of errands and with the happiest of news, my lady. Miss Lyndsey is to be wed."

"No doubt. At some distant future time."

"Immediately!" Merripace offered her a cavernous smile that confirmed her suspicion of his balding mouth. "I, myself, am the fortunate bridegroom."

"How . . . remarkable."

Embarrassment did not improve his complexion, she noted. Dear heaven! How could even the most hard-hearted of guardians expect a lovely young creature like Sabrina to sacrifice herself in wedlock with this bloated, filthy, decaying ancient? Better she be ruined in Darlington's embrace. The least she could do was throw them off the scent.

"In that case, I suppose it is safe to confide in you." She smiled sweetly at the aged reprobate. "You may find your bride-to-be at Mrs. Noyes'. Sabrina left here earlier this evening, packed and determined to return to the bosom of her family."

Merripace glanced uncertainly at McDonnell before addressing her. "Are you positive, Lady Charlotte?"

"Certainly, I am positive." She now glanced at McDonnell with frigid formality. "I believe your missive was the spur."

"Then she received my letter." He looked very satisfied. But only for a moment. A banked look of rage immediately overtook his rather ordinary features, making them quite severe. Poor Sabrina, thought Lotte, if this were the guardian she faced each day while in London.

"She has bolted!"

"Unlikely," Lotte replied, casting about in her mind for a method by which to put them off the mark. "I think you must be mistaken," she hurried on when it seemed both men were about to make objection. "Perhaps you did not visit the right cottage. They are all alike near the East Gate, and so cramped and filthy. I, myself, was quite horrified by the conditions in Mrs. Noyes' lane. You may have mistakenly visited the wrong abode."

"I assure you, my lady, I would recognize my kin," McDonnell answered stiffly. "She is my aunt."

"Ah." Lotte let the sound serve as dubious response.

"If she is not here and she most certainly is not with Mrs. Noyes," McDonnell exclaimed in annoyance, "then where is the chit?"

Lotte's eyes narrowed with intense dislike upon the man. "You make very free with my hospitality, Mr. McDonnell. I bid you both good night!"

She turned and swept into her hallway, feeling she had done as much to confound the pair as was possible without previous plan or strategy. "Sally, show the visitors out!" she directed as she swept past the sleepy maid who had roused her.

"Yes, Countess," the girl in nightcap and blanketed shoulders answered with a curtsey.

"A moment, my lady. Please, I beg you."

Lotte paused on the riser of the fourth stair and turned. McDonnell sounded genuinely distressed, yet she doubted the sincerity of the emotions behind it. "Yes, what is it?"

"If my niece be neither here nor there, where do you propose she could be found?"

"Found? You surmise she is lost?" Lotte cudgeled her brains and hit at once upon a brilliant retort. "How far could a young woman, traveling alone, get without attracting attention?"

"That is true," Merripace mumbled.

"Yes, certainly," Lotte concurred. "A young lady roaming the streets at night would be easy prey for all sorts of unscrupulous fellows." She allowed her contemptuous gaze to linger on McDonnell. "If she is neither here nor there then you must assume she has been taken elsewhere."

"Taken?" both men pronounced together.

"You do not suggest she may have been taken by thieves?" McDonnell questioned with open skepticism.

Lotte gnawed her lip, sorry she had sailed so close to Sabrina's own plans for her brother. "I suggest nothing. Though I suppose she might be ripe for ransom. She is, after all, an heiress. Some highwayman may have run off with her."

"Have ye then heard the news, my lady?" asked her maid from her place by the doorway.

Lotte frowned at the girl. "What news?"

"Jack Law is escaped this very night, my lady!"

"Ah," Lotte murmured sagely. "Perhaps that explains Sabrina's absence."

Her last very satisfying glimpse of the two men standing below her was that of a pair of faces registering disaster.

Chapter Twenty

"Where are we going?" It was the third such demand Sabrina had made during the past hour. "Is the road not lonely enough for you yet?"

Her companion did not reply, just as he had not on the other occasions since they left the inn.

"Very well, be mysterious, my lord." Her exasperation was absorbed into the woolen back of his overcoat. "What else could I expect from a gentleman willing to risk his life for tuppence!"

The goading remark did not draw so much as a snort from the man she hugged about the waist. Which was just as well, she supposed, since his remarks were seldom pleasant or flattering. At least he had agreed to see her safely out of Bath, if not all the way to Scotland. Best of all, she had escaped the machinations of Cousin Robert! What her guardian would do when he found out she was gone did not bear thinking about too closely. It was imperative that she find and rescue Kit before he guessed that Scotland would be the most likely place for her to go.

She had not ridden double on horseback since the days

when her father had allowed her sit up before him. Then she had been a small girl with no thought but innocent pleasure while they crossed the moors. Riding up behind Lord Darlington was an altogether different experience. Exhilarating, to be sure, but also a tormenting exercise.

In order to sit comfortably astride behind him, she had had to abandon her double paniers. Without the whalebone cage that held out her skirts and provided a natural barrier between herself and all else, she had discovered that each long, loping stride pushed her hips forward so that her body rubbed with unprecedented familiarity against her companion's. She was uncertain if he had noticed the repeated friction but it made her embarrassingly aware of their intimate proximity.

Hampered by the darkness and the unfamiliar road, the viscount's horse was forced to maintain a slow, steady stride along the ribbon of road snaking its way through the countryside. Sure-footed for the most part, the animal misstepped as they entered a copse of trees.

The stumble jerked both riders forward and Sabrina's chin collided with her companion's back, making her bite her tongue. Her cry of pain startled the horse and it skittered sideways. With a curse of anger Darlington brought his mount instantly under control as Sabrina felt herself slipping sideways off the horse's flanks.

"My lord!" she cried in alarm and clutched desperately at him. He reined in at once and then reached back with one hand and scooped his hand under her.

The shock of his hand gripping her buttocks through her shirts made her gasp. He pulled her up tight against him and held her until she had readjusted her grip about his waist and then released her, all without a word.

The encounter left the blood stinging through Sabrina's cheeks. Yet, she mastered her abashment and her inclination to apologize for her clumsiness. Why should she, when it was obvious that the moment had in no way affected him?

Though she was determined this time to hold herself apart from him, she was again forced to steady herself by holding on to the sides of his heavy cloth redingote. Before they set out he had draped her long cloak about her shoulders and tucked it together with her skirts up under her legs so that the materials would not flap and frighten his horse. Yet now her cloak had partially escaped and flapped in the breeze. As the minutes passed she became increasingly cold. Her fingers began to ache where they gripped his coat and her toes inside her boots were cramping. Only where her front met his back was she warmed by the heat of his body.

Resigned to the comfort of his warmth, she slowly and begrudgingly released his coat to more fully embrace him about the waist so that their bodies met. Her bosom pressed to his back and her thighs cradled his buttocks. She held her breath for several seconds, waiting to see how he would react. If he made one tiny remark, spoke one syllable of sarcasm, she would release him immediately. To her surprise and relief, he said nothing.

After several minutes she allowed herself to admit there was a pleasure beyond the mere necessity of warmth in touching him, a pleasure she had never before known when in the company of any other man. With her arms wrapped about him she could feel every shift of muscle and bone in his torso. How hot and hard he was, as solid as oak but as warmly and humanly alive as she.

She wondered what Lotte Lovelace would say if she ever learned that Miss Sabrina Lyndsey had run away with "Black Jack" Law? No, Jack Darlington was not the highwayman, though he had robbed her coach—she must believe it—for the devil of it! Why had she not realized who he was before? Or was it only that she had not wanted to?

She should have been dismayed, insulted, and enraged by his revelation. After all, he had hidden that secret while he pretended to court her. No, he had not pretended courtship. Their encounters could never be mistaken for that genteel exercise most often practiced between lady and suitor. He had never shown the least tender emotion toward her. He had exhibited disdain, disinterest, mild amusement at her expense, even a strangely aloof passion when he had taken her in his arms the night before.

Sabrina closed her eyes and rested her cheek against his back, lured by the inviting warmth of him into acquiescence. She had not felt in the least aloof in his arms, only a sense of wonder and a burning curiosity to feel more of his kisses.

Perhaps that was why she had refused to acknowledge the subtle hints of familiarity in his voice and manner. A phantom suitor on horseback was much easier to manage than a flesh and blood man. Viscount Darlington had a reputation as both a difficult and contrary soul. Loving him would be . . .

Sabrina's eyes popped open. Love Lord Darlington? Preposterous! She did not love him. She was infatuated, yes, she could admit to that emotion. Even enthralled by the temptation he presented. And he would likely, before they were done, be her downfall.

She was not a fool. He would ruin her, break her heart, and leave her unfit for decent men and unsatisfied by the ardor of any man. A woman did not love such a man, she merely desired to dance before the wicked allure in his gaze.

And desire him she did.

Her body tingled everywhere they touched. She knew, with a womanly instinct of which she had not heretofore been aware, that lying with him would be as fiercely sweet as his kiss.

So then why should she not behave as the libertine Cousin Robert had often branded her? Her life as a lady was over. After the indiscretion of running away with a man this night, she would never again be received at court or ever again be invited to associate with the aristocracy.

Even dear sweet Lotte would be scandalized. But what did that matter? If her plan succeeded, she and Kit might well spend the rest of their lives an ocean away from their homeland. The only moments that were certain were these now, with her arms wrapped about the one man who had made her feel that odd sensation that more weak-willed women called love.

Oh, but she must not make that mistake. To pin her hopes on that easily vanquished hope that he might return her feelings would drive her mad. Better to admit to lust than to expire for a man who avowed that he did not know the meaning of the word love.

Yes! If the moment presented itself before their parting, she would take Jack Laughton as her lover. What better revenge against all her former stifled and ruled life than to lie for one night with the wild and unrepentant "Black Jack" of her dreams?

She wanted him and he must want her, too.

She pulled her arms from around his waist and then reached behind him and pushed her hands through the slashes fashioned at the back of a gentleman's coat and vest so that he could ride astride.

"My hands are cold," she said loudly enough for him to hear. He said nothing.

Once underneath, she pushed her hands forward until her fingertips met. How warm he was! The heat of his body was very like that she experienced when holding her hands to a fire. She had not known anyone could be so hot.

After a few moments more, she began flexing her fingers against the fabric of his lingerie shirt, as thin and fine as any lady's chemise. He jumped once, as though she tickled him, yet he did not order her to remove her hands. Chagrined by her own temerity, she pressed her face into the natural valley formed between his shoulder blades and began to slowly rub circles into his skin. She did not think too hard about what she was doing, as yet uncertain of what roused a man. She let instinct direct her, seeking what would amaze her if he chose to touch her in such a fashion.

The first tentative circles with her fingertips became a more general caress, sliding slowly up and down from the waistband of his breeches up his chest as far as the restriction of his coat and vest would allow. How smooth his skin felt beneath the thin lawn fabric of his shirt. Gathering determination from his lack of response, she found his lower ribs and slowly traced the curving lines of them to his sides and back.

He shivered once and then again, taut muscles dancing beneath her touch, then muttered something she could not understand. Perhaps it was just as well. Unless he stopped her by direct order she had no desire to abandon her design.

The rhythm of his breathing came a little faster now, as if he had walked a long distance when in fact it seemed they plodded along with all the speed of donkey cart. She smiled when he sucked in a quick breath as she pressed a finger into his belly button. She had forgotten until just this moment that he had been breathing heavily when he broke their last kiss. She had assumed at the time that, like her, he was trying to master emotions of anger and resentment and uncertainty. Now she wondered if, like she, he had been also attempting to subdue the desire that flooded him.

Her fingers tingled as she stroked him. The heat from him seemed to invade her own body, swirling through her, flushing her face and bosom and low down where her loins pressed against his buttocks.

Squirming in unconscious response to the feelings she had aroused within herself, she hugged him tighter and whispered, "Is it very much farther, my lord?"

"I devoutly hope not!" he bit out, sounding in a cold fury.

Disappointed, Sabrina tried to yank her hands free of his garments but she was hampered by the tangle of clothing.

Rather than tear his clothing, which she was certain would further infuriate him, she balled her hands into fists and hung grimly on. How could he be so unmoved when she felt as if she held the sun within her embrace?

Jack found he was shaking. Never in his life could he recall ever being more coldly furious or so thoroughly aroused. How could she know that her innocent playfulness was pushing him to the brink of madness? He could have ordered her stop, but to his consternation he had found himself helpless to do that. He had not wanted her to stop but to do more. He wanted to push her hands lower and direct her to unbutton his breeches, to take him in her hands.

He sucked in a deep breath as she rubbed her cheek along his back. If she did not stop soon he would lose command of his lust and abandon his noble plan to take her to a place of comfort and shelter and instead pull her from the saddle and take her in a ditch on the side of the road.

To have her so close, to feel the subtle pressure of her breasts against his back with every roll of his steed's gait was torture. To know that she all but embraced him while he could not even touch her except passively, inadvertently, helplessly, was a more powerful aphrodisiac than he had ever imagined.

Her hands tantalized him, her unconscious flexing a massage that made him ache to reach down and move those fascinating fingers to a more effective spot. Yet a new complication had arisen.

All his fine plans of seduction and abandonment had been given a new context. She was no longer simply a conquest for his amusement, a spoiled, pampered, proud daughter of the merchant class to be used and cast aside. She had become a very real and unique person for him, capable of selfless acts of chivalry and moments of courage he had not suspected. She had a brother whose life she hoped to save!

The devil confound it! It was a desperate desire doomed to failure. What could a girl and a sickly boy do to protect themselves, even if she were able to liberate him from her guardian's kin?

Worse yet, he was encouraging her in her folly by helping her escape Bath. Where would he take her? What would he do with her? Women wed every day where there was no feeling of tenderness. She would be a marchioness, her future and those of her children secure. What could he offer her but debauchery and certain doom?

He could not touch her. He could preserve her maidenhead and send her back to her fat, elderly bridegroom intact. That much of her innocence at least could be proven. Yet, he was very certain he was not that good a man.

He shifted in the saddle and then reached back to embrace her, his hand finding and cradling the small of her back. "There's a cottage just ahead. I think we've traveled far enough to be safe. Shall we retire for the night?"

"Oh yes," she whispered.

Poor child, he thought with a protective tenderness he seldom felt toward his victims. She would be asleep before she understood he had other plans for her. Or perhaps he was not as depraved as he thought. Only time and opportunity would tell.

Sabrina contained her excitement as he turned into the yard of the farmer's cottage. Did she have the nerve to follow through with her plan? Perhaps, if she succeeded and he liked her, he would take her to Scotland. She knew enough of the world to understand it would be a gamble, her body risked against his offer of continued aid.

Jack threw a leg over his horse's neck and slipped to the ground. Turning around, he lifted his arms. "Come here, sweeting."

Sabrina slid easily from the horse into his arms. He took her by the waist and eased her down. But as the horse danced away from them Sabrina realized that he continued to hold her off the ground. For a moment she stared into his eyes, mere liquid shadows in the darkness, and wondered what her future held.

"If you come in with me, sweeting, we will lie together this night. Is that your desire?"

She did want him. But she could not find the words to say that to this superbly confident soul. She felt the awful push of tears at the back of her eyes.

Jack felt the hard tremors coursing through her body as he held her close and understood better than she the enormity of the temptation he had placed before her. He slowly lowered her to the ground, drawing her in against him as he did so. "You do not need to answer, sweeting. Let your kiss answer for you."

He reached down and tilted her chin up. Anticipation shone in the dark depths of her gaze and he felt almost sorry for her. She was curious and yet desperately abashed by the desire that rendered her mute before the honesty of a declaration.

Sabrina gazed back at the reckless curve of his rare and beautiful smile caught in the stark starlight. That smile touched her like a little caress and made her feel less afraid and even more reckless. She knew there would never be another time. If she did not meet his challenge with courage she would forever after wonder and regret what she had missed by turning away.

In the end it was so simple because he stood before her, looking down at her with the gaze of desire she had never before welcomed on any other man's face. She laughed suddenly and pulled him to her. To lie with him this once would be worth the gamble.

His kiss caught her. The stark beauty of it was no stroke of the victor's blade but a balm upon her battered soul. Here is where she belonged, her heart sang, in this man's arms, with his lips warm and pliant upon her own.

She wrapped her arms about his neck and lifted up to

tiptoe, letting her quivering mouth answer in the words she could not speak.

After a long moment of hunger-fed kisses, he lifted his head and ran his thumb across her damp lower lip. "Come inside, where we may both be warm and linger over this matter of kisses until we are quite satisfied."

To her own surprise, she found her voice. "Yes."

He scooped her up without another word, walked the short distance to the cottage, and struck open the door with a boot kick. To her surprise a fire burned low in the hearth, breathing its accumulated warmth upon them as they entered.

"Oh, someone must be here," she said in dismay.

"No," he answered with authority as he marched into the center of the room. "I am very certain we are alone."

"How can that be?"

He put her down and turned her back to face him. "Because, sweeting, I am responsible for the fire."

Sabrina gazed up at him as his words sank in. He had prepared this place before she left Bath with him. Had he meant to come here alone . . . or had he expected to bring her along?

"Yes, for you."

Once again the enormity to what she was about to do washed over her and she turned away from him to study the contents as though she were being offered the cottage for purchase. There was a small table with two chairs. On the table stood a bottle of wine and two glasses.

"I am thirsty," she said automatically.

"Later."

He turned her a little by the shoulders until she faced the one item in the room that she had purposely not glanced at. In one corner stood an old-fashioned cabinet bed, its doors thrown open to reveal the turned-back bedding glowing faintly in the firelight. He was responsible for that, too, she supposed.

She turned back to him very slowly. She wanted this, she

reminded herself. Yet she was silent and still, unable to breathe as he carefully turned her to face him and drew her unresistingly to him so that they touched from chest to hip. She was shivering though the room was quite warm. He was smiling, but the time for words was past.

The night was dark and now very still. Her world was the man in whose arms she stood and then even that bit of the reality exploded under the incandescence of his kiss.

Caught up in the rapture of his kiss, she did not realize he had unbuttoned her coat until she felt his hands sliding along the sides of her breasts. She stepped back but, as if anticipating her reaction, he stepped with her, holding her close, and his mouth never left hers. His hands found the hooks of her waistband and began unfastening them. Within moments the heavy woolen skirt of her riding habit slipped to the floor. He lifted her free of it and then stripped her jacket from her arms.

As each garment fell, she stepped away from him, and each time he stepped up to her and drew her close to apply another assaulting kiss which made her feel light-headed and a little drowsy, almost as though he was plying her with wine. Finally she realized that he had waltzed her back to the bed.

Without the ribbons of the cage-like paniers to hamper him, he quickly unhooked her petticoats and she felt them drop like the weight of her respectability to her ankles. Finally she stood in only her corset and shift.

Daunted by his gaze, she reached up to shield from his sight the deep décolletage of her chemise that served her breasts up like oysters on the half-shell.

"Nay, sweeting. Allow me to look my full. For you are beautiful. You are meant to be admired."

He slipped off his greatcoat and jacket and left them where they fell on the floor. In rapid succession, he shed his waistcoat and then pulled his lingerie shirt over his head. Finally he stood before her in breeches and boots.

Then he came toward her again and enfolded her against him.

She had never been this close to a man before, never felt the heat of another living body against her skin. It was like sliding under his skin, being absorbed by his more physically powerful presence. She had seen him defy and demolish the self-possession of his tormentors at the Thames-side tavern. He was a duelist, a man capable of vanquishing his enemies without reluctance or remorse. She stood no chance against his indomitable will, applied upon her now as the most beguiling of enticements, his kiss.

Suddenly she wanted to hold apart from the next minutes, to hide within some small place inside herself, a place where even Jack Laughton could not reach.

But that was not to be. He applied small kisses to her nose and then her eyelids. He feathered strokes of his tongue over her cheekbones and under her closed lashes and then traced the outline of her mouth. All the while he slowly pressed and rubbed the length of his body along hers, a soothing and rousing rhythm that she began to imitate without conscious thought.

There was no surrender as he lifted her up into the high bed with its pristine sheets. There was no resistance in her as he pressed her gently back into the tick and then framed her shoulders with his hands as he lifted a heavy leg over her to capture her trembling knees within the embrace of his legs.

His smoothing hands chased goosebumps from over her upper arms as he bent his head and tasted the full curve of one breast. She gasped softly as his tongue left a slick trail that quickly turned cold in the night air.

Desperate for some modicum of control, she reached up to touch his hair. The thick texture of it shifted effortlessly through her fingers until her fingers flexed and held. He was real, as real as she, and equally vulnerable to passion. She curved her other arm up across his back as he plucked free her corset strings. The strong, smooth surface of his back pleased her. And then his mouth found the exposed tip of her breast and she forgot everything but the exquisite feeling of being with him.

"Yes," she whispered when he murmured something gruff and urgent against her neck as his hands moved beneath her shift.

"Sweet," he murmured when he found the soft, wet center of her. "You weep for me, sweeting," he whispered tenderly as he stroked her. "Promise to weep only for me."

His voice came to her as if from far away. This was no longer the cool and mocking Lord Darlington who had frozen her with his disdain and ridiculed her for her interest. This was a flesh and blood man who needed as much reassurance as she. At last she understood. They were not enemies in this moment, or even adversaries. For now, in this moment they were equals, he as much hers as she his, if only for this one night.

He slipped off the bed long enough to remove his boots and breeches and then he was again sliding over her, skin to skin.

"You were made for this," he whispered in her ear as he spread her reluctant thighs with a knee. "Let me show you how, Sabrina." His hands stilled upon her thoroughly warmed and willing body. "Please."

The question was so unexpected that she opened her eyes, staring up into his taut face. He knew as she did, even in her ignorance, that he could have taken her without protest or even unwillingness. Yet, at this moment of his greatest authority over her he had thought to give her back a bit of herself, and the right to decide her own fate. That realization broke open her heart.

She reached up and entwined her arms about his neck to draw his head down to hers. "Show me," she whispered softly into his ear. "Show me how to love you."

She clung to him now, mindlessly, recklessly, feeling a soaring, a spreading and beating of the invisible wings of freedom that had lain closed and curled against her so long she had begun to believe she had only imagined such joy.

When the too-full moment burst upon them, his groans of fulfillment and her cries of startled joy mingled in the night, enthralling them as their bodies discovered the answer to the question as old as time.

Too bad, she thought a little forlornly as the last updraft of ecstasy deserted her and she drifted earthward. Too bad that he was not the kind of man a woman could love. For if he was, she was very much afraid she would.

Jack replaced the cigar he had taken from the humidor above the mantel without lighting it. The lure of aromatic smoke had lost its enticement for him. More alluring was the taste of Sabrina that lingered on his tongue. His lips were still damp and warm from her mouth.

He turned back toward the bed where she lay sprawled in innocent, naked slumber. He had taken her fully, completely, heard her cries of surrender and wonder before succumbing to the shudder of his own release. Yet his body was only slightly more satisfied than before. One glance at her was enough to return the tightness at the base of his belly. Naked as well, he reached down to adjust the sudden fullness.

She had come to be his so trustingly, so willingly, touchingly eager to experience his embrace, deliciously flushed in her passion. He should have been pleased. He should have been congratulating himself on the success of the seduction. She had been every bit as lovely as he had suspected and much more passionate than he had dared hope. Her kisses . . .

His body betrayed his brain again, his sated flesh rising hard and proudly from his groin at the memory of her lips on his feverish skin. When was the last time a woman, not his own perpetual capacity for lust, had directed his arousal?

His revenge was complete, his task accomplished. His involvement with her, though she did not yet know it, must now end. To continue the liaison would go against all reason. Why then was he feeling this flood of doubt about what he was going to do next? Yet he did feel it.

From the moment he had first spied her in the depths of her coach on that moonlit highway, the suspicion that they were fated to be together, to come together like this, had frequented him. He could not explain it nor did he doubt it. No gambler worth the name ever doubted his intuition.

Was it possible that he had lost the heart to act on the final part of his plan, to rise and simply walk away from her?

He had never subscribed to the more chivalrous aspects of the gentleman's code of *amore.* A gentleman's obligation to be considerate, courteous, and gallant toward his conquests, protecting her sensibilities, honor, and person had seldom crossed his mind. As long as they obliged and pleased him, he tolerated the peculiarities of the females who spent fleeting days or weeks within the orbit of his life. He had never before been equally attracted to any of them after their first interlude as before it. Anticipation, like courting luck at the gaming table, was everything. Some knew more than others, all tried to please him and thereby ensnare him. Despite the variation in packaging, once unwrapped, women blended together in his mind as so many tits and cunnys.

Sabrina had not attempted to dazzle or impress him. She did not possess the predator's instinct for dominance. Her wondrous heartfelt responses had been as unstudied as the pleasure he had derived from pleasing her. That, too, astonished him. He was a selfish devil and he knew it. Yet without a word she had urged him to outdo himself with care and tenderness and the need to guard her sensibilities, even in the grip of his own lust. The need to be tender instead of master her was absolutely unique in his experience. And that was the most dangerous revelation of the night.

He came to the bed with silent footsteps. In winning her to his bed, he had exorcised no demons this night. He had loosed all the furies of hell and they wanted his soul as payment.

He could not leave her now, not until he felt that bargain between them had been satisfied. If that meant making a fool's errand of a journey to Scotland, then to Scotland he would go. What the gods offered he always took.

He reached for her again.

"You were there in the tavern along the Thames?"

"I was."

Sabrina stared at the patterns of the firelight upon the ceiling, determined to match his worldly *sang-froid.* Never mind that she was secretly appalled to be lying naked under the coverlet they shared. She had done many more bold things this night. The urge to tell him about their chance meeting at the alehouse seemed as good a demonstration of her nature as any other.

He turned on his side and propped his head with his hand. "Why did I not recognize you?"

Her expression was smug. "No one knew. I was dressed in the borrowed wig and breeches of a friend."

The surprise in his face was unexpectedly genuine. She had never before known his expression was capable of so many subtleties. "Dressed as a boy?"

"A young gentleman on the town," she corrected. "Lady Charlotte and I had thought it an amusing diversion. It did allow us to visit a rowdier side of life that ladies never know. I believe I liked it rather more than she." She offered him a coy glance. "Shall I sing for you the ditty which I committed to memory that night?"

"Certainly!"

When she had finished the bawdy tune he laughed and then sprang up and pounced on her, rolling over her and pressing her shoulders back against the bedding as he leaned over her. "By God, you are a women after my own design. You are as much an outlaw at heart as I!"

"I very much fear that I am," she replied in a contrite tone that did not match the wide smile of joy upon her face.

He frowned at her then and she wondered what she had done to erase his former joy.

"Never seek mercy or tenderness from me, Sabrina. This is all that I have to give you." He folded her hand over his rigid flesh. "For now that will be enough for both of us. But one day you will find, as most women do, that it is too little to hold you to me. When that times comes, remember that I warned you. Do you understand?"

She opened her mouth to say yes, but the truth came out instead. "No."

"Good. At least you are honest. Honesty is something I can promise you in return. One day soon you will understand what I tell you. And then you will hate me all the more because I predicted your pain. I suspect you will find, when your wounds have healed, in that integrity you prize so highly the ability to forgive me."

"Then why speak of it at all?"

"A chivalrous attempt to protect you, perhaps." There was a quiet assessment in his voice. "Do not expect me to always be so generous. I want you and I will have you as much and as often as I can manage. Are you frightened by that prospect?"

She looked at him and forced away the hurt his honesty caused. She had expected nothing else from him. Her hand tightened provocatively on his rigid flesh. "No."

Desire leapt in his eyes. "She-wolf! Do you present me a challenge?"

She smiled provocatively, too happy to be abashed by

the hand sliding upward between her thighs. "You tell me, my lord."

"Jack. For now and always in bed together, call me Jack, Sabrina." He leaned forward and encompassed a sweetly puckered nipple with his hot mouth.

Chapter Twenty One

Scotland, November, 1740

"All out for Crailing!" The postillion appeared as a mere bulky shadow through the mud-streaked window of the public coach. "Crailing! Five-minute stop!"

The coach from Hawick to Kelso in the heart of the Scottish border country had just drawn up at a wayside inn to water its horses. The pause offered a momentary respite from the continuous jolting and bouncing of the ill-sprung vehicle that creaked and groaned ominously with every jarring descent into a rut.

Desperate for that release, Sabrina pushed eagerly ahead of the other passengers to be first through the door when it was opened by the postillion. She ached in every part; her feet and hands, her spine and hips, even her teeth from the bone-jarring journey over what the Scottish laughingly called a highway. She was certain she could have covered on foot the same distance the coach had traveled this day over the all but impassable roads. Twice in as many days a wheel had broken in one of the damnable ruts, delaying the journey even more. While making repairs the driver had taken great delight in regaling them with tales of coaches whose axles had broken and of passengers who had been robbed by passing marauders and then left stranded for days without food or shelter. If he had thought to cheer his impatient and bedraggled travelers, he had failed miserably.

Since before dawn she and six other passengers had been wedged tightly in together. There was an Edinburgh merchant who, when he was not sucking on his pipe, shouted useless abuse at the coachman for mishandling his team. Occasionally he pulled from beneath his coat a vile-looking wedge of cheese riddled with mold and smelling suspiciously of his own body odor, which he pared and ate in great yellow curls, then belched for the next half hour.

The other passengers included a Calvinist minister, his wife, and three children, all of whose Lowland speech was so foreign, Sabrina had given up trying to understand their conversation. The two boys constantly tussled and argued among themselves until their father occasionally cuffed one or the other, exclaiming in a rough voice that they were, "Shilpit wee bauchles!" After every pause to water the horses, he would pull out his copy of *The Paraphrases* and begin what seemed an incessant lesson of reading and repetition. Until, finally, the deadly dull drone of his voice subdued even the boys' natural boisterousness and they slept.

A girl, aged four, had been sick for most of the journey, occasionally causing the coach to pause, but not always before she had relieved the contents of her sensitive stomach.

If that were not bad enough, the weather had changed these last hours from mild and sunny to wintry dreariness. The northern winds sweeping across the wild Scottish moorlands brought leaded clouds weeping frigid tears of sleet and rain. The penetrating wetness found every weakness in the coach's design and gradually dampened the interior.

A blast of that frozen rain greeted Sabrina as she descended into the blustery weather that had turned the afternoon to twilight and made of the stark countryside dark and misty shadows. The wind snatched at her cloak and raked her hood from her head, baring her hair and face to the biting damp. Drawing the damp wool back over her, she stepped rapidly to the rear of the coach in hopes of finding shelter.

All her high hopes of a week ago were now subdued by the sheer difficulty of the journey. The determination within her had tired until she was no longer certain what she had hoped to accomplish by coming to Scotland. The sheer daunting specter of traversing these roads with a sick brother had shaken her courage and belief in herself.

She did not look for Jack as she stamped the ground to try to bring the blood back into her half-numb feet. They had agreed to travel as strangers. To that end, he had opted for a seat outside, atop the coach. She wondered now if she might not have preferred that location herself, if only because she might then have burrowed beneath his coat and shared his warmth. No, that would have been foolhardy in the extreme. In a few short days he had come to represent a strength that she could ill afford to rely upon.

It amazed her, though she felt no shame in admitting in her thoughts, that she had become his mistress. It was only also to be expected that, in the deepest dark of night, wrapped in his sheltering arms, she had allowed herself to imagine that she was in love. He had offered his aid and protection, gone more than a step out of his way for her sake. How natural that she would confuse his indulgence with love. She was equally certain the feeling would not last—it must not, or it would destroy her.

Refusing even to give into the tempting weakness to look for his face among the other passengers, she gazed instead about the coaching yard. Though it was not yet dark, the lamp above the inn door was already lit. Heartened by that beacon of warmth and friendliness, she headed toward it.

"We do nae stop long here-aboots, Miss."

She turned to find the postillion had addressed her. "We dinna dare, what with reivers n' such, ye kin." With his hat pulled low and his muffler wound up to just under his nose, he looked very like a highwayman in disguise himself.

A great wave of weariness buffeted her. "But I must have pot of chocolate or I shall perish from the cold!"

"Then chocolate you shall have."

She turned about to find that Jack had come up behind her.

He smiled at her, and it was as bracing as the wind but infinitely more warm. "The lady wishes to warm herself by the inn hearth." He glanced at the ostler who had come from the barn bearing a pail of water in each hand for the team. "She is as much entitled to a drink as your horses."

Sabrina shook her head briskly, refusing to return his enchanting smile. "That is very kind of you, my lord, but I am fit for travel, I assure you."

But Jack, who saw her white face and bluish lips and the plea in her violet eyes that were the only vivid color in her face, knew she had been pushed enough for one day. He placed a hand on her shoulder before shouting up a question to the coachman who remained on his perch. "When is the next coach through?"

The driver's gaze shifted away from the Englishman's as he rubbed his chin. "I couldna say. No' for another week or more, mebbe."

Sabrina gripped his sleeve. "No, I am ready to go on. I can do it."

Jack squeezed her shoulder in warning. "I know, sweeting. But I am mortally weary and thoroughly drenched. Have mercy on a man."

She knew he lied. Even pinched from the cold, he looked as fit as he had the evening they had ridden out of Bath together. It was her chest that ached from the cold and her fingers that could not seem to function. She could not release his coat sleeve. Puzzled, she gazed down at her hand, which refused to follow her command, and then up again into his face. "I—I . . ."

Jack caught her as her knees buckled and swept her up into his arms. With calm efficiency, he turned to the postillion. "Put my bag and saddle down in the yard. I will be staying awhile."

The near frozen ground crunched under his feet as he made his way with his precious burden toward the entrance to the inn. The cold, unyielding ground was good for his mood. He was in a cold implacable fury, with himself. He, and no one else, was responsible for her collapse.

The sight of her, wan and weary beyond all imagining, had shocked him. Why had he not talked her out of this precipitous, ill-timed journey? He might have insisted upon time to rent a private coach, to provide them with foodstuffs and better, warmer clothing. Day by day she has grown thinner, the trek wearing her down like an oft-pared nib. What sort of man did so poorly by his mistress that she all but perished from lack of comfort and sustenance? A man whose brain had been addled by lust—that was answer. He had been afraid that in her stubbornness she would set off without him. To prevent their parting he would have agreed to a voyage to Shangri-La in a dinghy.

He had only to be near her for his body to grow tense and hot. That tension ran though him now, carrying her unresisting body in his arms. Odd that she had only to look at him to make him heavy and ready. And yet, inexplicably, her trusting gaze made him equally ready to protect her from every danger, even from his own hunger.

The sound of the coachman's whip did not at first penetrate Jack's blighted thoughts. But something in the driver's anxious shout to his horses and the sudden rumbling of the coach along the cobblestones of the yard made him swing about.

"Damn and blast!" The coachman had made off with his bag and saddle.

" 'Tis my fault. If I had not collapsed, it would not have happened." Sabrina glanced sideways at Jack over the rim of her cup of chocolate. His profile gave away nothing of his thoughts. "I am sorry."

"If you expect blame, you won't get it from me. But if you offer one more sniveling apology, I shall wallop you with joy. Now eat your ham. There's a good girl."

Jack's laconic tone underscored his anger, but it was directed at himself. For, along with his belongings, he had discovered upon entering the inn that he had also lost his purse.

"I should have known the lass from Coldstream was a bit too friendly," he had said with a polished sliver of a smile.

Though new to this game of posing mocking disinterest in what most concerned her, Sabrina refrained from asking what the Scottish woman had been doing so that Jack had not noticed her slipping his purse from his pocket. She suspected he would tell her, in great detail, and that she would not like the answer. Despite, or because of, his off-putting manner, certain women seemed to find the viscount irresistible.

I am now among them, she reflected miserably.

She sipped the warming, bittersweet beverage that had cost Jack his bag, saddle, and purse. She did not delude herself with the notion that thoughts of her occupied his jaded mind. The loss of his purse was of greater moment than her lost virtue. According to the world's reckoning, all that she now possessed of value was her pearls. Did she dare offer them to him?

"How shall we pay for our accommodations?"

"It does present a challenge." Jack eyed her speculatively as he lifted his glass of local brew the Scots called whiskey. "I don't suppose you play an instrument? Or dance?"

She shook her head. "I'm a miserable hand with a lute. I avoided lessons at the harpsichord like the plague. My voice is little better than passable."

"Nay, you sing well, as I recall." Some fleeting emotion passed through his expression; a hint of bemusement? "But 'tis Scotland. Bawdy ditties will likely bring down upon us the ire of the kirk." He paused to gaze significantly at her. "The tried and true will not do either, I suppose."

She looked away from his wicked expression. It contained his falsely persuasive, rickety-coach-to-hell smile meant to put an adversary at a disadvantage. "I still have my necklace."

"Keep it."

She wondered what he really expected of her. "Then what shall we do?"

That plaintive "we" tugged at Jack but he rejected the unaccustomed twinge of his conscience. Did she not realize that he had as many options at hand as he could imagine? As a peer of the realm, he might seek the residence of the nearest Scottish laird and expect to be welcomed as a guest with all customary honors.

Then there was the matter of the guineas tucked into the lining of his greatcoat. No seasoned traveler ever put all his coin in his purse. Gambling had been good in Bath. With his winnings he could purchase this inn and all it contained. Yet he was an adventurer at heart and the idea of buying his way out of trouble before he had wagered his wit against the odds struck him as unsporting.

"So then we must improvise," he mused aloud.

Seeking to do something useful, Sabrina signaled to the barmaid.

The girl came forward eagerly, though her bold gaze

and steady smile were aimed at Jack. "Aye, what be yer pleasure, sir?"

"I should like to how much further it is to the McDonnell's Tweeddale farm," Sabrina said in a peremptory voice.

The barmaid jerked as if Sabrina had poked her with a stick; her smile dissolved in the instant it took her to switch from a contemplation of Jack to her. "Ye were for tha' place?"

She looked Sabrina up and down with brisling hostility before spitting deliberately beside Sabrina's boot. "Tha' for the McDonnells!"

"That was enlightening." Jack's face showed the first glimmer of interest in their surroundings as the barmaid swaggered away.

He stood up and slowly unbuckled his belt and let his sword, concealed under his coat, slide to the floor. "Drink your chocolate, sweeting. I've a bit of conversing to do."

As he was about to move away, he glanced down sharply at Sabrina. "You do have your pistol?"

A rill of fear tiptoed up her spine. "Yes. Why?"

"Primed and ready?"

She felt for the butt of the weapon in the deep pocket of her riding skirt. Pleased to learn she knew how to handle a pistol, he had provided her with ball and powder for the trip. "It was, but the weather—"

He cut her off with lift of a single finger. "If I give the signal, aim it as though it will blow to kingdom come any soul within its sights."

As it happened, his injunction was far from necessary. Within minutes he had struck up a conversation with the men crowded round the wooden plank which served as a bar. Sabrina watched them very closely, her nerves pricked by the possibility of danger, and saw several of the men glance repeatedly at her and then guffaw in laugher.

It was nearly an hour later when Jack strolled back to

where she sat, the summit of his bronzed cheeks blushed by his liberal imbibing of the Gaelic *uisge beatha.*

His smile did not sit quite perfectly on his face, but he maintained his footing with a grace she suspected required a great deal of concentration. "Come with me. I've arranged for a room."

Sabrina rose from her chair, a doubtful expression on her face. He took her arm as they moved away from the table to the narrow stairs that led to the rooms on the upper floor, but it quickly became obvious that he was leaning on her for support as much as guidance.

"You are foxed," she whispered indignantly when he misstepped.

"Aye." The Gaelic inflexion rolled effortlessly off his tongue as they climbed the final steps. "And a lovely feeling it is, lass."

Thoroughly put out, she did not guard her tongue. "Well enough for you. But what am I to do once you've retired for the night?"

His smile wobbled in a most endearing manner as he lifted the latch on the door to their right. "Here I've gone to great lengths with no thought but your benefit. And, like a woman, you criticize me for it."

"Indeed?" Sabrina's brows lifted in exasperation as she stepped past him and over the threshold into the dark and cheerless room. "How is your being flummoxed of value to me?"

He stepped inside and caught her one elbow and, to her astonishment, tapped a finger of his other hand along the side of her nose. " 'Twould seem, sweeting, your nearest and dearest kin the McDonnells are in dispute with their neighbors."

"Why?"

"Last winter they called down the wrath of the Kirk upon the owner of this inn for trafficking in that exquisite elixir made by the illicit distillers who flourish about. The inn was fined severely and the owner drummed out of the church."

"Oh." She did not have to imagine what the ordeal had been like for the innkeeper. Cousin Robert had threatened her often enough with a similar fate, though she was not Calvinist.

She moved forward into the room, quickly finding a candle and tinderbox, and struck a light.

Because she was only human and the covert glances of the men at the bar continued to haunt her, she turned with candle in hand to ask, "What did you tell them about me?"

Jack sat heavily on the bed, which creaked ominously under his weight, an expression of self-satisfaction on his handsome face. "You would rather not know."

The candle flame trapped as a flash of silver mischief in his gaze confirmed in Sabrina's mind that he meant it. "I think I must insist."

He eyed her lazily. "I told them you are a highbred whore and that I'd bought you for an evening's pleasure."

"You what—?"

"And that you were so smitten with me that you've followed me from England, though I've not paid a cent to ride you since."

"That's a horrid, terrible thing . . . and just like you," she finished in exasperation.

Feeling every bit the despoiled virgin she was, Sabrina sank down beside him on the narrow bed. What had he told them except the truth? An ugly, only partially revealing truth, but in barest sketch not a lie.

"You're wrong." He gently touched her shoulder. " 'Tis not how I view you." By her expression he had exactly guessed her thoughts.

"You are no whore, sweeting. You've not the talent." He went on smoothly, despite her stricken expression. "You like the exercise far too much and you lack the cold-hearted instincts of a mercenary."

Sabrina gazed down into her lap, summoning her courage. "Then why did you tell those men such a tale?"

"Because it was a tale men like to hear. 'Tis every man's hope and fear that the woman who however innocently stirs his lust is every bit as debauched as his imagination can make her."

She looked at him. "Do you share this hope?"

He smiled at her almost regretfully as he slid an arm about her shoulders. "I know better than most that 'tis often the case. There lies in the heart of many a woman the soul of a rake."

Sabrina turned away from him. He would not make it easy for her. He had warned her. Do not look to him for mercy, he had said. She must not fault him for that honesty, even if it was painful. "So then," she said in a small voice, "what shall we do now?"

He pulled her gently toward him, pressing her back against his chest as he bent his head to drop a light kiss on the curve of her neck. "We will sleep until a knock upon the door beckons us to adventure."

She resisted the urge to relax and mold herself more fully against him. "What sort of adventure?"

He lifted her hair and kissed the sensitive place just behind her ear. "You wanted to free your brother, did you not?"

She twisted around to face him. "You have thought of something?"

"I hope, sweeting, that I have thought of everything."

Her thoughts went back to the men in the bar, their wolfishly eager, envious expressions now explained by his words. "Those men are going to help us?"

"They have agreed to help me."

The weight of that final word made her lift a brow. "Why are they willing to help you?"

"Because it seems the Scots have a particular fondness for thieves and marauders." He tightened his arms about her until her bosom was flattened against his coat front. "Especially those who steal the wives of the English."

Sabrina arched away from him. "But you told them I was a whore."

He shook his head slowly. "You are going to criticize my tale? I told them you were wed to an old pox-ridden peer. Left to your own devices, you were in the market for a lover. Enter I, who bought you at a private auction where, to appease your lustful appetite, your English husband sold you to the highest bidder for a night of pleasure."

He watched her jaw drop in astonishment. "No one would do such a thing."

Jack stared at her. Was it possible that she was unaware of the sexual highjinks among the more jaded of London's Beau Monde? If so, this was not the moment to enlighten her. "I have a clever mind."

"You have a vulgar mind."

"To be sure." He leaned forward and caught her mouth in the embrace of his lips. When she did not respond, he lifted his head, a mild reproach in his expression. "Would you like the hear the rest of my tale?"

"I don't know. Yes."

"Since you ran off with me, we must hide from your pursuing husband. To that end, I have come to Scotland to pursue my profession unhampered."

"What profession would that be?"

"Highwayman and kidnapper. A man with no great love of the self-righteous McDonnells, I've come to kidnap the heir to the McDonnell family fortune in the hopes of redeeming him for a fat ransom."

"You told them all that? You are a madman!"

"Mostly likely you are correct."

She raised her hands and pushed firmly against his chest. "You may have ruined everything. There may be those below who will warn the McDonnells of our presence."

"And lose their prize? I do not think so. In fact, I am

quite certain they are setting in motion at this very minute the plot we devised to free your brother."

A nasty suspicion entered her thoughts. "What prize did you offer them?"

He reached for her. "I have missed you, sweeting. Come let me warm us both most thoroughly."

Sabrina held him back with a hand. "If what you say is true, your new friends could knock upon the door at any moment."

He reached for the buttons of her jacket and pushed open the first two. "They know better. We have an hour, at the very least."

Sabrina fell back against the bedding with him, wondering if she were not being a fool. In succumbing to the thrumming pleasure of his touch, was she not accepting the very temptation she had promised herself she would resist? He was a dark-hearted and dangerous man, capable of all sorts of villainy. In her escapades in London she had merely played at mischief. He lived it. Yet she could not say what she thought was more at risk in lying here with him—her life or her heart.

At the end of the hour, she did know one thing more than before. She pitied all those men and women who had never lain in joy as they had just done, who had never loved with lightheartedness and without shame, who came together without imagination and tenderness, who did not know what it was to love so fiercely that for an hour nothing at all mattered of the past or future, or of anything else at all.

She would be grateful. When he was gone and the long barren rest of her life lay before her, she would hold to this moment and nothing else and be grateful. She had thought she risked only her virtue in lying with Jack. Now she knew better. She had wagered with her heart, and lost.

Chapter Twenty-Two

"You are certain this will work?" Sabrina whispered as she hung doggedly to the side of the rough-boarded pony cart in which she and Jack were riding.

Jack held his temper and repeated yet again what she already knew. "The McDonnells have gone to Kelso to bear witness against a man accused of witchcraft and consorting with the devil. 'Tis the Sabbath. They will not return before sunset."

Sabrina's shiver had nothing to do with the cold or the wee hours. It was difficult for her to believe that right and reasonable people still believed in witchcraft. Worse yet, some wretched soul's misfortune was making possible her own chance for happiness. How happenstance life was!

"Suppose they have taken Kit with them?"

"There's an ailing child left behind in the keeping of a maid."

"How do you know that?"

Jack swore under his breath. For a woman who had had very little to say while she lay sprawled under him in stunned ecstasy two hours ago, she had become a veritable magpie under the stars. It was nerves. He felt it, too, but he was accustomed to the tension that came before the moment of action. He would have done better to leave her behind if he had dared risk it.

" 'Tis Evan Lachland who told me. He is going to pay court to the McDonnell's maid and we are along for the ride."

"I see."

Sabrina considered how often love lay at the bottom of mischief and wondered how the McDonnell maid would fair if it were known she was consorting with one of the moonshiners her employees had sought to run out of business. Did strife and trouble trail every love affair? Were there no easy and pleasant couplings? Did there not exist anywhere gentle courtships and contented marriages? She glanced at the man by her side and doubted she would ever know the answer.

Ridiculous, romantic, foolish, delirious; all those appellations and more she attached to the emotion quaking through her. Jack Laughton was no ardent swain out to prove his love by slaying his lady's dragons. He was riding with her this night because it pleased him to cause mischief. When the amusement value of her plight paled for him he would be gone without a backward glance, perhaps without even a warning of his departure.

"You are shivering." Jack tried to pull her close but she pushed roughly out of his arms, unaccountably angry.

"I'm cold, 'tis all. Let me be!"

Sensing that nothing he could do at the moment would win her from her strange thoughts, he released her. He had trouble of his own to ponder. Stealing a child was one thing. Secreting him long enough to whisk him out of Scotland was another. And then what? She had not confided that element of the plot to him. And he had not pressed her.

Because I do not want to know.

He did not fault himself for a certain cowardliness where

her future plans were concerned. He did not figure into them, so why should they be of interest to him? Yet that was only a half-truth. He did not want to know because he did not want to have to think about the moment of their parting or wonder how she would fare after that. He did not want the burden of concern. He never worried about himself and the welfare of no one else had ever mattered to him. He held a certain fondness for Zuberi who, if he were following instructions, had returned to London to pack his things and close his London residence.

England had lost its dubious charm. When this interlude was done he would go back to the West Indies. There were land holdings there that he had never seen. Jack Laughton had been a reviled scion without means nor standing. Now that he had inherited the title of viscount, all that would change.

He had no taste for the life of a slave owner but he did fancy the life of a rich man. Perhaps he would become an importer/exporter—no! He would open the finest gambling establishment in Barbados!

He would grow rich very quickly. Despite all the centuries of hostility, the English, French, and Spanish who peopled the New World shared one common love, that of risking their wealth on the toss of a pair of dice or on the turn of a playing card. They would come to his salon for the thrill and cheerfully lose their riches to him. He would, of course, then be looked upon as a traitor by the aristocratic classes and regarded with jealous skepticism by his mercantile, middle-class neighbors.

Neighbors?

His thoughts shocked him. He had never before in his life planned his life beyond a fortnight. Roots had never interested him. Next he would imagine that he would prefer to lie nightly snuggled against the same warm woman smelling of perfume and their commingled essences rather than to continue to seek comfort with a different partner each night. Bah! If he did not get away soon to some diverting debauchery the alarming notion of matrimony would soon creep into his thoughts!

He crossed his arms and sighed in bewilderment. Scottish whiskey must have softened his brain.

Unaware of his troubled thoughts, Sabrina strained her eyes in hope of spying their destination. But the land did not yield its secrets easily. Under a midnight sky the dark land stretched interminably into the distance. No trees, no lane that she could decipher, no villages, nor even a cluster of cottages glowing within from their hearthside fires.

When the shape of the lone farmhouse appeared on the shallow vale of the surrounding countryside, it did so suddenly, appearing as forbidding as any witch's hut.

"We're ta' stop here," Evan said, bringing his donkey cart to a halt. "We walk the rest."

Jack helped Sabrina down and then held onto her hand when she would have rushed ahead. "We do not wish to announce ourselves," he whispered when he had drawn her close.

He was right, she knew, but Kit was so close.

Falling into step behind the young Scotsman, they followed at a distance of several yards. The lane was hard under her shoes, every sound of stone slipping and tumbling over stone as loud in her ears as the crack and snap of a roaring fire. They would be heard long before they reached the house. Roused by footsteps, would the McDonnells' servants come running or turn their dogs on the unexpected visitors? She clung to Jack's hand, uncaring that her vise-like grip betrayed her fears.

Evan reached the black bulk of the house first, slipping around the side toward the rear. She did not see a door open, but a sudden spill of yellow light into the yard betrayed its opening. Jack drew her into the deeper shadow at the side of the house and then turned his attention to the windows.

"What are you doing?" she whispered.

He wrapped a hand about her mouth and then released her to motion upward. When her eyes had adjusted she saw the subtlest smudge of light coming from an eave high above the ground.

"Kit's room," she whispered, again breaking the silence her eagerness. He had told her in an early letter that his bed was shoved into a tiny room under the attic eave of the house.

Jack moved quickly to the front of the house with her close as his shadow. When he boldly reached for the front door latch, she held her breath but it gave without resistance. With a smile back at her, he pushed it open and beckoned her ahead of him. She felt in her pocket for the pistol she had brought along. She had come this far. Nothing and no one would deny her access to Kit. The precaution proved unnecessary, for the room was empty.

She scarcely noticed the room through which she passed save to note its orderliness and the richness of the fabrics at the windows and covering the floor. The kirk believed in plain living, but the quality of the austerity depended upon the wealth of the faithful. Venetian glass winked at her from the cupboard and the dull gleam of silver candlesticks caught her attention as she headed for the narrow stairway that led upward.

She climbed the dark passage by feeling her way along the walls, bumping a picture frame with her shoulder. The steadying presence of Jack's hand at the small of her back kept her nerve strong as she climbed into that bleak gloom, that and the knowledge that somewhere within these walls Kit lay waiting for her.

Once on the landing she went more slowly. Even so, she stubbed her shoe tip on a table and would have tumbled forward had Jack not caught her from behind.

"The last door," she heard him murmur. She found the latch and lifted it. The door yawned wide on more darkness and then she saw another stairway, this one much steeper and narrower. The way to the attic, she realized, and began climbing by using hands and feet this time. Near the top she began to see a glow, the same glow she had seen from the outside.

She scrambled up the last few steps, uncaring that her boot steps rang on the uncarpeted wood. Kit was here. She could feel his presence.

The room, incredibly enough, seemed colder than the night beyond the narrow window. Burning peat behind a small grate gave the only light. The first and only thing she saw in its glow was the small figure lying inordinately still beneath the covers of the narrow cot tucked under the slanted roof.

She approached the bed slowly, fighting down panic. It was too dim to tell from the foot of the cot who lay there. The head of the cot was tucked into a shadow created by the slanting walls. The figure was covered to the chin, as if it were laid out for a burial.

She moved to the bedside and reached out her hand. She was not a coward. Even if it was Kit's corpse, she had to know. The thin blankets were damp to the touch but when she felt beneath them there was the rapid, shallow rise and fall of a chest.

"Kit?" she whispered, as if she were not certain she wanted him to hear her.

The shape twitched and uttered an inquiry in the unformed sound it made.

She reached up and slowly pulled back the cover, exposing the heartbreakingly familiar features of her brother. With a sob of joy, she knelt down on the floor beside him.

"Awake, dearest. I've come with a friend to take you away." She put her hand on his shoulder and shook him gently. "You must help me, Kit. Wake up."

The boy turned his head toward the sound of her voice, his features contorting in confusion. His lids flickered opened and he gazed blankly up at her with feverish blue eyes ringed by sickly smudges. Except for two bright spots of color that burned in his cheeks, he was alarmingly pale. "Who?" he whispered wonderingly.

She touched his cheek and felt the fire that fueled the unhealthy flush of his cheek. He was every bit as ill as she had feared. But she tucked the information away for a less critical moment. "Sabrina, Kit. Your sister."

A flicker of recognition entered his expression and his chapped lips quivered. "Is that really you, Bree?"

"Yes, Kit. No other." Sabrina reached for his hand and squeezed it. How weak he sounded. Yet he was rational enough to remember the nickname he had given her before he was old enough to pronounce her name properly.

"Did I not promise to come for you? I am here." She worriedly brushed a few silky strands of pale hair back from his damp brow. "We must hurry, love. Are you well enough to travel?"

"Oh yes!" He levered upright in the bed and flung his thin arms about her neck. "I knew you'd come. They said you wouldn't, Bree. But I knew you would!"

Sabrina bit her lip as she hugged his frail body to her own. He was much too thin. She could feel his ribs through his nightshirt. Dear God, she had arrived not a moment too soon.

A coughing spell came upon him suddenly, a retching dry hacking that shook Sabrina as she held his spasming body in her arms. By the time the fit ended he was damp with sweat and gasping for breath.

"It—its my lungs," he said hoarsely. "The co-cold. So co-cold."

Fighting back weak and useless tears, Sabrina gave him one more squeeze before lowering him back onto the cot. "Don't fret, Kit. I am here to care for you now. No one will separate us again, that I swear to you."

He smiled a thin crescent moon of a smile that she had almost forgotten. "You pro-promise?"

"Cross my heart and hope to die," she answered.

"You ca-came, Bree."

She did not trust her voice again. If she began to cry, Kit would think he was even more ill than he must suspect.

"Put this on him, and this and this." Jack tossed articles of clothing into the bed from a cupboard he had discovered on the far wall.

"That's too much," she protested when he tossed a third shirt her way.

His mouth set in a grim line. "We must travel a way tonight. I won't see him die of exposure. And be quick! I don't like what I'm hearing."

Sabrina stiffened. "What do you hear?"

"Silence."

The house was very still, she realized, as if it held its breath in anticipation of the consternation and fury their actions were about to cause. If it unnerved Jack, she reasoned, there must be cause for concern.

She picked up a piece of clothing but could not seem to make heads or tails of the threadbare piece.

"I can dress myself," Kit said with a return of some of his old spirit. He reached for the garment.

"You must conserve your strength," she countered with as much motherly stricture as she could muster. "You are ill."

Jack walked over and took the shirt from her hands. "Kit's no longer a babe, to be dressed by his sister. We'll deal better together." He lifted her to her feet and then pushed her gently toward the stairs "Why don't you see what you can find of value in the kitchen, then wait for us in the yard? Bread, cheese, water, wine. Something to sustain a man like Kit?"

To Sabrina's amazement he winked at her brother.

Kit looked up at the stranger with widened eyes. "Who—?"

"Your sister calls me Black Jack. We've been sharing an adventure."

Kit smiled wanly. "Bree always was one for adventures."

"Yes, she is a rather cocky wench." Jack's smile sobered and his tone sharpened as he turned to Sabrina. "We've very little time."

She understood at once that the too-still house troubled him. She reached out in the first uncalculated gesture she had ever made toward him outside of the rapture of their embraces and touched his arm. "Thank you."

She saw his silver eyes widen at her simple gesture, as if she had touched a place in him that all their intimate embraces had neglected. In that moment the façade of the supremely self-sufficient noble who required nothing and no one in his life slipped to reveal the lonely man haunted by his self-imposed exile from life.

He is more alone than I. That leap of awareness at this unexpected moment appalled her. She had carelessly uncovered his vulnerability and the thrill of it was equalled by her embarrassment. She turned and fled.

It took Jack several minutes to pull on and button up the boy in the sum total of his sartorial belongings. Many were little more than rags. His mouth was a grim line of anger by the time he was done. The rightful heir to a fortune, if his sister were to be believed, had been treated as a foundling.

When he was done, he wrapped the boy up in his bedding. Thinking little of the protection it gave, he stripped off his greatcoat and swung it about the boy. Then he picked him up and carried him like a babe in swaddling down the stairwell.

He was not surprised that Sabrina met him at the bottom of the first flight.

"I fear I stole rather a lot," she said, as she held up the cloth into which she had stuffed and tied her booty.

"Let us hope it will do," he said and headed down the hallway toward the main stairs.

The sound of something heavy falling jarred the silence below, halting them at the top of the stairs.

Jack turned and quickly forced Sabrina back down the hallway and up against the far wall into the shadows.

"Don't move."

She heard his whisper and then felt him shift Kit's weight to her before stepping away from them both.

She tightened an arm about her brother, who leaned against her but stood on his feet. Then she heard the faint sounds of footsteps below and moments later the creak of a stair under the heavy weight of a man's tread.

She pressed Kit behind her into the shallow recess of a doorway, too afraid to make a sound. Had the McDonnells returned unexpectedly? If so, why were they sneaking about like thieves? Or were they about to surprise the maid Evan had been entertaining?

Finally she saw them, two dark silhouettes against the gloom at the head of the dim hallway. They moved with the furtive unease of thieves and one carried a shuttered lantern. She glanced away into the shadows opposite where Jack had melted but could not find him. Then she saw the distinct flash of metal in the umbra and knew he had drawn his sword.

The intruders moved with clumsy unfamiliarity. The only reason she did not cry out from sheer anxiety was because she held Kit as well as her breath. She felt a convulsive shudder pass through him and knew Kit was trying to hold back his cough. She reached for the pistol she carried, gripped with agonizing fear for his safety as the lead man came toward. But Kit could not contain the seizure of his lungs. It burst forth from him in an explosive sound that startled both the intruders and Sabrina.

A hot-breathed curse erupted from the man nearest her as he swung the lantern up and pushed open the shutter. She cried out when the light splashed across her, momentarily blinding her.

"Got her!" she heard him cry gleefully.

She tried to wrench away from the man who grabbed her arm, but his grip was like an iron cuff. Hampered by the wrappings of blankets and coat, Kit could do nothing to help her as the man dragged her from the shadows.

Sabrina heard the swish of a blade cut the air and then the scream of surprised pain as Jack leapt from the shadows opposite onto his quarry's back.

A gruff curse hissed through the teeth of the man who held her and he dropped the lantern. As it hit the floor, it cast a harsh light upon the blade he had drawn. She heard soft grunting sounds as men grappled on the floor. The sounds of a fist meeting solid flesh came to her ears. She cursed with an unthinking savagery as she was wrenched forward and her arm twisted painfully behind her back as the man forced the cold bit of steel to her throat.

"Stand back or I'll slit her, I swear."

"No, don't hurt her!" Kit cried. Throwing off his bedding he launched his thin body at the man.

Sabrina felt the blade leave her throat and knew without thought what she was about to do. She still held the pistol in her free hand. She saw Jack leap up from the floor but she knew he would never be in time to save Kit. She lifted the weapon and fired into the man who held her.

She was freed as the man's fingers sprung open.

Jack grabbed and pushed her toward the stairwell. "Hurry!"

Sabrina did not need a second urging. Her only thought was to escape with Kit. She moved quickly to his side and put both arms about him.

But it was much too late for stealth. The dancing flicker from a lighted candle was rising up the stairwell.

A moment later the astounded faces of Evan and the McDonnell maid appeared above the edge of the landing.

Sabrina followed their gazes and a ripple of renewed apprehension flowed over her. The lantern's illumination spread over the inert forms of the two intruders. The one nearest her stared sightlessly up at the ceiling, a broad dark blotch oozing blood from the center of his chest. The second man was grunting and rolling from side to side. Stiffening, she looked away.

"What's going on?" demanded Evan, though the look on his face was far from guileless.

Jack's voice contained its usual aloof boredom. "If you do not unblock my path, Evan, you will receive a measure of the same."

He picked up his saber, allowing the candlelight to reflect its blooded length. He did not hold it aggressively but the evidence of its violent potential backed Evan and the maid down the stairs.

Jack's gaze went straight to Sabrina. "Are you all right? And Kit?"

Sabrina nodded yes to both. "I—I," she stammered, as angry with herself for showing her fear as for her inability to be of aid.

He smiled at her. "You were magnificent!"

Sabrina tried to hold on to the steadying influence of the arrogant amusement she saw in his face, but her world had been too badly tumbled. "You threw yourself upon those men without knowing whose battle you fought or why. You might have been killed!"

Jack wanted to pull her into his arms and kiss her for that accolade but there was no time. Nor did he deserve the praise. He knew it was his fault they were attacked and that only her quick thinking had prevented tragedy. When she had a steadier head and time to think, she would realize that, too.

For the first time in his life, he felt the watery-guts sensation of his own shortcomings. Because he did not know how to defend against that overwhelming inadequacy, he retreated into temper. "Hurry along. Leave Kit to me. For God's sake, mistress, don't forget the victuals!"

Offended and indignant, Sabrina snatched up the bundle she had liberated from the kitchen and hurried down the staircase once she saw Jack pick up Kit.

Because she had a temper too, and fear always lit its

wick, she marched up to the young maid conversing in subdued tones with her lover and said, "Tell your mistress that I came to claim my brother and that he will never again be needing her care." She paused, then added, "And, if I were you, I would not know the direction I took or the precise hour I came or even who was with me."

She glanced at Evan, who looked as guilty as any accused man. "Nor you, either. I don't believe any imagined tale of bravery you may think to weave will satisfy the family of the man who died tonight."

With that, she marched out of the McDonnell farm and into the night. And ever after she would wonder where she found the courage to do it.

The pace Jack adopted once they left the house struck every other thought from Sabrina's mind but the will to keep up. Even with Kit in his arms, he would have quickly outdistanced her had she not concentrated on matching her stride to his. Stones threatened to trip her while the rough grasses and bracken continually snagged at her skirts. The earlier rains had left pools in every low place. Within minutes she had stepped in so many puddles that the water seeped through her boots and dampened her stockings.

It took every ounce of attention to find her way along in the darkness lit only by the cheddar rind of a moon that was ending its journey through the sky. To the right the barest hint of dawn was beginning to smolder, but it would be hours before it lit their way. If not for the sight of Jack's back, an ever-receding lure before her, she would have given up the first half hour and collapsed on the cold bare ground.

But he did not slacken his pace or even pause to ask if she were all right. Gaining strength from her rage at him, she propelled herself along by muttering under her breath malevolent incantations.

"Damned preening cockerel!"

"Arrogant whoreson of a pox-ridden nanny goat!"

"May he develop a pustule blight on the buttocks of his pride!"

She invented ever more colorful invectives as she went along, some dredged up from every curse she had ever heard and some she made up for added spice. But finally, even her anger could not be sustained.

The wind had torn her hood from her head so many times that it eventually worked free the pins from her hair so that it streamed in a thick dark fall over her back and shoulders. Still Jack kept his pace out over the wide, wild moor. If he had a direction in mind she could not guess it. She could only plow along behind him in mindless toil until her lungs ached and her feet swelled inside her boots and all that was left in her miserable heart was the desire to do murder.

She had killed a man!

No, she could not think about that or she would fall down in the mire and howl like a banshee. She had saved Kit's life. That is what she had come to do. Now they must make complete their escape.

She did not know whether they walked an hour or two or ten. Jack paused only twice, to give a little wine and water to Kit when he began to cough, and then he was off again before Sabrina could properly catch her breath.

The sky seemed only marginally lighter than when they began when Jack suddenly paused before her, looking out over an escarpment of hills, the lower slopes of which were darted by dark humps she recognized as grazing sheep.

"Now what?" she demanded at length.

He glanced sharply down at her. "See the river? That would be the Tweed. We're for there."

She saw nothing, for she did not care to look. She simply followed him down the incline, too weary now to even complain.

A little while later they entered a small stand of trees

near an unseen yet noisily gushing stream. Jack walked over to the largest tree and lay Kit at its base, propping the boy's head and shoulders against the trunk. He had been asleep some while. Which was just as well. It did not seem he would be fit for walking anytime soon.

Sabrina staggered over to them and would have knelt if her knees had not given way. Instead she collapsed in a heap beside her brother.

"We will be declared outlaws," she muttered as she bent over her bother and felt his cheek.

"No doubt." Jack squatted down beside her, his voice surprisingly gentle.

She glanced resentfully at him through the rising mists from the river that refracted the dawn into an opalescent cocoon. "We will be hunted, a reward set upon our heads."

"A most likely occurrence." He reached out to pull her to him as he leaned back against the tree and stretched out his legs.

Sabrina held herself stiff as he rubbed his hands lazily up and down her arms. Her natural courage and anxiety-provoked bravado had long since been ground away. Now the weaker emotions of worry and fear began unraveling inside her. "If we are caught, all this will be for naught!"

"Most probably." How reasonable he sounded, and unconcerned.

She sat up and twisted around. "Then why are you smiling?"

He angled his head toward her. "Am I?"

"Yes!" She was still furious with him over his treatment of her in the aftermath of the struggle at the McDonnells.

He shrugged and leaned back, closing his eyes. "I am too weary to match wits with you just now, sweeting. Will you wait an hour?"

"No." Now that he was tired, she must rest? Contrarily, that was the very last thing she wanted at the moment. She poked him in the chest with a finger. "I want to know why those men turned against us. After all, you believed they would help us. "

He sighed. "I suppose I embellished my story rather too well."

"You mean they intended to kidnap Kit and claim the ransom for themselves?"

"Perhaps."

"A fine mess you've made of things!"

Jack opened his eyes and stared at her. Even ravaged by weariness and cold, her care-worn face with its stubborn chin and angry gaze seemed the most pleasant sight he could imagine. He would spare her the knowledge that the men who attacked them were more likely interested in raping her than in taking upon themselves the daunting task of extracting blackmail from the McDonnells. He could not say he blamed them. If he were not as mortally weary as she, tossing her skirts over her head would have been the thing uppermost in his own mind.

But she would think him crude and selfish and unfeeling. She had killed a man. He understood some of her feelings, but she, he knew, would not understand his.

Instead, he closed his eyes and dreamed of a world where the sun rose hard and strong and sultry.

Sabrina sat a long time watching the closed sleeping faces of the men who shared this tiny plot of ground with her. From a distance a nightjar churred from the bracken on the hills, its song a lonely desolate sound. Dear Kit, he seemed less labored in his breathing now. She had Jack to thank for that. As her gaze drifted from one cherished face to the other the thought struck her as a pain in her middle that she loved them both, differently but equally.

Jack had carried her sick brother for hours. Though thin, Kit was no babe. There had been no good reason for him to do that, except for her sake. He had known what she had not realized until they set out, that neither Lyndsey could have made it on his or her own. He had stayed with them, fought for them in a battle in which he had no part.

Now his life was at risk and she had only harsh words to hurl at him.

Feeling the need to make amends she moved closer to Jack and laid her head shyly on his chest. To her surprise, for she had thought him asleep, his arm came up and enfolded her to hold her against him.

"I killed a man," she said after a moment.

"He would have killed Kit," he answered and turned her face up to his.

Leaning forward he kissed her trembling mouth, which sighed under the touch of his. He could not make love to her here, he told himself. They had no privacy, no comfort. Her brother lay next to them. Yet his arms went about her and he drew her softness tight against his chest, and ground his pleasure in her into her lips.

A cough from Kit finally made her tense and pull back. Jack blessed the breaking of the passion between them, though the throbbing at the base of his belly proclaimed him a fool as he backed away from her.

When she had resettled her brother to her liking, Sabrina moved back to him and placed her head trustingly on his shoulder. Within seconds she was deeply asleep.

This time Jack lay awake a long time, pondering the immediate future opening out before him. Not only was he tied to a mistress with a sense of moral rectitude that exceeded his own sense of duty to himself, but now there was a sickly child into the bargain to further enrich his life. Oh, he had chosen well.

The sun had climbed a hand's span into the sky before he heard the sound he had been listening for. The jingle of harness bells, the crack of a coachman's whip, and the rhythmic pounding of horse hooves.

A quarter of an hour later, he had handed both his companions up into the warm dry interior of the southbound coach and dropped enough coins into the coachman's glove to see them all the way to Gretna Green.

Chapter Twenty-Three

Bath, December 1, 1740

Lotte sat before the blazing hearth with Sabrina's kitten curled snugly in her lap. The late autumn days had resolved themselves into ones of cold drizzle under slate skies. She had not gone out-of-doors in more than a fortnight and she could think of no good reason to do so today, of all days.

Today was the first anniversary of her marriage.

The occasion was a most painful reminder of the one fact she could no longer avoid. She was alone and very likely to remain that way. Ran was not going to come for her.

"I must go home," she murmured as she stroked the sleeping ball of fur.

The decision had been made weeks ago, shortly after Sabrina had disappeared with Jack Laughton. She knew then, there was nothing to be done but face the truth of her situation. She was going to have Ran's child.

Yet her resolve had yet to translate into the necessary

action required by her decision. Nothing would change a moment of the past or the reality of the present dilemma.

How to proceed? Should she write Ran, informing him of her imminent return? Or would it not be better to simply present herself to him and plead her case in person?

In a bitter moment of self-recognition she had to admit to herself that she was to blame for so much of the strife between them, certainly this last act of disaffection. She had blundered and blundered badly by running away. By then, the trouble between them was months old, straining the once impregnable bond between them. Now that she had had the time to think deeply and at length, she had come to the conclusion that while he had taken a mistress to spite her and make her jealous, she had failed miserably in her part as the wife. Perhaps, if she had remained to fight for his affection he would ultimately have returned to her.

Was it now too late?

Pride was a dangerous commodity, she was learning. The cost of maintaining it was higher than she had ever suspected. What had the struggle to preserve it cost her? Everything!

She lifted the kitten from her lap, rose to her feet and placed it on the warm seat she was deserting, and then crossed the room to her secretary. Two documents lay unfurled on top. The first was a diagram she had been working on for nearly two weeks. It contained her plans for remodeling the children's wing of her London residence into a nursery. Beside it lay the most feared legal document of the land: a will.

It represented the truth that she had faced shortly after Sabrina's departure, that she was pregnant and that it might end, as it had for her mother, in her own death.

For the next weeks she had drifted through her home like a ghost: silent, secretive, and infinitely sad. Fears of her own death had been uppermost in her mind. And then last evening a remarkable thing had occurred. As she lay in bed paging though the local gazette in hopes of distracting herself from thoughts of her early demise, a vague tremble in her lower belly caught her by surprise. At first she thought she must be mistaken. Then she wondered if the broiled lamb chop she had consumed at supper might be the culprit. Finally she felt it a third time, unmistakably, a movement as light as butterfly wings.

Though she had heard Lady Henrietta, who birthed a child a year as regularly as a brood mare, speak of "the quickening" she had never considered that she might experience such a thing. Yet before rising this morning, she had felt again that mysterious stirring of life.

Lotte lowered a hand to her belly and pressed lightly, smiling in dreamy delight. Though she had been forced to loosen her corset strings, no casual observer would yet notice what she knew to be true. Those subtle little flutters were tangible evidence that she carried another life within.

The morbid whims that had preoccupied her for months had suddenly vanished before a more substantial realization. She would soon have a child to rear and she did not trust anyone with the job, certainty no straw-haired mistress!

"Lady Henrietta has survived six lying-ins," Lotte mused thoughtfully aloud. "And Ran has often said she has no more wits than a milch cow. Certainly then I, whom Ran once accounted prodigiously clever, can master the trick of remaining alive while giving birth."

This new life depended upon her well-being, and her well-being depended upon her close proximity to the man she loved.

She reached over and pulled the servant's bell. She would leave for London immediately. To waste even another day would be foolhardy. First she would set about winning back Ran's affections and then she would find a method to oust her usurper! After all, she was the wife! And soon she would be the mother of Ran's child.

She reached out and lifted the will from the desk and then tore it neatly in half. She would not need it, after all.

"I shall need a new dressing gown of emerald green, Ran's favorite color." She smiled a secret smile that added smoky depths to her eyes as a flush of carnal desire swept over her. It had been long time since she lay secure and happy in his strong protective arms. Much too long.

London, December 1, 1740

Ran stood with one foot braced against the brass fender of his library fireplace and stared into the flames of the blazing hearth. Beside him, his mastiff lay sleeping on the heat-warmed slate. Bleak, mist-enshrouded London was all but deserted in December as hunting parties and house parties heralding the approach of the holidays drew the inhabitants to their pastoral residences. Half a dozen invitations had arrived for the present weekend alone, yet he could not think of a single good reason to accept them at this of all times.

Today was the first anniversary of his marriage.

The occasion was a most painful reminder of the one fact he could no longer avoid. He was alone and very likely to remain that way. Lotte was not going to come home.

"I must do this," he muttered as he beat a fist softly against the marble mantel.

The decision had been made weeks ago, shortly after he had seen Lotte in the arms of Jack Laughton. By the time he had ridden back to London he knew that there was nothing to be done but face the truth of his situation. He had lost Lotte to another.

Yet his resolve had yet to translate into the necessary action required by his decision. It was useless to put it off, foolish, in fact. Nothing would change a moment of the past or the reality of the present dilemma.

How to proceed? Should he write Lotte, informing her

of his decision? Or would it not be better to simply present the document to her through a messenger rather than risk the inevitable scene that was certain to follow when she read it?

As much as it grieved him, he could admit it now. He was to blame for so much of the strife between them, certainly the last act of disaffection. He had blundered and blundered badly in allowing her to run away. Perhaps if he had gone after her at once—no, the trouble between them was months' old by then. She was right. He had taken a mistress to spite her and make her jealous, and had failed miserably in the enterprise. Perhaps, if he had listened to her and apologized she would have remained in town where he could have fought to regain her affection and she would ultimately have remained with him.

Now it was much too late.

Pride was a dangerous commodity, he was learning. The cost of maintaining it was higher than he had ever suspected. What had the struggle to preserve it cost him? Everything!

He lifted his foot from the fender and turned to cross the room to his desk. The document lying unfurled on top had been delivered two days ago. He had yet to sign it. It was the most scandal-making legal document of the land: a divorce decree.

It represented the truth that he had faced shortly after his return to London, that Lotte was lost to him and that their marriage might as well end.

For the past weeks he had stalked about London like a wounded bear: belligerent toward his adversaries at Whitehall, short-tempered even to his colleagues, and infinitely sad when left to his own devices. He had drunk enough to be named a sot, had he not had a head as hard as his will.

Fears of his wife's desertion becoming part of the Beau Monde rumor mill had been the uppermost in his mind. He knew of men who suffered in silence their wives' peccadilloes, in the hopes that the women would tire of their lovers and return home. But he was not such a man. He could not grind his teeth and pretend that it did him no injury that another man shared his wife's affections and body. There was only one remedy for it. He must file for divorce.

For two weeks the document had lain like an omen of disaster upon his desk. And then last night a remarkable thing had occurred. As he sat at his desk, poring over bills that his party hoped to introduce in the next session of Parliament, a visitor had been announced. Ordinarily, he did not receive unexpected guests, but the name of his guest caused him to rescind his rule.

Millpost had come to call. What could possibly have brought the gossiper to his door—except news about Lotte?

A quarter hour later, he knew. Darlington was back in town. Moreover, he was not alone!

Millpost had come to convey his latest *on dit* to Lotte, who Ran announced was still away taking the air in the country.

Unsatisfied to leave without imparting his scandal, the baron had offered his juicy bit to Ran.

"Rumor, though I know you do not indulge in thuch things," Millpost had lisped maliciously, "whispers about how the licentious viscount hath brought back with him a new mithtress. Thome thay he ith tho jealous of her that he will not allow her out of hith rethidence. Do you thuppose, ith her appeal tho great, that he dare not trust other men with even a glimpse of her?" His pale eyes had gleamed with salacious delight. "Fenwell ith recently back from Bath where he thwears Darlington attempted to path off a mythterious ebony-trethed beauty ath hith West Indian thithter-in-law! One mutht give him points for invention. He hath no brothers! We are all agog. Thoth island women are thaid to be prodigiously proficient in the amatory arts!"

So! Darlington had thrown over Lotte that quickly. Ran picked up the document and stared at the royal seal and ribbons attached near the bottom. Lotte was jilted! Darlington had never been known for the length of his liaisons, only the number. Now Lotte could be counted among them.

He stared at the names he had filled in and the blank space where the reason for the petition had yet to be written.

He should be pleased by this turn of events. The tryst was over before any of their set had become aware of it. He should be gloating at her comeuppance. By a few strokes of a pen he could make public her shame and salve his pride at the same time by the declaration of divorce. He should be pleased, he should be relieved, he should be triumphant . . . but he was not.

"Poor silly Lotte," he murmured as he returned to a contemplation of the degree. He would have ample grounds now to divorce her and leave her penniless. If she thought she could come back to him, contrite and on her knees, he would not—

No, that was as a lie. In the wee hours of every night of the last two months he had lain awake in his bed aware of a truth he had tried to deny, that he loved Lotte with every fiber of his being and always would. The affectiveness of his political life depended upon clear-headedness, and his well-being depended upon his close proximity to the woman he loved.

He could not let her go. He could not simply walk away from his feelings. She would be humble now, see the error of her ways, or would she be so ashamed that she would never come back?

He reached over and pulled the servant's bell. He would leave for Bath immediately. To waste even another day would be foolhardy. First he would bring her home and then he would set about winning back her affections and finally he would find a method to forgive her for her indiscretion. After all, she was still his wife! And, despite all, he still wanted her to be the mother of his child.

He reached for the top of the decree and then tore it neatly in half. He would not need it, after all.

"I shall soon be with you again, Lotte." He smiled the bold reckless smile of a conquerer who could afford to indulge in a rare show of mercy to a truly repentant and vanquished adversary. That thought added smoky depths to his dark eyes as the heat of carnal desire swept him. He had not bedded a woman in months, not since his last night with Lotte. That was a long time. Much too long!

Chapter Twenty-Four

London, December 3, 1740

"I'm feeling better, Bree, honest I am."

The scowl deepened on Kit's face as his sister continued to tuck a blanket around his legs. "What good is getting out of bed if I must sit on a moldy old chair?"

" 'Tis a very nice chair," Sabrina responded automatically and finished her last tuck. "You may sit here by the window for an hour and watch the carriages pass by."

" 'Tis not the same as going out to see them," he mumbled. "For all I am allowed to see of London I may as well be in his lordship's attic."

"Darlington House is so splendid I'm certain even the viscount's attic is spacious and warm. As it is, we must consider ourselves his honored guests."

"I'd feel more honored if I were allowed to go freely about."

Sabrina straightened and smiled at her brother. "You are better. I'm very glad for it. But you cannot expect me to allow you run amuck just when you are on the mend. Now eat your bowl of porridge."

Kit wrinkled his nose at the steaming bowl set on a tray in his lap. He glanced up at his sister with a guileful appeal in his wide blue eyes. "I'd so rather have a chop and pudding."

"Perhaps tomorrow, if you eat your porridge today."

The sulk returned to his young face along with a gaze of reproach. "You were never so strict with me before."

Sabrina laughed and tousled his hair. "That's all you know. I've always been quite an ogre. Just ask Lord Darlington."

"She is correct. Your sister is a veritable tartar."

Both Lyndseys looked toward the open doorway to find the subject of their conversation standing there.

Sabrina pulled at her bodice and then put a hand to her hair because she knew it was in mad disorder. She was sweaty and damp with the sleeves of her bodice rolled and her skirts showing dark wet streaks. How infuriating and embarrassing that he had come upon them just as she had finished bathing Kit. It had been a lively affair. Now that he was feeling better her brother had been quite mischievous, laughing and splashing water and pelting her with his sponge. In brief, she was nothing short of disgraceful.

Darlington, on the other hand, looked quite splendid. He wore a dark red fitted coat with wide skirts and brocaded cuffs, cream breeches, white silk stockings, and black shoes. The tricorner he carried under his left arm was embellished with the same brocade as his cuffs. A frill down the front of his shirt replaced the more formal lace cravat of eveningwear. His own unpowdered hair was curled above his ears and tied back in a queue. He looked wickedly handsome while she felt every inch a dowd.

"You are going out, my lord?"

"As usual," he answered carefully.

"I wish you joy of it," she answered lightly but turned quickly back to Kit, who looked a bit forlorn. "We will make our own fun. I shall bring out the chessboard and we will play until you are drowsy."

Beneath his flaxen bangs Kit's expression was belligerent. "I don't want to play chess. I want to get up and go out and see London." He turned a conspiratorial gaze on the viscount. "Lord Darlington has promised to show me his horses and even take me for a ride in Rotten Row."

Sabrina knew she should be grateful that her brother was hearty enough to be difficult but she was feeling quite contrary as well, though it had nothing to do with him and everything to do with the gentleman on whom she had ungraciously turned her back.

She folded her arms but kept her voice even. "We must not tax his lordship's hospitality to any greater degree than we already have."

" 'Tis no hardship." Jack approached the bed, pleased to see that while Kit was still too thin, the unhealthy pallor had left his cheeks. The boy's lopsided smile of greeting was all cockiness and charm. "Kit and I have had several discussions these last weeks about the sights of London."

"He's promised to take me to the menagerie." Kit looked eagerly from his sister to the viscount. "You did promise."

"I did," Jack agreed. "Perhaps your sister will favor us with her presence as well."

" 'Tis December," Sabrina countered, growing more peevish with every moment. "The days are chill and Kit can ill afford another fever."

"You spoil everything!" Kit crossed his arms and subsided into a sulk.

Sabrina gave up her efforts to placate him, for this was clearly not a battle she could win at the moment. She smoothed her damp skirts out of habit rather than of any effect it might have. "I must go and see to my own dinner and then I promise I will come back. If you do not wish to play chess then I will read to you."

"I am tired of books!" Kit turned his face away toward

the window to hide the fact that his chin had begun to wobble.

"Very well, you shall chose what we do when I return."

How quickly spirit reasserts itself, she mused as she turned to leave the room. On the one hand, she could applaud his show of temper. On the other, it had begun to weary her and make her fractious.

During the first week of their journey back to England, Kit had started or cringed at every new sight and sound. He had not been easily frightened as a small child but his experiences in the McDonnell household had all but crushed his spirit. Jack had insisted they stop awhile in Gretna Green in order that Kit might gain back his strength. He had even sent all the way to Edinburgh for a physician to treat the boy. The doctor was quick to point out that while Kit had a predisposition to weak lungs there was nothing essentially wrong with him that could not be righted by proper rest and nourishment. He was right. Once the fever had passed and the congestion in his lungs had eased, Kit had bounced back quick enough. Now three weeks after being reunited, they were in London, the very last place she ever thought they would be.

She was surprised when a hand caught her by the elbow to detain her.

"I should like a word with you." Jack's tone was clipped and impartial, yet it made her heart quicken.

"Of course." She said it automatically, without even looking up at him. "If you will but allow me to freshen up first."

"There is no time."

She did look at him then and saw in his aloof expression the aristocratic presumption that she would alter her wishes to conform to his.

She supposed this reminder of their differences in rank should have wounded her pride but she was much too weary to care. "Very well."

He indicated that she was to go before him and then followed her to the small salon at the end of the hall.

Lines of consternation informed Jack's expression as he followed her petite figure down the hallway. Her disarray did not disturb him but he was appalled by her appearance. He knew she had had very little sleep during the past three weeks and had never spent a single night in any of the beds at the coaching inns he had provided for her. She had kept a constant vigil by her brother's side, sleeping with her head on his mattress when she could no longer remain awake. Now that they were back in London nearly a week, and despite the fact that Kit was plainly on the mend, she continued her regimen. In short, her life had shrunk to the size of a bedchamber.

His thoughtful frown deepened as his gaze remained on her. Her usually lively step was sluggish. There was not an ounce of provocation in the movement of her hips. Even the hair tumbling from its pins had lost its deep blue-black gloss. Kit might be on the mend, but his sister was very close to making herself ill. He missed the heated words they had often shared and, more than that, their heated embraces.

His golden brows lowered ominously over his silver eyes. This abuse of her beauty annoyed and angered him. She was needlessly punishing herself.

He had not forgotten her stricken look of horror in the moments after she shot the intruder. It had haunted him as surely as the act haunted her. If he had been a fraction quicker or chosen the other man as his first target, she would not now be wrestling with her conscience over a life he would have taken without a second thought. He suspected she was attempting to make amends through her devotion to her brother, and by freezing him out.

A rare tender smile touched his lips. She was, for all her natural wantonness in his arms, a traditional girl at heart. Perhaps she thought they had sinned together. And, of course they had, delicious, delectable sinning that had only to be recalled to have him standing in his breeches. That full swelling spurred his thoughts.

They had shared few private and certainly no passionate moments since her brother joined them. He was unaccustomed to celibacy and eager to end what he considered to be an unnatural state for both of them. She was meant to be in his bed, naked and flushed from his attentions. It was time she remembered it.

When she halted a few steps inside the room and turned to him, he said without preamble, "How are you?"

"Perfectly fine, thank you." It sounded like the lie it was.

He walked up and put a hand to her chin. She was as pale as her brother, and nearly as thin. There were dark circles under both eyes and her lush mouth had lost its rosiness.

"You look dreadful," he replied dryly.

Her black lashes fluttered down over her violet eyes as if in great fatigue. Yes, my lord."

The humble reply disappointed him. This new subdued Sabrina annoyed him. "Come, sweeting. Have you no better barb?"

When she did not answer, he released her chin and took a step away, offended. "Is there something I have or have not done to please you?"

She looked across at him with surprise. "No. How could there be? You have done so much more than I could ever have hoped for, nay, dared ask of you. It is my one regret that I have no way to repay you."

"Have I asked for repayment?" His voice crackled with affronted pride.

"I did not mean to suggest—"

"God above, Sabrina!" Jack checked his next words. He never shouted, never raised his voice to women. There had never been any cause. They all knew better than to rouse his wrath. Yet Sabrina Lyndsey bedeviled him as no other woman ever had.

He touched a hand to his brow. " 'Tis clear I've ill-timed this conversation. You are exhausted and I am late for an—"

"Assignation?"

He glanced sharply at her. "An appointment," he finished mildly. So that was where her thoughts lay. She believed he was off to see another woman. Jealousy was an emotion he understood. If she were jealous, it meant she still cared. The anger died out of him. "I shall return for supper. I expect that you will join me." His gaze ran meaningfully over her attire. " 'Twill be a private evening." He started for the entrance, calling over his shoulder, "Do not be late."

"One matter, my lord."

He stopped short, biting off a nasty comment about her reversion to the formal "my lord." Before the night was finished he would have her singing his name in ecstasy. "Yes, what it is?"

Sabrina clasped her hands tightly together, braced for renewed hostilities. "You must not make promises to Kit that you shall not be able to keep."

His expression did not change but for the marked lift of one golden brow. "What makes you think I do not intend to honor my promises to Kit?"

"We are in hiding, my lord, though the matter seems to have slipped your mind."

"Not a bit."

That had been the bargain between them: if she came with him to London so that Kit could fully recover, no one must ever learn her whereabouts. She had not even dared write Lotte with the news of her success. Only when they were away from England would she feel safe.

"It is all very well for you to go about London. After all, no one would think to connect us."

Jack said nothing, though there was one person, Lotte, who knew exactly the nature of the connection between them. Nor did he think it politic to tell her that handbills were now circulating through London with the news that "The Lyndsey Woolen Heiress" had been kidnapped by the "Infamous Highwayman 'Black Jack' Law" and that a hefty ransom was being offered by her guardian for his capture. A month ago she might have shared his amusement that a price had been set on his head. Now he feared she would bolt.

Unaware of his thoughts, Sabrina continued with her own.

"I am certain the McDonnells will have informed my guardian by now that I have taken Kit. We cannot, therefore, so much as set foot outside your door for fear someone will recognize me and inform my cousin that we are in London. Therefore, no matter how kind your intentions, promises to take Kit abroad in London are wrong."

"You are perfectly right." His voice was again coolly polite. "Does that satisfy you?"

Sabrina blushed. "I know I may seem difficult, but it is only that Kit has not had much joy in his life. I do not want anything ever again to make him despondent."

"No further disappointments?"

"Yes." She looked away from him. "It is often better to have no hope than to have one's hopes raised by whim and thwarted."

He doubted she was still talking about her brother but he let it pass. "Very well, then I will bid you a good afternoon.

"You are gambling this afternoon?"

"No." He knew he could have eased her trepidation and salved her curiosity by telling her he was going to a shipping office, but some spur to devilment held him back. Thwarted hopes, she had called them. He would soon put to rest her unhappiness and cheer himself considerably into the bargain.

He left quickly and Sabrina did not try to stop him. In fact, but for one matter, she might have been perfectly content to remain forever in the viscount's lovely London house. The one matter, unfortunately, was the continued presence of the owner.

She hurried to the window to watch as he left the house. He descended the steps and then strolled off in the direction of Pall Mall, looking every bit a rakish member of the Beau Monde off for an afternoon's assignation.

Her heart gave an odd lurch.

He had told her shortly before their arrival in town that he would not stay in London and that she might therefore remain in safety and at her leisure in his home. Yet a week had passed and he had shown no inclination to depart. That might have seemed a promising sign had the case between them been other than it was.

When he had disappeared from view, Sabrina let the curtain fall closed. For all the attention he had shown her since that harrowing night in Scotland, she might as well be Kit. He had not even kissed her since they arrived in London. Their affair was at an end. He had not told her so but she doubted he ever explained himself to his mistresses. So why did he remain, his presence a tormenting, tantalizing reminder of all that she had lost and could never recover?

"Because this is his home and London his realm. He may do exactly as he chooses with whom he chooses," she said bitterly to the empty room.

With whom he chooses.

She did not know the women who now occupied his mind and his body, nor did she care to guess. He had once told her she did not have the disposition of a whore. At the time she had thought it a compliment. Now she was not so certain it was not a lack he found unfortunate.

Perhaps he had refrained from mentioning his current mistress out of consideration for her feelings, but that did not make it any less difficult for her to deal with the fact that he had deserted her bed.

She had lost him.

The pain that she had been carrying around inside her like the dull throbbing of a sore tooth erupted. She let it wash over her this one last time, let tears form in her eyes and run unchecked down her cheeks.

For several minutes the only sounds in the room were her sobs, and the intermittent hum of servants' voices too far away to be deciphered.

She did not hear the stealthy footsteps of Zuberi who soon stood just beyond the door, watching and listening in perfect sympathy with her. He too mourned a loss. Lord Darlington's order to leave Alvy behind in Bath had pained him greatly. He had pledged himself to the viscount and a pledge was not a matter for revision. Yet there were things the viscount could not order to his liking, like the sympathy of another's heart.

Eventually Sabrina took a deep bracing breath and stripped the bitter moisture of tears from her cheeks with both hands.

"Tears are all very fine but they don't earn a wage," her father, ever a practical man, would say when, as a child, she lamented a matter she could not alter.

She held no hard feelings for Jack. He had been more than good to her. He had been a true savior where Kit was concerned. But she could not go on hiding in shadows, waiting for the impossible.

She had heard about a place where friends of Countess Lovelace went when they needed to pawn their jewels. As soon as Kit was abed for his afternoon nap, she would go there and make her own arrangements for the purchase of her pearl necklace.

Sabrina moved away from the window, her lips compressed to still their trembling. She had been warned that Jack Laughton possessed a devastating charm. To be fair he had even warned her against loving him. She thought she had listened and heeded him. Now she knew the truth. She had made a most foolish mistake at the start. She thought her wager with the viscount had been for her virtue and reputation. Now she knew she had gambled with her heart, and lost. All she had left was a very little pride, and if she had any sense of self-preservation, she would leave, and quickly.

Chapter Twenty-Five

"Can you do no better?" Sabrina sat in the cramped space of the pawn brokerage while the owner peered at her necklace under the light of a candlestick fitted with a copper fender that amplified its flame. "This is a very rare piece."

"I see that, miss, but I am a pawnbroker not a jeweler. My clients more often recover their pieces when their fortunes rebound." The elderly man smiled slyly at her, revealing one front tooth in his lower jaw. "You will doubtless find it easy enough to persuade your next beau to redeem the baubles of the last."

Sabrina was past being put to the blush by insinuations of her supposed licentious life. Of more concern was the paltry sum he had offered in exchange for her only valuable. Whatever money she received in exchange for her pearls would have to last Kit and her for the foreseeable future. "Very well, I will try elsewhere."

She rose abruptly and held out her hand.

"There, there now, miss," the man responded, holding the necklace more tightly. "Don't fly away on me." He waved her back into her chair. When she was reseated he bent a hard look upon her. "They ain't stolen?"

"Of course not. My father gave them to me."

"Of course," he murmured cynically. "Of course."

He ran the strands between his gnarled fingers again and then rubbed them along the top row of his teeth, of which he had three. "They're real enough. Not one of them paste."

Sabrina held her tongue, but out of sight in her lap her hands were knotted into fists. Now he thought her a thief and cheat!

"You are certain you will not want to redeem them?"

"You may sell them at whatever price you choose, provided you sufficiently compensate me at present."

He crooked his head. "Two hundred pounds."

"Five," she countered implacably.

"Three."

"Four."

"Done."

"Guineas," she added with a small smile.

He frowned at her here, as though suspicious still of her real intentions. "I will need time to collect so large a sum. He brushed a caress over the strands lying across the back of his hand. "You must come back in a few days."

"I must have my money now for I am leaving London in the morning."

He squinted at her. "Why the rush?"

She stood up a second time and silently held out her hand.

"Now, now," he nattered, "I will see what I can do." He rose with arthritic stiffness from his chair, pulling his shawl more closely about his curving shoulders and tottered away, calling back over his shoulder, "You wait right here."

The moment he disappeared the bell mounted over the door tinkled as two more customers entered, a tall gaunt gentleman in greatcoat and muffler wound round his neck and a fashionably dressed lady who was openly weeping.

"I simply don't see how I can possibly—" she sobbed and dabbed at her eyes with her muff. "Family heirlooms? Think of the scandal, were it to be told!"

"Pleath, do not dethpair, viscounteth. 'Tith the very reason I brought you here, tho that you may provide againth the pothability your huthband will learn the truth."

Sabrina could not mistake that voice among a hundred others. Sir Millpost, the notorious gossip! Of all the damnable luck!

"You are too kind, sir," his companion went on to say. "I don't know what I should do but for your kind advisement in this matter."

"A friend in need," he crooned, bending over her gloved hand to salute it. "It shall be our little secret."

Sabrina attempted to back into a corner among the alarming number of hocked objects that included a full set of armor, but they noticed her the instant she moved.

"Who ith there?" Millpost called out and lifted his gold knobbed cane in a threatening manner.

"Another customer, of course," Sabrina said in a waspish tone and stepped forward, for there was nothing else to be done.

"Oh no! Oh no! We must go!" The lady, a rather pretty young noblewoman with rouged cheeks and diamonds at her throat, turned and hurried to the door.

Millpost obediently followed, opening the door for her but at the last moment, before he went through it, he twitched his head back toward Sabrina. "Are we not acquainted?"

Sabrina looked into his reptilian gaze peering at her out from under the brim of his tricorner and said succinctly, "Impossible."

He did not argue but left quickly.

"Who was that?" asked the returning pawnbroker as the bell tinkled behind the closing door.

"I haven't the slightest idea," Sabrina answered. Had Millpost recognized her? She could not say with certainty one way or the other. Now more than ever it was imperative that she and Kit leave London.

Minutes later she was hurrying home through the mizzle-filled afternoon, carrying more coins that she had ever possessed in her life. She told herself over and over that it was unlikely that Sir Millpost would recall her face. Like many of Lady Charlotte's friends, he had never seemed to find her as worthy of his attention, not when the juicier gossip lay in the activities of her betters. She had never even sat at table when the countess entertained gentlemen friends at cards. Besides, even if he had recognized her, it would mean nothing to him. After all, no one but Cousin Robert knew that she had run away and Millpost would be unlikely to know Robert.

Rattled but secure in the knowledge that she would be gone from London before her whereabouts could be ferreted out, she picked up her step, more worried that she might be late for her final supper with Lord Darlington.

"You are not eating your soup."

"I do not feel much like soup today," Sabrina answered.

"No soup? Then we must think of something else." Jack signaled for the footman to remove her dish. "What do you think would tempt you, sweeting? A chop? A bit of custard? Fresh berries perhaps? Or a freshly stewed fig?"

Sabrina gazed coolly at him down the length of the sumptuously laden table replete with Darlington House's best silver and plate and crystal. "Nothing, thank you, my lord."

"Come now, surely something at my table intrigues your appetite?"

He was baiting her. In her experience of him, his quite

rare high spirits could only have one cause. He was sexually spent. He had spent the afternoon cradled between some harlot's thighs!

The room seemed suddenly too warm, or perhaps it was only her temper heating up the air in her vicinity. She had cause. For instance, her suspicions about the lovely red velvet gown she wore, which he had gallantly supplied at the last minute. What else could she think but that it had once belonged to another of his mistresses? The fact that she had no other suitable garment was the only reason she had agreed to wear it. It was a remarkably good fit, seemingly made for her, which galled her all the same.

She looked up, feeling suddenly ravenous. "I believe I will have a chop. A very bloody one." Something she could stab and dismember with her knife.

Jack hid his smile behind his napkin. The color had come back to her cheeks. He did not know precisely the cause but its appearance was enough to cheer him. Her hair had been washed and brushed out in deep shining waves down her back, which added an alluring informality to their meal. Her skin was luminous in the candlelight, a perfect foil for the luscious red velvet of her gown. There was only one element missing. The deep décolletage begged adornment.

"You should have worn your pearls," he said as he set his wine goblet aside. "The gown requires them."

Sabrina regarded him steadily, noting the lace that adorned his shirtfront and cuffs. "I was unaware of the formality of the occasion, my lord."

"A tribute to you, sweeting. Do drink your wine. The vintage is a particular favorite of mine."

He watched as she begrudgingly followed his suggestion. Thanks to Zuberi's intrepid actions he knew that she had gone out this afternoon, where she had gone, and what she had done while she was there. Perhaps, if he drew her out, she would tell him.

"What did you do this afternoon?"

"Very little."

"Something, surely."

"I read a book."

"I see. My afternoon was spent far more enjoyably."

"I shouldn't doubt it." She did not attempt to subdue the scorn in her voice this time. "You are a gentleman who brooks no interference with his pleasures."

"Did I once say that?"

"Yes, to Countess Charlotte. You had come for tea but announced before even seating yourself that you were leaving. You said quite loudly for all to hear that you found her guests dull. That you were in search of exceptional pleasures and that you never brooked interference in their pursuit."

"I am flattered that you should recall my words upon so slight an acquaintance."

She lifted a brow in indignation. "I had never heard anything so rude."

He laughed. "You since know me better. I have been ruder in your presence, and bolder about it." The rare brilliant smile he sent her dimmed even the candlelight. It was as if he touched her, wrapping his long, strong fingers about her naked breast.

Shaken by so small a thing, Sabrina glanced away. With the length of the table between them and two footmen as chaperoning onlookers to the ordeal, she was finding it exceedingly difficult to share her last meal with him. He had but to look at her and she was half-afire with wanting him. She had once thought the suspense of not knowing what these feelings represented was the worst torment. Now she knew how very foolish those thoughts were. How much worse it was to be in perfect knowledge of what his hands and mouth and body could do to her!

Mercy's grace! She must get away before she shamed herself and disgusted him with her pleas to be taken back into his bed. When he went out for his daily rounds on the morrow, she would bundle Kit up warmly and hire a hack to take them to Greenwich, where she would book passage for them on the ship sailing out.

She glanced down, letting out a shuddery breath. She had lived well enough before she knew there was passion in her. She had thrived before his arms ever went round her or his kisses persuaded her that the love of a man might be worth seeking. She would learn now how to live with the knowledge of all those things, and with the absence of them in her life. She must.

"I've decided to leave London."

Sabrina's thoughts collided with his words, jerking up her chin. "What did you say?"

"That I have decided to leave London." His long fingers moved impatiently among the silver pieces arrayed beside his plate. "For good."

"I see." She held his gaze. "Where are you bound?"

"Does it matter to you?"

Oh no, he would not draw her out! He would not make her beg him to stay and see the satisfaction in his eyes a moment before he rejected her with the admonition that she had been warned not to expect anything of him but the hours they had shared in blissful coupling.

"What, have you no words of fond farewell for your fellow adventurer?"

Her mouth was dry. The words seemed to stick together as she pronounced them. "May you have good sailing, my lord."

"Ah, so then you think I should make a sea voyage." He looked splendid in the candlelight, every inch the nobleman at his leisure. "I was thinking the same. Do you like sea voyages?"

"I would not know." How stiff she sounded, like a green girl at her first soirée. "I have never sailed in anything larger than a skiff on a river.

"Doubtless you would find a sea voyage exhilarating." He picked up his wine goblet and held it toward her in salute. "Would you care to make such a journey?"

A frown of confusion puckered her brow. What game was this? Did he suspect her plans? How could he? "I have thought I should one day like to see the American colonies. My mother's brother resides in Boston."

Jack nodded and sipped his wine. So that was where the minx thought she was headed! "You might not like it. Boston is as cold in winter as Scotland and equally remote."

She shrugged elaborately, "It was only an idle thought, my lord."

He was accustomed to handling things with blatant threats or exquisite delicacy. Despite his two duels, he had walked away untouched from enough other untidy situations that he should have been presented a medal for finesse by the unsuspecting husbands he had cuckolded and the wives he had debauched. But none of that weighed in a jot when it came to the small, courageous, and exasperatingly stubborn young woman who sat opposite. She was as resolute as any opponent who had ever held a pistol against him. And just as potentially deadly . . . to his freedom.

He set his glass down, but his fingers tightened on the stem. "What will you do without me?"

Sabrina rose without answering. She did not trust her voice. She did not trust her feet or her heart or her resolve. She was tired of fighting battles alone. This once she would not rail against the injustice in her life. She would not protest or vow vengeance. She would not demand or plead or even murmur regrets. All she had to do was get beyond the door ahead of her. That was all that was required, that she put one foot ahead of the other. A simple activity that she most often gave no more thought to than breathing.

She nearly made it.

His chair sat between her and the door. As she passed by him he stood and caught her wrist. "Don't leave me."

A great shudder passed through her. He had said, "Don't leave me," not "Don't leave me yet" or "Don't leave me now."

She turned blindly to him, not wanting to read a correction of her hopes in his eyes.

Jack brought her in against him and, with no more than a look, banished his footmen from the room.

"Come, Sabrina, we are alone. You may speak freely now."

She lifted her gaze from a contemplation of his shirtfront, her expression as wary as any he had ever beheld. Gone was all pretence to raillery and arrogance. He knew he stared into the eyes of a woman in love, a woman who did not know if or how that love was returned. The power of that simple knowledge affected him more than any sword or pistol he had ever faced. Did she care so very much, then? For him? He did not, perhaps never would, deserve it.

"Don't look so." He touched her face tenderly, his fingers fanning out over her soft cheek. "Did you think I would leave you behind?"

Sabrina blinked back the hateful tears that had threatened her the whole day long. "I thought you were determined to try."

The statement drew laughter from him.

It was the last sound she heard before her world exploded.

There were heavy footfalls suddenly in the hall and then the door to the dining hall burst open and several armed soldiers, muskets at the ready, poured through the breach. In their wake came Robert McDonnell, who stopped short when he saw her. He pointed an accusing finger at her. "That is her! That is Sabrina Lyndsey!"

A surge of vertigo washed through her as the armed men rushed her. Dimly she realized that Jack had stepped away. She saw Zuberi's dark face loom momentarily in the doorway behind Cousin Robert, then vanish.

Finally a man in a long red coat was standing before her, speaking. "Miss Sabrina Lyndsey, you are under arrest for the kidnapping of your stepbrother Christopher Rodale and the death of Tom McKinley at McDonnell Farm."

It seemed as if the world had gone unaccountably mad as she was taken by the arms, her wrists whipped behind her back and tethered with a length of cord produced by one of the soldiers. She did not speak, could not find a single word to utter in her defense. All she could think of was that, if they were allowed to search the house, they could find Kit.

She glanced in mute appeal to Jack who stood some distance away. He was no longer even looking at her. His face was expressionless but for the slight smirk that lifted one corner of his handsome mouth. Did he know something she did not? Her mind fixed on that hope, and it bolstered her nerve. Of course! He would handle everything. There was no risk he would not take, no gamble he would not wager upon, no odds he could not bend to his design.

When his prisoner was properly secured, the man in the red coat approached the viscount and said, "I'm sorry, your lordship, for the inconvenience. Only doing my duty as it was charged to me."

"Don't be absurd, Sergeant." Jack reached for the snuffbox he carried in his pocket but seldom used. He flicked it open. "The young woman could not have harmed anyone."

"I regret to inform you, Lord Darlington, that you are mistaken."

Jack took his time in turning to the owner of that supercilious voice. When he did he was certain he would have recognized Sabrina's "Cousin Robert" anywhere, though he had never met the man. He was of a type, mean-spirited, small-minded, and smug in his deficits. So this was her nemesis. If his glance alone were sufficient to the method of murder, McDonnell would be gasping his last breath. "Who are you?"

McDonnell's self-important smile withered, frosted by

the nobleman's chill tone. "The name is Robert McDonnell, my lord. Sabrina Lyndsey is my ward." His nose quivered in distaste as he glanced at her, his pale eyes as hostile as they were merciless. "I cannot presume to know what lies the girl has told you. I don't doubt she has offered you persuasions all her own. She is steeped in every sort of calumny. You have been deceived in her. She is nothing short of a criminal."

"All that?" Jack kept his voice soft and mildly bored. "I had not guessed."

The man's baleful gaze continued to evaluate his ward. "If you know the whereabouts of my ward, Christopher, I should be grateful to you for the information. I will not rest comfortably until he is again under my care."

Jack inhaled a pinch of snuff before drawling, "I would not give a leech into your care, McDonnell, had I the direction of leech."

At last McDonnell's attention came back to Darlington. "I should have a care were I you, my lord. Else the courts may seek to discover your exact role in these matters."

With this threat to Jack, Sabrina found her tongue. "I took Kit!"

When her guardian turned to her, she struggled briefly but the two soldiers held her fast. " 'Twas no kidnapping. He came willingly with me."

"You have put your pretty neck in a noose, my dear," McDonnell said coldly.

"You do not believe her?" Jack asked scornfully. "She is lying to protect the true villain." His slow smile of licentious pleasure as he turned his gaze upon Sabrina was one that no man present could misunderstand. "I have that affect on women."

"I commend your chivalrous attempt to shift blame, my lord," McDonnell answered shortly, "but there are witnesses to her crime. A man is dead and she is accused of his murder."

Jack's gaze turned flat, dangerously absent of light as he

retrained it upon the guardian. "You will look the fool trying to convince a court that this mere slip of girl had the courage to fire a pistol point-blank at a Scotsman half again her size."

McDonnell's lids flickered. "What say you?"

His expression was one of hard contemptuous amusement as Jack held out the snuff to the Calvinist. "That I did it."

McDonnell's hand paused short of dipping into the fragrant tobacco. Suspicion made his face stiffen. "I must warn you, my lord, that the authorities take this matter very seriously. I cannot imagine any reason why you should wish to confess to murder."

"That is easily reversed." Jack snapped the lid of his snuffbox closed, all but clipping McDonnell's fingers. "The handbills flying about since my return to London advertise a reward for the fellow suspected of kidnapping Miss Lyndsey." Cool, calculated boredom informed his voice. "I am that man. I am 'Black Jack' Law."

Chapter Twenty-Six

Lady Charlotte Lovelace arrived back in London just three days after the arrest of the disreputable highwayman, Black Jack Law. The city was beset with talk and chatter of the man who had vexed and harried the countryside for miles around. Acts of piracy and robbery, as well as various abductions and rapes, were being laid at the feet of the rapscallion whom the wildest rumor claimed was none other than the new viscount Darlington, late of the West Indies.

Lotte could not believe her ears, could not in fact do more than laugh in the startled and affronted faces of the first five people who broke the news to her. Black Jack, *her* Black Jack, one and the same as Jack Law the highwayman? Absurd! Outrageous! And too juicy an *on dit* to forebear repetition. Just wait until she told Randolph of the wild rumor.

It was not until she was given to understand that Jack Laughton was indeed ensconced in Newgate that her absolute confidence in the fraudulence of the tales began to wane. A mistake had been made, a great horrid mistake which Ran would quickly clear up.

Dear, dear Ran! How she longed to be held in his strong arms again. How she longed to impart to him her news, but not until he had taken her to bed and shown her with the greatest of care how much he had missed her and she had reciprocated with all the loving enthusiasm of which she was capable.

In this frame of mind, she directed her private coach to her door without so much as a note to precede it. After all, things were worked out quite reasonably in her mind. Ran's fit of temper would long since have passed and she suspected he might even have missed her. How silly she had been. On the journey homeward she had had time to reflect and revise her view on many things. She could and did now forgive him his weaknesses. After all, he was only a man. As if a mistress could truly come between them! She was about to deliver to him the greatest gift a woman could offer her husband: an heir. By her reckoning, she was four months gone. A baby for May Day!

Nor would she again cavil against his musty friends and his dreadfully boring political schemes. She loved to host parties and even if his choice of guests did not inspire her, at least acting as hostess would ensure that he was home more evenings and that no one could detain him for one last drink on the way home. On other nights she would have the baby, who would quite satisfactorily occupy her time. How frivolous and wasteful she had been, gambling her money away for a transient thrill. In the future she would direct her financial expenditures on more permanent reminders of her very fortunate life. The first would be the new nursery.

In this state of blissful anticipation, she alighted from her coach and sailed up the steps of her London townhouse.

"Good morning, Geoffrey!" she declared as she sailed past the startled butler.

"Good day, my lady," the butler answered a little breathlessly, for he had just in time been warned by an under maid of the arrival of a carriage.

"Where is his lordship on this fine morning?"

"Still in his chambers, my lady. Shall I announce you?"

Lotte started. "Announce me, his wife? What are you thinking, fellow?"

She then smiled so charmingly the old retainer's heartbeat slowed. Who could resist her ladyship's smile? It was his most fervent hope that his lordship could not.

The lady did not wait for him to go ahead of her. Instead, she approached and began ascending the stairs, dropping articles of clothing behind her as she did so, a cashmere muffler, a large ermine muff, and finally her fur-lined cape.

As the elderly butler scurried to retrieve them, he wondered which of his noble employers would prevail in the contest of wills and proud hearts that was about to be enacted abovestairs.

Lord Lovelace had been in a mood so dark and foul these last weeks that the household had gone about on tiptoe lest the least thing bring down his wrath. The absence of the countess had been remarked by all. For all her frivolous behavior, she had brought a gentleness and joy, and one might even say a domestic touch, to these former bachelor quarters. Yet she had behaved very badly and his lordship had a prodigious pride.

Geoffrey smiled as the heady scent of her perfume drifted back through the hall. His money was on the countess.

Lotte paused just outside her husband's door to remove her silk traveling hood and pat a curl in place. She had deliberately left her flame red-hair unpowdered, for her russet curls had once stimulated Ran as much as the sight of her in only a corset and garters. If only she had dared to arrive so dressed today. Regrettably, the weather did not permit such naughty behavior.

She took a deep breath and without knocking thrust open the pair of doors to her husband's bedchamber.

The suddenly opened doors jarred Ran from his perusal of the criminal charges he had been sent to read. "Damnation Geoffrey! I've told you I do not wish to be disturbed!"

"Lud! If that is not a fine greeting!"

As that throaty contralto voice penetrated his amazed senses, Ran lifted his head slowly from the work spread on his desk. "Lotte," he said in a dull tone.

"Correct. Lotte. The Countess Lovelace." She offered him a saucy smile. "Do you know longer stand for ladies, Ran?"

Ran came to his feet but he felt as if the boards had opened beneath him and dropped him two floors. Lord, but she looked wonderful in a green brocaded gown with the new cinched waist. Yet his eager observation did not inform the monotony of his tone. "You might have informed us of your arrival."

"I might have, had I not wished my arrival to be a surprise." She came forward in a graceful slide that allowed her full skirts to swing provocatively.

Ran watched the motion and felt an answering sway low down.

When she reached him she placed both hands on his desk and leaned slightly forward so that a blind man would have had to notice the plump breasts straining against the fabric of her bodice. He had no spit to swallow.

"Despite all that has happened, Ran," she began in a breathy voice of reconciliation, "I could no longer stay away."

With great effort Ran forced himself to look into her face, which seemed more radiant than he remembered. Her coloring was of those glorious delicate shades that only a master portraitist could capture. She was even more delicious than memory. Then he remembered.

The door swung shut on his emotions once more. "You are back because of Darlington."

"Why would you think that?" Lotte's puzzled expression cleared and she smiled and flicked open her fan. "Ah, you mean this ridiculous rumor that he is a highwayman. 'Tis a tale so droll I had hopes of being the first to tell it."

The shock of her sudden appearance was wearing off. He watched her with a new detachment. "The charges are very grave. Aside from a hundred robberies he is accused of kidnapping your former protégée, Miss Lyndsey, for the purposes of debauchery and profit. I very much think they intend hang to him." He watched her closely. "I've been asked to stand for the prosecution against him."

Lotte's mouth fell open. "Don't be a fool, Ran. Darlington did not kidnap anyone, least of all Sabrina. The man's besotted with her. He all but told me so."

"That must have been very distressing for you." His hands shook as he mindlessly rearranged his papers on which the charges he had just mentioned were written.

"It was, to begin with," she allowed in a small voice, then shrugged elaborately. "But then I rallied to the spirit of it."

Ran found he could no longer look at her. "The spirit of betrayal?"

"Of course not. Of *amour.* He came to tell me that he was taking her away to become his mistress." She blushed and fiddled with her fan. "I know you will think me heartless in the matter, but I reasoned it was better for her to lie in the clean, virile embrace of a man like Darlington than to waste her youth in the clutches of a old roue like Merripace."

Anger formed an icy coating over his heart as Ran lifted his gaze hers. "You have had much experience of virile embraces?"

Lotte smiled at him, blushing. "I most certainly presume so." He did not answer her suggestive smile. After a moment hers drooped and she sighed against the pain of his hard look. "But I suppose nothing lasts forever."

"You are accepting this with remarkable aplomb, madam."

She nodded. "I am, aren't I? I think I have gained greatly in understanding of the way of the world since I have been away. It was most educational."

"So what am I to make of this matter of your return?" he asked heavily.

Her brows lifted in surprise. "Why, that I'm home for good, Ran. That I have thought it through and believe that I may owe you something of an apology."

It was his turn to lift a brow. "Something of an apology?"

She half turned from him, offering him a lovely view of her slim back and graceful neck. "Very well, a complete apology, replete with *mea culpas* and rending of my garments." She tossed him a coquettish glance over one shoulder. "Would that please you?"

"Not if it will require that your wardrobe be replaced by an enormous modiste's bill."

She chuckled in spite of her annoyance, for he was not responding as she had hoped. "Lud! You are such an antidote to romance."

"No doubt."

The clipped reply was not what she had expected. She turned back to stare at him, noticing his tight expression with its thin-lipped grimness. "You know what I mean, Ran. You will forever be counting up the guineas and pence. Life is too short to keep a strict accounting."

He fiddled with his papers. "You think I should not count everything you have done ill against you?"

The first tendrils of doubt crept into Lotte's mind. She had thought, regardless of his anger, that he would be thrilled, at least momentarily, to see her. "I should hope you would not. I admit, I have been frivolous. I have been vain and arrogant and, yes, even indiscreet." She poured her heart into the melting glance meeting his disdainful stare. "It was only done in an attempt to attract your attention."

He held her gaze this time, feeling the tug of old times and long absence. "You have always had my attention, Lotte."

"You know that is not what I mean. Your passion." She closed her fan with a snap of her wrist, impatient with his lack of ardor or even friendliness. "It had been lacking of late."

His gaze cut away. "I did suppose you had found other diversions."

"I admit I did try. But cards and gambling and idle gossip are poor substitutes for a man's arms."

"What of your friends?" he questioned levelly, waiting for her to come to her point. "Surely one of them offered you succor?"

"I have come to believe that you are right about my friends," she said quickly. "They are as idle as the gossip they exchange. I am determined to find better company or simply better methods by which to entertain myself." She trailed a finger along the satin finish of his desktop, wishing instead she were stroking his bare chest. "The most extraordinary thing occurred while I was in Bath. I quite believe I have taken the knack of architecture. I should like to try my hand at building something of my own one day. A little cottage in the woods, perhaps. Or an ornamental bridge at our country residence. Why not a folly? Then perhaps something grander, more substantial."

"What makes you think I'd allow you to spend another penny of my money?"

The flick of anger in his voice drew her first vexed reply. "Oh Ran, do not be tiresome!"

Ran watched her carefully now, trying to determine her

purpose. "This is why you've come back, to build monuments to your consequence?"

"No, of course not." Lotte fanned herself briefly, seeking the courage to say the words. She had hoped he would embrace her warmly and allow her to subside in his arms while she broke the news. Yet it was quite evident he had no such swooning reconciliation in mind.

"There is something I must tell you, something which you will find quite surprising."

"Lotte, I already know."

"You know?" She made a tentative gesture toward her still-flat stomach. "But how could you know? The weakness did first appear while I was still in London, but I did not fully succumb to it until I was in Bath."

Ran felt every muscle in his face move stiffly as he spoke. "I find that bit of news of little comfort."

"Don't blame yourself. How could you know what had occurred? I myself was startled by the truth. We had quarreled so the night before I left that I was much too miserable to sort out the source of one emotional upheaval from another." She sighed. "I should have supposed it was only a matter of time before it should occur. It is, after all, the way of the world. You said so yourself."

"Yes." He bit out the word. She was speaking of his explanation of his mistress, of course. "Perhaps I was hasty in my supposition."

"Oh no, you were perfectly right. And I am so happy for the eventuality. You see, we will both now have what we want."

The ice around his heart cracked under the pressure of rage. "I wonder that you can say that to my face."

She came round the table toward him, feeling more confident with every moment. "Now Ran, dearest. Who else would I confide in, if not you?"

He stared at her as if he had never seen her before. Indeed the brazen, self-possessed woman standing before him was as different from his former sweet Lotte as any stranger. "I do not want your confidences if they concern that matter!"

Lotte clicked her tongue impatiently. "Do not prove difficult at this juncture, Ran. I know you are angry. You have every right. I did desert you." She offered him another appealing glance. "But I am back. And, to be fair, you were more adamant about how our lives should be lived than I. I was reluctant. I will admit that I never wanted it to happen. I was afraid of the pain and disorder and the messiness of the affair. But now that it a fact, I cannot express my delight!"

Ran's self-control vanished. He stepped away from her before he did her harm. "I think I have heard enough!"

"But Ran—"

"No, madam." He turned on her a look of such fury that she backed up a step. "Perhaps I have underestimated you or overestimated myself but I am not so worldly that I care to listen to my wife rise in raptures about the bliss she received in her lover's arms."

Lotte gaped. "What lover?"

"Darlington!" he roared.

"Darlington?" Lotte stunned gaze reflected her utter confusion. "Jack?"

"You speak his Christian name with great affection."

"Well yes, but—"

"Don't touch me," he shouted as she reached for his arm, "or I shan't be responsible for my actions."

Lotte drew back her hand, her own temper set to the spark. "You are behaving quite extraordinarily bad."

Ran took a sobering breath. She was right. He had had weeks to think about this moment. Three short days ago he thought he had made his decision. He was ten miles outside of London before reason asserted itself and he had turned back from his mission to find and bring his wife home. If she wanted to come home, she would have done so, his practical mind told him. She had run away *because* she did not want to be with him. Bringing her back would not change that. If she did not return of her own accord he would have gained nothing.

Bitter, regretful, but certain that this cold splash of reasoning was more sane than the fevered passion that had set him on the road to Bath, he had returned home, sadder than ever.

Now she stood before him, as luscious as any dream of her that had haunted his nights, and he knew they had never been farther from happiness.

He raked a hand through his clipped hair for he had yet to don his formal wig. "Forgive me. I have no experience in the niceties involved in discussing the merits of my wife's lovers."

"Ran, you can't believe—?"

"Yes, I can. I do." He looked at her. "I saw you, Lotte. I was there in Bath. With my own eyes I saw!"

"Saw what?" Inexplicable panic rose up in her. "What?"

"You and Darlington in an embrace."

Lotte gasped, "That is not possible!"

"Don't lie. Just don't lie."

"Why should I lie?" She reached out to him only to have him jerk away from her touch. "Darlington never so much as—oh!"

Her stricken look gored him. "Ah, it comes to you at last."

Lotte turned pink as a new-budded rose. "Well, he does like to linger over his salutes to my hand."

"Lotte!" he roared, "Go away before I throttle you!"

"Go away?" She looked vaguely about. "Go where?"

"God knows I do not care. Go back to Bath. Go to the country, but just get out of my sight!"

"Well! Well!" Her bosom was heaving in a way that would have made any actress proud, but it was no artifice for feigned emotion. "That's a fine way to treat the mother of your first child!" She turned and stalked out.

"My first—? Lotte? *Lotte?*"

But she could move with remarkable rapidity when she

rose. She was through the door before he reached it, slamming it in his face with such force that the sound resounded throughout the house. Enraged, he stuck it with a fist. "What devil's trick is this?"

Chapter Twenty-Seven

London, January 1, 1741

"Once again I ask you, where is that bastard brother of yours?"

Sabrina held her chin high, too weary to think of a clever remark today. "I do not know."

She was dressed in a plain gray serge gown, her hair bound in a plait down her back. There were no adornments on her, not even the natural sparkle of her fine eyes. She had been a prisoner in her guardian's home for nearly a month. After the first week, when he had beaten her daily with his belt, he had curtailed physical punishment, but only because Merripace had arrived in the midst of the ordeal and had been horrified by the thought that his prize bride might be damaged.

He would bend her to his will in his own way once they were married, she had heard Merripace say in cloistered argument with Cousin Robert, but he would not take an openly scarred or battered bride. He needed an heir out of her. She must not suffer a ruptured womb.

Robert McDonnell paced the floor of his library, infuriated to be reduced to less overt methods of punishment and persuasion in interrogating his ward. He had put her on bread and water rations and sequestered her in a tiny dark closet for days when she was not standing before him, as now, being drilled by the same questions. Yet she had never varied from the first; she would say nothing about the whereabouts of her brother.

"You will tell me, Sabrina, eventually."

"Not even with my dying breath," Sabrina answered in a bare whisper.

Truth be told, she did not know where Kit was to be found, yet she suffered no deep qualms over his disappearance. She was certain Jack had had a hand in the boy's escape and was equally certain that he was being better looked after than he would have been under Cousin Robert's roof. She would withstand a great deal. Starvation would have killed Kit.

What she could not fathom was why Jack remained adamant in his story that he was a highwayman.

His announcement had electrified the soldiers. The startled sergeant had asked the viscount to repeat his assertion. Jack had, adding that the young woman they had come to arrest was not only guiltless of any crime but that she had been his victim. She was being held captive in his home.

Something in his manner, so calm yet so emotionally flat, had kept her from contradicting him. Over Robert McDonnell's vocal objections, the beleaguered sergeant had said it was all too much for him to untangle and that they would all have to be taken to headquarters.

Sabrina did not even know what Jack had said to the officers once they reached the Home Office because she and her guardian, mere commoners, had been held in the hallway while Lord Darlington was entertained as the aristocrat he was.

After what seemed an eternity, she was released, uncharged, and remanded into the care of her guardian.

On their way out of the military headquarters she spied a flyer tacked to the barracks door which offered a reward of five hundred pounds for the capture of "Black Jack" Law and the return of the Lyndsey woolen heiress. Jack had known about this. Why had he not told her?

Her gaze moved quickly toward her cousin as he stopped short before her. "Where is he?"

She flinched but did not cower as his hand swept with stinging force across her face.

Pain flared in her cheek and the dull ache of a hunger headache flared to full throbbing in her temples. The one question she had gotten an answer to just this morning was how the soldiers had found her.

She cradled her cheek as angry tears burned her eyes. "I should be careful, cousin. Sir Millpost will soon be here to collect his reward."

"Damned snoop!" She saw with satisfaction as the gibe found its mark.

"Merripace was most generous in the reward he put forward on your behalf," she continued, for words were her only defense.

"Too generous," he muttered and turned abruptly away.

Sabrina relaxed as he moved from her. Millpost the thief taker! And Cousin Robert forced to be his benefactor. What a merry pair they made! "I am amazed that you offered a ha'penny for me."

"I did not. That was Merripace's doing. I did not suspect when I suggested he return to London from Bath while I led the search for you that impatience would drive the old fool to plaster the countryside with the news that you had been kidnapped. Had he stayed out of the matter, I would have recovered you soon enough."

Never, thought Sabrina. She had almost won free. A few hours more and she and Kit would have been away to sea, sailing away from England and their cousin forever. The bitterness of that near escape was with her still.

"Why did you not simply allow me to vanish? What

matter to you—oh, of course!" Sabrina wondered why she had not thought of it before. The answer was that she had no interest in the legal ascendancy of inheritance laws. Since coming to London all her attention had been upon securing Kit's claim. Now she saw her error.

"You cannot afford for me to die, can you?" She smiled for the first time in weeks. "My father would not have been so foolish as to name as our guardian the next in line to his fortune. The temptation would be too great to simply do away with us. If I should die you would lose control of the inheritance."

He shot her a truculent glance that made her stomach quiver. "Now that Millpost has made public knowledge of the circumstance of your recovery, I can do little but play out the tarradiddle that you are a victim and that Lord Darlington is a highwayman and the true culprit."

"He is not guilty of anything and you know it."

"What do I care? They will hang him in any case."

"You cannot be certain." Sabrina played a desperate game and she knew it. The cards were stacked against her and at stake was her life. Yet she needed the challenge of matching wits with her enemy, trumping where she could, or she would go insane. "Lord Darlington is an aristocrat. The House of Lords will judge him. They may not consider it a genuine crime to debauch the daughter of a merchant. And if they free him what do you think he will do?" She smiled broadly. "He will come here and skewer you for the trouble you have given him."

McDonnell smirked. "He would not dare."

"You don't know him as I do. Believe me when I tell you, his methods are as ruthless as they are thorough," she continued confidently. "He will, most likely, confront you in a public place and offer you his challenge. If you refuse he may take a bullwhip to you in the streets. You are, after all, a commoner and you have set yourself against an aristocratic house."

He had turned very white and she saw his hand tremble

as he lifted it to adjust his cravat. "There's nothing I can do in any case. He freely made his claim."

Sabrina held back the opinion that Jack had done what he did for her sake. It would further inflame her tormentor. "Were I you I would seek to present myself as friend to him instead of a foe."

"How so?" he questioned in disbelief.

Sabrina shrugged. "You might allow me to speak for him at his trial."

He sneered. "Disabuse yourself of the notion. Until Kit is returned to my care, you are little more than a criminal yourself."

"Then you will have nothing, for all your trouble. Darlington will be freed. When he is, he will kill you or leave you as good as dead. Then who will wish to align themselves with a cowardly commoner and his wanton of a ward? There won't be enough guineas in all the world to buy back your respectability."

She knew he was listening to her, though he resented every moment of it. "You are free with your threats, but I do not see any profit to be had in allowing you to save him."

Sabrina met his eye and played her final trump card. "I will marry as you wish, if Lord Darlington is set free."

"Yes, of course, your word on that is sufficient inducement," he jeered.

She held his gaze. "I swear upon my father's grave to wed as you will it, if you allow me to speak in court for Lord Darlington and he thereby wins free."

She saw the calculation going on behind her guardian's pale stare. "And if he is not freed?"

She did not even blink. "Then you may murder me, for I will never again do your bidding."

The barest hint of a smile, as cold as it was unpleasant, lifted a corner of his lipless mouth. "Now that he's seen you again, Merripace is still willing to take you on." She felt the pricking of her skin as his gaze raked her shapeless gown. "It must be the smell of soiled goods that makes his prick puckish."

She ignored the ugliness of his remark, for she had already suffered the indignity of having him order Mrs. Varney to confirm the fact that she was no longer a virgin. "That is to your advantage and mine. So what is it to be, Cousin Robert? Is there a bargain between us?"

"You will swear, your hand on the holy Bible?"

The cell into which the Earl of Lovelace was shown by the gaoler was clean and spacious and sparsely furnished by a cot spread in heavy winter linens, a basin, chamber pot, a small trunk, and a chair and desk at which the prisoner sat.

Though the day was wintry gray, Darlington sat in his shirtsleeves before an open window, his bright head bent over his moving quill, his face bearing a tense absorbed expression unlike any Ran had ever seen on the man's face before. Boredom yes, indifference certainly, icy rage mayhap, and most often mocking disdain. But this concentration lent his features a wholly new and unsuspected refined and intelligent quality.

Or perhaps I am looking for excuses, Ran thought. Lotte was with child. Though she claimed different, how could he believe other than the man before him was the sire?

He stepped onto the small rug that had been spread against the chill of the stones beneath his feet. Regardless of the amenities available to many of the stateside residents of Newgate, the thick walls and the bars at the window were there to remind a soul that even on the best of days he was a prisoner.

"Darlington!"

The viscount looked up distractedly and then, seeing who his visitor was, stood and bowed slightly, but said nothing.

"I have received the remittance of your gambling debt."

"I am glad to hear it." Darlington's voice lacked its usual drawl of interest. "I regret it could not be tendered personally and in a more timely manner."

Ran loosed the top button of his riding cloak and shed it, laying it over his arm. "I hear you sold Rockingham Estate to raise the funds."

Darlington nodded. "You are well informed."

Ran frowned. This mild conversation was neither what he had expected nor come for. "Why do such a thing?"

"Contrary to the sentiment engendered by the ownership of such memorials, my ancestral home means nothing to me. One way or the other I do not intend to return to England."

"It would seem your life has caught up with you at last."

Darlington closed the lid of his inkwell. "So it would appear."

"You beg to differ?"

"Not in substance of your condemnation, only in the particulars of the events which have led me to this juncture."

Ran smiled. "You will now protest your innocence."

"Never innocence." He dusted his letter with sand as he spoke. "Yet I will own that I am not in fact the real Jack Law. Nor did I kidnap Miss Lyndsey. I did seduce her away from the safety of your wife's residence. I did take her to my bed. I did help her liberate her brother from what was little more than prison." He looked up a moment from his activity. "And, of course, I did shoot the Scottish fellow, but only because he was about to knife Miss Lyndsey's brother. All that, I fully confess. I do not believe any of it is accounted crime enough to hang a noble."

"We will see." Ran was suddenly impatient to be gone, regretting his decision to come at all. For this man, Lotte had ruined herself!

"The House of Lords is prepared to sit in special session in order to bring this matter to a quick and just end."

"How thoughtful of them. I do grow weary of my cage."

Ran felt the strength of personality in the gaze Darlington turned on him and took an equal measure of him. Had Lotte loved him? Why then had he not spared himself the humiliation? And why did he now wonder about the motives of a man whom he had wished most fervently dead these past weeks?

"If you are innocent, as you say, of criminal activities as Jack Law, why confess?"

Darlington met his question with a brief smile. "Miss Lyndsey may be wealthy, but she is a commoner. She would have been held in one of Newgate's common rooms where she would not have lasted a night. If she had not been killed for her garments, she would have been driven mad by the dishonorable attentions of the males. I would have done anything to prevent that."

Ran could not argue the truth of his words. The vileness and depravity of Newgate was notorious. A young woman of Sabrina's beauty would have been raped first by the guards and then any prisoner with coin to buy her, and then finally left to the rabble of the common cells.

An honorable impulse from a dishonorable man? Lotte claimed Darlington was in love with Miss Lyndsey. Yet he could not quite believe that there was not some other discreditable motive in the man's actions. "When you first made your confession, Miss Lyndsey is said to have cried out that *she* shot the Scotsman."

Darlington's face lit up briefly. "She is a noble thing, is she not? I doubt she realized they would hang her out of hand for that confession."

"You would have me believe that she was thinking only of saving your graceless neck?"

Darlington smiled. "I have that affect on women. Alas, in this instance, it is of little good to me."

"You use your mistresses hard."

"And cast them off just as easily," Darlington finished self-mockingly.

If he had had his sword Ran believed he would have

run the unharmed man through at that instant. "Lotte is with child."

"Yes." He smiled at Ran. "Congratulations."

Ran felt as if he had been slapped. His face burned with indignation. "Your salutations are misdirected. I am quite certain the child is yours."

He saw the old wicked humor return in Darlington's gaze. "Believe me, were the deed mine I would show no compunction in admitting it, even to you."

"If?"

"If."

Ran turned to pace the room. Now that he had begun this damned interview, he would see it through. "I know you were lovers."

"You know nothing of the kind," Darlington answered smoothly. "If you choose to believe so, that is your folly."

Ran paused a few feet from him. "Why should I disbelieve my own eyes?"

Darlington grinned. "You spied on her?"

"I saw you both together!"

Darlington held his gaze, as he seemed to give the matter fresh thought. "If your lady wife had given me any genuine encouragement, Lovelace, I should have taken her. You know me well enough to believe that," he said coolly. "But you know her infinitely better. If you believe other than she tells you, then you are a fool and deserve to lose her."

"I see." Ran could barely force the words through his teeth. "Then we have nothing else to discuss." He swung away.

"One moment, Lovelace."

Ran turned and looked him up and down, the act insulting in its silence.

Darlington hooked a thigh over the edge of his desk and sat. "You are an honest man, Lovelace, if sometimes a damned stupid one. Therefore, I have a request to make of you."

Ran stiffened. "Yes?"

Darlington picked up the letter he had been addressing, folded it in thirds, and then picked up another official document and tucked it inside the first. When he had set his seal upon it, he held it out to the earl. "I would ask that you see this delivered into the hands of Miss Lyndsey. Into her hands only, and without the knowledge of her guardian."

Ran did not move to take the missive. "I don't know that I can make you that promise. Don't know that I should."

Darlington smiled. "I sold my soul to the devil a long time ago. I am not going to die for my actions but I could remain imprisoned for a time. It is vitally important that she have those papers immediately."

"What are they?"

Something flickered in Darlington's gaze and Ran knew he was not accustomed to having his requests questioned, even by his equals. Nor was he comfortable with requiring assistance.

He stood up and came forward slowly. "I have never begged a soul on this earth for anything. I am asking you." He proffered the missive again, this time within arm's length. "Take this to her. It is passage for three to America. I have given her directions to her brother's whereabouts. She is to take my manservant Zuberi with her for protection. I promised her I would see her to safety. If you do not help me, her guardian will surely see her as good as dead."

Ran stared at him a moment longer before accepting the letter. Could Lotte be right? Could Darlington be risking his life in a selfless act to save Sabrina? Why, unless . . . "You are in love with her?"

"Doubtless you are correct." He managed a brief self-conscious smile. "Foolish whim for a man who was thought to own no heart."

Darlington turned away and ran a hand through his hair, a gesture of weariness and resignation. "Was there any other reason for your visit?"

"Yes, there is." Ran took his time with the news he had come to impart. "I have been asked to stand for the prosecution at your trial."

Darlington glanced sharply at Ran but his expression remained neutral. "How awkward for me."

"I imagine it will become more so." The first easy expression in weeks creased Ran's face. "I believe I may stand instead for the defense."

Chapter Twenty-Eight

The house was inordinately quiet when Ran returned, though it was early evening, just after dark. For the past three weeks he and Lotte had lived as separately as two people sharing a roof could. They had glimpsed one another only by accident in a hallway, entering or leaving a room, or coming or going on the stairs. Each time Lotte looked stricken, as if she had been caught in an unlawful act. He felt, equally, that she had.

After the first week she had stopped even attempting to speak with him during these chance encounters. He had preferred it that way. Now, after his conversation with Darlington, he was not so certain that he might not be the greatest fool in Christendom.

Darlington was in love with Sabrina Lyndsey.

Darlington was *never* his wife's lover.

Darlington was *not* the father of Lotte's child.

He had tried so hard, a hundred different ways a day, to accept the unacceptable, that his wife carried another man's child.

Now for nearly an hour, the time it had taken him to

ride from Newgate to his door, he had been considering the possibility that the adjustment was totally unnecessary.

Lotte carried *his* child.

He felt the truth of it in his heart, but his heart had proved a very unreliable organ these last months, prodding him to actions and words that had nearly destroyed his home and his happiness. Could he believe this swelling sense of hope inside him? However tentative, could he begin to repair the great damage his disbelief must have caused, and still caused, his wife?

His wife.

He climbed the stairs to their private chambers with a heavy tread. He did not know what to say to her. He, who always had words for every occasion, could not think of a single line to eradicate the hurtful, spiteful, ugly suspicions he had heaped on Lotte. She might not listen, even if he found them.

A cold hand wrapped itself about his heart. What if he had lost her? What if no reconciliation was possible? Would they go on passing one another in the halls as strangers until it no longer wounded either of them and they each, to ward off this chill he already felt in his soul, sought in truth to find happiness in the arms of another?

He went first to his own chamber to relieve himself of his outer clothing and wash away the grime of the day. Afterward, he took his brocade jacket off and put it on half a dozen times before he gave up in disgust and slung it into a corner. He had never before worried about how Lotte might interpret his intentions if he approached her in his shirtsleeves. Months before he had often passed through the door connecting their bedchambers wearing nothing at all and been absolutely confident in her reception.

He glanced at the discarded jacket. "Coward," he muttered and went over to the door before his nerve broke.

He did not knock for fear she would reject him. When

the latch gave under the pressure of his hand he sighed in relief. She might have taken to locking her side.

He entered so quietly that she did not at first notice him. She sat in bed reading by the light of a single candle. Despite the cold of the evening she was dressed in lacy dishabille with her fiery ringlets caught up in a green ribbon atop her head. She looked as delectable as a French pastry. But he knew that she was no mere puff and crème confection. She was a flesh and blood woman with real feelings and pride and an inviolate sense of self-worth. He would never again forget that.

"I have been to see Darlington."

She started badly at the sound of his voice. Her book tumbled from her grasp. Yet when she turned her head and saw him standing in the open doorway, she merely said, "I see."

How he had missed her voice, the throaty, almost boyish contralto that, in fact, could really only belong to a woman.

He took a step toward her, testing her reception. "I thought you would wish to know that he is well."

She reached for and closed her book before answering. "Thank you for the consideration."

When she looked away from him, he took two more steps toward the bed. "Lotte, I have something to say. I—"

"Please!" She held up a hand and shook her head, refusing to even glance at him. "I do not think I can bear another round of quarreling." She did look at him then and the expression of grief on her lovely face tore at his heart. "I give up, Ran. I concede to your desire to be rid of me. But in my condition I do not think it wise for me to leave London. After the chi—" She again glanced away. "Afterward, toward the middle of the summer, I shall move home with my parents."

She began nervously pleating the coverlet. "They are fond of babes. My sisters have given them half a dozen grandbabies. Another will hardly be noticed."

Ran hesitated. "If that is your wish."

She nodded slowly, still gazing at the coverlet. "I think it best."

"Best for whom?"

"Best for all of us." She lifted a hand to her brow and rubbed her frown lines as if they gave her pain. "You do not wish me here, cannot bear the sight of me. How much worse it will be after the babe's arrival."

Ran quietly approached within a foot of the bed, watching her every move. "You believe I would put you and your babe out on the street?"

"No, I do not." She lowered her hand to press the tremble from her lips. "You are a good man, a generous man. I know you would do all that is expected of you and more. But I will not burden you with a daily reminder of a lie that you prefer to see as truth."

"I was wrong."

"Of course, you are wrong—" She started a second time, as if he had interrupted her and not her thoughts. She turned her head toward him, her gaze disbelievingly wide. "Did you say you were wrong?"

He could not even smile. "Yes."

She shook her head, a tight little movement of confusion that set two loose curls dancing lightly across her brow. "I think you must make yourself more clear, Ran. I have given up the attempt to understand you."

He managed a shrug. "I was wrong, Lotte, wrong about everything. I may be a dunderhead but even I can be made to see reality in the end."

Her gaze was as wide as any ocean now, and perfectly blue. "And this new reality. Does it have a cause?"

He swallowed, wishing he had the right to reach out and touch her. For he would, gladly, wrap her in his arms and hold her so close she would never have to doubt him again. "The blinders of pride have been lifted from my eyes."

She looked away from him at last, her voice grown husky from emotion. "I would not be too sure. A reckless word spoken after dark often proves the height of folly with the morning light."

She knew him all too well. It was true, just gazing at her had brought him to tumescence. But that was not the reason he had come to her and she must never think that lust had overcome his better reason. Still, the joy of this familiar desire should not be denied. "I have always rather enjoyed my follies after dark with you."

She kept her gaze averted. "Do not! Do not tease me, Ran. I cannot take another false hope. I have put away my foolish dreams. You must allow me to remain in peace, for the child's sake."

"I will do that, I swear to you that I will never be the cause of another moment's alarm or pain. But you must hear me out, tonight. And then I will leave you."

She looked at him then and he saw his declaration came too late. Her brimming eyes spoke of great pain and he knew he was the cause.

Suddenly he was remembering the last fight they had before she ran away, when he had called her foolish and her friends idlers, and wished he could take back all the words he had ever spoken in anger and simply take her in his arms and kiss her breathless. He lived by his power with words, won through persuasion and argument men and causes to his side. Yet words had been the cause of his and Lotte's estrangement: accusations, warnings, retaliations and resentments. There had already been far too many words and not nearly enough actions to serve as antidote.

He moved to bend a knee upon the bed and though she stiffened he sat down, his knee a foot from her leg. She stared at his knee as if it were a red-hot poker and then, for no reason he could discern, she jumped.

"What's wrong?" He reached out without thinking and touched her thigh. "Are you in pain?"

A funny look crossed her face and then she glanced sidelong at him. "Nay, 'tis only the babe."

"The babe?" His voice rose slightly in alarm. "What's wrong with the babe?"

"Nothing, it is perfectly well." She turned bright pink. " 'Tis only that he or she has awakened."

He frowned at her in doubt. "How do you know it's awake?"

To his utter surprise she reached out and took his hand in hers and then pushed it, palm flat, against her belly. It took him no time to realize what his eyes had yet to determine, that her belly had grown convex and quite firm. While he was digesting this development the swelling did a most remarkable thing—it moved!

His eyes snapped up to her face to see Lotte smiling at him serenely. "The babe?" he whispered.

She nodded.

He lifted his hand and then pressed it back, hoping to feel another kick. "How far along are you?"

"By my reckoning, nearly five months."

"So much as that?" he breathed, inexplicably whispering as if the child might overhear him. "A May babe."

"I am thinking that if it is a girl I may name her Hyacinth or Columbine."

"And if 'tis a boy?"

She looked momentarily sad. "I am not certain."

He smiled for the first time. "My father's name is William. 'Tis a sound name, a family name."

She looked at him, doubting him. "Would that be wise?"

"Wise and sound and absolutely fitting." His eyes widened as he felt a second rolling pressure under his palm. "After all, my first son will one day be heir to an earldom."

"Ran?"

"Yes, love." He lifted his gaze of wonder to her face. "You heard me right. The child, whether boy or girl, may have a fool for a father, but father I am."

"Oh Ran!" She opened her arms to him.

Her breath was warm and sweet in his mouth. He did not think then of what he was doing, or even if he should be doing it, only that she had embraced him and that in doing so the icy hand unclenched from about his heart and the blood now flowed hot and heavy through his veins. His hand threaded through her tangled curls and he followed as she reclined back onto the pillows.

She did not protest as his hands found and pushed her gown from her shoulders. She held onto him, moaning softly even before his hands touched her skin. He found her breasts more voluptuous than before, and her nipples longer and pointed. He found that she smelled the same, a subtle sweetness at her neck and between her breasts. Then he tasted the pungent essence of desire as he dipped his head lower down. She came instantly alive in his hands and mouth, brought to the peak of need before he could even divest himself of his clothing. And then he slid into her, tenderly, softly, remembering only when he was buried in her that there was a new life within her, one that they had created together and which, to his everlasting joy, he now knew to be his.

They lay quietly a long time after that, just touching and whispering nothings, and touching again, as if each had thought the other lost forever across some great unspeakable divide.

"I was afraid to bear a child," Lotte said finally, having begun to try to explain the many cross-purposes that had motivated her behavior. "I thought I would die in childbirth, as my mother did."

Ran held her tighter to his chest, trembling with a new fear. "Dear sweet one, why did you not confide in me your fears?"

"How could I? You wanted children so badly and I wanted you. I thought I could make you happy enough that if there were no children for a time, I would be enough for you."

"You are, dearest." He kissed her brow, pushing a fiery curl against his lips. "But that will not change with the arrival of a child. I do want children, of course. Yet, had

I known your fears I would have taken precautions. There are ways to prevent conception."

"I know."

He lifted his head to look at her. "Do you?"

She blushed crimson. "They don't work very well, do they?"

He stared at her, aghast. Then his face eased into a smile. "You are a very naughty girl, Lotte."

"Yes, I suppose I am." She walked her fingers through the black silk curls lightly furring his chest and then hugged his neck. "But I am glad it happened this way. I was only a little sick at first and passed it off as indigestion. Now that the child is growing I feel stronger and happier with each day."

"Promise me one thing against the future."

"Yes, what?"

"That you will confide in me your fears as well as your joys. I cannot be expected to solve them but I can be there to share them with you so that you will be a little less afraid."

She kissed the side of his jaw. "I am never afraid when I am in your arms."

"Then we shall have to see to it you are here regularly and often."

"I should like that above every other thing. I do love you, Ran. I always have."

"And I you, Lotte. We have been a great pair of fools."

"Yes, we have. But is the making up not worth the pain?"

"No, and we must never forget it. We nearly lost one another in our folly. We must be very careful in the future to never take that risk again."

"I think we have learned our lesson."

Ran debated bringing up the subject but decided it was as well that they air all their differences at once. He took a deep breath. "I gave up my mistress a month ago. It was a stupid mistake which I should have corrected at once, but pride would not let me admit the error."

Lotte took her time in answering. "Many men have mistresses," she said slowly, "especially if their wives do not please them."

He turned on his side to face her. "Never think that, Lotte. It was never about that. In fact, I was with her only three times, and all within the first fortnight."

"Yes, certainly I believe that," she remarked lightly.

"No, truly."

"But, Ran, you set her up more than two months ago."

"Three, to be exactly," he supplied ruefully.

"And in all this time, you never bedded her after the first two weeks?"

"I swear it."

"Then what have you managed to . . . no, I should not ask."

"Cards," he supplied. "We played cards."

"But why?"

"Because I found that she could not cure me of my passion for you."

"Cure you? Why should you wished to be cured?"

His smile was liberally laced with chagrin. "Fool that I am, I was afraid of the passion you inspired in me by simply walking into a room. I cannot eat or drink, or think much beyond anything but you when you are near. I was certain it was but a form of madness that could be exorcised."

"Between another woman's thighs," she added acerbically.

"Folly, Lotte. I know now. Complete folly."

"Yet this desire to be free of your passion for me? Why was it so important to you?"

He shrugged. "Vanity. No other husband of my acquaintance held his wife so dearly. I know now they are the unlucky ones. But sometimes, a man believes he should be as other men. I found their disinterest gave them an edge in their management of other things. They could eat and sleep and drink politics while I could do nothing but dream of being with you."

"Well then," Lotte answered, hugely enjoying this declaration of his infatuation. "We must see what we can do to aid your career. I would not want you to fall behind on my account. I could dye my hair with tea leaves to take away its brightness and sit in the sun until I become very freckled. I could eat twice my usual fare at dinner until I become as corpulent as a pig—"

"And I would still love you!" he answered warmly.

She glanced at him askance. "I am not certain I would feel the same about you were you to subject yourself to the same regimen."

"Yes, you would," he answered confidently and rolled her over until she lay fully over him. "You will love me when I am fat and bald, and gap-toothed. Because. . ." He paused to kiss her soft mouth. "Because you love me, foolish soul that I am, just as I love you, gallant spirit that you are." He rubbed his hands in a molding caress down her flanks to her hips, which he cupped against his new-rising passion. "But I'm not so much of a fool that I will not enjoy this lovely form of yours for as long as it lasts."

"A moment, sir, before you begin your mighty exertions again." She rose up and propped an elbow in the middle of his chest and placed her chin in her hand. "There is still the matter of Darlington and Sabrina."

Ran sighed. Darlington again. He supposed he would become accustomed to the sound of that name without flinching. "What do you have in mind?"

"First of all, he's in need of the very best counsel."

Ran smiled. "I'm very much afraid he will have to settle for lesser fare."

"Because the fellow will go against you?" She smiled fondly at him. "Then you will have to try to do less than your best in prosecuting him."

He cupped her cheeks in his hands. "No, Lotte love, I mustn't. Darlington's counsel is none other than myself."

"You? You! Oh Ran, how splendid of you!"

She kissed him hard and swiftly. "But this is perfect. He will be set free, without doubt."

"I appreciate your confidence." He did not wish to dim her belief in him just yet. But the fact that Darlington would not recant his statement was a sticking point to his freedom. Also, she might again feel left out as he turned to concentrate on the trial.

And then he smiled, having had a brilliant thought. There was a way to insure that she would not be left out again, even in this matter. "I will, of course, require a woman's touch in the affair."

Lotte's eyes narrowed. "What sort of woman's touch?"

"Yours, Lotte love. I must find a way to speak to Sabrina Lyndsey alone. I have a message for her from Darlington."

Lotte's expression brightened. "Leave that to me. No one would think a thing of it were I to visit her. And we must hurry this up, Ran. We must find a method to free Jack so that he and Sabrina can be as happy as we are."

As happy as we are, Ran mused and he tenderly rolled Lotte onto her back so that he could make love to her again. He did not think a dozen people on the globe were as happy as they were at that very moment.

Chapter Twenty-Nine

Randolph Lovelace rose to his feet as the counsel for the defense with the full confidence of a man who had shared with his peers in the House of Lords the long tedious hours of this trial. Some members of this august body had fallen asleep during the recitations of witnesses for the prosecution while others contented themselves by gossiping. In the rear, a card game had sprung up. But all eyes were now alertly upon him, curious as to what defense he would offer for the West Indian-bred nobleman.

The trial had become a spectacle, with feelings running high on both sides as the prosecution had interrogated a parade of presumed victims of the notorious outlaw Jack Law. Some had called for hanging but most, predominantly women, carried bouquets to show their sentiment in favor of the romantic exploits of the highwayman. The benches as well as the galleries were full to bursting with the curious who had come to see to it that, as the prosecution had stated that morning, "Someone pay for the infamous variety of crimes."

It was his job to see that it was not Lord Darlington.

Randolph turned his attention to his first, and hostile, witness. "I submit to you, Sir Alan Buckley, that you must refute the prosecution's claim that the gentleman in the dock is Back Jack Law."

"I will not!" Sir Alan crossed his arms before his chest, his expression pugnacious. "Lord Darlington claims to be the highwayman and I stand here to second that claim. He was in Bath at the time of the recent robberies that plagued us."

"Then do explain to us, Sir Alan, why during that same time you arrested another man whom you claimed was the real Jack Law?"

Sir Alan snorted. "No need to explain anything. The rascal confessed."

"Under the administration of a whip," Randolph added.

The witness's smile was complaisant. "Many a confession has been got by the use of the lash. Loosens the tongue of the miscreant."

"I should imagine a useful lie would serve as well, if it halted the application of torture," Randolph said sharply.

The knight shifted on his feet. "I took his confession in the spirit with which it was rendered."

"Under duress." Randolph knew he should move on from this point, for there were more sympathizers in the House for Sir Alan's methods than not. "Are you certain that it was not the wily fellow's escape that led you now to accept another candidate for the role of Black Jack?"

"Nonsense. Lord Darlington gave himself away."

"Then you forced an innocent man to confess?"

Sir Alan's face reddened with ire. "I cannot speak for the fellow. All I know is I did my duty as I saw fit under the law."

Ran smiled and turned a sly expression on members of his constituency. "Gentlemen, I should take care if you are ever so unfortunate as to come under Sir Alan's jurisdiction. His persuasive manner leaves something to be desired."

The contemptuous snickers and guffaws from both sides of the aisle heartened Randolph. Buckley was a pompous braggart who deserved no less than to be hoisted by his own petard.

"Are you equally certain, sir, that your testimony is not corrupted by a personal enmity toward Lord Darlington?"

Buckley's eyes narrowed. "I don't know what you mean."

"I refer to an encounter in a gambling salon in Bath on the evening of the very same day you boasted of your arrest of Jack Law. There are witnesses to an altercation between you and the viscount. I believe he remarked upon your—" Ran pointed to a line of text on the table before him. "Lack of prowess in the boudoir."

Sir Alan turned an alarming red. "Might have done," he muttered. " 'Twas said more to impress his whore."

Randolph moved quickly from that point, as well. "I stray from the matter before us. Your certainty of Lord Darlington's culpability baffles me. We have all heard the testimony, testimony that described Jack Law variously."

He reached for the foolscap upon which he had scribbled a few notes. "Ah yes, let me read a few samples. 'A dark fellow,' 'a brooding hulk of a man with bad teeth,' 'a thorough-going gentleman in rich garments,' 'a monster with flaming eyes,' 'short and thick-necked,' 'tall and handsome,' 'rapier thin with a thatch of red hair.' "

Randolph glanced up with a bemused smile as the chamber hummed with comments and chuckles. "I defy any individual to step forward who can answer that description in total."

Sir Alan's lip curled in disdain. "Some may be mistaken, or perhaps the fellow wore a disguise."

"Or perhaps in the extremity of the moment," Randolph suggested, "they saw nothing at all, or only a cast of their own worst nightmares."

Buckley crossed his arms high on his chest. "I will not call a single one a liar."

"Nor do I," Randolph replied cordially. "The witnesses

were robbed." He turned to face the Lord Chancellor. "I only contend that they were not, any of them, robbed by Lord Darlington."

Amid the mutters and murmurs that rose in the wake of his comment, he flipped through his notes, smiling to himself. The prosecution, in their haste to submit a large number of charges, had not bothered to exercise any regularity upon the testimony they had allowed.

"But now we come to the greater perplexity. Sir Alan, you apprehended the fellow you suspected to be Black Jack Law on November 2nd in the environs of Bath. Yet that very same night Squire Hellum declares Jack Law held him up in Derbyshire. I submit that Black Jack would need Satan's own nag to ride from Derbyshire to Bath on the same night."

Sniggers and querulous mutters again rolled through the chamber.

"Perhaps not every robbery was committed by Black Jack," Buckley conceded testily. "That don't negate the fact that Lord Darlington confessed himself to be Black Jack." He nodded, snug in his assertion. "That's good enough for me."

Randolph offered him a blighting glance. That parting shot struck at the very heart of his defense. Darlington had yet to recant. For that he needed other help. "I am done with you, sir. You may step down."

As the man left the witness box, Randolph strolled over to his side of the aisle. "How goes the course?" he inquired of Lord Stilton, who sat on the front row.

"They are listening, which is rare enough," his colleague and advisor answered.

"I believe that the next few minutes shall entertain them mightily." He stepped away. As he did so, he allowed himself a rare glance at his wife. She sat in the first row behind the lords on his side of the aisle, looking splendid in rose brocade and fox fur. Despite his desire that she remain away from the stress and strain of the day, she had insisted upon coming to the trial.

"I wish to be there in your hour of triumph, Ran," she had declared at the breakfast table. "I should like to be able to tell our child of your glorious victory over small minds in the name of friendship."

Ran doubted he would ever account Darlington among his friends, but he owed Lotte her pound of flesh in a public forum for he had once, to his everlasting shame, believed the worst of her. His defense of the gentleman presumed by rumor to have cuckolded him was a small price to pay.

Lotte's eyes shining with loving devotion made him feel as though he had tiptoed past the gates to hell and found the devil sleeping. He had nearly lost her! Her frank adoration in a room of disinterested parties made his heart beat quicker with gladness that he had not.

He turned to face the Lord Chancellor, who acted on this occasion as judge. "The defense calls Miss Lyndsey."

From the corner of his eye Randolph saw Jack rise to his feet and he approached the defendant to keep it from appearing that anything untoward was occurring.

"What the devil do you think you're doing?" Jack demanded in a deadly whisper.

"Saving your neck," Randolph responded under his breath.

Jack eyed him coldly. "I don't need to be saved."

Randolph smiled slightly. "I know, old boy. But there's my reputation to think of. Sit down before you do her testimony irreparable harm."

"If you insult her in any way, I will kill you."

"You must needs be free to do that."

Randolph moved quickly away and turned his attention to his next witness. What he was about to do was harsh but necessary. Since Darlington would not defend himself, he was now forced to do it for him. "My lords, the defense again calls Miss Sabrina Lyndsey."

Sabrina ignored the swelling of comments as she rose from her seat beside her guardian. But McDonnell trod hard on her toe as she made to move past him. "Remember our bargain," he hissed between clenched teeth.

She moved quickly away, the feeling of revulsion running high in her. She had pledged to wed Merripace, this very day, if Jack were set free. The lavender silk gown she wore, an elaborate affair with a formal arrangement of pleats that showed off her neat, corseted figure to full advantage, would either be her wedding dress or her shroud.

As she walked between the rows of benches, she could not help but hear the murmurs of the lords who sat in judgement of Jack.

"Darlington's whore."

"Fine-looking filly."

"Strumpet."

" . . . the merchant classes above themselves!"

"Money don't make for breeding."

"Can't blame Darlington."

" . . . abscond with that piece meself!"

The alternating waves of hostility and suggestive puerile comments battered her until her legs trembled by the time she reached the witness box. Yet she kept her head high, though the effort cramped the muscles in her neck. She knew what most of London thought of her. She was either the disgraced maiden of abduction or a common wanton who had led one of their own astray. Their sympathies lay elsewhere.

After she was sworn in, she folded her hands before her. During the entire ordeal, she had not so much as spared Jack a single glance. She feared that Cousin Robert would notice the looks that passed between them and refuse to allow her to speak. Now she was about to risk everything on a gamble to save Jack.

"Miss Lyndsey," Ran began politely, "are you acquainted with the defendant, Lord Jack Laughton, Viscount Darlington?

"Yes."

"Did he pay address to you in your position as companion to the Countess Lovelace? Or was it your habit to undermine the lady's generosity by conducting idle flirtations with any and all of her aristocratic male guests?"

"I did no such thing!" Sabrina answered, surprised by this unexpected attack from Jack's counsel. Lord Lovelace's expression gave no hint of his purpose.

"No? Then perhaps you were opportuned upon by the viscount without encouraging him. His reputation is that of a seducer."

Sabrina quickly reeled in her temper. She knew she must keep her wits sharp. The slightest mistake could cost Jack his freedom. "Lord Laughton never made any improper address to me while I was companion to the countess."

"Then must we assume, as the prosecution suggests, that Lord Darlington, in the guise of Jack Law, stole you for ransom."

Sabrina forced a smile. "Preposterous. I left Bath with Lord Darlington of my own free will."

"As would half o' London!" came a catcall from the upper gallery.

"To what purpose?" Randolph questioned at the back of the laughter.

Sabrina began to breathe a little easier. She could now tell her story. "He offered to help me free my brother."

With one eye on his colleagues, Randolph offered her an incredulous expression. "Why should a viscount wish to help you, a commoner, steal a bastard child?"

Sabrina's mouth tightened at the use of the word bastard but she refused to let it hinder her. "Lord Darlington is a remarkable person. He saw my need and offered his aid."

Cynicism colored the counsel's tone in suspicious shades. "For no perceived consideration or recompense?"

"I cannot claim to know the workings of his lordship's mind," she answered crisply. "You will have to ask him."

"Yet the most grievous offense against my client is that he abducted you for nefarious reasons."

"I was not abducted," she maintained with dignity despite the contempt and sneers directed toward her by the room of leering males. Suddenly she felt the need to declare the truth, though it made a fallen woman of her. "What I did, I did freely and I would do so again."

Randolph allowed himself a quick glance at his client to gauge his response to her declaration, for it made momentary pandemonium of the chamber. He saw with relief that Darlington's features held no expression whatsoever. He appeared bored, disinterested, and even inattentive.

As the Lord Chancellor banged his gavel for order, Randolph decided to offer her an escape, if she chose to use it.

"There is another possibility, of course, Miss Lyndsey," he declared in the sonorous voice that made him a great orator. "You are possessed of a goodly fortune. Could it be that the viscount, whose circumstances at the time you left London were, to put it delicately, indigent, might have conceived of the notion to follow you to Bath in order to woo your substantial fortune?"

This was one answer she did not have to consider. "Lord Darlington has never proposed marriage to me."

"O' course not, lovey!" came another taunt from the gallery. "Not when ye were swivin' 'im for free!"

That drew shouts of ribald laughter, but they quickly subsided in the avid desire to hear more.

Randolph looked away from her, resigned to the necessity of delivering the last, most damaging blow to her character. "Your guardian had determined at the time you went to Bath that you were to be wed. Is that not so?"

"Yes," she answered guardedly, wondering anew at his purpose.

"Yet there is a witness who will testify that you meant to spite his rightful authority in the matter."

"Mrs. Varney," Sabrina murmured, anger gusting her breath. She had witnessed her argument with Cousin Robert. "I will not deny that I was averse to marriage. That is hardly a crime."

"And what better way for you to foil your guardian's plan than by comporting yourself outrageously with a known rake?"

The spitefully-worded question startled Sabrina. It seemed Lord Lovelace had taken the role of prosecutor and she was the accused. Well then, she knew how to treat an enemy.

"I had thought the word 'no' might answer as well," she said coldly. "I cannot be wed without my consent."

As the audience once again freely offered comment that required the Lord Chancellor's intervention, she glanced at Jack for the first time. There was nothing in his mask of indifference to hint at his feelings about her presence in the courtroom, or whether he even cared. Dressed in severe black and white, he looked like a mourner at his own funeral. She looked quickly away as her heart filled with tamped-down emotion. Oh, but she had missed him, had never thought to see him again.

For four weeks memories of him had been her only company. During her lonely hours of enforced isolation she had kept her sanity by calling to mind every detail of their moments together. She dwelt upon the exact shape of his smile, the intoxicating taste of his lips, the strength of his arms about her, the inexplicable glory of their ecstasy. How long ago it all seemed, how far away they were from that time . . . how little it changed her feelings.

"Miss Lyndsey?"

Sabrina started at the sound of her name. For the duration of that one glance she had completely forgotten where she was and why. She refocused on Lord Lovelace. "Yes, my lord?"

"Did you not tell the tale in Bath that you yourself were robbed and mistreated at the hands of a highwayman?"

How did he know that? Sabrina felt as if she had stepped onto a frozen pond only to find it less solid than she had supposed. Trepidation tiptoed up her spine. "My coach was stopped and the thief relieved my companion of forty pounds."

"Is that all?"

"Yes."

"But you are too modest, Miss Lyndsey. I'm told you vowed that you had shot the villain with his own weapon."

"Oh, that." Sabrina glanced down, as if horribly embarrassed by the admission when she would have liked nothing better than to take a shot at the too-wily Lord Lovelace. She could not guess his purpose and that unnerved her all the more. One slip and she could ruin everything.

She looked up, summoning a smile that was all disarming charm. "I believe I may have embellished the tale. Perhaps, I made a too generous estimate of my skills with a pistol."

He looked at her sharply. "Who robbed you, Miss Lyndsey?"

She did not look away from Lord Lovelace this time. "The fellow did not give his name."

"Did you not declare before your traveling companion that you recognized him to be none other than the notorious Black Jack Law?"

She silently wished Mrs. Varney to blazes. "I might have. I was frightened and cold and in no mood to be detained." Dear lord, what had that old harridan told the authorities?

She turned deliberately away from members of Parliament to address the Lord Chancellor. "I had the evening before been teasing Mrs. Varney, my companion, about the perils of highway travel. We had discussed specifically the highwayman Black Jack Law. Quite naturally, as I had had no other acquaintance with villains, I thought of the name when the fellow who took her purse accosted us. Had I known the name Lovelace as that of a notorious outlaw, I might have been put in mind of the counsel for the defense, my lord."

The twitters and outright chuckles at this recounting heartened her. When she turned back to her interrogator, to her surprise she found Lord Lovelace was now smiling at her.

"So now, will you explain how Lord Darlington came to be party in a scheme to kidnap your half-brother for ransom?"

" 'Twas never for ransom but only to ensure Kit's safety." She sent a resentful glance to where Robert McDonnell sat. How much could she say and still keep her promise? "I thought that I could care better for my brother than anyone else."

"And so you stole him?"

"Kit came willingly. He knows I would never do anything to harm him."

"Where is your brother?"

"Out of harm's way."

"Can you prove that?"

"It would seem that the whereabouts of a child whom the king has disinherited would be of no concern to anyone but the sister who cares deeply for him."

This time the murmurs from the lords' benches were unanimous in their agreement with her. Though many of them had sired bastards of their own, none of them were interested in fate of a commoner's by-blow.

Ran turned to the opposing counsel. "Your witness."

The Attorney General rose to his feet, his face an expressionless mask beneath his impeccably groomed wig. His lazy-lidded gaze put her instantly on the alert. Here was a most dangerous adversary.

"One question only, Miss Lyndsey. Do you believe that Lord Darlington is Black Jack Law?"

Sabrina laughed. "I do not!"

His long sober expression altered to one of amused disdain. "You disappoint me, Miss Lyndsey. I should have thought that a young woman of your perspicacity would have noticed the most obvious, and damning, connection between the two."

"What connection would that be?" Sabrina asked cautiously, sobered by that sliver of a smile that in no way warmed his haughty countenance.

"Why, that the names lend themselves to interpretation. Darlington's given name is John, hence the nickname Jack. His family name is Laughton. Jack *Law*. Jack *Laughton*." He drew out the syllables of each to stress the similarity. "Is the highwayman's byname not self-evidence of a wit at work?"

"That would depend upon the wit, I suppose," Sabrina answered slowly for, surprisingly, the thought had never before occurred to her. Jack had always been Lord Darlington to her and then, once she fell in love, her own dear Jack. But she saw in the flash the danger of the connection. She must sever it at once.

"Jacks abound," she continued. "Yet who but a halfwit would conceive so obvious a ploy? People might label Lord Darlington many things but never a fool!"

Supporting laughter from the galleries echoed her sentiment, just as she hoped.

"Do you mock this court, *Miss* Lyndsey?" the prosecutor asked in a tone that quelled even the throng.

"Certainly not, my lord." Sabrina smiled at the Attorney General though she knew her temper flared in her gaze. He had made it clear that he considered her less unworthy of his consideration, as both a female and commoner. She knew she should bow to his superiority but she could not. Still her voice was all feminine difference as she applied her own brand of wit. "I sought only to answer your question in the spirit in which you proposed it, my lord; a frivolous question answered in kind. If I have erred, I beg your pardon."

The Attorney General stared at her a fraction longer, as though pondering his next move, then he seemed to change his mind. "Thank you. You may step down, Miss, Lyndsey."

Randolph watched her leave the witness box with great admiration for her performance. She had managed to diffuse the matter of kidnapping and abduction, and offer Darlington a plausible alibi, though it was at the cost of her reputation.

He glanced at the first row in the gallery where McDonnell sat looking like thunder. Lord Merripace sat beside him, pulling thoughtfully at his lower lip. He did not like to think what else her testimony would cost her if Darlington were unable to act quickly enough when the trial was over. But first he must win it.

"The defense now calls Jack Laughton, Viscount Darlington, to the witness box."

Amid the buzz and push and shove from the upper galleries as men and woman vied for a better look at the handsome defendant, the viscount was sworn in.

"Lord Darlington," Randolph began, "did you not introduce yourself in Scotland as the highwayman Black Jack Law?"

Darlington shrugged. "I might have. The Scots seemed more impressed by a man who lives by his wits rather than one who lives off the sweaty brow of his fellow countrymen."

A hiss of disapproval that arose from the benches of aristocratic landowners, whose lives of ease were maintained by the toil of their many tenants, did not disturb the viscount one whit.

"Then you admit you are the notorious Jack Law?"

"Certainly not. I merely stated that I found the sobriquet useful."

"Useful? Were you not arrested after you told the authorities that you had kidnapped Miss Lyndsey and her half-brother in order to hold them for ransom?"

He smiled, drawing his scar into a valley of a laugh line. "It seemed more prudent to admit to a lie than to allow

Miss Lyndsey to be taken away to a place where a different lie might have been beaten out of her." He glanced pointedly at Sir Alan, who shifted uncomfortably on his gallery bench. "Such things are not unheard of."

Randolph cleared his throat in amusement but did not comment. "Would you care to explain your relationship with Miss Lyndsey."

"No."

"No?"

"No."

"Will you not speak, if only to defend her honor?"

"Her honor requires no defense. She is none other than she seems, a splendid girl with a brave heart full of only the best of intentions."

"A commendable sentiment. Yet hardly the kind of declaration expected from a gentleman who seduced her away from her family and traveled alone with her all the way into the wilds of Scotland."

Darlington gazed at his counsel with lazy indifference. "You are unfamiliar with the tropical temperament. We do not require much inducement to adventure."

"Are you certain that the inducement was a not a financial one? Miss Lyndsey's future husband will inherit a great fortune upon her marriage."

"Miss Lyndsey's wealth has never weighed with me. She was in need. I offered my services."

"With no incentive of any kind on the young lady's part? I am impressed. Unless your intentions were less than honorable. Perhaps you had not aid but seduction in mind."

Jack stared at his advocate for a moment. "Perhaps."

The softly spoken answer caused a startling response. The lead counsel for the prosecution stood up and declared in ringing tones, "You stand in this court of law and admit that you are a heartless seducer?"

Jack turned a complaisant gaze on the Attorney General, as the collective audience in the room seemed to strain forward from their positions to catch his every word. "I admit that my interest in Miss Lyndsey has never been wholly virtuous in nature. I defy any gentleman here to attest to such a paltry lack of passion for a woman he claims to love."

"Love?"

Sabrina's startled question sounded clearly in the one moment of stunned silence.

"My lord! This will not serve!" The Attorney General came forward on long quick strides. "My lords, this is but a charlatan's trick, a sham of feigned emotion aimed at winning the court's sympathy!"

The lead prosecutor glared at the defendant in contempt, waiting until the calls for silence hushed the crowd. "This is clearly a bid to manipulate the emotions of the bench. Miss Sabrina Lyndsey is to be wed this very evening to Lord Merripace."

"What?" For the first time Jack's expression lost its indolence.

The prosecutor smiled. "Have you not heard, Lord Darlington? The marriage banns have been read these last two Sundays. She gave herself freely to the offer."

"I see." No emotion animated the words.

Jack turn to look at Sabrina for the first time. She looked stricken and pale. It was true then. He knew it with a certainty no amount of explanation could cushion.

As he turned back to the prosecutor, there was a strange expression on his face, at once tender and regretful, something a little desperate and resentful, and an infinite quality of utter amazement. She had gambled away her future for his life! It was the dearest, most precious gesture anyone had ever made on his behalf. Yet, it was totally unnecessary. He had found a method by which to save himself. How could she doubt it?

"The lady has my felicitations. But I should like to get on with the matter at hand." He smiled the smile of a man who knows he holds an unbeatable hand. "I can prove that I am not Jack Law." He turned to look at the gentleman who had sat in silence through the full day of court proceedings with a bemused expression on his lean, saturnine face.

A tall, thin, elegantly dressed man in black silk and gold lace stood up. By his flamboyant dress he could not be mistaken for other than a continental. Though his accent was faint, when he spoke his origin was quickly pinpointed as French. "I should beg the indulgence of the court for a moment, my lords."

The Attorney General squinted down at the man from his high perch. "And who, sir, are you?"

The Frenchman smiled, making of his saturnine face a mobile composite of charming villainy. "But, of course, I am Monsieur Jacques Justice de Tristesse or, as you so vulgarly prefer, 'Black Jack' Law."

Chapter Thirty

Jack sat in the small room at Westminster, awaiting the judgement of the House of Lords. His coat was shed and his shirt dangled free at the cuffs and open at the throat. He should have been cold, for the room was little warmer than the temperature outside where frost was beginning to etch lacy fingers on the windowpane.

He was a man who had never given a damn about anything, certainly not others and scarcely more than base-level creature concerns about himself. He had always suspected, deep in his heart, that he was as his mad father predicted, the devil's spawn, damned by his very existence. So there was no need to be better than his worst self, no need to care and suffer as good people did. No need, especially, to seek comfort in this despairing world. No need to strive or sacrifice or plan or hope. No need to deal in the minor emotions that weaker people claimed made life easier or more bearable, or even just worth living. No need at all, until Sabrina.

How droll, what a canard was fate! At last, certain of the origin of emotions that he had never before felt, or thought he would ever feel, he had nearly sealed his birthright and heralded his own defeat.

He drew in a foot upon the chair on which he sat and dangled an arm over his knee. He had been ejected from the judgement portion of his trial in the council chambers at Westminster and placed in a private room with a guard beyond the door. Without Sabrina, he was equally indifferent the outcome.

He loved her.

The realization abashed and appalled him. He could not speak the words in her ear in a private loving moment. No, he had let her drift and dangle in doubt for weeks and then tossed the word out to her from a witness box with all the snooping, spying, uncaring world to hear. No wonder he was damned.

He threw back his head in bitter laughter.

The door to this temporary cell swung wide at that moment and Lord Lovelace entered in a quick stride and a swirl of melting snow that dampened his clothing as he crossed the yard. He stopped short at the sound of laughter. "You've heard, then?"

Jack sobered a little slowly, wiping a tear of mirth from one eye. "Heard what?"

Randolph frowned. "You're free!"

Jack sat a moment in silence. When he did speak, the old mocking disdainful drawl was back. "Did you ever doubt it?"

"At least half a dozen times today." Annoyed, Randolph stomped to rid his boots of the last of the snow, really slush, which had begun to accumulate. It seemed his rush to deliver the news was wasted. Then again, when did Darlington ever say what he meant?

"You might at least have told me of the existence of Jacques Tristesse."

"And miss the opportunity to astonish? I think not."

"Half of them wanted to hang you for your impudence this afternoon," he said as he unwound his muffler. "The other half wanted to give you a parade for the very same reason."

"Human nature is so easily swayed by sentiment."

"Yes, well, there are stipulations."

Jack's expression lost its humor. "Such as?"

Randolph began unbuttoning his favorite heavy coat. "You did not think they would thank you for tantalizing them with the specter of a notorious criminal only to discover when they attempted to arrest him that he had gained the king's own pardon?"

Jack smiled. "It was a necessary evil in order to persuade the gentleman to expose his masquerade."

"How the devil did you manage it?"

"I'm afraid I was party to it." Lotte's voice drew both men's attention to the open doorway. She stood wrapped in velvet and fox fur like some winter fairy just sprung up from the new-fallen snow.

"You?" Ran approached his wife and took her gently by the shoulders. "Lotte, what have you done now?"

"Very little," she assured him with a smile. "I merely spoke with the queen on Jack's behalf."

Ran's expression darkened. "When?"

Lotte flung back her fur-lined hood to reveal her unpowdered hair. "A week ago. Jack wrote me, asking me to." Seeing her husband's frown deepen, she added hastily, "I but carried a letter to Her Majesty to be delivered to His Majesty. I had no idea of its contents."

Ran glanced over his shoulder at Jack. "We now know it contained a request for a carte blanche, the king's immunity from prosecution, for Monsieur de Tristesse."

"Wasn't his the most romantic story?" Lotte breathed happily.

Ran basked in the warmth of her gaze. "You are partial to love stories, though I wonder if his tale of a Jersey Islander's love for a Devonshire lass was but a sham to win hearts."

"I would not doubt it," Jack rejoined, thinking of his

own mad escapade on the highway and how it had brought him love. Monsieur de Tristesse had told his story of being a privateer, bedeviling the English coast, when he met a girl in the port town of Exeter. He decided to take up his trade on land, substituting highway robbery for marauding on the high seas, until he had won her. "Did he say she was a year in the wooing?"

"That would explain his gallantry to his victims," Lotte mused. "No woman would wed a man who had actually committed atrocious crimes."

The men exchanged knowing glances that belied that fact. Women often loved wastrels.

"How did you know where to find him?" Ran asked.

"I've had weeks to think about the man," Jack answered ruefully. "I did not doubt that the outlaw once existed, but it stood to reason that the proliferating number of robberies could only mean that others had taken up the colorful nickname. As legend springs up in the wake of reality, I assumed the real 'Black Jack' was dead or retired. Friends made inquiries to discover which theory was correct."

"You have friends?" Ran asked skeptically, still smarting from his exclusion in the matter.

"I have acquaintances. Once the calendar year turned over I also had money enough to bribe the tightest maw."

"I commend your ingenuity."

"Thank you. I believe Monsieur de Tristesse rather enjoyed setting the record straight. As a good citizen of the Isle of Jersey these last twenty years and with a family of six to rear, he wanted his name cleared of the worst infamy that has become attached to the reputation of 'Black Jack'."

"I'm glad you can be so philosophical about it, for your generosity to him will cost you mightily."

Jack lifted a brow. "There were stipulations? What are they?"

"You must leave London, immediately," Randolph

answered grimly. "If you are discovered within the borders of England after Friday, you shall be summarily arrested."

Jack nodded. "A pleasant alternative to exile. Does Sabrina know?"

Randolph paused fractionally before answering. "McDonnell waited himself to hear the verdict."

Something ugly moved in Jack's expression. "So then, she will know."

"She is very likely being shoved before a minister at moment."

Jack stood and reached for his coat. "I wish her every happiness, I'm sure."

"God grant me mercy!" Randolph cried in disgust. "If you love her, take her with you! If not, be damned to you!"

Grinning, Jack stuck an arm in the first sleeve. "I rather think I will."

Lotte eyed him with fond admiration. "Which is it, Jack?"

Jack shoved his arm into the other sleeve and hoisted the coat up onto his shoulders. "I rather think I shall take her with me."

Randolph nodded his head once. "Here, you will need this."

"What is it?"

"Miss Lyndsey's passage to America."

Jack's expression altered. "You never gave it to her?"

"She refused her portion. Her brother and your servant received theirs. They are waiting for you in the port town of Plymouth. I have a message from the tall blackamoor."

"Zuberi? Yes?"

"He said to tell you that he did not leave a certain person, his words, in Bath. He is sorry to disobey you in this one small matter but as she is leaving England with him, it will no longer inconvenience you."

Jack chuckled. "Loyalty is no match for love. It is a new lesson for me."

Randolph dug into the pockets of his formal coat and pulled out another sheaf of papers. "This is yours as well."

Jack did not reach for these. "What is it?"

"Christ!" Randolph slapped the furled pages against Jack's chest. " 'Tis the deed to Rockingham."

Jack backed up a step. "You won it fairly."

"Actually, no." Randolph reached up and pulled open the neck of Jack's coat and tucked the papers into the opening. "I could no more afford the wager than you. I had hoped to ruin you when I thought you had won something infinitely more precious from me."

For a long silent moment their gazes met and held, two very strong and determined men, and each was glad that the other was a man he would never have to meet on a field of honor.

"So then, we are even." Randolph returned to her side and hugged his wife close. "Lotte thinks I am a hero for saving you." He smiled down at her, feeling the luckiest man alive. "She now intends to build monuments to my consequence."

Jack smiled at them. "You are the better man, for her."

"Indeed. Consider Rockingham our wedding present."

"Mind your own damned business!"

"You will find Miss Lyndsey at—"

"I know where," Jack said grimly and looked at Lotte who nodded in confirmation.

"How do you know?" Randolph asked testily, for it seemed he was missing a great deal of information.

Jack smiled. "Your lady wife. She has a most remarkable talent for intrigue."

Lotte blushed. "I simply had my maid slip over to Merripace's side during the trial to ask where the ceremony would take place so that I might attend."

"You are a wonder," Randolph said in affection.

Lotte blushed. "Our carriage waits below, Jack. The driver has orders to take you anywhere you wish. If you hurry you may just prevent a tragedy."

Jack stopped short at the door. "I do not suppose either of you have a pistol on you?"

Sabrina had never been colder. As she stood in the rear of a small side chapel of a church whose name she did not even know, the chill had started deep within her, against her spine, and radiated outward until she could no longer feel her hands and feet.

The ceremony was to be a private one, the chapel rented for a half hour. Only two candles burned, one on either side of the altar. There would be no cakes and ale, no toast to the new bride, or even a simple wedding supper. She was marrying in haste in a dark and cheerless place, and it seemed only fitting.

"Come, Sabrina," Robert McDonnell called impatiently from the front of the chapel. "Take your place at your husband's side."

Sabrina paused and compressed her lips hard. She must not think about anything, nothing at all. She must not look at Merripace or Cousin Robert, or she would begin to think and feel a dozen angry things. She could go through with this. She must not think of herself now. Kit was safe. Jack was saved. She had done all she could for those she cared most about in this world.

She forced herself to move forward awkwardly on feet that felt like blocks of wood. Mrs. Varney and her guardian's driver stood to one side as witnesses. It would be over so quickly she would scarcely realize it. A few words, ordinary words, and it would be over.

When she reached Merripace's side the minister opened his book.

"Dearly beloved, we are gathered here together in the sight of heaven . . ."

His voice droned on but Sabrina forced her attention away. She would not participate, not in her thoughts, not in her attention, and never in her heart!

"Repeat after me. I, Sabrina Lyndsey. . ."

"I—I . . ." Sabrina looked up into the face of the old and shallow man who was to be her husband and released her full revulsion with this travesty. "I will not!"

McDonnell's features contorted as he reached for her. "What say you?"

"The lady demurs, sir! And that is enough for me!"

That voice! Sabrina swung round, her heart leaping in foolish helpless joy even before she spied her savior at the back of the church.

A tall figure in a gentleman's overcoat stood at the back of the chapel, his tricorner pulled low and his face muffled by his cravat. Nearly as welcome as he was the pistol he carried.

"What the devil!" cried Merripace.

"The unholy soul himself," the masked intruder answered as he came forth, the pistol in his hand as steady as it was deadly.

"Darlington!" McDonnell spat.

"I would not be so certain in my judgement, fellow, lest I decide your life is forfeit in my need to escape."

He came up beside Sabrina and motioned Merripace back with the barrel. "You may now continue, *padre.*"

"With the ceremony?" the small man asked doubtfully.

"Yes, but with one minor alteration. Miss Lyndsey is to pledge herself to Jack Laughton."

"You cannot do that!" cried McDonnell.

"Can and will." He leveled the pistol at the man's middle. "Do you wish to stand as witness here or in heaven?" The man visibly paled. "If you are uncertain, then I suggest you remain mortal a while longer."

Sabrina tucked her hand in her outlaw's as the minister began. He faltered several times at the beginning, then went on more strongly. The vows were quickly exchanged, though Jack could not spare her a glance away from their enemies even as he pledged himself to her, "Until death do us part."

"It is not binding," McDonnell jeered when the ceremony was complete. "I have not given my blessing."

"It will serve my needs." Jack backed over to where the document lay open, waiting for the wedded couple's signatures. He dashed Merripace's name from the text and then recorded his own.

Sabrina followed suit, smiling foolishly as she did so. When she looked up, there was mischief in her eyes.

"I did not know your middle name was Larchmont?"

"Only one of the many dubious surprises married life is bound to serve you," he answered. "Are you ready to forsake all others for me?"

"Yes, yes!"

He drew her quickly with him back down the aisle up which he had come. McDonnell started after them, yelling quite crude oaths that Sabrina would never have expected from so pious a man.

Once through the doors, Jack paused to stick a key he drew from his pocket into the lock and turned it.

" 'Twas on the other side as I entered," he explained and then tore off his mask, put his pistol away, and picked up Sabrina to carry her the few short yards to the waiting coach.

It was snowing again, the crisp white flakes falling softly through the twilight to kiss Sabrina's cheeks. And she laughed aloud, thinking them as beautiful as any blossoms showered upon any bride and groom.

The earl's traveling coach pulled away the instant Jack slammed the door behind them. Darkness descended about them as he drew closed the leather curtains, wrapping them in a dreamy world where nothing existed but themselves.

Sabrina felt suddenly shy. He had seated himself opposite her, as if uncertain he would be welcome by her side.

"They will give chase," she said, because she could think of no other topic.

"I doubt even the hounds of hell can outpace the earl's best team," he answered lightly.

Sabrina gazed at him through the dark, wishing she could see his expression. His voice sent flushed ripples though her body. "Where are we going?"

He leaned forward and placed his hands at her throat. "Ah, well, there was a stipulation in my release."

"Was there?" she whispered faintly, feeling the heat of desire in his touch.

His hands unbuttoned her cloak and pushed it from her shoulders. "I am, it seems, an undesirable person in my homeland. I've been charged into exile."

Sabrina gasped softly as his hands found and strongly traced the curves of her breasts to her waist. "For how long?"

"Forever, sweeting." His hands went round her back and begun plucking the strings that held her gown closed. "What do you think of that?"

"Where shall we go?"

He smiled. She had not hesitated to ask. What a woman! "First to Plymouth, which is where Zuberi has been hiding Kit." He quickly pulled her free of her bodice. "Then I had thought we might sail to Barbados. The trade winds are sweet this time of year."

"I hear it is very like—" His thumb found and circled an instantly puckering nipple. "Paradise," she breathed softly as his lips touched her neck.

"So some say," he murmured against her throat. "You will have to judge for yourself, my love." He raised his head and brushed his lips across hers. "You are my love, my life, my wife."

"Wife!" The word rang with sudden intense truth inside Sabrina's thoughts. She was Jack's wife!

The joy of it made her fall back against the soft leather squabs of her seat in giddy, abandoned laughter.

Given the invitation, Jack quickly moved over to her and lifted the hem of her skirt, fighting petticoats and hoops and a half dozen other impediments until he found what he sought.

"We will be cast as outlaws wherever we go."

She sighed and closed her eyes and hugged him closer. "I have always been accounted an outlaw by those who knew me best."

"You'll be gambling your life away on a thorough-going devil."

She reached down between them and cupped him through the fabric of his breeches. "Then I see I shall have to practice my she-devil tendencies."

"I beg you, do," he gasped softly as she kneaded his swollen flesh.

When she had released him from his breeches, he pushed into her, sliding home where he belonged. "Then the West Indies it shall be," he answered in laughter.

"And what will we do there?" she whispered as he plied the soft, melting center of her.

"Oh, we shall do this, and this, and most especially this!"

As the coach rocked briskly along the road south toward the coast, Jack and Sabrina lay wrapped tightly in one another's arms and legs, riding their own way to paradise.